J. B. Aspinall

John Brian Aspinall was born in 1939 and grew up in Rochdale. After reading History at Oxford he taught English in comprehensive schools around England, and now lives in France. His poetry has been published in various magazines but *Gringo Soup* is his first novel.

J. B. ASPINALL

GRINGO SOUP

SCEPTRE

Copyright © 2001 J. B. Aspinall

First published in 2001 by Hodder and Stoughton
A division of Hodder Headline

The right of J. B. Aspinall to be identified as the
Author of the Work has been asserted by him in accordance
with the Copyright, Designs and Patents Act 1988.

A Sceptre paperback

2 4 6 8 10 9 7 5 3 1

A CIP catalogue record for this title is available from the British Library.

ISBN 0 340 73378 0

Printed and bound in Great Britain by
Mackays of Chatham plc, Chatham, Kent

Hodder and Stoughton
A division of Hodder Headline
338 Euston Road
London NW1 3BH

For Frances

'From whatever place I write you will expect that part of my "Travels" will consist of excursions in my own mind.'

S. T. Coleridge

Baluth Tour BT15, 'The Magic of Mexico' is an in-depth, once-in-a-lifetime voyage of discovery, by coach, boat and aeroplane, of Mexico and its ancient Indian heritage – from the fascinating kaleidoscope of the metropolis through the upland vistas of Oaxaca and San Cristobal to the mystic Mayan marvels in the rain-forests of Palenque and the Yucatan. Our adventure ends in relaxation on the dazzling white sand beaches of Cancun beside the azure Caribbean, where there is a special-offer extension (optional) in a four-star hotel.

LISA MANDERS

Titchy pricks of stubble in my armpits. I towelled then sploshed myself with floral lotions and Body Shop syrups – but didn't dress. I used the dryer on my impulse-buy corkscrew perm and tilted the kitschy dressing-table mirror to help me put on lipstick and eye-shadow.

Deano likes me to use make-up – he says lots of feminist concepts seem winners on the drawing-board but are party poopers if you wheel them into operation. They emasculate males by denying them the whiff of power that braces their balls and make females frigid by associating shame and betrayal with the idea of them making themselves delicious to blokes. The net result – results – Deano says – are 'limp cocks and parched twats'.

Deano has a lot of admiration for Islam in which he claims the cock is pampered and female satisfaction assured. Islam okays aphrodisiac drugs and no-nos alcohol which is a downer and the Great Western Sexual Calamity according to Deano. He would be a Moslem if it wasn't for the unhip side – that women are supposed to put their heads in bags and not wear make-up – plus which there is – are – the problems that Deano does a lot of boozing and doesn't rate God.

I pulled on the white silk stockings slow and easy so as not to snag them. Deano bought them for a giggle but they have come to be our code. He likes me to wear them for bonking because they make him think simultaneously of hookers and virgins. When I bleated at that he said I was being 'parochial'. 'Hookers and virgins – outer limits – see? Men are scared by them and fascinated. To me the words are both compliments and insults – and at the same time neither. Weird, eh?'

5

I lolled on the bed with the cool plastic phone on my tummy. High time Baluth issued its reps with portables. I tell the punters hotel phones are a rip-off. Buy a phone-card – I say – and find a street booth. But a public box would have cramped the style of this particular inter-continental liaison which I planned would be both soppy and hyper-erotic.

Twenty past eight in the morning, which meant about half eight at night in Hyderabad.

'Is that the Commercial Hotel?'

'I beg your pardon?'

'Is that the Commercial Hotel?'

'This is the Commercial Hotel, Hyderabad.'

The same jerk as last week. His whacky way of plonking out every phrase was typical of the way Indians speak English but also reminded me, yuk, of the way Kelvin talked when he was in an iffy temper and looking for a bust-up.

'Can I speak to Dean Boswell? Room thirty-three?'

'One moment please.'

I could feel my pulse ker-thumping as I waited to hear Deano's doleful smoker's growl that a week ago had set my pussy purring across oceans and continents by asking me what I was wearing. This time I wouldn't have to tell him porkies to tease us both with tiny warm wavelets of tender frustration. Whereas I knew him for a hapless fibber and wouldn't ask him anything. I could picture him most carnally in his boxer shorts with an erection shoving at the orange fabric. Those little sunbleached hairs all over his bronzage. Those goofy sunglasses and the tufty ponytail held together with a rubber band.

'There is no answer from room thirty-three.'

'There must be. Please try again.'

'I beg your pardon?'

I put on the slow, posh Baluth voice that I use on native boors and dumbos. 'Room thirty-three, hurry please, this is long distance.'

'I have tried. There is no answer.'

'There must be some mistake.'

'I beg your pardon?'

His tone was definitely not user-friendly now I'd called his competence into question. It was as if he was judgementally beholding me in my skimpy freaky finery. I turned my head and spotted myself in the dressing-table mirror – an amateurish effort at a snap from a wank mag.

'Shit,' I croaked, then, 'Sorry, thanks, I'll be in touch.'

I peeled off the stockings not bothering if I did them an injury then put on my knickers and bra and sat on the bed a million miles from nowhere like it says in the song, ashamed of my naff project and livid at Dean. After a bit I phoned East Grinstead.

'Colin Manders speaking.'

Since he took early retirement and discovered he detests golf Daddy has plenty of time to man the phone. His voice, twangy and nasal with all the vowels squeezed flat, is just what you'd imagine once you knew he was a quantity surveyor from East Grinstead. It used to make me grind my teeth but now he sounded homey and a lump came into my throat. I could picture his slippers and specs, the spice rack, the garden frosty beyond the velvet curtains. Bracken the labrador would be dreaming, thudding his tail under the stove. He lies too close to the heat, the stupid mutt, so you can actually smell his pelt singeing.

'How are you keeping, Daddy?'

'Lisa?'

'What time is it there?'

'Your mother's in the conservatory . . .'

He'd faffed off without answering either of my questions. If our relationship is disappointing it's because he's never kept abreast of my developing persona. I despised and defied him for years, complaining about him to Mummy, till later in my teens when I came to loathe Mummy and Daddy seemed relatively harmless. It was Mummy I wanted now, though. He was spot on there.

'Lisa?' Mummy has kept her Northern accent that is calming and comfy over the phone even when she's being remote and sly.

'Can you ring me back?' Always worth a shot.

'I can't,' she lied. 'I've got to go out in a couple of ticks. What's up?' She knows I rarely buzz her unless I'm in crisis.

'Nothing. Can't I ring my own mother across half the world without something having to be wrong?'

'There's that note in your voice. What's up?'

'Nothing apart from I hate Mexico and my work and Deano's not there when I phone him.'

'Deano? Is he the one . . .'

She pretends to confuse Deano with other blokes though I've spoken of nobody else for two years and she's met him twice. She doesn't like his lack of manners and 'prospects'.

I yelled: 'You know who he is! He's the selfish scumbag shit on whom I've wasted my agenda, the last of my youth!'

'He's in Bombay?'

'Hyderabad and out with some scrubber when I call him.'

'How many times have you called him?'

'I called him just now. What do you mean by that? How many fucking calls do you reckon it takes to find out somebody's not there?'

'Calm down, Lisa! What do you expect me to do about it?'

Right. It's a kiddy thing, this yelling at my mother when things go wrong. I do it out of spite so she can worry that I'm in the dumps.

'Stupid of me to expect you to be interested in my problems.'

She'd be perched on the arm of the sofa, turning in her fingers the little biro on a silver chain that lives next to the phone-pad. She is slim with short grey hair and unlike me in all respects. When she was my age she had three kids.

'What's the problem with the job?'

'The last lot were supershits, there were seven Belgians who bitched about absolutely everything. On top of which somebody imported a cold from winter in Europe so we've all been spluffing and splorting including me. Plus which my next batch arrive today instead of tomorrow, I mean yesterday instead of today, so I don't get a sodding break.'

'When are you coming home?'

'Middle of February, I told you last time I rang.'

'You didn't. You said something about Belize.'

'Belize and Guatemala till the middle of February, round about the fifteenth, I told you!'

'Only Carol said something about fetching the twins over this February half-term and I said they could use your room if you aren't back by then.'

'Let them have it anyway. I can stay somewhere else.'

'No, that's not right, pet. It's your room.'

It isn't. It's a shrine to a teenager who died long ago when I went to University. It still has soft toys and Save the Wildlife posters and even Adam Ant records. The only evidence of the living me is in a cardboard box on top of the wardrobe. I also have a tea-chest in a cupboard in Julian's Docklands flat and a big trunk under Xandra's bed in Islington.

'And is that it then? After Guatemala in February you're finished?'

'No, I dunno, if they offer me another contract for the summer . . .'

'Lisa, you promised! You're frittering . . . waste of a good degree . . . tell by the wages it isn't a proper career, just a way of seeing the world for kids after University . . . thirty years old – already past the ideal age for motherhood . . . get your priorities sorted . . . Watsisname.'

Ringing off, I thought, she's D.R.A.B., detestably right and boring. It's drab to have a mum who's so morally and mentally solid when you're in love with a slob who's out contracting sexual disease in Hyderabad while you miss him in Mexico.

In the bathroom mirror I gave myself a once-over which didn't do a lot for my morale. The perm – all those facetious ringlets with added bounce 'n' shine that are supposed to proclaim my fiddle-de-dee – just looks spoof. Un-hip. I'm going to be an up-yours skinhead with a pin in my nose if Baluth don't come through with another contract. Smoking and whatnot and the sodding Mexican sun have ravaged my complexion so that even when I cake on the make-up I can see the zits and wrinkles biding their time below. And I've been getting fat – fatter – for years. I liked it at first (I was long and skinny as a kid), and thought 'firm' and 'voluptuous', but now it's hard to stop other terms springing to mind such as 'podge' and 'blubber'.

Five years is a long stretch for a Baluth tour leader: the burn-out rate is frantic. I don't know anybody else who has served as long without getting a home posting or being given special assignments opening up new routes and regions.

Even if I swallow the fact that tourism is a frivolous luxury I still have to admit that mine isn't serious work. When I started I felt like Hannibal or Vasco da Gama with the fate of a whole expedition in my hands but pretty soon realised I was a zero. The tours are ordained by Central Office in London; day-to-day details are sub-contracted to local agencies and guides. My job is PR and social, like a Butlins redcoat or a Thomson courier – answering complaints or passing them on translated into Spanish – helping the punters think they're being cherished and having a happy-clappy time.

I pouted a bit longer then flounced from the mirror to find I had half an hour before the briefing at nine thirty. I spent some of it skimming the reports of the last group, checking my tour leader score. One 'fair', six 'good' and four 'excellent'. But only half of them had handed in the reports, which was miffing – partly because it's usually the ones that mark me down lower than dogshit that are shy about giving me the forms – and partly because I know some of them, once they get home, will never bother to post the forms to Baluth, and the number of responses is taken into account assessment-wise.

There seems no correlation between my efforts and my grades. Some who moan and snarl throughout put 'excellent' on the report, whereas others zap me with 'poor' who made delighted noises to my face. And anything I do to oblige is sure to get up somebody's nose. What one welcomes as a helpful tip another resents as bossiness. One person's swank social evening is another's squalid piss-up.

Yup, a fairly typical bunch of reports. A couple on their end-of-holiday high put 'excellent' for every aspect. Otherwise hotels were mostly considered good, food and arrangements good or fair, guides good or excellent and overall value good. In response to, 'Do you think you will go on other Baluth tours?' only a couple had entered a grudging 'maybe'.

The 'most memorable parts of the tour' were almost always the big Mayan ruins, which are self-evidently brain-boggling. Nobody admits to being disappointed by them though a lot look pretty blank on the sites. One or two – as usual – bragging rather than carping – said there was too much regimentation, or that the guides were ill-informed. Cancun was panned by some who were not beach people and thought it pricey, 'common' and an anticlimax.

Most grumbles were main-stream humdrum: cockroaches, noisy hotels and draughty buses, the delays and discomforts of the internal flight between Villahermosa and Merida. Damien, once a Methodist minister in Argentina, was fixated on the Catholic Church in Latin America and had left me a diatribe in tiny green writing.

More irritating than moaners were those who used the 'additional comments' area to splodge out the feel-good bull-shit that infests visitors' books in museums. Reading these, I could hear Paulette's contralto wobbling like an old thesp: 'I am shattered – elated – broke – and deeply grateful.' Gordon brayed, 'WELL DONE, MATES, A CRACKER!' Celia's handwriting was loopy and lollopy, like her mind: 'Viva Mexico! Viva Baluth! Ole! Ole!'

Then I leafed through the short questionnaires which my new group had filled in. Only sixteen because there had been late drop-outs. Baluth advertise themselves as small group holidays and when I started we used to have about a dozen but there is a tendency to push up the numbers, sometimes to over twenty.

Eleven women, five men. Three couples, two women travelling together and eight singles. Five from the Home Counties, four from the provinces, two from Ireland, one from Wales, an American, an Australian, two English now living in France. One over seventy, four in their sixties, two in their fifties, two in their forties, five in their thirties, two in their (late) twenties. A housewife, a nurse, two schoolteachers (retired), a publican, a civil servant, an accountant, an optician, a biologist (genetic research), a marketing representative, a company director, a travel agency clerk. The middle class at play. One had written 'private income' and three had left the 'Occupation' section blank. 'Reasons for choosing this tour' were the usual guff, varying in length from a question-mark to a close-scrawled ten-line treatise on pre-Columbian artefacts and 'extramural seminars' at the University of Wales in Aberystwyth.

I had met most of them at the airport, nine thirty the night before. Gabriel was with me – he's the guide supplied by the local tour agents in Mexico City. We buzzed the airport first, as usual, and as usual discovered that the flight had been held up for two hours in Madrid. Gabriel suggested a drink in the bar, as usual, and as sometimes happens I thought, fuck it, and went and had two Tequila Sunrises to brace myself for meeting all my new chums.

Gabriel is a cliché Latin male with slobbery brown eyes and bristly tash, constantly playing for touchy-feely vibes, putting his knee against you, resting his hand on the flesh of your arm and so forth. He's forty two. His wife is older than him and insanely jealous. He values the sympathy of a lovely señorita who deserves better than a boyfriend at the other end of the earth. Shyness, sobriety, our professional relationship and his respect for all women and me in particular are keeping him from telling me what is really in his heart. At this point he gives a slow wink and lets the tip of his tongue peep from under his tash then leans forward to capture my hand like a counselling daddy but I dodge him by reaching for my drink.

Ever since puberty I've been irresistible to blokes I didn't rate whereas nobody I yearned for ever gave me a second sneer. When I was brushing Deano off he was besotted, but after I fell for him and became his concubine his affections swung straight back to the spliffs and scrubbers he had given up to make himself presentable to me. It's just the same when it comes to the actual bonking. If I'm indifferent, even unconscious, mad-for-it Deano is all over me – but if it's me that fancies a shag and takes the lead it's a turn-off. Whatsitsname? Anxiety impotence? It's as if I let out an off-putting pong as I warm up. But perhaps this is more about the blokeishness of blokes than about the me-ness of me.

Gabriel always knuckles down to duty and stays control-freaky even when half-pissed and love-lorn for frigid Lisa. When we got to the arrivals gate he sported a large card painted in red aerosol: BALUTH. A wheeze that I always forget till I get to the gate, when I have to wave a wibbly bit of Baluth-headed note-paper out of my dossier. Gabriel's placard was much more up-front and speedily spotted by the punters as they trooped out of customs.

They thronged round us and dropped their baggage onto each other's feet and in the way of other travellers. Through their jet-lag and weariness you could see the haloes of relief now that they were somebody else's problem and their holiday had really started. A big, middle-aged woman with her hair in a long grey braid bounced up to me and hollered, 'Doctor Livingstone, I presume?' then let out a peal of silvery mirth. A haggard-looking blonde in her thirties loomed up dressed all in black and asked, 'Do you know where there is a toilet?' She sounded German or Dutch: speaking slowly and moving her lips very carefully as if she thought I might be deaf but able to lip-read. I pointed at the illuminated sign. A fat, cross-looking man with floppy brown hair and a fuzzy beard plonked down two fat cases and squonked in a cross fat man's voice, 'I fail to see why there is any need to go to Madrid to get from Heathrow to Mexico City.' A striking black woman, straight and stately with strong, handsome features, came and stood next to me without saying anything. A gaunt old woman asked if she might change some money at once. She had blue-rinsed ridges of hair and a swanky voice but a brown wrinkled face like an old fisherman. I beamed at her and chanted brightly, 'Just a minute! There'll be time for that!' A gangling bloke with a blue chin slouched up and said in a Northern accent, 'Doctor Livingstone, I presume?' and chuckled.

I was keeping aloof so as not to give the same introduction and explanation umpteen times. At the same time I was counting. There should be twelve. The other four, from France, Australia and the States, were 'land-only' customers already booked into the hotel – I had so far managed to avoid them. When there were twelve, including the woman who had disappeared into the toilet, I semaphored at Gabriel but he went on grinning and waving his placard.

'Hello and welcome to BALUTH BT15, Magic of Mexico. I'm Lisa, your tour leader. This is Gabriel, your guide to Mexico City.'

Several mumbled how-de-do. Somebody said, 'Ooh goody! Super!' Somebody said, 'Liza Minelli.' Somebody let out a mad laugh like an impaled zombie. Somebody said, oh-so-testily, 'Where's the bus?'

You couldn't tell anything important from the questionnaires. You couldn't tell who were going to keep the group waiting all the time, catch malaria and lose their wallets. Who were going to puke in the bus. Who were going to be paralysed with vertigo on the pyramids. Who were going to have nasty laughs, be mean with money, tell filthy jokes, wear puffa jackets, want their food vegan or kosher or boiled in special disinfected plastic bags. You couldn't tell (though there were clues) who would set themselves up as authorities, lecturing the rest of us about Mexican history, archaeology, astronomy and wildlife. Which would be the wise-crackers, the grumblers, the claustrophobics, the cheer-leaders, the thugs, the pressure-cases, the wannabes, the enigmas. All you could be sure of was that they would be a bit worse than the last group. They always are.

Thing is, fun-seekers, over the last five years the standard of Baluth punter has nose-dived. The problem is that group tours

– any group tours – attract people who are deservedly lonely: people used to finding space around themselves as strangers and acquaintances cringe away. The more such people show up and feed on a captive audience, the less normal people enjoy themselves on Baluth tours and want to repeat the experience. So Baluth tour groups contain a greater and greater percentage of nerds and pariahs, and a time can be foreseen when an entire one-hundred-percent group of detestable scumbags will detest and murder itself.

Nobody in the first-floor lounge where I had fixed to hold the briefing. Some were finishing breakfast: the rest had either not heard my spiel or had forgotten it. Downstairs I found several sitting in the foyer where they'd filled in the questionnaires when they arrived. An agitated woman dashed up to me brandishing a slip of paper.

'You must help me!' she commanded, in one of the public-school voices I'd kept hearing the previous night. 'I've been overcharged, I mean given the wrong change.'

She was a wispy little woman with a hennaed hairstyle, including a silly fringe, that was supposed to make her look younger. Looking beyond her, I could see the waiter, Alfredo, peering round the door of the dining-room like a sniper.

'I've spoken to him in Spanish but he pretends not to understand,' she said. 'Two pesos.'

'He'll have deducted his tip,' I said. 'It's normal practice here.'

'But it said on the menu that service was included.' She was red faced, screwed up.

I said, 'It's only twenty pence.'

Wooh! Her face went even redder and she cried out in a shrill voice: 'It said on the menu that service was included!' She was staring like a nutter and other members of the group were watching us.

'Did it?' I said sweetly. 'Okay.'

Plucking the bill from her fingers I took it to the dining-room. Alfredo intercepted me, as I knew he would, before I could get to the cashier.

'*Dos pesos por la señora.*'

Alfredo nodded gravely. He reached some change from his pocket, counted out four fifty centavos coins and placed them with exaggerated care into my hand.

People who back home blithely let themselves be ripped off for hundreds of quid by plumbers and solicitors will frantically count every penny abroad, as if bandits will cut their throats if they show any sign of being an easy touch, or as if the whole reputation of a glorious empire rests on not being conned by local wogs. In a poor country like Mexico they get especially stingy. They'll haggle with a market-woman over a sum that wouldn't buy a blob of lime with their beer in an East Grinstead pub.

Baluth policy condones this. We are encouraged to tell the punters the natives expect them to haggle and are disappointed if they don't, which is a frigging lie because the natives don't do it for fun and are delighted if you give them their first price, in the case of textiles about a tenth what you'd cough up in England. Haggling adds to the feel-good factor of the trip. Something to boast about when you get home, as real seasoned travellers – not just sniffing out bargains but earning them by squeezing the natives. As if it's even more fun being rich and privileged among rat-poor folk if you've done them at their own game and got them to take twopence less. I used to trot out the recommended line as part of the cheerful service, but now I say what I think.

'You've all had the itinerary – (Yes, that's right.) – so I shan't go into a lot of detail but there have been one or two alterations. We spend three full days here in Mexico City. (Hooray! Sorry.) Today is an extra, because of the rearrangement of the flight schedules. In half an hour, at ten thirty, a coach will arrive to take you to Xochimilco, the ancient water network of Tenoctitlan, known as the Floating Gardens. (Ooh goody, super!) You can hire boats there after lunch and cruise the canals to Mariachi music and there's plenty to eat and drink. It's great there and I'd love to come with you but unfortunately can't – (Oh what a shame!

Why not?) – because I have a lot of paperwork to catch up on, but Gabriel speaks excellent English. (Who?) Gabriel. (Sorry.) Tomorrow morning we spend in the Archaeological Museum – (Tomorrow morning? Roger!) – followed by a visit to the Zocalo in the afternoon.'

The big woman with the long grey plait who kept interrupting me had a notebook in which she was scribbling, hardly watching what she was writing. Otherwise what I said was received in silence apart from one or two formal murmurs of appreciation. Dennis the Welshman was nodding his head as if he had written my speech for me and was reasonably happy with how I was delivering it. I struggled on with the itinerary, then with some blurb about not getting their knickers in a twist over hold-ups and agenda-loops. Enjoy it all, said I, as part of the Mexico experience.

'Finally, I need a hundred and eighty dollars from everybody for the tour kitty. This pays admission fees for sites and museums and all tips to guides, drivers and so forth. I'd also like a volunteer to look after this kitty.'

I looked around oh-so-radiantly but everybody avoided eye contact. 'Aw, come on! There's nothing to it. I'll tell you how much to tip and stuff like that.'

Always an iffy moment. There was no reason why any of these punters – who had come on an organised tour to avoid this sort of hassle – should take on work I was paid to do. Also, if they thought beyond my blah-de-blah-de-blah, they'd see it made no sense, because it would be as much trouble for me to help and advise the kitty treasurer as to do the job myself.

Thing is, if I looked after the kitty I would have to dish out what was left at the end and trust somebody to take the plunge and make a collection for me. Sometimes this didn't happen, even at the end of a really smooth trip – and it was difficult to do anything to inspire it. But if I appointed a tips monitor it was odds on that what was left in the kitty would form the basis for my tip.

It was one of the tricks Kelvin taught me when he nursed me through my first assignment. Since he's been on the board at

Baluth HQ we've had a Team Leader Circular forbidding the tips monitor scam under the description of 'unacceptable delegation of responsibilities'. The poacher turned gamekeeper, hmm? None of the other things have happened – the longer contracts, higher pay and improved health insurance – that Kelvin used to sound off about when he was a poor bloody gubbins like the rest of us.

A dumpy-looking woman with an Irish accent said, 'One of the boys.'

I looked at Martin, the tall, skinny publican from Manchester. 'No, no,' he said. 'I'm useless with money. Simon's the man you want.'

I turned to the fat geezer. He had a permanent sulk about him but first impressions can be misleading. At first glance, for instance, you would say he didn't care about his image – but his beard had surely been grown to camouflage his fat jowls, and brown wings of hair groomed and deployed to cover his bald dome. I simpered (deep breath), 'Simon, would you mind?'

'I most certainly would!' he retorted in a testy whine that exactly matched his features.

H.A.B.W.A.G. Hide a blunder with a grin. Never let the punters think you're rattled. I smiled radiantly, thinking, arseholes, fat git. Once a couple refuse you don't get any takers. Even the woman with the plait had shut up and was deep in her notebook. 'We'll leave it for now,' I chirruped. 'Maybe somebody will volunteer in the course of the . . .'

Part of Baluth Induction was Simulation. We were difficult punters – pretending to be ill, demanding changes to the itinerary or heckling the team leader with questions while he or she was trying to deal with the rest of the hassle. The one who had the team leader role was supposed to maintain various principles. (i) Never let the punters think you're rattled. (ii) Never promise anything you can't deliver – and remember that you aren't empowered to make decisions. (iii) Treat every demand or request, however stupid, with a show of attention. (iv) Put a positive spin on things. (v) Keep a high profile – 'I'll personally have a word with the chef . . .' etc. This not only lulls the punters but gets you a better tip at the end of the tour. Samantha – she was a head-banger who dropped out during the training course – was fiendishly bloody-minded – picking at everything the team leader said, quoting the brochures, insisting on her rights, making impossible demands and complaining about everything at the top of her voice to the extent that nobody playing the team leader could handle her. When some of us complained that Sam was over the top, Terri, who was running the simulations, just grinned and said, 'You'll see.'

I don't think I can go to Xochiwatsit because my glands are swollen. Where's the action, you know, round here? This is a photo of my second cousin in Felixstowe. What's the Spanish for suppository? Explain to me again about the exchange rate. I speak several languages but very badly. Could you arrange for me to sit near the door of the bus? The prices at the hotel desk are less than we are charged. Haven't I seen you on TV? Can you inform me of the current figures for quasi-urban aggregation in Mexico and how they have been quantified? There is a creature in my lavatory. Are you a transcendentalist? Can you mend zips? Ignore me if I'm a nuisance. The friskiest mandrills are in Tanganyika. My life has been a shambles. Where can I buy a very expensive hammock? Explain to silly me again about the exchange rate. I hope you're going to be tough on dawdlers.

When they were gone, phew, I had a beer and rang Deano. He was not there.

There's a film whose title I forget but it has Daniel Day-Lewis in it. The heroine – because the bloke she loves (DDL) is always screwing around – falls into the fix of blaming herself for her judgmental attitudes – and goes out to get shagged in a bid to clear the cobwebs and reconstruct the relationship. I mention this just to show I had no such guilt thing going on and wasn't doing anything for Deano's sake, not even taking revenge on him.

Okay, so that last bit is a porkie. I rang Lee.

He's a Harvard post-graduate researching in Mexico. I first ran into him in the Olmec room in the Archaeological Museum, a grizzly gloomy womb for our cool and hyper-modern relationship; since when we had met three times – the first time by accident – in Chapultepec Park. Once a month for three months, whenever I was in the capital at the start of a Baluth cycle, we shared a fast food lunch while watching the voladores.

Lee gave me scholarly snippets I could use to wow the punters. He was a good listener, too, and I told myself ours was an intellectual thing. Even when we'd progressed to swapping life histories I reckoned our relationship had zero chemistry. For one thing, his personal stuff was a tad *no simpatico*. It was blatant that he had everything going for him – handsome, brainy child of the stinking rich – yet he presented his life so far as an injustice he was struggling to endure. Tears of self-pity rimmed his eyes as he spoke of his disastrous childhood, the teachers who picked on him, the buddies who betrayed him, the parents who starved him of affection. Yuk. Plus there was no way I could fall for somebody who'd be so acceptable to Mummy.

A couple of times he tried to make an evening date but I was committed to my tour group. His third shot, at our last meeting, was nearer the target. After chatting about his enthusiasm for pre-war Mississippi blues – about which I confessed to knowing nothing but not that I couldn't give a toss – he claimed to have samples on CD at his digs and suggested we go to shelter from the swelter.

I nearly picked up the offer as casually as it was dropped. Then I stood bolt upright off the log we were using for a bench. 'I'm engaged to Deano!'

A dumbo thing to blab. It smashed the sophisticated image I'd been beaming towards Lee and blew the tact that was letting our relationship breathe. It was also redundant. I'd told Lee plenty about Dean, which he'd have taken on board before he made his proposition.

Lee spread his hands. He's one of those big athletes who seem to tiptoe. A collection of slow, soothing gestures go with his voice and spiel. I've occasionally thought him creepy, like an undertaker, but usually he seems beguiling and a bit hypnotic. 'I've bugged you,' he said.

'Don't flatter yourself.' I strode off without looking back. Fled. Social disaster. Done for that utterly oblivious bastard Deano.

'Lee Schumacker?'
    'Yeah. Lisa?'
    'See you at the voladores? I'd love to hear some pre-war blues.'

I got a bus by the statue of Cuauhtemoc and rode through the pink zone to Chapultepec Park. A bit of Mexico that could be Madrid or Atlanta or almost any city centre – busy carriageways between plate glass buildings. That suited me fine because as I had said to Mummy I hated Mexico now. I hated Montezuma and Zapata and Popocatapetl, the ball courts and cathedrals, tortillas and iguanas, priests and mariachi musicians and little bald dogs.

I can remember getting a buzz from the crowds in Chapultepec but now all I could see were stereotypes – leery men, stumpy women, sticky kids – everybody little and dark and rowdy.

There was a crowd round the voladores where Lee was waiting on our tree-trunk bench scoffing a waffle splodged with raspberry syrup. He seemed gobsmacked to see me, which made no sense till it hit me that he was reacting to my appearance – I'd donned my maroon stretch leggings that make my thighs and buttocks look predatory. (I'd considered a minidress and those white silk stockings but that would have been too clunkingly symbolic.) Maybe he hadn't fathomed the coded message about the blues. Certainly he didn't look decked out for a passion-fest. He was in full nerd mode – sandals, Bermudas and a Hawaiian shirt. His squatting position on the log meant his knobbly kneecaps were just about level with his cropped blond brainbox that glistened in the sun.

I had two cans of Tecate in an insulated bag for lunch, along with a chocky bar (and I hadn't had breakfast – when I'm not eating restaurant nosh with the punters I starve). I offered Lee a beer but he had a Coke between his feet. He moved over on the log, I squished in next to him and he loomed over me. I'm tall myself, and used to looking down at Deano. The voladores in scarlet and white were climbing the pole, the musician last of all.

Neither of us spoke for a while then Lee murmured, 'You unhappy about Dean?' A quite impressive reading-between-the-lines thing to say. It also – in case my nerve had cracked – offered me the alternative agenda of a shoulder to blub on.

'I don't want to talk about relationships.'

Lee put a big mitt on mine and said softly, 'Take it easy, Honey.' It was the first time he had ever called me that. He set off telling me about his latest research on the Olmecs who are part of his doctorate project. Zzz. The four voladores flipped backwards off their platform and came spiralling slowly down with their arms spread. The musician was standing there scarily high, playing a flute and stamping his foot on a drum.

Mexico City has the best metro in the galaxy, kept sweet and safe by busy cleaners and smiley cops. The commuters never have the psychotic look they get on the Bakerloo line. We travelled across to Balderas then down to Copilco where Lee lodges, handy for the Ciudad Universitario.

Now it was me talking. I told him about the dribbly loony in San Cristobal and gave him the plot of *Pulp Fiction* in detail. I told him about my first cigarette, the alligators in Regent's Park Zoo, hand dancing, winter in East Grinstead, why I hate poetry, stonewashed jeans. I chattered all the way out of the metro, up a tree-lined street like nowhere I had ever seen in Mexico City, and through a wrought-iron gate into a small colonial villa.

A big cool room with a leafy vista. The walls were glimmery-white, the furnishings Spanish – even Moorish – with dark wood and crimson fabrics. There was a battery of techno hardware – a hi-fi deck, a TV and video, a computer layout – that must have cost more than I've ever earned.

Lee said, 'I don't have anything alcoholic.'

I said it didn't matter, though it did.

Lee said, 'What would you like to hear? We'll start with Charley Patton, the daddy of them all.' He seemed under the delusion that I actually wished to listen to some gloopy old dork.

We perched our bums on a high-backed settle like they used to have in the Dark Ages and listened to three tracks. Taken from wrecked old seventy-eights, they sounded as if somebody with a sore throat was singing in a shower on a train. Lee started to feed me a lot of technical stuff about the guitar tuning and blah-de-blah but I hushed him and wriggled myself up against him pretending to drink in the dreary racket. If this surprised him he didn't let it show – he put his pectorally advantaged arm around me like a good old pal. At the end of the first song he asked, 'What do you think?'

I peered up his nose. 'Okay,' I sighed. 'Very much okay.' And snuggling my head into his shoulder I added, 'And so are you.'

At the end of the second song we kissed. At the end of the third dollop of gunge we set off for the bed like slowed-down Apache dancers, clinching and grunting all the way and leaving a trail of shoes and garments.

It was B.A.N.G.O! Big, reliable Lee. We moaned and pulsed and slid on a slow-motion tsunami while old Charley grizzled away like he was on Mogadon in the next room.

Later we lay in one another's arms treacly and gratified while Lee did a lot of talking. I was somebody he'd been looking for all his lonely, thwarted life. It had been love at first sight among the spooky carvings of the Olmec room. Our lunches in the park had been anguish because he could see they were no big deal from my point of view. When I'd fled from the third meeting he'd been devastated, cursing himself for being impatient and pressuring me. When I'd rang him that day he'd been struck stupid, unable to credit his luck. Now, this minute, he was less desolate than he could ever remember. He'd found me – we'd found each other – and he wasn't going to let me go, ever.

The more I listened to his gentle Yankee voice the less I felt able to put out a response. Impossible to go along with his stampeding propositions after I'd only known him for a few hours of easy-spent time – and difficult to turn them down with my legs still tingling from orgasm. It was a relief – and a bit miffing, too – that it didn't occur to him to ask me for my verdict. Sex-wise, Lee seemed to be in ethical timewarp – he took it for granted, like a medieval wotsit or a Victorian virgin, that we wouldn't have screwed if I didn't intend to spend the rest of time with him.

I pretended I thought he was joshing me, though his personality doesn't seem to include either malice or a sense of humour. Then I said (which was true) that thanks to him I was in no state to take anything heavy on board. I pointed at the pendulum clock, checked my watch and squeaked, 'Shit is that the time? Gotta get back to my punters.'

A cheap ruse – Lisa taking flight again. But I could tell the suspicion never entered his noggin. He was perfectly sure of me.

As the cab Lee had paid for took me north along Insurgientes to the statue of Cuauhtemoc I triumphed over Deano. Sex with Lee had none of the hassle of a session with Deano. No frantic fumbling and repositioning. No squirty anticlimax that left me stranded on a prickly raft on a swell of quease. No excuses or recriminations or pleas for kinky stunts as the only means of saving the bacon. Even if he wasn't on the other side of the moon Deano would have had no chance of competing with Lee as a stud. Add to which Lee was a rich, smiley brain-box who adored me.

Tough, Deano. Next time be in when your bimbo phones.

The punters were back from Xochimilco and I didn't manage to get my keys from reception without listening to rapturous buzz-phrases ('Enchanting as Disneyland') and dishing out a lot of repeat info about schedules, currency, the nearest drugstore . . . Some of them were already gathering in the lobby ready for the evening.

When I got to my room the phone was ringing. At first I let it ring in case it was Deano. Then I laughed out loud at my naïveté. The idea that Deano would actually ring me – pay for an intercontinental call – was as bonkers as the notion that he would be conscious at all at seven in the morning even if he had managed to seep back into his room.

It was Lee, of course, the fuss-pot.

'Lisa, you got back okay? I wanted to be sure, and to let you know that I love you and miss you. I wish we could spend the night together.'

'Me too,' I said, 'but it's tricky.'

'And I want you to know how much I'm counting on seeing you tomorrow. Twelve hundred at the voladores?'

'No, I have to lunch with the group at the museum. I'll be along as soon as I can.'

'I'm listening to Charley. He's even better now he reminds me of you.'

I was supposed to be with the punters in the Zocalo on Sunday afternoon. I rang Gabriel and proposed we include the Zocalo in Monday morning's city tour, leaving Sunday afternoon free – which I knew would suit him because he'd recently suggested it.

When I announced earlier that I was 'going to Shirley's for supper' I recommended various other eating spots, hoping that 'Shirley's' sounded untrendy enough to put folk off and give me an easy evening. Zilch effect. Most of them maybe felt a bit neglected and exposed at Xochimilco, enough adventure for their first day in Mexico – and now wanted to flop and be pampered. Twelve were lurking in the lobby for me to lead them fifty yards up the squalid little street, past the garage and the twenty-four-hour drugstore to the back entrance to Shirley's. The two Irish women didn't show up. Neither did fat Simon from Plymouth and the stunning-looking black woman, Pamela, who I was amazed to discover is his wife.

As we traipsed into Shirley's I thought, what an ill-assorted bunch. There were only two couples – Donald and Dorothy, the gumpy schoolteachers from France in their Reeboks and Rohans, who are white-haired and look incestuously alike – and the couple from Basildon who are as different as the teachers are similar: Brian a dapper little plump nerd in with-it labels whereas Millie is twiggy and fluffy, frumpish, flushed and forlorn. The other eight came separately but are sharing rooms – and six are mis-matched. Martin, the lanky publican, is already doing his best to avoid his Welsh room-mate, Dennis. Rose, the woman with the plait, is likewise being shunned by Isabel, the little posh-voiced woman with the hennaed hair who complained at breakfast. Stephanie the Australian nurse and Katrin the boffin from God knows where via Shepherd's Bush are blatant loners – misfits who won't hit it off either with each other or with anybody else. The only pair likely to click are Sunita from the Midlands and Tonia from Detroit who are relatively normal human beings.

Shirley's wasn't crowded and we put six tables together without bugging the staff. It's Baluth policy to foster a togetherness thing by doing this when we can. I spent time circulating with a menu and helping people order – even though Shirley's is an American chain with a menu in English. Then I'd sooner have sat near Sunita and Tonia but found myself boxed in with party-poops at an end of the table – Rose, Dennis, Isabel, Brian and Millie.

Rose said, 'It's super fun with the tables put together like this. It reminds me of Refectory at Cloisterhouse. I came to school in England whereas I was born in Rhodesia and my grandmother was Spanish, an Andalusian blonde. That's where I get my golden complexion.' She's a bright-eyed, straight-backed, strapping woman in manically crisp condition. She made Isabel, who despite her efforts had finished up next to her, look pallid and wizened though caked with make-up and several years younger.

Dennis was next to me, and though his contributions were factual and objective he aimed them quietly in my direction as if they were top-secret. At close range his waxy complexion was at odds with his Zapata tash, intrepid quiff and cool metal-rimmed specs. 'Infralux Varitint,' he told me proudly. 'They are particularly appropriate to the tropics, since they are multiglare-resistant and so obviate the necessity to have resource to sunglasses.'

I was thinking, I'm old, it will soon be too late for me to have children, Lee is my last chance. Deano was a detour, a bad trip. When did I ever have rapport with Deano? When did anybody?

Brian said, 'Little Millie was a demon at school, top of the class in more or less everything, weren't you Millikins?'

Millie rewarded him with a sheepish little grin. 'This brown stuff is horrid. We had it for breakfast too. What is it?'

'*Frijoles*,' said Dennis. 'Free – hole – lays. Their usage is wide-spread in Mexico and they are decidedly nutritious.'

Up the table Martin was sitting among the younger women with a slightly sloshed smirk on his face. Tonia and Sunita were tiffing about something that had happened at Xochimilco. Dorothy gave me a friendly smile but her husband was slurping water and staring ahead, not taking any notice of anybody. Katrin wasn't saying much either, but watching us all with her foreign, baffled look. Stephanie, who was managing to get Katrin to answer her from time to time, is squat with frizzy brown hair and a cast in her eye so you can't tell if it's you she's looking at.

I could see Deano sprawled in the squalor of his pad eating cold rice pudding out of a tin with a teaspoon. Sitting cross-legged and picking at the grey sole of his bare foot while he recited some of those screwy lyrics he can never get his musician buddies to use. Listening to the Doors with a goofy look on his face while he crumpled hash into a fold of tobacco. The expression he has if I beat him at chess – like the look a dog gives you as it dangles the paw you just trod on. Or if I've said something mega-sarcastic – really reached him – how he sulks up at the ceiling, swallowing, with his big Adam's apple bobbing about on his long neck, looking like a broken-hearted camel.

'Are they the same Indians in Peru as in Mexico?' Isabel asked. 'Somebody told me they're all Orientals really – like Japs and Chinese – but that makes no sense to me.'

Rose cried out: 'The lakes of Kashmir! Super! Utterly divine!'

Dennis said, 'Authorities are not agreed that the human race has a single geographical origin, the "out of Africa" theory having fallen into some disrepute recently.'

'Isn't it tomorrow we visit the archaeological museum?' asked Brian. 'Millie's little guidebook says one visit isn't really enough.'

'There's been a change of plan for tomorrow,' I announced in the hip'n'happening bray I use for group leadership initiatives. 'The museum in the morning will be quite enough guided tour for one day. After lunch you'll be free to explore for yourselves . . . or spend more time . . .'

I was thinking, I.D.I.L. It's Deano I love. Deano. He's so dysfunctional compared to Lee that what I've done is unfair and terrible. Better, less of a betrayal, if I'd found comfort and revenge with some smarmy gigolo or pissed sugar-daddy. Lee is just the sort of wally Deano wants me to despise. All because Deano was not in his room when I called him! I was like a kid that got a swish new teddybear and threw the tatty old favourite into the stove. Every blemish of the old toy seemed suddenly precious. Deano.

Isabel fixed me with a plaintive look from under her naff fringe. 'I'm nervous of wandering around on my own. That's why I come on tours like this.'

Rose, however, was beaming at me euphorically. 'The onion domes of Samarkand,' she intoned. 'The shingle beaches of Killarney. The sunset over Mandalay.'

I grinned and looked out the window. There were a couple of musicians in the street – a bloke in the usual wide-brimmed hat playing the guitar and a woman in flamenco togs singing in a sort of bruised contralto. They don't let musicians in Shirley's but they were leering in at us through the plate-glass windows as they performed in the hope of picking up a tip from us when we left.

Dennis said, 'The mariachi bands of Mexico City are usually composed of trumpets, violins and guitars, whereas the marimba, a variety of xylophone, is popular in the south of the country and Guatemala.'

I had been careful to tell the head waiter to give everybody separate bills. One bill for all risks chaos and bitching – and it's me that pays up and has to collect. Just the same there was a lot of hassle at the end of the meal. Isabel, encouraged by the success of her breakfast-time bleat, was the first to claim her bill was wrong, then others caught the itch and discovered things they wanted me to 'sort out'. In every case the fault lay in their own crap arithmetic and the galloping paranoia of the Brit abroad. Martin was a bit pissed and wouldn't believe how many beers he had swigged but the waiter had left the empty bottles on the table.

Just as I was set to drift back to the hotel Tonia and Sunita fancied going on to a night spot. I was directing them to the Sombrero when Rose chimed in with, 'Super! Why don't we all go? The night is yet young!' This gruesome wheeze caught on like sodding wildfire among my charges, several of whom were on a first-day high and blobby with alcohol. Even Katrin, who had sunk into a spooky stupor, suddenly perked up like a dog that hears somebody say walkies. Typical! Gloops and wrinklies, couch-potatoes tucked in bed by ten at home, yearn to turn into raving nightowls as soon as they get abroad with a bit of vino inside them. I usually take them to the Sombrero or the Hotel Emporio, keeping clear of the real clubs where I went with Deano in my black lips and silver eyelids phase. One or two make fools of themselves – the majority are deafened by the racket, too shy to dance and too mean to pay night club prices for drinks.

'Not for me,' said I, pretending to yawn. 'I'm for the sack.'

I should have known better. First a silence fell, then Isabel raised her eyebrows and said, 'So you're not coming with us?'

Sheer malice and hypocrisy. The snide cow had not the slightest intention of going to a night-club, with or without yours truly, but for once in her life she had hit the mark and was representing public opinion. All those eyes not coldly quizzing me were swapping significant looks. I was being assessed and marked Poor. Hadn't gone to Xochimilco. Was leaving them untended tomorrow afternoon. Wouldn't take them on an all-night bash. Three derelictions of duty on the very first day of their holiday of a lifetime.

No way would I relent. Never let the punters change your mind, Kelvin said. If you show self-doubt you lose all trust and the loonies take over the asylum. 'Come come!' I said brightly, trying to keep that flat tone out of my voice that Mummy says I get when I'm rattled. 'We're adults aren't we? I'm sure you can go clubbing without me to hold your hands.'

Dodgy vibes. Nobody laughed to lighten the thud with which my utterance fell. Isabel went bright red. I went on, less bitchily, 'The Sombrero is particularly suitable because there's a salsa club, a disco and a rumba-tango-paso doble spot on the premises, something for all tastes and ages.'

I was glad fat Simon wasn't there, or Annabel the Irish woman who looks a tough old cookie. Nobody let out a mutinous peep but only Tonia and Sunita went to the Sombrero. The rest trailed back to the hotel with me, blonky and pathetic. Bad karma. Only one day of the trip gone and already they're riled by my antics. I'll have to take them rockin' an' ravin' soon.

Back in the hotel I buzzed Hyderabad. The same desk clerk, twelve hours later!

I strained my ears through a babblement of voices and phones ring-a-linging half a world away. Then Dean's voice came naked and intimate as if he was in bed next to me. 'Uhuh.'

'Deano?'

'How goes it Lisa?' His husky voice made me want to weep.

'Not too fucking good. The last group were supershits and this lot are worse. I been missing you. I dressed in those white stockings and rang you, you pillock. Where were you? I've met a hunky rich American who wants to wed me.'

'Uhuh.'

My bafflement turned promptly to temper and I yelled down the telephone, 'Is that all you can fucking say?'

'Uhuh. How goes it Lisa?' Then he giggled dopily. At least, somebody did. 'I got stoned.'

After a while I asked, 'Have you got somebody there with you?'

There was silence, as if several people were holding their breath.
'Naw. Nawbody. Nobody.'
I rang off.

DENNIS BOWEN

Opening the window I inclined with my Taishitsu Quick-Shutter Free-Zoom to photograph the city skyline, which was sufficiently imposing from the seventh floor room but nevertheless gave an inadequate impression of the dimensions of the conurbation sur-rounding us. Mexico City has the world's largest metropolitan area, 2,018 square kilometres or 779 square miles populated by 18,000,000 people; and the city itself, with a population of over nine and a half million, is said to be the second largest city in the world after Shanghai, though such claims are invariably the subject of dispute since they depend on the terms of reference employed.

The narrow street below was littered with beer cans and other rubbish presumably spilled by people entering and exiting from the club opposite the hotel. In the course of the night both the club and its customers had made a lot of noise, augmented by police sirens, the burglar-alarms of vehicles and the clamour of guard-dogs. Notwithstanding this racket I had slept well, because I furnish my mind and body with healthy exercise so never suffer from insomnia; but Martin, despite the excessive quantities of alcohol I had observed him consume at the evening meal, must have been troubled by the din, for at some point during the night he had risen and closed the window which I had purposely left open. I have never been happy about sleeping with the window shut and could only regard his action as 'high-handed', devoid as it was of any pretence of consultation, but being of equable disposition I chose not to protest. Instead I inhaled the morning air, as I am in the habit of doing from my apartment on Machynlleth Road in Aberystwyth, then comically pretended to cough and called over my shoulder: 'The pollution count here in Mexico City is among the worst in the world. The closure of the huge Pemex Refinery is supposed to have reduced lead and sulphur dioxide emissions to acceptable levels, but citizens are still advised not to take outdoor exercise.'

Martin, 'humped' in bed with one eye glittering unpleasantly from the 'cave' made by the coverlet he had pulled around his head, made no response to my jovial sally except to turn himself laboriously round so as to present his back to me. Regrettably, since we are thrown together (as the only two unattached males) for the duration of the trip, it is already evident that we are incompatible. Martin, when his mood is propitious, can be affable and entertaining, not dissimilar to certain colourful old characters back in Ceredigion who are the 'salt of the earth'; but his presence on this holiday is hard to explain, since he possesses neither knowledge nor curiosity about either modern or ancient Mexico, his only interests being drinking (which could just as well be done where he resides in Rusholme, Manchester, with less bother and expense), and 'flirting' with the younger females in our group in a way that is pathetic at his age although harmless: Tonia and Sunita have made quite a pet of him.

'It takes all sorts to make a world', but I could not exist in Martin's state of intellectual inertia: just as I take pride in keeping my body trim and healthy by conscientious 'workouts' with my Ramrod Muscletoner, so I would not contemplate leaving my intellectual faculties unexercised. People are invariably astounded when I tell them I was not considered very 'bright' as a child; but unlike the majority who abandon all educational ambition the day they leave school, I have taken opportunities (and contrived them if they were not readily available) to extend my knowledge and enrich my understanding; with the result that I am not only better informed than most but have acquired academic qualifications and now have rewarding, responsible work in the office of the Controller of Postal Communications for the Ceredigion Administrative Division in Aberystwyth. Instead of promptly spending my stipend on beer, cigarettes, gambling and carnal solace, as is the practice of many young fellows with a similar background to mine, I invested my earnings and leisure time in self-improvement: taking, in recent more affluent times, one holiday a year in some exotic and instructive region of the earth and spending my evenings and weekends at the Adult Education Institute or in the Extramural Department of the University of Wales in Aberystwyth. If in consequence I have deprived myself of the normal socialising available to a working-class youth, then so be it: instead of studying in what the ignorant call the 'University of Life' I have been garnering a broader and more cerebral experience that will 'stand me in good stead' both in my career and as a husband and father if I am privileged to undertake those responsibilities.

Martin is not only indifferent to the notion of improving his understanding but actually happier if unaware of his own inadequacies (and the incongruity of his spending money on a culturally orientated holiday) and unappreciative of information or advice. A striking example occurred late on Saturday night when, entering the bathroom while Martin was cleaning his teeth, I could not help recommending the advantages of my toothbrush, which has rubber bristles that admittedly seem 'squeaky' until one is accustomed to them but have proved in scientific tests to be 40% more effective against plaque and 30% against gum disease. Martin continued to scrutinise himself in the mirror while he cleaned his teeth as if entirely unaware of my presence, only acknowledging me, when he had finished spitting and rinsing his brush, by saying, 'Don't put it in the same glass as mine.' The stance he had adopted to obstruct my ingress made me conjecture that his reaction was coloured by resentment of my entry into the bathroom while he was utilising its facilities. Of course I retreated at once, not being the sort of person who wittingly intrudes on another fellow's notion of privacy, but I could not help reflecting how an important benefit of the group tour is the comradely informality of an impromptu community and how pitiable are people who burdened with the inhibitions of their workaday lives are self-excluded from the experience.

It is against my philosophy as well as my temperament to 'bear a grudge' so just before setting off down to breakfast, I made a further effort at sociability. 'Wakey wakey Martyboy! We're off to the *Museo Nacional de Antropologia* at oh-nine-hundred-thirty.' Several seconds later when the figure on the bed had given no sign of arousal I remarked sympathetically, 'I expect you didn't get a lot of sleep, since Mexico City is as famous for its decibel count as for its levels of pollution.' It seemed that he was dead or determined never to speak again, then I caught a slovenly mumble, and using the encouraging tone which one employs towards people with difficulties I asked him to repeat what he had said, which he did but I still failed to 'decipher' it. Walking around the bed until I was in close proximity to the 'shrouded' head I made my request again, at which he said clearly, 'You snore like a pig.'

Breakfast in Mexico normally consists of coffee or *jugo* (juice), a sweet roll (*pan dulce*), or *pan tostado* (toast) and eggs variously prepared and served: *huevas revueltos* are scrambled eggs, *con chorizo*, with sausage, or *con frijoles*, with beans; *estilo mexicano* is scrambled with chillis, garlic, onions and tomatoes; *fritos* is fried and *rancheros* is fried, bedizened with spicy ketchup and served on a *tortilla*. I perceived a 'degree of justice' in the circumstance that Martin's hangover and resultant curmudgeonly refusal to accompany me to breakfast meant I was able to share both the meal and an uninterrupted chat with Tonia and Sunita, whose company Martin had so monopolised at Shirley's.

As an 'eligible' thirty-eight-year-old with a responsible job and satisfactory status in my home community I am finding the prospect of a wife and family increasingly appropriate. Unfortunately, since not many young women attend the courses that attract me at the Adult Education Centre in Aberystwyth or the Extramural Department of the University of Wales, the only two marriageable females with whom I am in regular contact are Glynis and Janine in the office of the Controller of Postal Communications for the Ceredigion Administrative Division: and Glynis as well as being a heedless and derisive type of person is engaged, whereas Janine though more civil is too 'dowdy' to answer my requirements. Therefore, though I do not regard myself as a 'lady's man' and have no intention of impairing my annual cultural experience by pursuing romance, I have found myself paying attention to the younger women on the tours; and at the conclusion of last year's trip exchanged addresses with one young lady, though subsequent correspondence proved abortive.

Baluth Tour BT15, 'The Magic of Mexico', is not well-endowed with 'eligible' females; and two of those within a satisfactory 'age-range', Stephanie the wall-eyed Australian and the trance-like Katrin who seems to be some sort of European 'displaced person', are too unconventional to qualify. Sunita I also discount, though my humanist studies have rendered me tolerant in racial matters: for example, I admire the childlike imaginations and mystical artefacts of the Australian Aborigine, and am highly impressed by the complexity of the click-language of the Bushmen of Central Africa, but that is not to say that I would want an Aborigine or pygmy woman for a wife. Furthermore Sunita, though not uncomely, has short, spiky, 'brilliantined' hair and is deficient in the elegance for which Asian Indian women are celebrated, as well as a bit 'lower deck' as regards her career status and academic attainment: she is a travel agency clerk who (in her own words), 'got cheesed off fixing holidays for other folk and started to read the brochures'. Tonia, the remaining candidate, is superficially impressive: a plump and friendly woman with cool blue eyes in a pleasant, 'open' countenance, her attractiveness not significantly qualified by close-cropped russet hair, abundant freckles and a startlingly deep voice. She has prestigious and responsible employment as a representative for an international pharmaceutical company and though her availability is impaired by the existence of a 'long-term partner' back in the States, it is significant that she is here alone and their relationship has not been cemented by wedlock.

Unhappily my breakfast-time reconnaissance of Tonia's deportment was disillusioning; though as a relative stranger she was not, of course, blatantly offensive like the creature Glynis at my workplace in Aberystwyth, who mimics my mode of utterance and grins at other people as I am speaking, endeavouring to orchestrate a conspiracy of derision. Tonia's is a more inattentive rudeness, well illustrated by the lack of consideration with which she let me exercise my modest linguistic proficiency in translating the menu for her, then proceeded to give the waiter complicated instructions in fluent Spanish. Her eyes were vague and her face averted while I recounted a shocking and hilarious anecdote concerning the disaster that befell a German couple who could speak no Spanish and took their dog with them into a Mexican restaurant; and when I had delivered the punch-line at the grisly 'dénouement' (Sunita had the grace to giggle and say 'Ugh!'), Tonia just said, 'Yeah?' as though I had been disclosing humdrum facts. She made no effort to conceal her indifference to me, and the only occasion on which she betrayed any degree of animation was when she enquired about Martin and the extent of his hangover, at which her features assumed a fond and indulgent expression which was as incongruous in reference to an inebriate old enough to be her father as the rest of her behaviour was offensive.

I was confirmed in a suspicion I had entertained since the previous evening: that if this holiday was to produce an ancillary benefit by furnishing an introduction to a compatible female it was not towards my fellow-customers that I should direct my attention but towards our Tour Leader, Lisa: an attractive and vivacious woman, several years younger than myself as is suitable, who has the wit to acknowledge wit in others and the intellectual resource to sustain intelligent conversation.

The *Museo Nacional de Antropologia*, designed by Pedro Ramirez Vasquez and built during the 1960s at a cost of 20,000,000 US dollars, has a 350-metre façade and a vast patio overshadowed by the world's largest concrete expanse supported by a single pillar – a giant mushroom 4,200 metres square. On the ground floor, after orientation to Anthropology and the Meso-American civilisations, there are exhibitions of the Teotihuacan, Toltec, Zapotec, Aztec, Mixtec, Huastec, Totonac, Olmec and Mayan cultures. On the upper floor the Ethnography of Modern Mexico is introduced then exemplified by displays relating to the Cora, Huichoi, Purpecha, Otoniano, Totonac, Nahua, Otomi, Tepehua, Oaxacan, Mixtec, Chinantec, Chuicatec, Mazatec, Huastec, Chiapan, Lacondon, Yaqui and Tarahuma Indians among others.

It has been my practice, before embarking on any of my three foreign tours, to equip myself for the experience: firstly by taking full advantage of the Library facilities at the Extramural Department of the University of Wales in Aberystwyth, then by the purchase and conscientious perusal of such convenient sources of information as the *Globetrotter Megaguide to Meso-America*. The effort and expense of such a course of 'crash' study is fully recompensed by both my own heightened awareness 'in situ' and the benefit the others get from the advice and assistance I ungrudgingly offer. This was particularly true of the visit to the *Museo Nacional de Antropologia* because the whole display is too vast for a single visit and the majority of my fellow tourists appreciated not just the practical tips I could give them (such as a timely reminder that cameras are only allowed into the museum on payment of a fee and flashes not permitted in any case), but also the way I was able to draw their attention to a particularly significant exhibit or detail which they might otherwise have missed in two bewildering hours of a too comprehensive guided tour. My services were particularly valuable in view of the inadequacy of the guide Gabriel, who though a personable, fluent and amusing publicist of both modern Mexico and its history was guilty of several inaccuracies and spurious assumptions. An example was when he preposterously supposed that the existence of jade among the Olmecs in 500 BC might be explained by trade with China: the sort of irresponsible hypothesis that imposes upon the ignorant, and indeed aroused no sort of surprise or incredulity from any member of our group apart from myself, who had been fortunate enough to attend the Pre-Columbian America lectures of Professor Ivor Simkins at the

Extramural Department of the University of Wales in Aberystwyth, so had the information that jade was surface-mined in Guatemala from earliest times.

Martin and Tonia took trouble to avoid my proximity; Stephanie entirely ignored me in the Meso-American room, turning abruptly away in the middle of my explanation of the architectural principles of the pyramids of Teotihuacan; Simon gave a similarly ungracious display in greeting my comments on the Tula figurines (remarks directed not at him but at his remarkably charming and intellectually receptive wife) with scornful snorts and irascible muttering; otherwise my contributions found grateful recipients and benefited their response to the *Museo Nacional de Antropologia*. For instance, I was able to decipher the animal symbols on the Aztec stone calendar for Brian and Millie, instruct Dorothy on the details of the scale model of Tlatelolco market which according to Cortes was visited daily by 60,000 people, and help old Annabel to find her way round the Oaxaca room where artefacts from some of Mexico's most important and impressive archaeological sites, particularly Monte Alban, Mitla and Yaqui, are displayed, including Monte Alban pottery and gold burial jewellery. Even when we took a breather while Gabriel went outside for a cigarette I was able to entertain and enlighten Donald, a taciturn but attentive listener, with Professor Ivor Simkins's preference for Pizarro, who conquered Peru by consciously following the Mexican script, over Cortes whom the professor considered a 'lucky blunderer'.

In the Museum Restaurant I was careful to obtain a place at the same table as Lisa, who had adopted a low profile in the museum, leaving all the elucidation to Gabriel. Isabel, a middle-aged woman whose conversation consists of censorious platitudes, shared our table, as did Katrin, who utters English with difficulty, though it transpires that she has lived in the United Kingdom for many years and is employed in scientific research at London University. I gave a detailed but light-hearted résumé of the impact of the museum and the occasional flaws in the discourse of the guide, perceiving that the onus of conversation must reside with me; particularly because Lisa, even more than the previous evening, seemed distracted by some secret problem, though this detracted little from the professional aplomb with which she tended the bleak conversational needs of Isabel and Katrin, or the more spontaneous reaction of unaffected interest and enjoyment, expressed both vocally and via the intelligence of her brown eyes, in her reception of my remarks. After a bowl of *sopa de aroc*, a rice soup which proved to be 'more rice than soup', I lunched on four small *tacos* of beans, cheese and chicken seasoned with *salsa* and wrapped in crisp corn *tortillas*.

In response to demands for information not just from Isabel but from others who either approached our table or intruded upon our conversation by simply shouting across the room, Lisa said she could not accompany any of us in the afternoon because of 'something that had come up'. She went on to enumerate possibilities open to us: including a further visit to the museum; either to the ground floor again, since our tour had been too fleeting to do justice to the wealth of material displayed there, or to the upper floor which our visit had not touched. She listed other places of interest which would not be included in the next day's scheduled city tour, but said that she could not recommend Chapultepec Park, though it was temptingly adjacent since the museum was situated within its purlieus: on Sundays the park was not only unbearably crowded but infested with muggers, pick-pockets and contentious drunken beggars. Return to the hotel could easily be effected by the 'multitude' of little buses that plied Reforma and Insurgientes: or we could try the Metro if we felt brave enough, though this would take us out of the comparative safety of the *Zona Rosa*.

She left abruptly after lunch and I went with Brian and Millie to the upper floor and assisted their enjoyment of the ethnological exhibition. We were particularly impressed by the Tarascan wood cabin with carved cedar pillars, the basketwork and leatherwork of the Toluca valley, the fascinating presentation of Oaxacan Indian herbal remedies, the costumes and musical instruments of the

Gulf region and the diagrams and photographs relating to the famous *voladores*. Since Brian and Millie are keen ornithologists I suggested that we next disregard Lisa's warning, which was at odds with the information supplied in my *Globetrotter Megaguide to Meso-America*, and visit the zoological gardens in Chapultepec Park. But Brian said Millie had a headache: they withdrew to the hotel and I resolved to strike out alone for the zoological gardens, thinking to obtain matter with which I would later be able to 'regale' Brian and Millie, compensating them for the opportunity which her indisposition had compelled them to forgo.

The history of Chapultepec Park has its beginnings in the popular legend that one of the last Toltec rulers fled from Tula to the woods of Chapultepec, which means 'Hill of the Grasshoppers' in the Nahuatl language; the hill after which the park was named later sheltering the Mexica tribe then serving as a fortress for Moctezuma 1 (1440–1469) and being utilised as a vacation residence for Aztec nobles until the sixteenth century when the lord of nearby Texcoco, Netzahualcoyotl, consented to let the area be made into a park. The second section beyond Boulevard Manuel Avila Camacho was added in 1964 and the third, to the south-west, in 1974, so that the park now covers more than four square kilometres (1,000 acres).

The park was as crowded as Lisa had prognosticated, though I could perceive little of the threatening ambience of which she had complained as I pressed through the 'bewilderment' of stalls and music and the concourse of families at their Sunday afternoon recreation; till I was beguiled from my search for the zoo by an exhibition of those very Totonac *voladores* about whom I had been informed in the *Museo Nacional de Antropologia*. Having witnessed the whole of one 'hypnotic' spiral descent and recorded it with my Taishitsu Quick-Shutter Free-Zoom, I was wondering whether to await another performance when I became aware of Lisa, 'perched' on a tree-trunk that served as an improvised bench in my close vicinity.

I did not recognise her at first, and afterwards only with a degree of incredulity, because since quitting the museum restaurant she had radically qualified her appearance. The 'intricate' brown ringlets of her coiffure, which during the museum visit had been confined within a 'cloche-type' sun-hat of inexpensive fabric, were now but lightly ordered by a black velvet fillet, otherwise permitted to 'flounce' 'as they wished'. In addition she had changed her apparel from the shell suit in bottlegreen and mauve to a short dress in yellow shantung silk and white silk stockings which seemed to cause her legs to 'loom' in an immodest and unapologetic manner, particularly in her present posture.

Since I am bluff and direct both by nature and moral preference I took her to task at once, employing a tone of jovial belligerence to demand what she was doing there and the purpose of all the 'balderdash' concerning the perils offered by the park and its denizens. While uttering these interrogative pleasantries I seated myself beside her on the log, despite some obstruction from the person on her right, a crew-cut American in T-shirt and shorts whose muscular definition seemed not inferior to my own and who displayed a boorish reluctance to make space for me. Lisa made no attempt to satisfy my first question but defended herself against the accusation 'couched' in the second by reaffirming that the park was full of scoundrels and while I might consider myself safe enough those older and feebler in our tour party would be distinctly vulnerable. She herself, she declared, would not care to trust herself to the park without a manly escort: and seeing me bemused by this assertion she introduced the American as a friend of hers and graduate student in the Anthropological Department of the Mexico City University.

Someone with less social resource might have been constrained by the predicament into which chance and good faith had blundered me, but my Cambrian ease of manner and the great fund of information I have mastered came simultaneously to my assistance: I gave Lee the benefit of what I knew about the Olmecs, whom he specified as his particular field of study, and enquired as to whether he was familiar with the scholarship of Professor Ivor Simkins of the University of Wales in Aberystwyth. From his manner I deduced without remorse that my 'coming upon the scene' had disappointed him by intruding upon his 'tête-à-tête' with Lisa, who suddenly rose and proclaimed it necessary for herself and Lee to depart since they were late for a rendezvous at the University. The regret in her voice was so unfeigned that I had no compunction in suggesting that I accompany them, since I would be interested to see the campus; but Lisa explained ruefully that their appointment was with a 'stuffy' old professor friend of Lee's father, and it would be a breach of Mexican etiquette for them to take along an uninvited companion.

Compelled to surrender Lisa to whom I jocularly termed 'my rival', I comforted myself with the consideration that for the next fortnight I would have preferential access. Although I was unfavourably impressed by the vulgarity of her caparison (the white stockings and suspenders were particularly ill-advised in conjunction with the brevity of her frock), the 'dominant male' in me was piqued by the existence of her American admirer as well as flattered by the genuine reluctance with which she had left with him for their prior engagement. I was able to congratulate myself on the encouraging aspects of the encounter as I perused the 'denizens' of Chapultepec Zoo: the first zoo in America, founded by Netzahualcoyotl in the early sixteenth century.

Having boarded a bus on the Paseo de la Reforma which took me straight to the statue of Cuauhtemoc I strolled from there to the Hotel Reforma, purchasing en route, for a purpose that shall later become apparent, an inexpensive bottle of *tequila* (authenticated with the letters D.G.N. which signify *Direction General de Normos* or 'Bureau of Standards'), and entered the foyer of the hotel with my jocund spirits undiminished. In my opinion one of the most agreeable benefits of a group holiday is the pleasure of returning, after independent exploration, to a hotel base where there is companionship and the ancillary delight of comparing adventures. My apartment on Machynlleth Road in Aberystwyth, in a 'spanking new' block with communal gardens around a fish-pond, is more than I could ever have hoped to achieve when I left school to take up menial employment at Mrozik Fabrics Ltd; yet it must be admitted that when one returns to it after work, or worse still later at night after having attended an Evening Class, there is an emptiness in the acoustics, a 'doomy' hollowness to the parquet and a 'moan' to the lift, that might have an oppressive effect on someone less self-contained and optimistic. My good humour was even proof against the discovery that Martin had of course taken the key to our room, despite my reiterated instructions to the contrary, to wherever he was now 'propping up a bar' and leering at Tonia and Sunita.

Only with great exercise of my 'flimsy' Spanish was I able to prevail upon the desk-clerk to entrust the spare key to a porter so that he might admit me to the room where after showering I settled to read my *Globetrotter's Megaguide to Meso-America*, firstly to acquire information about the Plaza Garibaldi, our venue for the evening, and secondly to prepare for the next day's city tour and trip to Teotihuacan. I had of course thoroughly 'digested' most of the material before setting out for Mexico and on the plane journey, so that it was only a question of refreshing my memory on one or two details, some of which I jotted onto my Scoop-pad to have them available to enhance the experience of the 'morrow' for myself and others.

After satisfying myself that I had sufficient relevant and fascinating 'lore' at my disposal I began to 'furnish' with messages and addresses the postcards I had purchased the previous day.

I sent Mam and Dad a black and white photograph of a Mexican revolutionary, fierce and 'dapper' with his wide-brimmed sombrero, his rifle and sabre, his moustache and bandoleers. Since I myself have no concern for politics and only a limited interest in twentieth century history I could think of no comment on the photograph, nor could I summon any 'distillation' of the impact of the cultural experience of Mexico which would be within the depressingly narrow scope of my progenitors. Though they are nowadays assiduous in expressing pride in my career success, they are somewhat in awe of my academic progress and much more comfortably affectionate towards my brother Dave, who is still an underskinker at Mrozik Fabrics and a toper with a fat stupid wife and four children. Dave and I refrain from all contact (save such as occasionally and coincidentally occurs via our parents), an arrangement I would be happy to extend to my parents were it not for my sense of filial obligation: which may be praiseworthy but is surely illogical, since my achievements have been despite the influence of Mam and Dad, who were incapable of offering either assistance or encouragement when it mattered and to whom I consider myself indebted for very little beyond the actual accidental 'gift' of life. I wrote on their card: 'It is hot here, 33 degrees centigrade at noon, but I am in good health and profiting from the experience of Mexico. Forward my regards to Dave, Patricia and the "nippers".'

To my cleaner, Mrs Prosser, I sent a panoramic view of Mexico City, addressed to my apartment on Machynlleth Road where it is arranged that she call twice a week to water the plants and feed the fish. Mrs Prosser has manifested wistful appreciation of the exotic scope of my holidays; which I now rewarded with a card full of solid information: 'The population of Mexico City is over nine and a half million; the population of the Greater Metropolitan Area is 18,000,000. The city is the world's largest metropolitan area, of 2,018 square kilometres or 779 square miles, and is reckoned by some to be (after Shanghai) the second largest city in the world.'

At this point my labours were interrupted by Martin, who used our key to effect a somewhat fumbling entry then was startled to find me already in possession of the premises. I could not refrain from protesting, albeit amicably, concerning his forgetful comportment with the key and the inconvenience which it had occasioned that very afternoon; whereon he accorded me a brusque and even belligerent apology, further qualified by the asseveration that he had not wanted the bother of looking after the 'bloody item' in the first place and henceforth would appoint me sole custodian. I demurred from this offer on the grounds that it would produce an unwieldy and unnecessary arrangement, when all that was required for convenient mutual usage of both key and room was that whichever of us happened to have the key should remember to leave it at the hotel desk and on no account take it with us out of the hotel. At this he shrugged in a heedless manner which confirmed my burgeoning opinion that reason does not have high status with Martin and it is accordingly difficult to enter into any negotiations with him by using it as a basis. Even so early in the evening the olfactory taint of alcohol was upon him and he was swaying perceptibly as he 'endured' a little of my logic before entering the bathroom and emphatically shutting the door.

I sent the most intriguing postcard, a photograph of *voladores* in action, to Gareth Batt, barman at the Northgate Arms, where since my promotion in November I have taken to refreshing myself with two gills of bitter on Fridays on my way home from the office of the Controller of Postal Communications for the Ceredigion Administrative Division. Gareth confesses himself a frustrated globetrotter; and though often distracted by the exigencies of work and the importunity of customers he provides a gratifying audience for my 'travelogues'. I wrote to him: 'This is a traditional Totonac rain dance performed on a thirty foot wooden pole surmounted by a rotating structure. A musician and four *voladores* ('flyers') ascend to the platform, where the musician dances accompanied by his own pipe and drum while the roped *voladores* fling themselves spreadeagled into space and spiral slowly to earth.'

My card to the office of the Controller of Postal Communications for the Ceredigion Administrative Division was deliberately calculated to arouse the envy and admiration of my colleagues while avoiding as far as possible the derision of the obnoxious Glynis. It featured folk being feasted and serenaded aboard a colourful *trajinero* and bore the message: 'At Xochimilco (which means 'place where flowers grow' in the language of the Nahuatl

Indians) in the thirteenth century the Chinampaneca Indians constructed rafts on the lake in order to grow flowers and food, which
rafts (now named *chinampas*) took root at the bottom of the lake,
eventually transforming Xochimilco into more than 80 kilometres
of canals.'

By the time I was hesitating whether to send my last card to
Professor Ivor Simkins at the University of Wales in Aberystwyth
Martin had re-emerged from the bathroom, his shaggy grey locks
erratically combed and parted, and donned fresh clothes as
unsuitable as the last: plimsolls, flannel trousers and a check
shirt buttoned up to the neck. I myself lay no claim to being
stylishly or trendily apparelled: I wear Bushcraft Limberwear not
because of the 'macho' image derived from its 'combat' camouflage
but merely because it is light, durable and easily laundered; yet I
cannot help being depressed by the mentality of people like Martin
whose very habiliments proclaim his inability to break the bounds
of environmental conditioning and enter into the spirit of a Baluth
trip. But it is a maxim of mine that the behaviour of others ought
as far as possible to be tolerated when it is disadvantageous only
to themselves: and adjudging Martin's garb to fall within this
category I subdued my exasperation and proposed to him civilly
that I accompany him downstairs where we could have a drink
(another drink in his case) and a chat until everyone was gathered
for the evening excursion. He left the room without responding,
in that reckless, headlong manner characteristic of him, so I was
forced to hurry in his 'wake' and almost physically restrain him
while questioning him as to whether he still had the key on his
person.

'Key?' he 'mechanically' intoned, staring as if the word had no
meaning for him; then his gaze ranged beyond me towards the
door of our room which I observed was slowly but 'implacably'
closing, either because incompetently hung or as a result of the
vagaries of the air-conditioning system on the landing. Envisaging
'in a flash' the humiliation and annoyance of being shut from
our room with the key inside I leapt back with the alacrity of

a Rugby Union footballer in a defensive crisis and by lunging onto my knees with one arm outstretched was able to prevent the door closing and automatically locking. Martin having meanwhile entered the lift and departed from the action, I went back into the room and searched it, including feeling into the pockets of the trousers which he had untidily 'jettisoned' onto the floor, but without locating the key. The difficulty which now had me 'beleaguered' was that unless I was sure that Martin had the key with him I could not leave the room to go to seek him in case the key was after all in the room and I locked myself out. Nor did I like to leave the door open, since I had several possessions including my Taishitsu Quick-Shutter Free-Zoom which it would be inconvenient to leave in the deposit box in the hotel office and which were sufficiently valuable to reward an opportunist thief. I compromised by taking the camera with me in my Screemarcher Routepack and by employing a leather thong detached from the same Routepack as a discreet doorstop so the door was unable to lock itself against me but might appear shut to a prowler on the seventh-floor landing.

I expected to find Martin in the bar or the foyer, since he had said nothing contradictory to my sociable proposal, but he was nowhere on the ground floor of the Hotel Reforma and the key had not (of course) been returned to its niche behind the hotel desk. Meeting Brian and Millie I began to regale them with the motmots (family *momotidae*) which I had seen in the aviary of Chapultepec Zoo. Closely related to kingfishers, with which they share the characteristics of burrow-dwelling and a similar foot structure, they are remarkable for their long tails shaped like rackets and heavily serrated bills, and are vocal at dawn: the call of the common and widespread blue-crowned motmot (*momotus momotu*) may have given the family their name. But I was distracted by the constant consciousness of that door slightly ajar upstairs and had to make my apologies to them, assuring them I would be in the bar or the foyer presently to offer them all the information they might wish. Back upstairs I subjected the room to a diligent and systematic search, even taking the liberty of 'rooting' in the hold-all full of inappropriate clothes which Martin refused to keep on its proper luggage-rack, before I reached the unavoidable conclusion that he had the key. Since I could be confident of 'running into him' in the course of the evening, and since the time for gathering for the 'soirée' was approaching, I collected together such possessions and garments as I might need then boldly shut the door behind me as I left.

I could not find Brian and Millie in either of the places where I had suggested we meet but I came upon Annabel and her companion Maureen in the bar, which is an extremely ill-lit place full of loud Mexican music. Seeing Annabel's bandaged ankle reminded me of a droll anecdote reported in the miscellany section of the *Aberystwyth Advertiser*, concerning the Pope, a group of cripples awaiting his blessing and a weary medical attendant who fell asleep in a vacant wheel-chair; but when I had recounted it the constraint of their response left me with the impression that they are either Roman Catholics or otherwise credulously devout. Meanwhile the barman was hovering to take my order, and I advised Annabel and Maureen that the 'rest of the gang' would be assembling in the foyer as on the previous evening, and that it would be all right for them to take drinks out of the bar provided they took care that the waiter did not overcharge them in order to compensate himself for the loss of the tip he might have anticipated if they had remained on his premises. Maureen got up to go at once but Annabel, who somebody told me is actually a Lady, informed me that she had no wish to 'assemble' or to submit herself to an evening of *mariachi* racket, but was dining in the Reforma; and when Maureen gasped 'forlornly', 'Oh, but I . . .' Annabel leant back and sneered 'implacably', 'That's up to you, isn't it?' The nuances evaded me but I have observed that although both women are supposed to be Irish Annabel speaks with the 'posh' accent of the English upper class.

Simon, Pamela, Donald, Dorothy, Tonia and Katrin were in the foyer; where Simon was 'waxing wroth' about the day's arrangements, declaring them to be a 'scandal' since according to the Baluth brochure we had been entitled to a trip to the *Zocalo* in the afternoon, whereas in fact we had been deserted to our own devices after lunch and actually warned off visiting Chapultepec Park which was the most convenient attraction. I did not betray Lisa by making mention of my encounter with her and Lee; instead taking her part by repeating her admonitions concerning the multitude of hoodlums and importunate persons in the park. I also, with a hint of judgemental rigour 'tingeing' my utterance, suggested that one of the charms of a Baluth tour is the rough-and-ready extemporisation which 'flavours' itinerary and facilities alike; and that those incapable of responding to the fun and challenge of 'mucking in' and adapting to circumstances should, if their financial circumstances allow, take a more expensive and predictable trip with a more prestigious firm. Simon reacted to my insinuations by ignoring them, reiterating his grievance at increased volume and in greater detail; and was declaiming about the laws of contract and our entitlement to the advertised itinerary when Lisa arrived, whereat he shut up at once, like a schoolboy whose insurrectionary diatribe is interrupted by the advent of the pedagogue.

I was relieved that Lisa had removed her intemperate gear in favour of the track suit she wore for the *Museo Nacional de Antropologia*. She discountenanced me a little by responding to my arch enquiry as to 'how the afternoon had gone at the professor's' with a haughty, baffled stare. I pride myself on being a shrewd observer of motives and as 'quick on the up-take' as the next man: I understood that she preferred her 'off-duty' activities not to be discussed, and putting my forefinger vertically across my lips I gave her a conspiratorial grin but she had turned from me so abruptly that my gesture was lost on her.

To arrive at the Plaza Garibaldi from the Hotel Reforma it is necessary to head north up Milan to the Paseo de la Reforma then north-east for a couple of kilometres, past the Estatua del

Colon and two major intersections, with Juarez at Revolution and Hidalgo at Esmeralda, before turning east along Republica de Honduras.

This was the first time that we had walked any distance as a group (our morning trip to the *Museo Nacional de Antropologia* having been effected by bus), and I was ruefully forced to the conclusion that Lisa's expertise in conducting a party of pedestrians through a strange city was even less impressive than that displayed by Quentin in Trebizond. Assiduous marshalling is essential, restraining those who would forge ahead impatiently while encouraging the 'laggards' to maintain closer contact; because the majority of the group have made no effort to ascertain the route beforehand and are easily distracted from prudent progress by both the architectural features and the exotic denizens of a foreign metropolis. Yet Lisa walked along 'chatting' with Tonia and Sunita as if she was oblivious of her responsibilities; and although she had said something further, prior to our departure from the hotel, regarding the prevalence of thieves in Mexico City, and particularly in the Plaza Garibaldi after dark, she had offered no instruction about appropriate comportment and the safeguarding of valuables in such conditions. I 'took it upon myself' to make good some of the deficiency in leadership, but the reactions of my fellow-travellers were either unappreciatively listless or resentful of what they clearly regarded as my unauthorised officiousness.

I was exhorting Donald and Dorothy, whom I took to be the 'back-markers', to accelerate, and at the same time trying to interest them in the way I was wearing my Screemarcher Routepack back-to-front as a device against pick-pockets and bag-snatchers, when my gaze lit on Martin, whom I had decided was absenting himself from the expedition to the Plaza Garibaldi, but who was now discernible 'mooching' along on his own at least thirty yards behind everybody else. I moved back to meet him, intending to insist that he searched his person immediately for the key to our room and/or searched his memory and divulged where he had left the item: but as I approached he turned aside, either on a coincidental whim or from a guilty inclination to avoid my encounter, and disappeared through what proved, when I reached them, to be the swinging wooden portals of a cantina styled after a 'cowboy' saloon. I pushed through the doors to discover the bar was almost empty, it being an establishment intended to cater for tourists and businessmen, both of whom were 'in short supply' at eight o'clock on Sunday evening. What was more surprising and pertinent was that Martin had vanished, so that I came under the impression that I must have miscalculated his point of egress from the street and backed out of the saloon in order to scrutinise the adjoining properties: a travel agent and a cash dispenser chamber, one shut, the other empty. Exasperated by behaviour at best random and at worst offensively 'insouciant', I entered the bar and 'braved' the laconic indignation of the barman by marching through to the back corridor where I resolved Martin must be lurking behind a door adorned with the silhouette of a cowboy and the legend *cabaleros*. A cursory inspection of the cubicle proved my supposition erroneous; but an open door at the end of a corridor afforded a perspective of a narrower, whitewashed corridor then another open door out onto a thoroughfare presumably parallel to Reforma. I now had to confess myself mystified by the lengths to which Martin had gone to avoid my remonstration, unless I ascribed both this instance and the bulk of his conduct to the sodden sportiveness of chronic inebriation.

Back on Reforma I set off in pursuit of the group now out of sight but did not succeed in overtaking them since, as I learned later, instead of following the logical route along the Paseo de la Reforma and the Calle Republica de Honduras they had turned east at Esmeralda onto Hidalgo, past Almeda Park then north along Lazaro Cardenas. My annoyance was augmented by the fact that the street-map of Mexico City in my *Globetrotter Megaguide to Meso-America* which I was soon forced to produce from my Screemarcher Routepack gave no acknowledgement to a maze of busy little streets to the east of Reforma: all full of foodstores and shops selling cheap jewellery and all bearing either no name or the name of a Latin-American or Caribbean republic other than Honduras. I was reduced at last to the indignity of asking the way and so making myself vulnerable to a variety of misleading directions: a difficulty compounded by the fact that Mexicans (contrary to the assertions in guidebooks and brochures) understand very little English and their pronunciation of Spanish is so far removed from Castilian as to constitute an impenetrably different language. As a consequence of all the foregoing our group were ordering dinner by the time I arrived, Martin 'ensconced' smugly among them, and I was not only forced to sit remote at the very end of the table but subjected to what I assume was the cumbrous irony of a reprimand from Simon for having lost contact with the rest of the party.

The Plaza Garibaldi is where one may hear Mexico's most extensive collection of *mariachi* musicians: as many as two hundred on a Friday or Saturday night in their traditional costume of wide *sombrero*, silver-embroidered tight trousers, gun and blanket. It is a lively and festive place with several *pulquerias* (specialising in fermented *maguey* juice) and *cantinas* where one can 'hob-nob' with Mexicans if one so wishes, and on one side of the square there is a huge 'dining-hall' with various stalls offering the different courses. There were as yet no *mariachi* musicians evident (10 p.m. to 3 a.m. are the principle playing-hours according to the *Globetrotter Megaguide to Meso-America*), but the square was nonetheless crowded and noisy with numerous sources of recorded music, both Mexican and *gringo*, adding to the din. Though there seemed to be plenty of room inside our restaurant the tables in the 'alfresco' portion where we were situated were almost all occupied and I was later told that the waiters had shown reluctance to put tables together for our convenience since the process was wasteful of seating-space: six tables that might have accommodated twenty four people being required for the construction of one long table to seat fourteen.

Lisa was circulating, as on the previous evening, to assist us in our orders: a gesture welcome for its implications regarding her approach to her responsibilities, even if it was not strictly necessary for those of us who have mastered a little Spanish (albeit Castilian) and made ourselves at least theoretically conversant with Mexican cuisine. I ordered *gazpacho*, which is a cold vegetable soup spiced with chillis, then turkey with *mole*, a sauce made from more than two dozen ingredients including chillis, spices and unsweetened chocolate; the latter dish being served with *frijoles*, *jicama* (a root vegetable resembling a cross between a potato and an apple that should be eaten with a sprinkling of lime) and *guacamole* (mashed avocado with tomatoes, lemons, onions, chilli sauce and so forth). I also took the opportunity to inform Lisa, as discreetly as circumstances permitted, that I was willing to 'put myself forward' as tips monitor and holder of the kitty if she had not yet found another volunteer. It was not the most appropriate or convenient time to make this offer, but having regretted the modesty and diffidence which originally caused me to demur I was now anxious to assume the responsibility before somebody else claimed it; both from a realistic sense of my own suitability and because I had perceived that the office of tips monitor would furnish occasions for negotiation with Lisa throughout the trip, even if such a 'special relationship' should at the outset be only banal and impersonal in its application. Lisa disappointed me by retorting that Tonia had declared herself willing to 'shoulder' the task and was admirably qualified by virtue of the fluent Spanish she had acquired during a year's residence in Barcelona.

Clockwise round the table, beginning next to my end seat, were Donald, Dorothy, Sunita, Tonia, Martin, Millie, Brian (on the end seat opposite me), Simon, Pamela, Lisa, Isabel, Rose and Katrin; I noticed from the first time that Stephanie was not of our company and coincidentally remembered something said about her having a gastric disorder. Seating for meals on this trip, just as on the 'Golden Road to Samarkand' and the 'Enchantment of Nepal', is arrived at without any intervention by the team leader; whereas I maintain that superior community spirit might be engendered by organisation: separating couples, intermingling sexes and preventing alike the formation of cliques and the ostracising of the socially inept. I am more concerned with general benefit than my personal interest, though a sketch of the seating order in the Plaza Garibaldi at once discloses the extent of my disadvantage: immediately proximate to me were Katrin and Donald, the two most 'laconic' members of the company; and I was further segregated from the majority by the schoolgirl shouts and vociferous 'prattle' of Rose, whose lack of discretion, allied to the copiousness and belligerent volume of her utterance, is already threatening to make her into a 'persona non grata'.

It is difficult to communicate with either Katrin or Donald, who one might think were suffering from similar 'dysfunctions', except that whereas she looks seriously alarmed when addressed (and seems to undergo several moments of crisis before coming out with some brief, 'brutal' answer that precludes further enquiry), he seems perfectly at ease in an inattentive silence he only breaks, when absolutely forced to do so, by uttering either a grudging monosyllable or a 'limp' trite phrase injurious to the impetus of the conversation. I endeavoured to entertain Dorothy, 'faute de mieux', with an account I once read in the Miscellany column of the *Aberystwyth Advertiser* about a gruesome yet risible incident involving a 'skin-diver' and a forest fire on the French Mediterranean coast; but though she seems educated and receptive to instruction she proved herself on this occasion to be deficient both in a grasp of detail and a sense of humour, in addition to which my narrative was repeatedly fractured by interruptions from Rose who alternated a résumé of her experiences while snorkelling off the Barrier Reef near Cairns in Northern Australia with a series of questions to Dorothy about living in France, every one of which I had heard her level at the same person the previous evening at Shirley's. Meanwhile merry chatter was interspersed with choral laughter at the far end of the table, where I could see Brian and Millie giggling helplessly, Sunita flashing her vivacious eyes, Pamela parting her dark lips, that rather uncouth 'shit' Martin leering as he 'scrooched' forward and even Simon looking as if he was enjoying himself: wobbling his fuzzy chops, tilting up his 'snout' and surprising himself with a spate of guffaws.

When desserts had been ordered by such as wanted them (*calabaza enmielada*, sweet pumpkin pie topped with cream, for 'yours truly'), I produced what was not merely my scheme for the enhancement of the evening in the Plaza Garibaldi (particularly in need of enhancement since the *mariachi* musicians who were advertised as the principle feature and 'raison d'être' of the locality remained 'conspicuous by their absence'), but my long-term contribution towards the amelioration of the 'esprit-de-corps' of the troop for the 'perpetuity' of the tour. I removed from my Screemarcher Routepack the bottle of *tequila* I had purchased in the twenty-four-hour store not far from the statue of Cuauhtemoc and placed it with a flourish on the table. '*Tequila* challenge!' I announced, sufficiently vigorously for all to hear; but in fact it seemed to be heard by nobody if one excludes Katrin and Donald (who were too close to be oblivious to my ejaculation but nevertheless gave no 'inkling' of having heard), until Rose clapped her hands in moronic delight and with 'macaw-like' cries of '*Tequila* challenge! Ooh super! *Tequila* challenge!' compelled the whole table to focus on my initiative.

I had intended to stand this little treat at the conclusion of the meal when the 'musical entertainment' had lost novelty, but in the changed circumstances was anxious to provide it before the arrival of the mariachi bands constituted both a distraction and a sonic impediment. My scheme was that, once I had introduced the company to the traditional method of drinking *tequila* (according to the *Globetrotter Megaguide to Meso-America*: lick the back of your hand, sprinkle salt on it and lick the salt; suck at a slice of lime, 'toss back' the *tequila*, then lick more salt), everyone would then drink one measure, the 'braver spirits' two, the 'seasoned' drinkers three, and so on until the winner of the challenge was drunk, the bottle empty and the rest of us highly entertained. Though you will have gathered that I myself am abstemious, I am tolerant of those who 'imbibe' less moderately so long as they are not thereby rendered a shame to themselves and an offence to others; and recognising the contribution that can be made by alcohol to the process of social bonding, I envisaged that my lead would be followed by others generously providing the drink on other occasions, and that the *'tequila* challenge', redolent of the *macho* ambience of Mexico, would be a popularly recurrent feature of our trip.

The first problem to beset my doomed project was the difficulty I experienced, even with Lisa's help, in getting the waiter to bring salt and lime: by the time these arrived I had decided to make do with the water tumblers already on the table rather than persist in my earlier request for more suitable glasses. By this time, too, I had lost the first impetus, my audience having dispersed their momentary heedfulness into desultory conversation; and although Rose came to my assistance with another 'spate' of ringing and ecstatic cries, I perceived this as not unequivocally advantageous to my enterprise, since she was already resented by the bulk of the gathering and was compelling their attention at the expense of their goodwill.

Launching into a brief introduction (to the effect that *mescal* and *tequila* are both made from the sap of the prickly *maguey* plant; but while *mescal* can derive from several species of the plant, *tequila* is exclusive to a variety restricted to the environs of the town of Tequila in the province of Guadalajara), I faltered long before I reached the demonstration stage, discouraged by inattention. There was, as I have said, a lot of noise in the square, and it was difficult for one raconteur however skilled to dominate a long table of fourteen people refreshed by alcohol: the people at the far end simply continued with their own preoccupations as if I was only addressing those in my immediate vicinity. Simon had emerged from his brief 'attack' of hilarity and was resenting the non-appearance of the *mariachi* bands featured so glowingly in the Baluth brochure and itinerary. Martin was leaning forward so that his face almost made contact with the tablecloth as he narrated what was probably a 'smutty' story, in tones so confidential and with an aspect so furtive that he gave the impression of discussing somebody actually at the table. Others were greeting the various desserts, as they made their capriciously timed appearances, with 'fusillades' of appreciative analysis disproportionate to those unambitious dishes. Lisa met my gaze and accorded me the smile of affable interest with which she had charmed me on several occasions that day; but observing how she was bestowing the same smile generally and impartially I concluded it to be a feature of her professional deportment rather than indicative of feeling.

I might have abandoned the effort altogether had Rose not kept my 'nose to the grindstone': nodding with manic eagerness as she 'drank in' as much of my discourse as she left uninterrupted by her irrelevant interjections, obtuse questions, snippets of contradictory doctrine and profuse apologies for interrupting me. She insisted I proceed with my 'demonstration'; which I did in a more subdued and sheepish fashion than I had intended, just for the benefit of those around me at my table-end, among whom only Rose and to my astonishment Katrin would consent to joining me in imbibing. Rose then pronounced *tequila* 'super'; and after essaying further missionary work, 'altoforte', with markedly less success than earlier, she commanded me to make a tour of the table supplying everyone with a measure of *tequila*, which she assured me would guarantee the attention and co-operation of all. I was foolish enough to accede to this, subjecting myself to a humiliating round of rejections issued at various levels of civility: of the fourteen only Martin, Tonia, Sunita and Katrin ('encore') accepted *tequila*, salt and lime, Rose unaccountably switching allegiance and refusing my offer as if I were being pesteringly importunate. Martin, Tonia and Sunita drank without awaiting my instructions: their use of the salt and lime, together with a trick of 'crossing themselves' with the drink before 'knocking it back', indicating that they had been coached by some barman since their arrival in Mexico City. I was galled enough to contemplate pouring my own portion of *tequila* back into the bottle but Katrin was sprinkling salt onto the back of her hand and licking it while watching me expectantly: I therefore felt compelled to go through the prescribed motions again, after which my head was 'invaded' by a queasy instability which made it necessary to concentrate hard while pouring the third *tequila* which Katrin demanded.

At nearly eleven o'clock our party was breaking up: the majority returning to the hotel while a few were determined to await the *mariachi* musicians. At first, when it seemed that only Martin, Sunita and Tonia were going to stay in the Plaza Garibaldi, I had the notion of forgiving Tonia her earlier mannerlessness and making up a 'foursome', if a gathering of three relative youngsters and one near-geriatric can be so described. But Katrin, who had now consumed her third *tequila*, asked me abruptly in her atrocious English if I was staying in the square, and I soberingly saw myself in danger of a 'liaison' so unprestigious as to render me a laughing stock. I said that I preferred to return to the Hotel Reforma so that I might retire before the sufficiently late hour of midnight: whereat Katrin came back too, but for some reason Brian and Millie changed their minds at the last moment and decided to stay in the Plaza Garibaldi and await the musicians.

I confess without shame that I am unaccustomed to alcohol: I blame the two 'swigs' of *tequila* not merely for my failure, on the return journey down the Paseo de la Reforma, to ensure that our group kept compact order, but also for the fact that I was halfway back to the Hotel Reforma before I remembered that Martin probably still had the key to our room. Back at the hotel I was forced to follow the same 'rigmarole' as in the afternoon, with the additional aggravation that the night clerk, diffident about the extent of his authority, would not entrust the duplicate key to me even if it were 'chaperoned' by a porter. Lisa, herself impatient to retire for the night, intervened with a 'torrent' of Spanish that dismayed me by its unladylike vehemence but obtained the abrupt compliance of the functionary.

In my room, reluctant to 'embark' upon a slumber that would sooner or later be dispersed by the inebriated stumblings of

Martin's advent, I sat again at the cramped little table by the barred window and considered the last of my postcards: the one I was seriously considering not sending to Professor Ivor Simkins of the University of Wales in Aberystwyth, though on previous holidays I have given the choosing of his postcards the same worshipful care that I have applied to composing my messages upon them. In those days the professor was as affable a recipient of my grateful homage as he was an accomplished feeder of my intellectual hunger; but in time he has 'drifted' into adopting an arrogant and dismissive attitude towards me which I assume is fairly typical of a 'career academic' more interested in fame among coevals than in fulfilling obligations to dependants. This culminated at the end-of-term buffet in the Extramural Department of the University when the professor was the worse for drink and greeted my reasoned response to his recent controversial lecture on the Mayan ball-game with the brusque words, 'Piss off, Dennis.' I dare say he woke next day full of remorse as deserved as his hangover, though he has shown neither the courage nor the manners required to contact me with even a private apology for the public humiliation. My continuing admiration for his scholarship, plus my wish to demonstrate that he has wronged a man whose comportment is superior to his, now motivated me to send him a postcard, as if the insult had either been magnanimously forgiven or gone blithely unnoticed. I sent him the view from the Pyramid of the Moon at Teotihuacan and wrote on it: 'A town was built on the ancient sacred site as early as 200 BC and by the commencement of the seventh century AD Teotihuacan was one of the largest cities in the world with 250,000 people, exceeding the population of Rome at that epoch, occupying 150 square kilometres. Toltec invasions are cited by one school of scholarship as the likeliest cause of the ultimate abandonment of the city (c. 700 AD) – but other authorities speculate that erosion and deforestation may have rendered Teotihuacan incapable of supporting a rapidly swelling population.'

DOROTHY HEMINGWAY

Arthritis in my knee and hip makes it difficult to fall asleep. If I have a chicory and cereal drink then read until drowsy I can slip away if Donald doesn't spoil it. The only times he talks to me are last thing at night when I yearn for sleep and first thing in the morning when I want to doze on or wake in my own time and come to terms with the day. He asks me about things I explained to him the previous day when he wasn't listening, or he answers a question he ignored when I asked it days before. Or he soliloquises, in automatic mode, about how the world has ill-used his merits. It doesn't lull me to sleep or help me face the new day cheerfully. Sometimes I shut him up but often I tolerate it, because it's something he's always done and reassuring now that he's so changed in other respects.

The worst is when I fall asleep at last then wake momentarily refreshed under the impression that it is morning, to discover that it is just after midnight and hours of stark insomnia await me. This is the dog-watch of the soul when the future slants to horror and nothing of the past is either pleasant or to my credit.

Sunday night, Monday morning, neither Donald nor arthritis were to blame. I couldn't sleep because I was excited about Teotihuacan. Then I was anxious about not sleeping, not being fit next day to do justice to Teotihuacan. I drowsed but woke abruptly as if from a bad dream, vividly recalling something that happened long ago in Wakefield.

I was beautifying myself for Donald's return from an education seminar, making an oval O of my lips to put lipstick on them, then rubbing them together. I remember that *Desert Island Discs* was on the radio: Connie Francis singing 'Carolina Moon', quietly, so as not to wake baby Jonathan. All the same when the doorbell rang I didn't hear it at first.

The woman had a bush of long dark hair, streaked with grey and tangled, that made her look like a widowed squaw. Her bleak form was clad in black rags. She held a basket in front of her and leant over it in a beseeching pose reinforced with a gapped black grin. The boy was not as dark – he might even have been blond under the filth. He had a green candle of snot in his left nostril. Keeping the woman's rags clasped tight in his fist he silently witnessed what followed.

'Pretty missie buy some peggies?' She had a Scottish or Ulster accent.

'No thanks.' Nowadays I'd have paid up out of political guilt and rage, but then I was playing the bourgeois housewife. Donald would scoff at me if I let myself be ripped off by hawkers. I could see they were not proper carved gypsy pegs but the sort with metal springs you can buy anywhere.

She promptly hid her fangs, scowled and let out a little gasp of frustration. 'Buy a little brushie then! Seven years luck for ten bob.'

Ten shillings was ridiculous for the little plastic item being offered. I was interested in real Romanies but this was at best a tinker woman of the sort that (everybody says) give gypsies a bad name. 'No. I don't want one.' I almost shut the door, then stared in amazement through the chink.

The woman drew herself up to as commanding a height as she could manage. Holding the basket in one claw she raised the other and nodded and waved it, like a drunken band-leader, in time to her utterance. What she was shouting in a high harsh voice sounded more like baby-talk than a curse: 'Ubbu ub grub gubble! Urbu glud guddle!'

And so on. The little lad was staring at me as if to say, 'Look what you've done now!' I laughed, shocked, and shut the door. The double glazing blotted out the curse but the gesticulating woman could still be seen through the warp of the bullseye window.

In Mexico City thirty-eight years later I listened to the little click that Donald makes at the beginning of each sleeping breath and thought, *the curse worked*. Then I tried to move the gesticulating crone from my mind, replacing her with film of the Pyramid of the Sun, but she came back as Alison waving her arms and contorting her face.

'It's pitiful, Dorothy!' she shouted at me on a bridge in Toulouse, where we'd gone to change the present that didn't suit her. 'It's a cowardly betrayal that makes it very difficult for me to relate to you.' She was in her uniform, the big boots and shorn head. Once she was a bubbly, imaginative kid but is now a thirty-three-year-old Lesbian Separatist who is doing me a favour by still accepting Christmas presents and including me in her vindictive agenda.

I said, 'I know all about the sodding bourgeois family, how it upholds capitalism and male dominance. But it's too late for me. I'm trapped. I yearn for my children and grandchildren.'

Alison gave her cigarette a morose squint and lobbed it into the Garonne. 'Let's face it, Mother, even as a bourgeois family we're dysfunctional. I'll never forgive you for not having properly channelled my development. Jonathan feels the same.'

I got up and showered at half past six. As I walked with Katrin to the twenty-four-hour shop I said how unexpectedly cool it was. She said, 'Your face look yellow een the 'otel. Now eet seem peenk.'

Everybody agrees she's weird. She wears flowing black garments that look as if she buys them second-hand or runs them up for herself. Her peroxide-pale hair is cut short and square like a medieval page. Her eyes are like brown buttons in a white face she keeps twisting and twitching as though she is being whispered insults by fiends. The movements of her lean limbs are more subtly weird – slightly uncoordinated, as if she's been implanted with a tiny receiver and is being fed remote-control instructions from more than one source. Tonia told me that Katrin arrived at the check-in at Heathrow accompanied by a big man in a suit and sunglasses who looked like a bodyguard.

The shop was closed but a girl softly told us to wait. Then she put her face to the grille and yelled '*Hola!*' loudly. Katrin gave a prolonged twitch.

On the way back I asked Katrin where she lived and what work she did. After a delay so long that I thought she had not heard me she said, 'I don't have any ordinary conversation.'

I laughed. 'Compared to my husband you're a chatterbox! You've just said more to me than he'll say all day.'

People think he's weird, too. Later on the bus up to the Zocalo Brian asked him, 'What's it like living in France?' I dare say he didn't expect much of an answer. The question was equivalent to the French *ça va?* or a remark about the weather. But Donald didn't answer at all. He shifted his gaze towards Brian, so acknowledging that he had heard the question. Then he simply gazed out of the window. It shocks me sometimes to see him as others do who are not used to him. I saw Tonia and Martin exchange a merry glance, and Rose squint significantly at Isabel.

I comforted myself by thinking how distinguished he looks compared to the other men on this expedition. I'd also rather have his company. Mind you, that's not saying a lot. Men are in general offensive, but these are a particularly grim selection. Dennis is aggressively tedious. Simon is a bloated bully. Brian is a creepy nerd who treats Millie as if she's a half-wit. Martin is sexist, racist, platitudinous and always half-pissed.

Donald wasn't quiet forty-four years ago when he was a trendy young teacher and I was in his O level class. The years have cut down his vocal output as they abolished the other attributes that first besotted me: his fleecy fair hair, his flannel and corduroy, his flushes of embarrassment or enthusiasm, the glasses he wore on a stern black cord. Many of my memories of courtship and early marriage are of him talking, especially after a few drinks, in that fervent and extravagant way he had: preaching social revolution and reciting poetry as he puffed away at his Woodbines.

A demanding wife, two unrewarding kids. Years teaching resentful teenagers in city schools. He was quelled slowly, so I hardly noticed, until acquaintances were telling me how quiet my husband was and I was saying, 'He wasn't always like that.' Sometimes when he drank he would revert to his old garrulous bravado. And there were nights when he would keep me awake talking in an awful whisper: gnawing at his failures and anxieties as a teacher and husband and father. Since his stroke put an end to both teaching and drinking silence has really set in. He is a writer now, which involves no need to speak to anybody. He has made no effort to improve his ancient school French and after seven years in Gascony is happily oblivious to most of what is said.

He was the sensation of the 1955 season in Spotland Technical Mixed. Even among my own classmates – never mind the divas and loreleis of the sixth form – I saw the advantages possessed by rivals: blonde Annette with the spectacular boobs and pert grin, Linda of the delinquent languor and mischievous eyes – even petite, mousy Pat, my best friend, could bring out Mr Hemingway's self-conscious flush if she stood at his table with work for his scrutiny. Those flushes, watched for and scored up, were never provoked by dowdy, gawky Dorothy with her big ears and bashfulness, though I hit on a tactic that distinguished my passion forever from the casual crushes of the mob. I became his star pupil.

When I quit school that summer he told me I should stay to the sixth form, but all teachers say that. I went back after the holidays – in a pair of bright red high-heeled shoes and my face plastered with make-up – and was dismayed by his abrupt, distracted manner in a corridor outside a rowdy classroom. I slunk off, wrote him a long letter about *The Great Gatsby* but never posted it. Two years later I met him in a fish and chip shop. I was with Keith, my boyfriend. Donald had frayed cuffs and a button missing from his jacket and he had been drinking. That was the first time he ever blushed for my sake. The second was a few weeks later when I walked into his A level class at the Evening Institute.

*   *   *

71

The impact of the Zocalo was diminished by Christmas decorations still being in place. As it was Epiphany a lot of kids had been brought to the square to be given presents of plastic trash – the same sort of patronising show that the Rotary or Lions organise in England.

Rose said, 'Oh, how sweet!'

I said, 'Ugh!' Tonia glanced at me enquiringly.

'I hate Christmas,' I explained. 'Religious twaddle and cynical rip-off. Drunken men, greedy kids and enslaved women.'

She raised her eyebrows. 'Yeah?' she said indulgently.

Everybody else was beaming up at the baubles or laughing at the kids scrambling for hand-outs, but for me the decorations made the Zocalo look tawdry and banal. And among all the historical grandeur – between the cathedral and the Templo Major – there was a stall where they boiled sheep's heads amid a stench of corrupt mutton – scraping off the meat and brains, plastering them onto hunks of bread and selling them as fast as they could furnish them. Another irritation was Teocalla, the first archaeological site of the trip, next to the National Palace. For some reason the site walkways were closed on Mondays and we had to make do with looking down from the pavements of the square, which wasn't much better than looking at a photo. *You're out of humour*, I told myself. *Not enough sleep and too many ghosts. Pull yourself together. Today is Teotihuacan.*

I was looking at a pavement display of little animals carved out of wood and painted. Stephanie, the Australian girl, said, 'They're cute, but what would I do with them? I don't figure on having kids of my own.'

Why has she never had her eye fixed? Apart from that her blunt features are pleasant enough. The cast makes her look slow-witted, and Australian accents always, to me, sound dopey. But she is a highly qualified nurse in charge of a children's unit.

I said, 'You've got the best deal. Hundreds of kids, and you never get to see them grow up and despise you.'

'Yeah, but I mean kids of my own . . .'

There was something wistful and brave about her. I admired what I assumed to be her celibate, useful life and wanted her to feel better about it.

'Listen, to have kids of your own you need a man. And that's what screws it up. Forget it.'

She grinned, but I decided that her dead eye was towards me and she was grinning at the little carved animals. I studied them again. I was considering buying some for Tom and Ginny but was worried that they would suck off the paint, which was probably full of poisonous lead, even if that bitch Heather let them have them. Then I looked up and Stephanie was gone, and so was everybody else. I was alone in a foreign city, a foreign continent.

I thought everybody must have gone round to the west door of the cathedral so I hurried round the corner but none of our group was to be seen either in the entrance or the gloomy interior. I panicked. It was amazing. It wasn't just that I was terrified of missing the bus and not getting to see Teotihuacan. I had to see Donald. I suddenly knew how I would feel when I was a widow and all the world was as indifferent and alien as the Zocalo.

My heart leapt as I spotted him inside the Church, in the black and grey Rohans I have kitted him out in, standing before the altar and chewing his beard as if being vouchsafed a heavenly vision – whereas I knew very well that he was working out some twitch of plot or trick of style. I galloped up and said, too loudly for the hushed interior, 'I got lost. I panicked. Aren't I stupid?'

His eyes focused on me with a hint of amusement but he didn't say anything of course. I'm so used to his silence that it rarely affects me. I chatter away at him the way a solitary person might talk to a cat. My children say I am mad. Or rather, Alison says that her father is mad and that I must be mad to put up with him. At the moment Jonathan (like his father), is not saying much to me at all.

Religion is invented by liars to subjugate fools. I particularly detest the desert monotheism that has swept away all the pantheistic fertility cults and replaced them with the sky-father who hates the world. The fanes of the grey Galilean, the Gringo god, seem specially despicable in places like Mexico and Peru, where they have been imposed on the just as murderous but less arid culture of the Indians. So I hated Mexico City Cathedral full of darkness and candles and mumbling and ugly, unconvincing images.

But I enjoyed the Palacio Nacional, where the Rivera murals raised my spirits. It was good to see Karlos Marx peering down from a place of honour in the revolutionary pantheon with Zapata and Villa and the rest. The previous afternoon I had lugged Donald round the Museum of the Revolution – Mexico still pays lip-service. There has been a lot of betrayal and back-sliding but Marx and Co. are still lording it in the National Palace, if only because Rivera is a cultural hero and his efforts cannot just be scrubbed off the wall.

In front of this particular mural Gabriel our guide told of Russian businessmen who on that very spot admonished him that Mexico should never let itself become communist.

I blurted out, 'Well, they would, wouldn't they?'

People looked perplexed, and Simon said severely, 'They were quite right. Communism can never work. It goes against human nature.'

I said sarcastically, 'If God hadn't meant us to eat each other he wouldn't have made us out of meat.'

This was met with silence, as if I had broken wind. I have to bear witness every now and then for my own peace of mind, regardless of whether I am ignored, laughed at as a daft old woman or taken seriously enough to give offence. I spent years not bearing witness, listening to sexist, racist, religious, capitalist bigots sounding off. It was Donald who used to raise my awareness and embarrass me sometimes by protesting, whereas these days he just grins and nods.

I don't like Gabriel or any of his crap. He's sexist and credulous and ignorant. His image of Mexico is strictly tourist hype and stereotype and an insult to the intelligence. He gives us the religious stuff about the virgin of Guadeloupe with exactly the same authoritative sincerity as he uses on actual historical facts or architectural details. And he likes to brag about – and impersonate – the macho Mexican male, with his stereotypical pride and passion and fondness for wine, women and song. A lot of men are so proud of having bollocks, as if they were a reward for merit. He's at his worst on the bus when he has us captive, and leers over the front seat with a microphone poised to help him deliver his slime.

Except for his strut and leer he's no worse than most of the guides I've come up against on Baluth holidays. They give you what they think you want, because they calculate that to be the way to get you to tip. So in Peru the guides constantly praised the Inca civilisation and ran down the Spaniards, because that makes Peru most poignant and rewarding to tourists. In Bombay the guide ridiculed both Indian popular cinema and (by implication) the population in general – then went on to tell us never to give anything to beggars, who were not only obdurately lazy but employed and exploited by the local mafia – and this of course was what tourists wanted to hear, to be rescued from the guilt.

Occasionally a guide can suddenly illuminate the tour – like Ran in the Hindu Ghats who made the shrine ring and shimmer with the perfect pitch of his song. But otherwise they are a dead lumber – at best telling you either what you know already or what you don't need because it isn't within the scope of your interest. I've come to Mexico to see things I've studied for years – I don't need telling about them.

When the bus let us out at the Plaza de las Tres Culturas Gabriel dispensed more of his smelly green blobs of bigotry, though he had to compete with the traffic noise and the street musicians. 'Furthermore to all that, this square has become sadly renowned for the shooting in 1968 of students during the problems that were world-wide at that epoch. Mexico is not proud of the death of these of her children, though the blame for the slaughter should not be laid at the door of the authorities who had no option but to keep the peace and quell disturbance. It is the Communists and other stirrers of strife who should be brought to justice for this blot of shame on Mexico's history.'

I gave a grunt of disagreement, shook my head and gazed round at the others, most of whom were not giving either Gabriel or me much attention. Tonia and Sunita were chatting intimately. Martin was lighting Pamela's cigarette. Dennis was grimacing coquettishly at Lisa as he drew her attention to some architectural feature.

We were given too long to study the Plaza, where the historical message is easily absorbed. The three features are the ruins of Tlatelolco, the seventeenth century church of Santiago and the modern Foreign Affairs building that is still a bit wonky from the 1985 earthquake. The allegory is more satisfying in Cuzco where the Spaniards built their stinking stucco cathedral on top of Coricancha, temple of the sun. Centuries later an earthquake destroyed the cathedral and the perfect heathen stonework re-emerged.

The Spaniards conquered civilisations inferior to their own in the arts of war and metallurgy, the utilisation of the wheel and the serious development of written communication. In most other respects (astronomy, architecture, irrigation, social organisation), the Indian world was superior. A lot of the inefficiency of Latin America – and the lousy, lukewarm food – stems from Spain. Social injustice and superstition were always here but haven't got any better since the conquest.

Not that we are in any position to criticise the Spaniards. Ronald Wright has a story about an American in Peru sympathising with the Incas by complaining that whenever Latins move in the neighbourhood goes down. That's a joke in pretty bad taste, if you consider the principle of 'manifest destiny' and the genocide of the North American Indians by the English and others. The Spaniards did better in Mexico and Peru – if only because they wanted the Indian labour as well as the land. Some of the churchmen have actually had a conscience about what they were doing – in contrast to the Yankee missionary sects who are still cheerfully killing Indians with loony diets and gospels.

My obsession with American Indians started when I watched western films with Keith – my only serious boyfriend prior to Donald – and always wanted the Indians to win. They seem to me an exotic, brilliant and tragic people. And baffling. Utterly other. In Peru they never discovered writing but had a social system which eliminated poverty. They never used the wheel, but Inca masonry is the world's wonder, and their irrigation conduits were just as miraculous, siphoning water to the tops of mountains. The Nazca people produced textiles finer than has ever been produced since by hand or machine. And they drew great shapes in the desert for the stars to see. Mayan masonry may not compete with Inca, but their architecture is on a quite different scale, both in terms of size and artistic ambition. Vertiginous pyramids, temples that are massive sundials, ball-courts where a whisper will carry a hundred yards and where the players of the intricate game were ritually slain at its conclusion. And the Mayans used not merely the wheel but the cog-wheel of European industry, not for practical mechanics but to produce a preposterously accurate astronomical calendar.

The amazing relics of the Mayans come later in the tour. Today was the day of Teotihuacan, greatest of all pre-conquest American cities. It was annoying that today was going to be shared between this major event and a tour of Mexico City – because I knew I could spend a whole day – a week – at Teotihuacan without any difficulty at all. I'm interested in Modern Mexico, the Revolution and all that – but I did it, to my satisfaction, yesterday after the Anthropological museum.

There were two little pigtailed sloe-eyed girls sitting entwined, singing tunelessly and begging, in a coign of the ancient foundations of Tlatelolco, one of them banging a tambourine. Rose started cooing and exclaimed, 'What *adorable* little bambinos! Couldn't you just *cuddle* them?'

I gave them some coins and took a photo. I've always taken

photographs and hope my Mexico album will equal Peru, though I don't know how it's going to manage it. Actually I have fifteen albums along the bottom shelf of a bookcase back in Gascony. A lot of the earlier volumes are full of children, mostly mine, cavorting, sulking, preening. Jonathan astride a stuffed leopard, Alison as a swathed maggot, Jonathan humiliated in a Fairisle sweater, Alison hugging a pissed-off cat. And our wedding pictures – Wakefield Registry Office – my mother was horrified I was marrying an atheist. Donald's suit had shoulder pads and narrow trousers. He still had his James Dean sideburns but his hair was already beginning to thin on top. He dominated me in those early years and sneered and bullied a bit, but I'm sure no worse than other husbands, even if being seven years older than me and my ex-teacher gave him an excuse for feeling morally and intellectually superior.

I have memories like snapshots from a lost album: a summer picnic by Sandy Bridge, Alison and Jonathan splashing in the beck; Donald asleep in the sitting-room and the kids painting his face with felt-tip pens, hoping he would wake up and go to the pub without looking in the mirror. The infancy of my children was the happiest time of my life. I've always loved little children – watching them open presents, tucking them in bed at night, hearing them stampede into the house or shout across the snow. It's a pity I couldn't have more than two. It's a pity that children grow up, and that time makes every curse come true.

Jonathan has split with his wife in acrimony and has given up the painful slog of maintaining access rights in the face of her obstruction and the disturbed conduct of the kids. He's a sales statistics workaholic comforting himself by misusing bimbos in what passes for his spare time. He never initiates contact or replies to letters, and his phone has an answering device which makes it impossible to reach him unless he permits it. He's less overtly hostile than Alison but just as disapproving. When he was a happily married daddy he couldn't resist making snide remarks about how he was going to bring up his kids better than he was brought up. When the marriage folded I got blame both for the short term events (Heather never liked me, he said) and for the upbringing that has left him 'insecure'.

Even in their thirties my children blame me assiduously for their faults and catastrophes, while awarding themselves exclusive credit for any success that comes their way. They both wish they had been the only child, and both upbraid me for not providing them with a wider selection of siblings. They complain that I was too permissive, too disciplinarian, too indulgent, too stingy, too cold and remote, too smotheringly and embarrassingly demonstrative. They blame me for the time I, scatterbrained, drained the chicken soup down the sink, and for the inexplicable deaths of both guinea-pigs (suicide pact?), and for the globe of snow they had collected for the head of the snowman that fell asunder in my cold, clumsy hands.

All big capitalist cities resemble each other. The modern centres are structured by the fat cat corporations: when you are on the Zona Rosa in Mexico City you might as well be in Tokyo or Paris or Birmingham. But the poorer areas are more distinctive. We drove between hills of shanties that looked solider and more cheerful than in Lima or Bombay. Just as in Lima, there were forests of TV aerials – the impoverished here too are comforted with American soaps and advertising glitter, action-man heroes and gringo bimbos.

I wanted to get to Teotihuacan. I knew what it would be like. I wanted to stand on the Pyramid of the Moon and look up the long wide thoroughfare, the Causeway of the Dead, to the mighty Pyramid of the Sun. And from the Pyramid of the Sun I wanted to overlook the entire site – the religious precinct with the houses of the royalty and nobility – the living quarters enclosing small patios and gardens like Roman villas – and surrounding these, stretching far away, the crowded alleys and cubicles of a vast and ancient city. It's all been excavated and investigated and displayed, awaiting my wonder. After that there would be the temple of Quetzalcoatl to the South . . . It doesn't need a degree in psychology to work me out as I console myself with ancient ruins and alien lands.

The morning was more or less gone and I was becoming increasingly impatient, but I wasn't going to get to Teotihuacan just yet. Gabriel solemnly recounted the miracle of the virgin of Guadeloupe as we were transported to her fatuous and disgusting place of pilgrimage. There are two basilicas now, because they can't get all the suckers into one building, so they've built a trendy new church a bit like Liverpool Catholic Cathedral. Inside the hackneyed ritual churns from dawn to dark – candles, clouds of incense, tinkling censers, hundreds of folk stumping around on their knees and crossing themselves, the nasal drone of the sky-father's music, and the priests in their Middle-Eastern desert gear. I thought of Gore Vidal's warning about trusting the followers of the sky-father – they're only passing through our world, and they wish it no good.

I watched a couple of young Indian pilgrims – I assumed they were man and wife – crossing the patio on their knees, not even in the building yet, shuffling a couple of feet at a time before stopping to pray and making the sign of the cross. I felt angry with them. I wanted to tell them not to submit to this abasement, this sepia imposture, betraying the spectacular technicolour of their history. On a more practical level, I wanted to tell them that they were being cheated, that religion was part of the social hoax, and that they should be in the jungles of Chiapas with Marcos and the Zapatistas.

Even if I had had the courage, I could not have communicated with them in my vestigial Spanish. And even if I could my political and psychological assumptions would be irrelevant. I knew nothing of the needs and personalities of this young couple apart from their poverty and piety. I didn't know if they were there to cure infertility, or in gratitude or expiation. They might be brother and sister for all I knew.

I have seen other pure Indians in Mexico City – *voladores* in the Park and beggars on Reforma – as well as plenty of evidence of

Indian blood in the city crowds and the kids being shown round the Anthropological Museum. Just as in Peru, the encounters are unsatisfying. Face to face with my favourite people they still seem a very long way away. I can't even talk to them about their astonishing ancestors.

The frustration of a tour is being cocooned from the people of the visited country. Your group surrounds you, redolent of the all too familiar world you have escaped. The country is remote, as if you are watching a video through the wrong end of a telescope. The 'free time' when we can get away from the others doesn't lead to much deeper involvement, because apart from the language barrier there is the sundering fact that I am a mere sightseer whose needs and purposes are as superficial as the contact I make with the natives. To them I am another big, pale, ugly gringo, rich and ridiculously clad, a commercial opportunity. Apart from the stereotypes they learn from television, my personality is as irrelevant to them and hard to decipher as it is for me to empathise with a dancing shaman or a kneeling pilgrim. And what I see of them is what they think I expect, or what is to their advantage. I remember in Peru a bunch of beggar children whimpering as they offered pitiful flowers. Their pleading voices were heartbreaking, weary with four hundred years of desolation, slain gods, enslavement by aliens . . . But when our guide told them off for begging they all promptly broke into broad grins.

For there to be meaningful dialogue I would have to go to the country for years and learn the language – as I have in Gascony. I'd like to open a curry restaurant in Cuzco, where all the food is lukewarm and insipid. But I wouldn't want to do it alone.

Maureen believes. I saw her crossing herself as we traipsed past the enshrined cloak that is supposed to have miraculously acquired the features of the virgin, and as we came out of the basilica she said, 'Amazing, truly amazing.'

I said, 'What's amazing is that they can impose these morbid absurdities on the real needs and destinies of people. And that people let themselves be intimidated by the clap-trap till they're incapable of defending their own interests.'

She gave me a long stare of insufferable pity then said, 'Yes, I dare say you're right.' I've noticed that she invariably agrees with everybody, even if it means abruptly contradicting her own proposition. She went off, unconverted, to repeat her original remark to Annabel, who I was gratified to hear growl, 'Don't be so bloody stupid!'

Tonia is convinced that Maureen is Lady Annabel's personal attendant, nurse or paid companion, pretending, for some reason of Annabel's, that they have come as friends. I find this plausible – but that may just be evidence of my own stereotyped picture of the British aristocracy – pardonable in somebody whose hereditary ruler still needs several people to dress her every morning.

My political development has been the reverse of most people's. According to the cliché, there must be something wrong with both my heart and head. When I was twenty Donald was just starting to chide me into political awareness – whereas now I'm a daft old Trotskyite mourning Socialism as the last lost chance for humanity on a planet soon to be wrecked by Capitalist technology.

My children have always detested my political views. When Jonathan was an engrossed father he made it clear that I might make more effort to be an acceptable granny for his children. It was more or less the same complaint that he used to make as a teenager – 'Why can't you be like other people's mums?' – meaning, with a blue rinse, a twinset and trite opinions. Alison was the same till she found another point of purchase in Lesbian Separatism, since when she is no longer mortified by the extremity of her mother's views but scorns my cowardly moderation and slags me off for a lifetime of compromise.

In my social Paradise there are no parents, no ownership. Love is allodial. Blood compels neither guilt nor greed. Children are raised by Dedicated Carers (among whom include me, please!) till they are relinquished to the Dedicated Carers for Adolescents. Each adult has a Habitation Module that can be linked by mutual agreement to another – others – many others – for a couple of weeks, or for life ... But I am not a fit citizen for my Paradise. Too guilty, too greedy. I am fearful my Module will sit sundered forever in a suburb waste of Hell.

We passed out of the city into a semi-suburban countryside littered with squalid-looking industry: corrugated hangars, railway gantries ... then into a scrubland of cactus and agave that could have been any hot, arid land (Northern Spain) – until a massive sandy-coloured pyramid loomed onto the horizon and my heart leapt.

We were late for lunch when our bus pulled into a restaurant complex – near Teotihuacan but tantalisingly out of sight of the Pyramid of the Sun. By then I was becoming seriously worried about the little time left us on the site. I mentioned it to Lisa but she just did her twinkly smile and said, 'Don't put all your eggs in one basket,' which I found irritating and not at all reassuring. She is not a convincing tour leader like Vicky in Peru, but I think there's a personal problem hindering her. A tall American with a crew-cut was pestering her when we got on the coach in the morning – he was pleading frantically and almost followed her aboard. I haven't yet talked to anybody who heard what passed, but Lisa seemed pretty sharp with him and as a result was in a sulk for most of the day – luckily she had little to do, since Gabriel was keen to bear the brunt. She's an intelligent lass and I wanted to say to her, *Don't throw it all away on messy biology. Don't subjugate yourself to the master sex with their callous angst and their silly bollocks.*

Teotihuacan was still at an almost hypothetical distance – and lunch was only vaguely adjacent. We were shown the entire processes of how pulque and tequila are made, how obsidian souvenirs are ground and polished, how sisal can be dyed with geraniums. We were coached in the drinking of mescal and tequila – all the stuff Dennis bored us with the previous evening in Garibaldi Square – and were encouraged to drink several free samples to soften us up for the next stage, when we were funnelled into an emporium full of trashy merchandise. Gabriel has some arrangement with the proprietors of that stopping-place. It was quarter past two by the time we sat to lunch.

I was next to Isabel. On Saturday she learned that I used to teach at a school for handicapped children and confessed that she had put her autistic younger son in a special boarding school. I told her that she had done the right thing, both for the child in question and her other child. Today she sat next to me on purpose, looking for another dose of anti-guilt. You get into these relationships on a group tour: a conversation a day with seven or eight different people. Sometimes each brief exchange fortifies the first impression, sometimes you're forced to change your verdict with each new day's revelation. Isabel seems a foolish, pampered person, wealthy and self-absorbed. She can't count change or understand instructions or stop complaining for ten minutes. She has an enormous wardrobe and changes two or three times a day – her hairdo and make-up must take hours – her voice is a snobby whine. She is a caricature, then I discover that she has an autistic son with whom she struggled for years and guiltily failed. She becomes a person like me. Like me she is lonely: her husband is dead and her elder son has buggered off to Canada and vanished. Like me she is getting old and scared.

My flesh and spirits have sagged, my hair is dropping out and my face is starting to fold into jowls and bags like my mother had. At the same time I am becoming invisible. Old folk don't exist for the rest of the population. This is particularly true of women, because to most men they only exist for one purpose. When I was walking through Toulouse with Alison a couple of fellows leered down at us from a lorry – I pretty soon realised that it was her they were leering at – but not before I'd remembered how it used to be to be the object of predatory male attention. It's not as welcome as it should be that I'm not harassed and offended any more.

Loss of allure is a minor problem. Since I reached the age of fifty-five I have been afflicted with high blood pressure, arthritis, kidney stones, a suspected slipped disc, chronic constipation, a piles operation that went wrong and spots like blobs of custard that interfere with my vision. Nothing fatal. The rewards of longevity.

Life seems very badly organised, dependent as it is on individual suffering and disaster. You only need to look at an arrangement like human teeth to know that if there is a God, a creative intelligence, he is a moron. And incompetence is the least of the charges against him. (I'm not in any doubt that God is a he if he has the bad taste to exist.) His systems of breeding and cleansing make Hitler seem benign. It wouldn't seem difficult for the human race to come up with something that was an improvement. But of course, there is nobody to bring to account – no bearded semite in desert robes, no cursing witch. Only ourselves and lousy luck to blame.

My health was nearly as bad in Peru but I didn't let anything stop me on the Inca Trail. Not the lung-bursting climb to Dead Woman's Pass, resting on my hands and knees for some of it with a red mist in front of my eyes, a hundred-year-old knackered silly bitch. Nor the day of knee-jolting descent to Macchu Picchu, down steep steps quarried and tunnelled into the Andes, when for the last hour I had to shuffle sideways like the cripple I'll soon be, falling behind everybody till it got to the point where even Donald noticed and started waiting for me. I wouldn't let anybody carry my haversack. It's not that I'm tough – if I was caught in a blizzard I'd pretty soon curl up and die. But I wanted to endure it and earn it and make it mine – that carved Inca stairway – (among the humming-birds and black butterflies, and the fag-packets and bog-paper of privileged unnecessary tourists like me) – on the mountain slopes falling dizzily down to the silver trek of the Urabamba. It let me forget the mess I have made, and the mess life has made of me, and turned me into Baluth fodder for ever. *Maybe in vain. Maybe you only feel like that once but I haven't lost hope and want to stop pissing around and get to Teotihuacan.*

Service was slow at lunch in order to submit us to mariachi entertainment by a wolf-like tenor and a stern-faced contralto. They sang several songs then stood at our table awaiting payment. Lisa murmured to us not to be embarrassed into paying if we didn't think their performance worth it – and everybody took this as a recommendation to give nothing. Eventually the man snarled sarcastically, '*Gracias!*' and turned on his heel. I for my part had little sympathy for the performers but would have been happy to tear their hearts and entrails out to relieve my own feelings, as I saw the day passing in footling tourist pursuits that should have been spent at Teotihuacan.

Nobody else was bothered. Most of them would be bored after twenty minutes at Teotihuacan. That's what people are like. At one time I admired just about everything Tony Benn said, with the exception of a phrase with which he often destroyed his own credibility and made himself ridiculous. 'I know that the vast majority of people in this country will agree with me when I say . . .' – then he would go on to say something just and perceptive which most of his countrymen would regard with derision. The depressing truth which casts a big shadow over the whole democratic process is that most folk are feckless, ignorant and stupid. Nazi Germany was the result of a democratic process.

The coach set out for the site, a handful of kilometres from the restaurant, at three fifteen. Even when we arrived I was frustrated. Gabriel took us into the priests' dwellings and trapped us there for about half an hour, lecturing us on the method of construction, the decorated friezes and the ancient sacred en-suite facilities, almost all of which was obvious at a glance and not particularly enlightening. I bitterly wished that we had had the courage to come on our own to Mexico instead of putting ourselves into the hands of Baluth and its guides. *You tedious git! We've come across the world to see the wonders out there. Why are you lecturing us here in these dark narrow rooms about load-bearing walls and plumbing systems?* I contemplated striding out on my own – but the cowardly habits of a lifetime are difficult to break, even when you can feel the chance of a lifetime sliding away.

In the end he gave us an hour – one pitiful sodding hour – to look over the whole breathtaking complex, including the Pyramids of the Sun and Moon which are almost a kilometre apart. We had time to climb the 248 steps of the Pyramid of the Sun and gaze out for fifteen minutes over the great ghostly outline of the city.

And even that fifteen minutes was spoiled. My concentration was deflected and I wasn't able to float and soak in the experience. It wasn't the fault of the guide or the schedule, or Dennis reciting his memorised guidebook or Tonia chattering in Spanish to some schoolchildren. It wasn't even my knee, that was singing after the climb. (It's got to climb all the pyramids in Palenque and the Yucatan.) It was because when I turned to Donald, out of daft old habit, I saw that he was sitting oblivious to the dazzling vista. His gaze was fixed on some internal event, as it nearly always is, and he might as well have been in a garage in Accrington.

The sun was suddenly gone from Teotihuacan. The city stood drab and dusty in the sepia weather of the witch's curse.

Why do I drag him everywhere? To France. To Peru and Mexico. To Gascon feasts. To theatres and museums. On trips to the sea and woodland walks and mountain rambles. It's just hassle and nuisance to him, if he notices it. And by taking him along I take the very thing that I'm trying to escape.

He has given up almost everything. Neither his family nor education – topics that tormented three decades – arouse a flicker of interest now. He doesn't read or watch television or smoke or drink or notice what he eats. Sex was discontinued after his stroke twelve years ago and never resumed. After a couple of years of rejection, occasionally sweetened by appreciative comments, he gave up submitting anything to agents or publishers. He plays chess against himself or the computer when he is not writing. (I've suggested he joins a chess club but he isn't interested.) The rest of his waking time is requisitioned by me for what I imagine is his good, keeping him in some contact with the world. When I am not making him accompany me somewhere I send him on errands or set him jobs in the house and garden. He accepts this interference without protest though reluctance sometimes shows in the set of his face or the hint of a sigh.

Drafts wrapped in yellow freezer-bags load the shelves above the computer. It's hard to keep track of his output because he constantly rewrites everything, changing it from stage play to film script and back to novel. Amnesia is one of his big themes. Chance is another. The style is annoyingly mannered, the personality of the author inscrutable. At one time he would ruefully give me a page or two to read if I asked, but now he says, 'It's not ready.'

He has given up almost everything, but the terrible thing is that what he has left doesn't matter at all to him. He doesn't care whether he is producing great literature or crap. I've got all his love of literature, his politics, his wit, his initiative, as if like a Drassodes spider after impregnation I had sucked him dry of everything to strengthen myself for the sequel.

The sun struggled back out. There was a brisk wind blowing onto us at the top of the pyramid but down below the ancient city lay still and golden as if sculpted from the finest sand. I tried to imagine a crowded thoroughfare down there along the mile of the Avenue of the Dead: smells and tumult, brilliantly painted buildings; masses of humanity, a bit like the mob in Mexico City, but everybody more exotically kitted out in festive textiles and even feathers. But maybe the Avenue of the Dead was kept silent and empty except for days of ceremony. Normally my fascination with the past either coincided with my political and moral scruples or overcame them, at least for a while, but this time the quibbles thundered through the breach in the dream. My mood was spoiled and I realised that even if it had been given me (by some leap of time or quirk of mind) to witness it all direct I wouldn't have liked it. I wouldn't have liked the swaggering strong and the grovelling weak, the rampant men and flinching women, the posing priests, the fools who were honoured to be this year's sacrifice, the anxious living and the laughing dead . . . I had to face the fact that I would have liked almost none of the living truth of Teotihuacan. What I had wanted time to glory in was the inoffensive romance of space and ruined stone.

I walked back to the bus with Brian and Millie. He has this blatant habit of calling her 'Little Millie' and talking to her – or about her – as if she was a child. When he suddenly left us, skipping off among the booths to 'buy a surprise for Little Millie' I couldn't stop myself asking her: 'Why does he talk to you like that?'

She laughed and said, 'I'm an accountant and he's an ophthalmic optician. We have to be professionally mature and responsible. When we escape from the work environment we become a bit infantile.'

'He's not being infantile,' I said. 'He's treating you as though you were an infant.'

She flushed with meek resentment of my interference. 'We're not going to have children. We've decided to be selfish, spend the money and affection on each other.'

I winced at her evasive rationale. *Is that why he is demeaning you?* But feeling I had spoken my mind enough I said instead, 'It isn't selfish. There are too many people in the world.'

In the coach which was now to take us to the temple of Quetzalcoatl at the south end of the site we waited quarter of an hour for Tonia and Isabel, who were shopping at the stalls between the site and the carpark. (Tonia and Sunita, inseparable for two days, were no longer talking and sat apart on the coach.) Gabriel, who had been so infuriatingly leisurely in the earlier part of the day, was now angry at what he described as the inconsiderate conduct of the missing women – and proposed that we visit the temple without them to teach them a lesson. I suspect this was a bluff aimed at us non-offenders – the way the children in school who have shown up get lectured about attendance if there are a lot of absentees. In any case, Lisa emerged from her sulk to veto his suggestion.

Isabel was suitably flustered, but Tonia seemed unmoved. For the first couple of days I admired her bland poise, wishing I had that sort of grown-up daughter. But I've realised that Tonia's surface confidence is anchored in stupidity. 'There's always a maverick, huh?' she now breezed in her jocular contralto, and we set off for the temple of Quetzalcoatl half an hour before the site was due to close.

Even then, as we walked from the coach to the frieze temple, bloody Gabriel stopped at a bush and gave a spiel about Mexican coffee and cactus fibres. In front of the great friezes of Tlaloc and Quetzalcoatl, as he droned out his encyclopaedia drivel, I did my best to ignore the voice-over and sink into an absorbent reverie. Next thing I knew only myself and Sunita were sitting on the terraces that confronted the friezes. Gabriel had ushered everybody else round the corner and back towards the bus.

I said, 'I don't believe in religion.'

Sunita flashed her eyes contemptuously. 'Me neither. It's bollocks.'

I said, 'This lot were screwed up by religion long before the Spaniards arrived.'

She said, 'I went to a carol service this Christmas. A mate of mine talked me into it. I found myself actually listening to the words and thinking, what absolute bollocks! As bad as what my mum believes – she's still into all the Hindu stuff.'

I blurted, 'Tell you what, though, if I was forced to believe in a religion it would be about important things like planting corn – not a con-trick that insults the intelligence with sin and guilt and pie-in-the-sky. The Aztecs slaughtering thousands to keep the sun shining is less horrible than the Inquisition slaughtering Albigensians over nit-picking doctrine or the Nazis slaughtering millions in a quest for racial purity.'

Sunita wobbled her head non-commitally – a mannerism she must have picked up from her parents, since she says she has never lived in India. Yet I hadn't said anything that she wouldn't have agreed with, argued with or scoffed at, if it had come from somebody her own age.

I was left alone, for precious minutes in the failing light, with the mad geometrical masks of Tlaloc the rain-god and the giant serpent heads of Quetzalcoatl. They were the carvings that we had seen copied the day before in the museum, but these were without the colouring – I prefer just the bare stone, though I know that that is not how it was. They have the frantic, terrified vitality that's typical of ancient American art – an utter contrast to the timeless calm of Egypt.

They were waiting when I got to the bus. Gabriel was looking mean and Simon gave a snort and Rose shouted accusingly, 'Ah, here she is!' but I didn't deign to say anything.

On the way back I talked to Pamela across the gangway – our husbands were in the window seats, hers scowling out at the Mexico City suburbs, mine with his eyes shut, perhaps asleep. She's Simon's second wife and he's her second husband – she's at least ten years younger than him. She had four kids from her first marriage but none from the second. And she admires Simon. It's hard to recognise him from how she speaks of him in her soft, West Country voice in which there's also a trace of Caribbean. She's a spectacular-looking and intelligent woman – maybe a bit insubstantial (talking to her is painlessly disappointing to an intellectual snob like me), but in every way such an improvement on her petulant gross husband that it is impossible to see why she is wasting herself. I was thinking also of Brian and Millie when it suddenly came to me how humiliated and desolate I feel when people show they are thinking the same sort of thing about me.

That night most of the others went to Garibaldi Square, but we decided to eat in the hotel and have an early night.

I asked Donald, 'What did you think of Teotihuacan?'

Teaching handicapped kids has taught me to ask open-ended questions so that he can't just shake or nod his head. He could

have said something brief and finite like 'Terrific,' or 'Not bad.'
But he just gave me that vague, enraging, lop-sided grin.

'Don! I asked you a question! Give me the courtesy of an
answer!'

He peered at me as if I was something gesticulating on the
horizon. 'Sorry?' he said.

I couldn't bring myself to repeat the question that was already
drained of whatever vitality it had possessed.

A couple of months ago, in a grey dawn full of calling birds, he
talked about the games he used to play by himself when he was
a kid. He talked for an hour, as if it was the most urgent topic
in the world, till I begged him to let me sleep. It was about some
sodding camel-coloured carpet they had in the lounge, and how he
used the pattern as a landscape – the russet border for mountains,
the wobbly blue rectangles for water-holes and so forth. How he
populated this landscape with dozens of marbles, and divided them
into tribes and regiments, and gave them names like racehorses:
Tomahawk, Entrails, Black Abbot, Milky Way. The lonely child,
self-absorbed. Maybe he is contemplating an autobiography.

Yet every so often there is a sign that he is still there. In his vacant
grin there lurks a ghost of the shy, reassuring smile he used to have.
Occasionally he lays his hand lightly on my arm or shoulder, as if
to steady a boat or quieten a nervous horse. This is not the stranger
he impersonates. We've shared everything, forty years, our only
lives. Enthusiasms: Trotsky, Tarkovski, murghi massala. Anxiety:
a blue-faced child, a traffic-light, a lighted corridor. Passion and
mirth. The squeaking four-poster bed in the Cerne Abbas hotel, two
hundred yards from the flagrant giant. Or the morning when a knock
on the bedroom door interrupted our lovemaking and we were forced
to gratefully eat, snorting with swallowed laughter, the appalling
breakfast (solid egg, soggy bacon, black bread) which eight-year-old
Alison had cooked for my birthday treat. I can't just let him sink into
his quag and see the bubbles plop and lose him for ever.

*   *   *

In the bathroom mirror there was an old woman with wild white hair. She remembered the face of a girl painting her lips thirty-eight years ago. And seven years before that the awful and delicious occasion when Mr Hemingway called back Dorothy Clifford at the end of the lesson.

Dorothy was suddenly bitterly aware of the defects of her image; her thin frame in its bottle-green uniform and the way her ears protruded between the rat's-tails of hair.

'Is this your own work, Dorothy? Or have you had help with it?'

'Who would have helped me?'

'Have you seen the film?'

'I didn't know there was a film.'

The classroom door clicked, creaked, then gaped open about nine inches. Annette inserted her frizzy fair head into the aperture, calling out impudently: 'Dotty! Are you coming?'

'In a minute!' Donald Hemingway said sternly. 'Go away! Don't interrupt!'

Annette made a face of comic indignation then backed off giggling and closed the door. Dorothy kept her attention gravely on the teacher and resisted further impulses to glance towards the door.

'You've read the book then?'

'It's on the list you gave us.'

'It is but I didn't expect anybody would read it. You write about it . . . remarkably.'

'I'm reading *Brave New World* now.'

He stared at her half-appalled, confronted so soon in his teaching career with a hungry talent. She waited, greedy for more praise.

'Remember to say "sir", Dorothy, when you speak to a teacher.'

The door burst open, several eavesdroppers being forced against it by the mischievous pressure of others.

That was it, then. I stood on the Pyramid of the Sun. That was the day of Teotihuacan, a rendezvous with wonder for which I had schemed and saved and travelled. It had been a day like many others, disappointing, like the Mexican revolution, the twentieth century, marriage, motherhood, my life. Another day spent in distraction and frustration, political rage and personal despond, numbering my afflictions, lamenting my children, missing Donald. I might as well have been at home in Gascony. And when I'm in Gascony I might as well be in Wakefield. It isn't your fault, Teotihuacan. And it's not mine, either.

I lifted my hand in front of the mirror and saw that it was withered, and that the hand in the mirror was withered. I ran my finger down my withered chops. *The curse of the witch has worked. Now I am the witch.*

MARTIN JACKSON

I got up while twat Dennis was snoring and went round to Shirley's for breakfast because Tonia likes it there and Rose doesn't.

In case by bad luck or judgement you finish up on a trip like this I can give you one or two useful tips. Not that I'm an expert on these capers, this is my first and last, but I've been around and know the ropes. I've been in the army seven years and as good as married three times and tried my hand at all sorts. You can't get experience like mine without learning to look after yourself. Nobody puts one over on me. A trip like this is like everything else, you have to work out the angles or you finish up a sucker.

The first tip is take a hard look at the others and be quick off the mark before they have time to fix onto you. You'll be able to cross most of them straight off your list of people worth spending time with. Cross off the elderly women and the ugly bitches and everybody with loud posh voices and all the loonies and foreigners. Cross off all the men who are with their wives or girlfriends because men who go on holiday with women are wankers. Then cross off anybody else you wouldn't talk to in a pub.

On this trip that only leaves three people not crossed out, and most have been crossed out at least twice. There's Tonia and I reckon she's a dyke. More of that later. And mousy little Millie. That's the lot if you don't count Lisa who looks as if she wouldn't say no to a fuck if she was off duty.

It's not a lot of scope, and I have to make a second list, two lists, of people who are just about bearable and the ones to be avoided at all costs. In the last category are fat Simon, that smarmy twat Brian and those posh awful bitches Rose and Isabel and Lady Annabella Murphy.

Top of that category, the prize-winner, is my room-mate Dennis, the biggest cunt it has ever been my bad luck to meet in forty years as a boozer and barman. He lectures me and tries to organise me like the bullying old bag of a wife I'll never have once I'm shut of Fiona. He farts and snores and his socks stink, he does press-ups at seven in the morning, and he won't let me smoke in the fucking bedroom. We're the only two unclaimed males on the trip and I'm working up to refusing to share a room with him. More of this later.

The trip was Fiona's idea. She told me, lying bitch, she won it in a raffle, she thinks I'm too stupid to know that a raffle prize like that is always a trip for two. She wants me out of the pub for a month, the slut, so that twat in a toupee who drinks Black and Tans can fuck her in her pink boudoir. She never thought I'd come but I suddenly thought why not, why shouldn't I get away from that fucking pub and sour-faced cow?

Tonia wasn't at Shirley's. Her and the Paki were probably still in bed. They fell out over something yesterday but made it up when they were pissed at night. I'm broad-minded, I go along with the view that it takes all sorts. If women want to wank each other off that's not my problem. If a bloke wants to pay a nigger or a wog to bugger him I say good luck to him, though I personally don't like darkies or perverts and have never paid for sex unless I was pissed.

I ate breakfast by myself. The waitress was a cracker, a thin little slut with big brown eyes like on the post-cards. I wouldn't have touched her sober at that time in the morning, you don't know what sort of mess you're getting into with a foreign woman. I was put wise on that in the army in Aden. But she had a way of perching her arse inside that tight black skirt that made it easy to imagine her snug cunt.

The bus left at nine o'clock and I was one of the first in line, as

if by accident. Don't let the others twig you. If you look anxious
to be first aboard it will set people thinking and there'll be a
scramble for the prime seats. So look casual, dawdle around a bit
and let somebody else on in front of you, but not too many.

One good tip is not to take a lot of luggage on tour, just a
bag you can get into the main cabin of the aeroplane. That's
convenient during the flight, not having to fuck about with
baggage checks and collection, all the suckers sweating round
the carousels, worrying whether their baggage has gone to Abu
Dhabi while they're in Mexico, and you sitting pretty. And when
you come to the buses you can count your baggage as a sort
of day-sack and take it on with you, put it on the rack or
under the seat, while the others, if they're on their own, have
to wait to see their baggage is loaded into the boot or onto
the roof.

There's quite a lot to choosing a seat on a tour bus. Near the
back you'll be jolted sick. On no account must you be over a
wheel. But the front of the bus is not good either, because the
guide and tour leader launch their broadcasts from there and the
driver sometimes has smelly buddies, buckshee passengers who
infest the area.

Another thing to watch out for is the window. Make sure
you're near a window that actually opens or you'll roast and
choke. But also be sure that any window that opens is placed
so you control it and aren't at risk of a gale from the seat in
front or a draught from behind.

If the bus has more seating than the group needs it's a good
wheeze to claim two seats by sitting in the gangway seat of a
pair. Then nobody will sit with you unless you invite them.
You can put your bag on the seat next to you and have its
contents handy, such as toffees and pullovers and the inflatable
rubber collar that's supposed to help you snooze. Later you can
choose whether to sit in the window seat and admire the view or
next to the gangway if there's a draught, which there often is on
Mexican buses. And if some twat in front of you invades your

space by tilting back the seat you can swap seats with yourself and get a bit more room.

My plans were interfered with by Dennis. There was no boot or roof-rack on this bus and the baggage had to be loaded onto the back seat, so that boring cunt organised us 'fellers' into a chain down the bus. That is, organised me, Brian and Donald. Simon would have nothing to do with it, like the wide-awake twat he is, and I'll follow his example in future and walk away.

It was a bad business. Dennis brought the bags onto the bus to me, who passed them along to Donald, who passed them to Brian, who stacked them along the back seats. Dennis was acting like a fucking sergeant-major or PE instructor, setting the pace, cracking the whip and shit like that. He's an athletic bastard too, from all those press-ups he does, with a slim waist and big biceps like a body-building ad. He would lug a heavy suitcase into my belly so that all the wind was knocked out. Donald was always looking the other way, or would take the case off me so slowly and dreamily that I hadn't time to turn and brace myself before Dennis zapped me again.

While I was struggling those fucking bags up that gangway some of the others got on and got in our way while they claimed the prime seats. Dennis made an effort at disciplining them – 'Nobody must board the bus till we've installed the baggage, please!' – but Simon and Lady Annabella and loony Katrin took no notice.

I'd had the wit to reserve my two seats by putting my bag on a gangway seat about halfway down the bus – but it was a rush job, hassled as I was by Dennis, and when the bus set off I found I wasn't ideally placed. Maureen and Lady Annabella were in front of me and they were the sort who would tilt back their seats as far as they would go. Behind me was loony Katrin and I was going to have bother with her because of a fucking sliding window which was out of my control. More about this soon.

As soon as we were away Lisa leaned over the front seat and babbled at us through a little mike full of static. I was too busy weighing her up to pay attention to what she was saying. She wasn't wearing a bra under a scarlet Palenque T-shirt and her nipples were nuzzling through the cloth.

She looks like a bubbly and enthusiastic fuck. She's a tall lass, big-boned and square-shouldered, with trollopy ringlets round her face like the girl in *Last Tango*. She's got a shapely arse and firm tits and is just at the point when a woman is starting to put on fat, when her skin seems stretched over her flesh like the skin of a plum or a cherry. It was easy to get a hard on as I watched her.

I often get randy since my operation. That was another of Fiona's ideas, I was having problems getting a hard on and keeping it, so she packed me off to this specialist. Falk is a Jew-boy but he knows his stuff. I've wrecked the little arteries that feed my prick by smoking Woodbines for forty years, so he's re-routed an artery from my leg.

I still have a leaking valve at the base that can make my prick deflate in the middle of a fuck. A rubber band can help with this, like male models and strippers use to keep a semi-hard on. But rubber bands, condoms, any tricks and gadgets put me off, I lose interest if I suddenly see what I'm up to and who with and how fucking absurd it is. I remember once in Southport, I'd bent Sharon over the bed and was fucking her from behind when I found myself looking at us in the wardrobe mirror. Sharon saw it too and just gave a giggle but I stared myself in the eyes while my prick collapsed as if it had been punctured.

I'm meaning to get back to Falk and ask about this new stuff, Viagra, but any case fucking is over between Fiona and me, she reckons she's too old for the caper, the lying bitch. The irony is I'm left with a prick that wakes me in the night or gets hard like it did when I was a lad at the sight of a tart in a short skirt on a bar stool.

It's good to get away from the Talisman. It was a nice pub a few years ago. The regulars were nearly all male, with not many Micks and no coloureds. We had a couple of handy lads who worked behind the bar and some of the local cops used the pub when they were off-duty so we could count on a bit of support. But three years ago Fiona did a deal with Watkin's Brewery, they redesigned and refitted the pub, put in their own range of 'Real Ales' and jumped up the prices. The dart-board, the snooker-table and most of the old customers have been stuffed into a sort of barn at the back. The rest is all posh rooms with thick pile carpets, red leather stools and wrought-iron tables. We've got a new clientele of couples and foursomes having bar meals, yids with portable phones and youngsters meeting for a drink before they go clubbing. On quiz nights and karaoke nights we're packed out with tossers and old bags from the semis along Wilmslow Road.

I didn't get much of a say in the matter because Fiona's name is over the door, she ran the pub by herself for five years between Willie's death and our marriage. Willie was a red-headed Glaswegian, a thick-set sod. Fiona is sturdy herself, with massive thighs and her tits stuck out like nose-cones in a heavy-duty bra. They married young, had two sons and two daughters, and she's got seven grandchildren now. I'll have nothing to do with them, I've never liked kids. I only claimed access to Darren to spite Brenda and dropped it like a hot brick when I saw what a circus she made of it, practically giving me a fucking breathalyser before I was allowed within range of the little twat.

Some of the others got excited by whatever was passing the window and made a pest of themselves by wanting to share their discoveries. Maureen was burbling about purple whatnots, white morning glory, lemon schlotziums, till Lady Annabella told her to shut up. Dennis gave out bullshit about crops, identifying items like wild avocado and castor oil plants, probably wrongly. We passed a volcano called Popocatapetl and Rose, the silly bitch-bag, started shouting poetry.

The big lads behind the bar have been replaced by barmaids, a nigger in a leather skirt that shows her crutch and Nadine from Withenshaw who looks about thirteen. At one time Fiona wouldn't countenance a barmaid in the Talisman apart from herself, she reckoned girls weren't tough enough to deal with the customers, but I flatter myself it was also a back-handed compliment to me. When she signed on Nadine and the nigger I knew she either thought I was past it or didn't give a sod.

I've never had the whip hand with Fiona. For one thing, she's physically stronger than me. I don't hold with knocking women around but with bitches like Brenda, and Sharon once or twice, a corrective knock with the flat of the hand was a useful option. I can't even imagine trying that with Fiona.

Why did I wed her? She's a handsome fit woman, like a discus- or javelin-thrower, but not a type that ever attracted me. She never gets to feature in my fantasy fucks, unless the image of her padding towards the bed in that maroon nightie bursts in to bugger up some better daydream and the hard I've got. But just before closing-time, when I was pissed and swaying on my stool, and she was framed against the optics and wooden mottoes . . . I was selling double glazing and too old for the job. Since Brenda divorced me I'd been five years in a fucking bed-sit paying rent to old Mrs Armitage. The notion of waking in my own pub and listening to the bars being Hoovered while I scoffed breakfast seemed like Paradise. What's more I'd started to struggle trapping cunt. Until I was thirty it was no problem, I could have had a different woman every night. When I was with Sharon I turned down some good offers, but it was Brenda that put me out of practice, because I tried to be a good husband and father, though you'd never get that bitch to credit it. And then I was pushing fifty, and the only women I got to fuck were old bags, other blokes' wives, and my prick had begun to give problems.

It's bad at the Talisman now. Fiona doesn't think I'm posh enough to serve behind the copper bar, and since she doesn't let the staff smoke or drink while they're serving I'm not going to argue. I've got to a point where I prefer to go into town, to the

Norman Castle or the Belgrade. Quite apart from Fiona looking down her nose at me, I don't like the attitude of some of the customers and staff. There's disrespect in some of the things that get said, and in their eyes. I'm the landlady's tame drunk, old Martin, the customer that got to stop after closing-time. Everybody knows Fiona is being fucked by that smarmy twat Gavin. Fiona doesn't give a shit what she says, either. I'm sure she's told them all the details of my fucking operation, so some of them have only to clap eyes on me to start to smirk.

I felt a draught on my neck. Loony Katrin had pushed open her window. I turned round and closed it, smiled and said, 'Excuse me, but there's a fearful draught.' She looked stricken but didn't protest.

Maureen had already worked the fucking mechanism and tilted back. Old Lady Annabella was about to do the same and cut down my space into a little triangle. I thrust my knee against the back of her seat in the nick of time. She gave a couple of shoves with her arse then gave up, thinking there was something wrong with the tilt-back mechanism. I knew I had only held off a first assault and the old crow would try again in a couple of minutes. They always do. I was tempted to tap her shoulder and ask if she would mind not tilting back her seat as it caused me discomfort. Nine times out of ten you get away with that sort of approach. But I was sure Lady Annabella would be in the ten per cent.

I was distracted by hysterical choking noises from Katrin, as if she was being throttled under a tarpaulin. Before I'd even time to curse the window was open and the draught was trained on the top of my spine.

I turned round and knelt up on the seat. Katrin was doing deep breathing as if she'd been dragged out of a canal.

'If you've got to have the window open, Katrin, open it wide so I don't get a draught.'

I slid the window wide open. Katrin's yellow fringe fluttered. She was compressing her lips and her eyes were stubborn brown buttons. She was going to half close the fucking window as soon as I sat down.

And when I turned round fucking Lady Annabella had worked her trick with the seat and I'd no room at all.

I moved into the gangway seat where the draught was nearly as bad and leaned and asked Maureen if she'd mind moving her seat forward. She did mind, but she did move it forward, about an eighth of an inch.

I relaxed as much as I could and thought about Sharon. It's usually Sharon I bring to mind, even thirty years later, when I want to feel randy. Sharon with a white coat collar pulled up round her face, putting her tongue in my mouth while I dive my fingers inside her knickers. Sharon padding towards me in just a black bra, with that big bush of pubic hair. Sharon leaning and grinning while she spreads her legs to open her cunt. Lisa is taller but will be built like Sharon, with big nipples and plump thighs.

We stopped for lunch at a round, pink building with a mock thatch on the top. Fat Simon and a few of the others settled in for a meal but I was happy with chocolate and beer and a couple of fags. They'd a cold box with lots of cans of Dos Esquis and Tecate. At home I drink draught Guinness, I wouldn't touch lager, but in Mexico you've to learn to like lager if you're going to drink beer.

The Mexican beers we get in England are bottled, Sol, Corona and so forth. If I can't get draught I'm happier with a can but you can only get the cans in shops, in cafés and restaurants it's almost always bottled beer. Sol and Corona are both a bit bland for my liking, especially Sol. Dos Esquis is my favourite bottled item but I prefer Dos Esquis or Tecate cans.

Back on the bus I sat on the other side of the gangway. I reckoned the stumpy little Aussie would either not be bothered or too shy to let out a squawk. But she stood over me and fixed her good eye on me and said, 'Hey! That's my place you got.'

Dennis called out helpfully, 'Best if we keep to the same places, Martyboy.'

'Your place is it? You want to come back here do you?' I gave her my famous grin that used to make even the plain birds wet their knickers.

'That's the idea,' she said.

Everybody was sitting in the places they'd been in through the morning, even the ones who'd been jolting along over a wheel. I lugged my stuff back across the gangway to where Maureen and Lady Annabella had already thrust their seats back as far as they would go and Katrin had the window open.

Lisa was staring down the bus. I tried my grin again but she didn't see me.

Bitch, I thought, I've had better than you. I shut my eyes and started reviewing my top ten fucks.

I've always fantasised about women. At one time I'd have thought wanking as much an admission of defeat as paying for a tart, but in recent times I've started buying magazines and hiding them from Fiona and taking them with me into the lavatory.

Some of my memories have got confused with poses in those magazines. Carol from Luton, pouting over her shoulder and churning her arse. Brummie Mandy in a dayglo T-shirt, pressing my arse onto the stool as she settles on my prick. I've a useful prick, of average length but thick and with a good head on it, which comes as a nice surprise to those being fucked by a weedy-looking twat like me.

Sharon with her white teeth and dark nipples. She'd silky flesh and an educated cunt, Sharon. Yet it wasn't all arse-end between us, we were fond of each other. She'd a gruff, tender way that can make an old codger's eyes water to think of it now. I hear her say – she'd a husky, friendly sort of voice – 'Fasten your coat, you pillock, it's cold.' When she was cutting my hair she'd lean and kiss the back of my neck. More of this later, maybe.

Number one was Brenda, which is funny, because she wasn't a talented fuck. A bit lifeless. What wins her the number one spot is the weekend in the Black Bull at Coniston just before we wed. She was timid and her frilly nightie made her look young and vulnerable. I propped a big cushion under her arse and was bang on form, enormous. I fucked her four times that night and morning and got horny again when we were eating the egg and bacon and fried bread and sausage.

When we got to the Hotel Christobal in Oaxaca I put my bags in the room then went straight out while Dennis was fussing with the zips on his fucking rucksack, because on no account did I want that twat tagging along with me. I got away with it because he'd the fucking key in his possession which is the best arrangement for both of us because he never lets me out of his sight if I've the key. That's since Monday when the cunt locked himself out of the room.

There was a bar right next to our hotel, but I crossed to the other side of the Zocalo.

In a lot of Mexican bars you can't just go and get served. There's nowhere to sit at the bar, or only a couple of stools that are already taken. Sometimes there isn't even standing-room at the bar. Especially if you're a tourist, they like to insist on you sitting at a table and waiting for the fucking waiter or even worse some clueless tart to get round to you. Some places the staff seem to disappear altogether, so you sober up between drinks.

I have two tips about this. First, it's less annoying if you only have one drink in each bar, because the waiters give you attention when you first arrive. Make sure you pay as soon as they bring the drink or you'll be waiting to pay for fucking hours after you've supped up. The other tip is buy two beers at a time and start looking for the waiter as soon as you've supped one of them. This keeps the supply flowing but you don't get a lot of time to relax.

I wasn't looking for anybody from the hotel to come and drink with me, that's never been my style. I'm the bloke who branches out, the squaddie who grins at a tart on the next table and his buddies know they've lost him till tomorrow lunchtime. I picked up Sharon like that, at Steve's stag night, though I didn't meet her till next morning.

At first it wasn't like the luckiest waking in all my life, but just another morning after. The light was like cheese through the curtains. I didn't know where I was or why. The bed was a hard flock mattress with a pellet of a pillow.

She'd stolen most of the bedclothes and had her back to me, I could only see a brown tuft of hair and didn't know who the fuck she was. From the long sighs she was giving I could tell she was asleep. Then I saw her football scarf with all our clothes on the carpet and I remembered she'd been with a gang in the pub, singing anthems and spilling beer from a pint mug as she jigged up and down. Her teeth had gleamed white and her eyes dark. Sweat had stuck her fringe to her forehead. But I couldn't remember chatting her up. I'd been across the room with Steve's stag-night piss-up.

Still pissed, I sat up for a closer look at her, which woke her. She turned over laughing, then put an arm over me and pulled me down into the bed. That was Sharon. I'd an iron erection but I couldn't come. I went on sawing away till we were both knackered.

'That was better than last night, eh?' I guessed.

'It was,' she said, ' but I'm surprised you remember.'

She asked if I remembered the pub carpark where she'd let go of Malcolm's hand, whoever he was, and taken mine. I lied and we sat up in bed and had a fag. Her flesh looked like china in that light.

'Is this your room?' I asked her.

She said, 'Christ, you don't remember anything, do you?'

I came here to Mexico with the idea of having a fling at finding a bit of lost youth. Tank myself up with alcohol and fix myself up with a bit of cunt, even now when I'm an old git who a couple of pints can put to sleep. I've never forgotten hitting the jackpot that night when I got pissed out of my skull and woke up next to Sharon. But so far on this fucking trip I've woken up every morning next to fucking Dennis.

Saturday night I didn't try hard enough to get rid of him, even after I'd seen he's the last twat in the universe I'd choose as a buddy. Sunday night I was with Tonia and the Paki in Garibaldi Square. I'd decided they were the best company to be had even if they were dykes and one of them was a darkie. At midnight I went back to the hotel with them though the mariachi musicians had arrived and Garibaldi Square was swinging. I told myself I was maybe in with a chance of fucking Tonia but that was bullshit. Monday night there was a group of us, Brian and Millie, Katrin, Lisa, fucking Dennis, Tonia and the Paki, what Rose calls the Late Night Gang. I was well tanked up and feeling in form, I tried my grin on a Mexican bird on the next table. She fluttered her menu as if it was a fan and gazed at me over it with big dark eyes. Then the cow giggled and shared the joke with all the fat drunks round her who probably included her husband. Suddenly Lisa sprang up and announced that she was off back to the hotel and I said I'd escort her. I told myself that I was in with a chance of fucking Lisa. Then of course Dennis said that he was coming back, and Brian and Millie . . . I could have changed my mind at that point but I didn't, I gave up my last chance of a night on the razzle in Mexico City. I'm a timid old twat. I shan't wake up next to Sharon again.

Maybe I shan't wake up next to anyone, not even Fiona, so maybe it's time I settled for counting the cunt I've known and awarding the prizes. Brenda at Coniston was the best one night fuck, but that was a fluke. Sharon is the overall winner by miles. Why I took up with Brenda and lost Sharon is one of the unsolved mysteries of the universe.

I could tell I was going to marry Brenda when she wouldn't let me fuck her and I didn't lose interest. She was the sort of nice girl I'd always reckoned I'd look for when I gave up having a good time. She was eight years younger than Sharon and thirteen years younger than me. I even stayed sober for the cow. I went to the pictures with her and on shopping trips and picnics and trips to the zoo, places where you can't get alcohol. I'm still amazed to think what I went through for Brenda, eating dinner with her parents who thought I was too old for her, trying not to slurp too much of the wine I'd taken along. Watching quiz-games and soppy films in that comfy fucking lounge where her parents left us tactfully alone. January, got my tongue in her gob. February, undid her bra. March, hand up her skirt. April, fingers in her cunt. If I wasn't kissing her she'd chew her thumb and watch TV while I mauled her. Even then she wasn't as good-looking as Sharon. She was thin and her eyebrows met on the bridge of her nose. She was okay, though, good enough so that you didn't feel awkward to be seen with her, and a nice girl, the sort a bloke marries. I thought being older and experienced would give me the whip hand.

In my eagerness to escape from Dennis I'd been the first out of the hotel. From my vantage-point across the square, where I was pestered by an old woman pretending to be blind and a kid murdering an accordion, I could watch the others come out to explore the town. Dennis appeared with Lady Annabella and Maureen. He had his guidebook with him. I couldn't see Lady Annabella putting up with that for long, for she's a tough old bitch and used to having other people put up with her.

Brian and Millie came out with Dorothy and that dozy twat Donald. All four came out together laughing and talking (well, three of them), then they went off in opposite directions. After that a bunch of women came out together – Rose, Isabel, Stephanie, Katrin. I wondered what Tonia and the Paki were doing and decided they were having a shower together.

I was thinking about that when Simon and Pam came past my table, which shook me because I'd not seen them leave the hotel. I thought they were going to sit with me, she nodded and hovered, but he wobbled on without giving me a glance and she followed. I wasn't sorry to be denied his company because when he's not complaining about everything he's bragging about all the other places he's been that are better than where he is. But she seems civil enough, for a nigger. I don't mind niggers quite as much as wogs. At least they talk English and have fun. And Pam is a good-looking woman if you like that sort of thing, younger than Simon and wasted on the fat twat. She looks supple for her age and has a jutting arse and strong thighs like those black runners you see in skimpy outfits on telly. Tonia told me that Simon owns half the real-estate in Plymouth and Pam's the secretary he divorced his wife for.

Simon has been everywhere but learnt nothing. I don't need fancy degrees and book-learning to know what makes things tick, I've lived in the real world and kept my wits about me. I don't give a fuck for scenery and ancient ruins and history books, I can't speak Spanish and I don't like foreign food apart from curry, but I can get along with my fellow men and women, even niggers and wogs. You'll learn more about England from a couple of hours in a Manchester pub than from days trailing round Buckingham Palace and the Houses of Parliament. Barriers soon break down when you're buying a bloke a drink or watching a woman's arse and I bet I get more out of Mexico than these frumpy bitches and teetotal twats.

I tried to picture a juicy fuck with Pam, curly black minge, muscular thighs, but I can't always concentrate these days. Other images came into my brain for no good reason and I started thinking about the hospital test that found my leaking valve. I had to scramble up and perch naked under a bright light, then they partly covered me with a plastic sheet. They injected my prick with something that made it stiff and timed it with a stop-watch. I couldn't see what went on but could tell the result from the chuckles of the doctors, two young twats who treated it all as a joke. The nigger nurse pitied me. She got hold of my hand and talked to me as if I was a baby, the stupid bitch.

I was finishing my fourth beer and vaguely thinking of getting brave enough to look for cunt when a husky young Yank sat at my table and asked if he could join me, in that order. He sent the waiter off to fetch me another beer and something for himself that I didn't catch. I was wondering if he was a queer, or otherwise on the make, when I remembered where I'd seen him before, and just as I remembered he said, 'You're in Lisa's crowd, aren't you?'

He'd been at the hotel when we set off by coach on Monday and had made a scene by trying to talk to Lisa about what were obviously personal matters. He explained that he and Lisa were engaged but that she was threatening to break it off because she thought she didn't love him. He knew for sure she loved him, that was no problem, the only problem was how to stop her fooling herself. He was playing hooky from University in order to follow our tour until he'd had a proper heart-to-heart with Lisa and set her straight.

He spoke reasonably and quietly enough but I noticed one or two disturbing things about him. His left wrist was bandaged, not too well, and on the inside of the wrist blood had seeped to the surface of the bandage. He constantly picked at the nails of his left hand with the nails of his right, the nails on his left hand were jagged as a result. And he blubbed whenever he talked about Lisa. Tears gathered in the red rims of his eyes and he swallowed and gasped for air.

I told him Lisa's got a bright manner and a great arse but no woman's worth the state he's got himself into. What's more, showing a woman you're desperate for her isn't the way to either get or keep her. You've to be cool and cruel with women to keep the whip hand. Keep your distance, your mystery, for once a woman has found your weaknesses she'll use them to make you miserable then want nothing more to do with you. A man besotted with a woman very soon becomes contemptible to everybody, including her. More of this later.

He thanked me but said it wasn't so much advice he was after as information. He wanted to know the itinerary of our tour, so that he could make plans where to have a showdown with Lisa and could follow at leisure without having to keep our bus in sight.

I wasn't keen to help. From Lisa's attitude on Monday I gathered that she'd sooner see no more of him and wouldn't thank me for helping him dog her tracks. And there was something fishy and sick about him. I told him we were going to Yucatan, which I knew that he already knew, but that I was the sort of bloke that just went along with the flow and didn't give a sod for schedules and itineraries.

He thanked me again and apologised for bothering me. He left his drink half-finished, which was probably just Coke with ice, I couldn't smell rum in it. I wasn't keen on the idea of this loony trailing us, as if we didn't have enough on board, but I now had an excuse for a confidential chat with Lisa, which I want for a couple of reasons. One is, I don't want to share rooms with fucking Dennis. I've broached the topic once, complaining about his snoring, but she just shrugged and said, 'Get some earplugs and see how it goes.'

The fact that Dennis had left the Christobal was a good reason to go back into it. Also I'd not seen Lisa leave and thought I might seek her out at once. I wasn't drunk enough to go to her room like a callow lad but went into the hotel bar in case she was there, for she's a keen drinker of Mexican beer.

There was only Sol and Corona for sale and no other customers except an old git all in white, white golf-hat, white sweatshirt, white whiskers, who turned out to be another Yank. I've been short of like-minded male boozing company since I said goodbye to Clive and Pete in Mexico Airport. The Yank told me he was a retired 'druggist' from Kankakee, south of Chicago. As soon as he knew I was a Brit he said how much he'd admired Margaret Thatcher. Ed, I think his second name was Schwartzenbeck, said Thatcher was the exception that proves the rule that women are a dead lumber in the real world of politics and business. I dished up my quip about it being no wonder the world's in such a mess, half the population being women. Sure is a mess, Ed said, and a lot of it because nobody knows their place any more. Not only do children and bartenders show no respect but folk of all races and colours are leaving their natural habitats and spreading disease and making trouble. I took up the last point and made a speech about Manchester being given over to foreigners, especially Pakis, degenerate twats who make no effort to speak English let alone copy our ways. Ed and I agreed that invasion by the Third World is a disaster for both Europe and America and wishy-washy do-gooder idealism is letting it happen, rewarding queers and psychopaths, discouraging the teaching of correct English and making abortion trendy. It was amazing what a lot we had in common and how like each other we were in many respects, though he's German American and I'm a Mancunian Brit. We even knew the same jokes, but his were about niggers and mine about Pakis.

All of a sudden he was gone. This didn't bother me. Back home I like to get in the pub early and onto a corner stool at the bar. A typical evening is a series of chats like the one with Ed. When I've had a few drinks the bloke on the next stool has a tendency to change without warning.

Except in bed, I'd rather be with a man than a woman any time, though it's women that are always on my mind. I now tried to entertain myself with memories of fucking Sharon but all that would come to mind was the day we broke up. Sharon in her bright red coat with the upturned collar that matched her lips and plastic earrings and made her face seem pale. The room was littered with all my clothes she'd thrown around while packing hers into the suitcase or the bin-liner. Both these now stood at the door with the rest of her stuff, the pot-plant, the cassette-player, the standard-lamp, the keep-fit bicycle, the cat-basket. She'd a half-empty shoe-box ready for last minute finds. Her high heels clicked along the hallway linoleum, four paces, four clicks to the door of the flat. The chain-bolt, then the Yale, then a pow-wow all in whispers. She came back in and asked me, 'Have you seen the cat?'

I asked, 'Who is it?'

'Binky.'

'I know who the fucking cat is. I mean who's that out at the door? Is it the bald twat with the hump?'

She went into the kitchen. Returning with the baffled cat she stuffed it into the cat-basket and fastened the lid.

'It's that hunchback Graham, isn't it?' I asked. 'How long has he been fucking you?'

'Not as long as you've been fucking your virgin,' she said, 'and he's not a hunchback.'

I said, 'He's like a fucking camel.'

A bit later, looking out of the window, I saw a Datsun, red to match her coat and lips and earrings, drawn up onto the hard-standing. Although it was off the road its hazard lights were blinking. Graham was stooping with the weight of the exercise-bicycle. Sharon was carrying the cat-basket. They had shoved the rest of her stuff into the open boot or onto the back seat. I wanted her to come upstairs one more time so I could tell her I'd give up Brenda but there wasn't anything she suddenly remembered.

Tonia and the Paki had taken the place of Ed. I told them about the young Yank, which was a pity because earlier I'd decided to keep it to myself until I'd talked to Lisa.

Tonia said, 'The guy's an intern at Mexico City Hospital. A gynaecologist. Lisa had an abortion there last year.'

The Paki said, 'Tonia, Martin knows you're a pathological friggin' liar.'

They laughed but I didn't because I don't like to hear women use bad language, and it irritates me to hear the way Pakis talk, even when they've got Midland accents. I bought a round and we amused ourselves by slagging off the others. I'd no new stuff about Dennis since I spend all my time avoiding the cunt but I told them about Katrin's performance with the fucking window. Then the Paki launched into a weary story about Rose's stupidity in the women's loo on the motorway, something about messing with the flushing device. I wasn't listening because I was weighing up Tonia.

A lot of her features are only so-so. She's twinkly eyes and a good-natured curve to her lips but her ginger crop and freckles stop her from being pretty. She's fattish, too, and her man-like voice is a bit of a put-off. All the same I'm interested. She'll have a ginger minge and soft white thighs and arse and big, floppy tits, the sort of full-bodied bird that looks good in just a pair of black stockings. She says she's got a live-in boyfriend in Detroit but I'm convinced she's a dyke and is having it off with the Paki.

Funnily enough while poofs turn my stomach I find the idea of lesbians erotic. Buggering women seems okay too, though the only time I tried it I was pissed and got no co-operation. As these two went on scoffing at Rose and Simon and Isabel and Donald I got randy by picturing them in various states of undress at work on each other's cunts.

Tonia is a laugh and buys her round like a man. When they're together the Paki does the same. By the time I remembered my plan to seek out Lisa it was dinner time. We went out to where the others were gathering in the outdoor bar next to the hotel. I'd to watch that I was walking straight but this was no problem for an accomplished drunk like me. I hadn't given up the idea of going off on my own and looking for cunt in Oaxaca, but it was on the back burner for the time being.

Six or seven were there when we arrived. They'd crushed round one table and Dennis was delighted to be able to instruct us to start another table, which we did together with Brian and Millie. I made my drink last, because I was getting worried about my rate of intake. In my mind I could hear cow Fiona making sarcastic remarks about the way I was walking and talking. We moved off soon to a spot only four doors from our hotel.

It's time I dropped a few more tips. My advice was to be early onto the bus so you get the pick of the seating, but this wheeze doesn't work with restaurants. If you sit down first you've no control over who sits next to you. On the other hand, if you hang around till the table's full you've to sit in whatever place is left. Somewhere near the middle towards the end is best, but there are other considerations. I've noticed, for instance, that both Rose and Dennis like to sit down early and claim seats in the middle of the table where they feel at the heart of things. In fact the table usually fills up from the middle outwards, with Lisa nearly always one of the first to sit, because a lot of folk won't do anything without her lead. So by arriving last you get a choice of seats at one or other end of the table, avoiding the major hazards of Rose and Dennis and choosing which end of the table is offering the least irritating bunch. Not that this is any guarantee of a good time. There are too many shit-heads and bores on this trip for it to be possible to avoid them all, and wherever you sit you'll be able to hear Rose braying.

This time my calculations were thrown out by the way the tables were arranged. There were fifteen of us, everybody except Simon and Pam, and the space was only wide enough for four tables to be put together to make a ten-seater, which the waiters had done by the time I rolled up. I was following close after Tonia and the Paki, to sit by them if possible, but they took the last two places and Dennis called to the rest of us, for the second time that evening, 'Start another table will you?' The waiters put together two tables for the five of us who were left.

It was like a fucking table for geriatrics, Donald and Dorothy, Lady Annabella and Maureen and me. I could see Tonia pointing and grinning, she knows how much I hate most people my own age. Also she has a habit of taking the piss out of me as soon as we get in a crowd. It's flattering that she thinks me a bit of a character but there's something I don't like about it. If Dennis is there he latches on to it and tries to make me the butt of his lame humour.

The menu had an English translation. I ordered a chicken curry, which sounded less weird than most items. Curry is the one good thing to come out of Pakistan. I was drinking bottled beer, easing it into the tilted glass so it didn't froth and spill and show the world how drunk I was. Maureen made some snide remarks about men. 'You men so love your drink, eh? What would you do without your bottle?' Lady Annabella was talking about her husband Lord Cairncross, she actually refers to him as 'Cairncross', telling us fondly what a twat he is. I watched Lisa, who was in better spirits than last night. All her ringlets were lolloping around as she did the actions to some yarn she was telling. Fucking Dennis shouted at me cheerily, 'Martyboy, you're blushing!' He reckons I go red when I've had too many and always shouts out the same shit whenever he sees me drinking. Even more annoying, Tonia and the Paki threw back their heads and pointed at me and cackled like witches. I might as well have been back in the Talisman.

I waited a long time for my curry, long after everybody else had been served their main course, which gave further scope for folk to ridicule me, and for Maureen to say, 'Typical man, no patience at all, especially when his tummy's rumbling.' At one point Lady Annabella said, 'You're not going to light that, are you?' and I discovered I'd a fag in my mouth. When the curry came it was a paella, which everybody found fucking hilarious, but I didn't send it back. Another tip I can give you, and I'm in the catering trade myself, is never send food back, wherever you're eating, or if you do, don't eat anything else they dish up for you unless you don't mind including a bit of spit and piss in your diet.

Dorothy had an argument with Lady Annabella about education, Lady Annabella used to be a Governor of some Irish school and Dorothy is a daft old lefty. I joined in, just to be sociable, by saying that teachers get too much holiday – and in my opinion are overpaid. It had slipped my mind that Donald and Dorothy were retired teachers. The funny thing was I was looking at Donald as I said it, and instead of showing any annoyance the twat put his head on one side and pursed his lips and nodded slowly as if I had made an interesting point.

Dorothy said, 'Yours were.'

She was glaring at me as if she was trying to turn me into a toad.

She's been a good-looking woman but now there's something washed out about her as if she's been left out too long in bad weather. A sort of beatnik granny with wild white hair.

Before I could say anything Lady Annabella laughed and said: 'That's a good one! I haven't heard that before!'

'I have,' I lied.

Suddenly I came to my senses in a dark little loo. It was frightening because I didn't know where I was or how I got there. When I was young I had blackouts after I'd drunk a lot, but this was in no way like waking up in that doss-house next to Sharon. It was more like waking in a coffin and finding I'd been buried alive. What was more, I hadn't actually been asleep. It was like my life was a spool of film and somebody had cut a few inches out of it and pasted it back together.

I was leaning against the wonky hard-board wall and trying to piss into the basin that was dimly lit through the gap above the door behind me. Some of my piss was missing and sprinkling the floor and my left foot. Since I spent three days with a catheter in the end of my prick I've had trouble pissing straight, and in my drunkenness I had not pulled back my foreskin properly. Since the operation, because of the increased blood-supply to the prick, the foreskin has been tighter and is sometimes tricky to budge. What's more when I pull it back into place, if I'm not careful, I catch pubic hair in it and have to start again.

Coming out of the toilet I didn't recognise the corridor at all. Even when I was back in the restaurant I couldn't at first remember which way I had to turn to get to the table.

People were leaving and there was some problem over my bill. The waiter said I'd had four beers and I was sure that I'd only had three. I could hear people sniggering because the same thing happened the night before. The waiter could point to the four empty Corona bottles on the table but this time I was convinced that I'd been carrying a bottle with me when I arrived. I don't know how this matter was finally sorted out and don't intend to ask anybody in case they get the idea I was drunker than I was. Here's some more advice. Never say anything that might be taken as an admission of guilt. Never apologise, especially to a woman.

I was sure I hadn't drunk enough to justify the state I was in. A couple of thirty-three centilitre cans at lunchtime, and after that nothing but beer in quarter-litre doses. No shorts, no wine. Half a dozen in the bar across the Zocalo, half a dozen before dinner, about a gallon of beer altogether, which is what I used to quaff in a lunchtime session when I was a boozing man. Foreign lager is stronger than Draught Guinness, and I had almost certainly lost count, but more to the point is the fact that I'm a pathetic old twat whose time is gone.

Suddenly I was back in the foyer of the Hotel Christobal, trying to persuade Lisa to come to the bar for a drink.

'I've something urgent to tell you.'

'Come on, Martin! If you've kept it to yourself all night it can't be so urgent it won't keep till tomorrow.'

I could see her perfect nipples again through the scarlet T-shirt she had been wearing all day. Her stretch-jeans showed off her arse a treat. We were surrounded by other Baluth tour members – including Isabel who wanted Lisa to go back with her to the restaurant for some reason, and Katrin who was worried about the hotel safe, and Tonia and the Paki who knew as much as I did about my big news, the mad Yank. Tonia was amused by my proposition to Lisa. She gave me a wink and a thumbs-up sign, then the Paki whispered something to her and they both laughed.

I remember walking back to the main door of the hotel and looking out at the Zocalo. It gets confusing after that. There was a fountain splashing on the pavement, lamps like orange globes and little coloured lights that dangled from trees. A fat man was selling balloons and that kid was still playing his accordion and singing, 'Ay, ay, ay, ay . . .' There was a three-legged dog bobbing along a path between flower-beds. A blind old man was sitting with a tin strung round his neck, listening for coins. A woman was walking along in front of me in flimsy leggings that made her arse look like two boiled eggs in a handkerchief.

Then I was staring up at a girl leaning out of a window. The room behind her was scarlet and full of guitars and voices. She was only a silhouette but I could see she had long, straight hair like an Indian squaw and was wearing a frilly white blouse that left her shoulders naked. I climbed an unlit staircase towards the music, pushed a door open and found a light-switch. I was in a sparsely furnished bedroom, a wardrobe, a table with a jug and wash-basin, an empty bed, a cot with a sleeping child. It looked like Darren, till I remembered that Darren is now a twenty-seven-year-old layabout and could see it was a Mexican kid. Footsteps came along the landing and scared me so I pressed myself against the wall next to the wardrobe, drunks can suddenly be clever like that. The footsteps stopped at the door of the bedroom. After a couple of seconds the light was switched off and the door closed. I listened to the footsteps going away along the landing, heavy, weary feet. Then I groped my way back in the darkness towards where I hoped the door would be.

Then I was at a bar talking to a little Mexican twat. I was trying to tell him the joke about the Chinamen and the nymphomaniac but he didn't speeka de Eenglish and was even more pissed than I was. There was hardly anybody in the bar which was full of dim blue light and loud rock music. Some sort of fracas occurred which got me into the fresh air again. A young soldier with a pistol in his belt was pushing me in the chest and shouting Spanish at me. A fat woman was protecting me and cajoling him away.

Then I was being wheeled along a hotel corridor on a trolley, through some rubber doors, and lifted off the trolley onto an operating slab. The surgeons and nurses were all wearing masks but I could see one of the nurses was Fiona. One of the surgeons took my limp prick in forceps and lifted it for the others to look at. Everybody pissed themselves laughing. As soon as I could tell I was dreaming I woke up and knew where I was at once because

Dennis was snoring like no other twat ever did, like boulders dropping onto a corrugated fucking roof.

I put on the light. My watch said half past three. My wallet and money-belt and passport were all intact on the bedside table. All the same I was in the panic drunks suffer when they wake up not remembering everything that passed. Experience has taught me that I don't always get away with it. Sometimes in the blotted bit I've said or done something that can't be ignored or laughed off.

It was going to be tricky to get back to sleep. I tried to picture Lisa astride me in stockings and suspenders, but she soon turned into Sharon, and then I was watching that Datsun move out onto the main road, its hazard lights still stupidly blinking and the pot plant nodding out of the back window.

Then I was opening the front door of 15 Nuttall Street, where I lived with Brenda for eight years. I came home not quite as pissed as usual and switched on the light and discovered I'd been burgled. The rug was gone out of the sitting-room along with the table, the suite, the curtains, the television and the stereo. I called to Brenda but got no answer. Upstairs both our bedroom and Darren's bedroom were stripped, bare floorboards, curtainless windows, bare bulbs in the light-fittings. I ran back downstairs. The burglars hadn't bothered with the tatty stairs carpet. They had kidnapped my wife and son, driven them away in a big van with all the furniture. I'd heard about that sort of thing. In a few days' time they'd get in touch with a ransom demand, unless the twats realised by then that they'd picked the wrong house and I hadn't any money. The telephone was still connected but sitting on the hall carpet, the cute little table it had stood on was gone along with the address-book and telephone directory. I was about to dial 999 when I thought of something and replaced the receiver.

I suddenly knew that there would be a message for me somewhere in the house.

In fact there was more than one message but nothing in

words. In the kitchen the fridge and the cooker were gone and all the drawers and cupboards were empty. I thought, these burglars must be fucking loonies, they've taken all the crockery and cutlery, the cooking-pots, the tea-towels, the rusty bottle-opener, the broken egg-whisk, everything. But on the unit work-top next to the sink had been left, neatly stacked, a plate, a bowl, a cup, a knife, a fork and a spoon. And in the spare bedroom that was still left furnished was the rest of the evidence. My driving licence and other personal documents were jammed into the drawer of the bedside cupboard. My suits and shoes, shirts, socks and underclothes and pyjamas were piled on the floor of the wardrobe. A towel and toilet kit had been flung on the bed.

ROSE SMITH

I woke from a scrumptious dream and reached out for the Dreambook which I keep under my pillow so that I can catch the fleeting alchemy instantly on waking – before it is banished from the memory forever by the salutations of the new day. It was still spooky dark so I invoked the delicious orange miracle of the bedside lamp. Isabel – that unquiet spirit – gave out a groan but said nothing – she has come to comprehend a little of what burns in me when I reach for one or other of my books – and that the Dreambook must be written in immediately if the vision is to be cherished.

I wrote: *Voladores flying – circling – descending – like Peruvian condors to the haunting anthem of a pentatonic pipe. I was a child again – beholding and applauding in my turquoise and white school cookery pinafore – and Dru and Mumps were beside me – the other two of the Terrible Trio from Prep School in Bulawayo – and my dear dead parents there too – she in her high shoulder pads and natty little hat with a veil – he in his jodhpurs and silver spectacles. The music soared and I was flying – first like the voladores in ordained circles – then like the condor – high – high above everything – but lapsing down onto a lovely landscape of trees and rivers – losing altitude – the forest-top yearning up towards me. Unafraid I laughed and lilted above the leaves and boughs then skimmed the levels of a brilliant river. I was surfing rapids in a trance of spray and a noise like Seraphs singing when I woke.*

I am blessed with gorgeous dreams. Dreams reflect that inner Essence which mystic savants have identified by the word 'soul' – I am therefore proud as well as grateful that dreams delight me.

Nine out of ten people do not dream in colour – whereas I am
constantly aware – as my Dreambooks testify – of the most dazzling
and subtle hues – as well as odours, textures, and an enchanting
music which extrapolates my dreams like the score of a film but
resembles no tunes I have ever heard – I dearly wish I had the art
to reproduce that music after waking! *Could I revive within me
that symphony and song* . . . And I never suffer distasteful dreams.
While there are romantic interludes involving both Roly Poly and
other persons – (represented by rows of asterisks to thwart any
snoopers into the Dreambook!) – nothing occurs that leaves an
unpleasant aftertaste – *a burning forehead and a parching tongue*.
Nor do I have nightmares – if my dream is awesome to the verge
of peril I confront it with the sanguine pluck which characterises
my waking life.

I dare say Freudians could hold seminars on my Dreambooks
but I scorn all such materialistic science. *Reason has moons but
moons not hers are mirrored in her sea* . . . I have known many
mystical experiences – I have gazed into a clear night sky from
the Hennin monastery, twelve thousand metres above sea level,
and heard the heartbeats of the stars – I have watched a butterfly
in a shaft of sunlight through Amazonian verdure and known the
immortality of the soul. In the dunes of the Sahara – the ashen
slopes of Sinai – the tumbleweed of Arizona – I have understood
the ascetic ecstasy of the saints.

My Dreambooks are the journals of my immortal soul in which
I recount the unexplored potential of an alternative and transcen-
dental Being. I do not dream every night and sometimes wake
remembering little, so my Dreambooks fill up more slowly than
my Lifebooks – in which rarely an hour goes by but I am jotting
something – as a result of which I have a great hoard of Lifebooks
in an exotic camphor-wood chest chez moi in Wimbledon. They
are my testament to phenomenal existence – the outpouring of all
my delighted perception of the material world. When too old for
the old trail, my own trail, the out trail I shall edit my Lifebooks
and bequeath them to those who have been denied my panoply of

experience. I have seen the sunset on Lake Titicaca – the red disk sinking like a drowning fiend behind the vertiginous black crags of the Andes. I have chortled to watch the flame-striped zebras roll their mares among the trampled lilies of the Serengeti. I have bobbed in time to the dervishes and the plaintive cries of castrati on the Golden Road to Samarkand. I have crouched in a coign of the Forbidden City listening for its history and have watched for mermaids through a glass-bottomed boat in the ultramarine coils and currents of the Maldive Sea.

I get the notebooks from Frobishers, Bleeding Heart Yard, Holborn, EC1 – a darling olde worlde nook full of artists' materials and quaint stationery. They are 'traditional vellum' – feint-lined – 90 leaves, A5 size or thereabouts – with veined, bottlegreen covers and crimson spines. Something luxurious – even sensuous about them – seems to have rapport with my literary powers. I used to use an antique, gold-nibbed fountain-pen, but good-quality fibre-tips are better suited to my headlong scribble.

I opened my current Lifebook and wrote: *Wednesday 11th January. This morning we go to Monte Alban – mystical magical city of the Zapotecs. My utter being is focused like a quivering arrow onto the lodestar of the event. Yet even as I sit ravished with anticipation I spare a thought for poor Isabel on the bed beside me – maimed by the disenchantments of an undemanding history with which she has nevertheless failed to cope – full of mundane neurosis and incapable of response when the Angel sings. For I have travelled on horseback through the cathedral of a great sequoia forest – snorkelled on the Barrier Reef where shoals of a million fishes pass playfully in echelon – beheld a thousand Himalayan peaks glitter emerald and topaz and sapphire, deafeningly aware of the silence and the ineffable mystery of my own being clamouring for identity. 'Only the silence, only the sky, and God and I.' Having trodden breathless in those holy places I know full well that it is not where one goes that matters but what one takes there – 'it's always ourselves that we find in the sea' – the marvels of creation might as well be confined to a bed-sit in Wimbledon or a tea-room in Cheltenham if one does not have the wonder and courage of a Child.*

Getting to breakfast soon after seven o'clock as requested by Lisa at our last briefing was a hardship for many – impossible for some – but for me, pish! I wake each morning eagerly. *Bliss is it in this morn to be alive!* They appointed me dormitory monitor in Aylward House for three years running when I was at Cloisterhouse because I could be counted on to rise with a song on my lips and fling back the curtains and pester all the slugabeds in my jolly way. And when I was married to Roly Poly – who was scowly Mister Grumpy in the mornings – I never let him daunt my chanticleer spirit nor detract from the spell of our African vista where the lyre-birds wailed across the turquoise veldt of dawn.

Those of us early to breakfast were on top form despite the hour. I quote from my Lifebook: *Hilarious larks at breakfast – we discussed traditional breakfasts all over the world – Korean raw silverfish and the goatsmilk curds of Mongolia – the hominy grits that are served up in Mississippi, Home of the Blues – and the thin gruel flecked with slices of banana that is to be had on the legendary slopes of Macchu Picchu. We lit on the comical and astounding fact that the French are the only civilised nation that do not eat eggs for breakfast. The egg – a repository of latent life – is a symbolic encapsulation of unexplored Potential – so appropriate for the first meal of the day. Dennis had interesting things to say about the calorific content of eggs and the etymology of the word 'breakfast' – the Welsh have always struck me as a scholarly and articulate people. But it was Lady Cairncross that was the life and soul of the party. She is not only a true-blue aristocrat – her husband is Lord Cairncross of Argh, pronounced Oh, an ancient Irish family – but she has a laconic wit that is evidence of centuries of inherited culture. Eggs disgust her, she maintained, coming as they do from the posteriors – she used a more risqué expression! – of farmyard birds! It was irresistibly droll – I fear I got a fit of giggles that lasted long after everyone else had forgotten the topic! I can tell already that this is going to be one of those festive, rollicking days that are friendly fun from dawn to shut-eye and make it a privilege to be an inhabitant of the planet.*

The jollity continued after breakfast – when we assembled outside the hotel where the bus was stationed - but no driver! We were supposed to hit the trail at eight o'clock but at a quarter past there was no sign of the scamp and Lisa set off to look for him. Five minutes later she was back with the news that he had overslept! We had to wait another ten minutes before he showed up looking sheepish – and we all gave him an ironic cheer! Such fun! I wanted to give him further stick with choruses of 'Why Are We Waiting?' and 'Why Was He Born So Beautiful?' but nobody else knew the words and I was laughing too much to sing properly.

I never tire of the multifoliate diversity of my fellow humans – *the old, proud pageant of man* – and looking round the bus I revelled in the colourful bunch of characters who had chosen this trip. Working round the bus – from the front seat behind the driver where Isabel and I were the dullest codgers on show – directly behind us was Simon – larger than life in more senses than one – a mighty mogul in the South West Coast property market – and exotic Pamela who was his secretary before Romance defied boundaries of class and colour to blossom between them. Then there was Lady Cairncross – a blue-blood of the old school, who can boast a castellated manor set in Celtic twilight, its feasting-hall bedecked with the armorial bearings of her ancestors – *where none has lived that lacked a name and fame* – and her companion Maureen – a devoted family retainer whose demure demeanour cloaks a passionate history of which she confessed a little to Tonia – an illegitimate son who is now a University professor, her shame and pride. Behind them lurked Martin – the canny old Northerner – salt of the earth – with two seats to himself as usual. He's a card! Then came the Hemingways who used to be schoolteachers and now live in quaint and lovely Gascony – he taciturn and enigmatic, a brooder on internal events – she, poor dear, restless and voluble, still assailing the world with the firebrand notions of her youth – Marxism, feminism, atheism and what have you – *sands upon the*

Red Sea shore. The only other person on our side of the bus was Dennis at the back, the vigilant custodian of the baggage, whom I call the Welsh Wizard. As well as an authority on a multitude of topics our cheery Taff chum is an organising genius and Lisa must thank her stars that he is on this trip. On the other side of the bus – by coincidence – were all the youngsters. Tonia is from the Land of the Free – a career-woman with a manner and personality that invites confidence – and a mine of information about everybody. Sunita is an Asian Indian who displays the stunning loveliness and refined deportment of her race. Stephanie – a spunky Aussie lass – has dedicated her existence – like a latter-day Gladys Aylward – to the care of handicapped and endangered infants. Katrin is some sort of brainy boffin, believe it or not! She's a hoot – Clueless Kate, I call her! Brian and Millie are top-notch professionals in their respective spheres yet just like love-birds – absorbed in each other – so sweet – like Roly Poly and me in the early days when everything was the excuse for a cuddle – before Mister Grumpy came along every morning and stayed all day. Then there is Lisa – our trendy, sassy leader – a New Generation Girl who is being stalked by a love-sick American giant! A soupçon of drama to add to the composition of a group as various as humankind – except that we are spared the company of any ill-mannered young men.

All the way up the twenty minute drive to Monte Alban I could see mounds on other hilltops which demonstrated the size of the bygone settlement. I could sense one of my mystical experiences looming – so my heart was pitter-pattering as we alighted in the carpark and moved through the ticket office and museum. Then I was on the North Platform – gazing out over the flat, brown, grassless plaza, the pyramids and terraces of brown stone.

I narrowed my eyes and flung myself back across the aeons and generations. Suddenly – just as at Teotihuacan – the buildings were plastered and painted like the models in the Mexico City museum. I could see a copper-skinned, black-haired multitude – the priests in their masks and feathered robes – the warriors in their wicker-work armour – the civilians in the bright-dyed uniforms of their tribes. I could hear the market-costers' cries – the bells of the temple dancers – the grunts and thuds of the athletes in the ball court.

My sensitivity sometimes affords me glimpses of previous emanations. I have sipped the sherbets of a silken harem, latest and friskiest of a sultan's concubines – I have felt the alabaster throne of a mighty empire cold against my jewelled spine – I have nursed my wounded warrior in a buffalo-hide tepee – I have jingled the bells on my anklets as I descended the marble steps of a temple. Nor have all the avatars of my soul been feminine – I have swung a cutlass on a tilting quarter-deck – mushed my dogs across moonlit snow.

But there is something ineluctably other about the ancient Indians of America. I have no recollection of an incarnation among them.

I wrote in my Lifebook: *Monte Alban, the city of the Zapotecs, is particularly magical because of its situation – high in a dry moonscape of hills and valleys. Within the confines of the site are many particular and delectable treasures – the observatory, aligned with the bright star Capella – the plangent mystery of the ball court – the scary tomb to which we descended half a dozen at a time with torches – above its portal an urn in the shape of a person wearing a mask of Tlaloc the rain god. The carvings are particularly astounding – a jaguar wearing the rain-god's mask – Xipa Totec, the flayed god and god of renewal – Pitao Cocobi the maize god with his big snake and feathered head-dress – and the Dazantes – carvings of slain enemies with open mouths and closed eyes and blood flowing from their lopped genitalia. Ugh!*

A mystic vision transported me back through the centuries but I had no sense of a specific avatar.

Tomas, our guide to Monte Alban, claimed to be descended from the Olmecs. 'You are indeed!' I cried at him – clapping my hands – 'Just like the statues and carvings! Those very same thick lips and pudgy limbs!' – Yet it was a far cry from the weird Olmecs – who seem to have spent a lot of their time flaying and trepanning each other – to this scholarly young man. I'm afraid I interrupted him a lot and put him out of his stride – I apologised to him when he finished. He gave a shy grin and did not open himself to me but I felt that I had most definitely made contact. There is a wonderful moment when cultural and racial differences fall away as spirits touch across the void. *But there is neither East nor West, Border, nor Breed, nor Birth.* I have felt this bonding countless times – when bargaining jovially with a shrewd old aborigine woman – or when pressing a coin into the hand of a Bombay beggar – or on that euphoric day when the wise withheld their misgivings and Nelson Mandela walked out of captivity.

We met Nathe and Sherry again! They are an American couple we first bumped into at Teotihuacan – then we spotted them again in Oaxaca. It's terrific fun when one keeps running into the same people – they become old friends. I dashed over to see what they were up to – they were looking down into a deep hole that Nathe reckoned was some sort of irrigation system. I asked Tomas and Lisa and Tonia and Brian and Millie about it but none of them knew what it was. Simon looked as though he knew but said nothing. Dennis said it was a sewage system but his voice did not have its normal confident ring and he went into no further detail! Nathe is tall and slow and drawly – reminding me a bit of Roly Poly when I first fancied him. Sherry is plump and jolly and a bit vulgar – what the Americans call a trailer-park sort of person. I have spent time in the United States – marvelling at the vertiginous splendours of the Grand Canyon – *cliffs of fall, no-man-fathomed* – the glass and neon symphony of the Big Apple – the wicked, jazz-exuding riverboats of New Orleans – and am in harmony with the soul of America – because I too am eclectic and international – *everything human I understand* – born in Rhodesia, a quarter Spanish, a quarter Scottish, and living now in London where the races of the earth – white, black, brown and yellow – are intermingled in a tumultuous kaleidoscope of interacting destinies.

I go to Yoga in Wimbledon and Blodwyn has explained the philosophy to me. I accept the notion of the pursuit of Perfection through a series of lives and think that my present existence is a crucial one, wherein I have moved from the concept of individual love to that of Universal Love. For whereas my relationship with Roly Poly was abortive and I have been denied the fulfilment of child-bearing, despite this – even because of it – I have attained an insight, *hearing oftentimes the still, sad music of humanity*, that links me to the Eternal and triumphs over selfish, transient desire. Not only is Blodwyn a whiz at Yoga but she has translated the Bhagavad Gita into Welsh – and is a member of a White Magic coven in Wimbledon. She has her eye on me as a possible recruit – but while I am attracted I am not prepared to desert the Anglican Church whose doctrines and ceremony have supported me since infancy.

I have tried to imbue Isabel with something of the concept of Universal Love. She – poor turbulent spirit – is full of animosity and mistrust. I've shown her my treasured photograph – myself and my sister in the kitchen garden with Jock the Ridgeback and Pollydoodle the cook and Polly's tiny little piccaninny sitting grinning inside an enamel pee-pot, so cute. This is what the world could be like, I said to her. It's how it was in Rhodesia when I was a child. *Fair seed time had our souls.* It is our fault, the civilised and educated, that the idyll is destroyed. We lost the trust of those in our care. We let them have power too soon – when they were young in wisdom and full of rancour and easily gulled by communists.

When we got back to Oaxaca Lisa told us (again) that we had a free afternoon. Super! I wrote in my Lifebook: *The afternoon is for our own devices! I adore this sweet alternation of routine and liberty – guidance and permission. 'Glory be to God for dappled things!' It reminds me of Cloisterhouse when after the lessons – the scintillating maze of Mathematics with grim old Prodger – or the aching poetry of Geography with fey and interestingly flushed Miss Robespierre who was rumoured to have a midnight cyclist for a lover – we were accorded two delicious hours of Options between Refectory, Chapel and Prep.*

Some girls could not respond to Options. They shilly-shallied and were discontent. That was never my way. Whether I doughtily held my own in the hockey goal – compensating with intrepid effort for my lack of flair – or watched absorbed as Matron demonstrated the sheep-shank bandaging technique for a dislocated socket – I brought to each activity my brimming soul. *But to be young was very Heaven*. I have always been religious – a rapt mystic rather than a devotional drudge – and have considered every exhilarating moment a debt we owe to God. *If you can fill each unforgiving minute with sixty seconds' worth of distance run . . .*

For three years I had a tremendous crush on Djina Martindale. She was only a year older than me – though we were never in the same class for anything – so it wasn't like the pashes that sprogs got for prefects and teachers – or the rather naughtier interest one or two older girls showed in sprogs. Djina was tall and slim and dark – she had a helmet of black hair that covered her ears and neck. She was quiet, law-abiding and average at games – a mathematician and the best chess-player in the school. I adored her for three years and never told her. I got myself into the lacrosse team because that was Djina's game, and was rewarded by getting to share a shower with her once a week! She had a lovely slender body with identically perfect breasts at which I did not dare to gaze. She was a very composed person and everybody respected her. Nobody bullied her, like they did me.

I was determined not to get lumbered with Isabel – or Katrin – or Stephanie. Katrin is comical enough in the short term but her weirdness soon becomes wearing. Stephanie is super – the salt of the earth – but her limitations prevent her – poor dedicated drudge! – from being a rewarding audience or chiming in with the gang. I was resolved on spending a vibrantly congenial afternoon in the company of Lady Cairncross – and Maureen, perforce, because Lady Cairncross goes nowhere without her paid companion.

One or two girls at Cloisterhouse came from well-connected families – Djina Martindale was related on the 'distaff' side to the Norfolk Howards – it was Lord Howard of Effingham who commanded those hardy sea-dogs Drake, Hawkins and Raleigh against the seemingly invincible might of the Spanish Armada! But most of us were ordinary girls – except that our parents, while

not exactly rich, were not exactly poor either. Lady Cairncross
clearly isn't simply married into distinction but comes herself of
noble stock. Her venerable, craggy features scintillate with the
effortless authority of those born to command and in the courage
with which she heaved her rheumatic and angular frame up the
pyramids of Teotihuacan I discerned the dauntless spirit of warrior
lineage. *Behold the forebears' ancient lineaments.* She will have an
escutcheon! Heraldry has always thrilled me, with its plangent or
and sable, its formal plants and heraldic beasts. I quote from my
Lifebook:

*I who have roved the world unfettered by social restrictions –
who have watched the ineffable splendour of dusk in the Canyon
de Chelly – seen the winking, watery lanterns of Rangoon – while
not presuming to be one of her own kind, might be able to offer
Lady Cairncross a brand of comradeship which she will not obtain
among the endearing but vulgar stereotypes of our little band –
good fun as they all are – and which can hardly be compensated
for by the ministrations of a hireling. I have made several attempts
at conversation but so far in vain. When not sightseeing she
spends a lot of time resting and is rarely at the evening dinner
venues. Furthermore she has an imperious deafness which abruptly
prohibits conversational advances. I understand how aristocrats
have to be firm and even rude to keep respect. On the farm in
Rhodesia I soon had my easy-going permissiveness qualified and
became versed in the exercise of power and the responsibilities
entailed. The servants could be obstinately stupid and sharp words
were sometimes necessary – even with Pollydoodle my old nurse –
for their sake as well as mine. I was hardly more than a child
– fresh from the democratic hurly-burly of school in England –
and married to Roland who expected me to keep the household
in order!*

I took my place determinedly on Lady Cairncross's table.
Maureen was with her of course. Maureen looks and speaks
rather like the housekeeper Janet in *Doctor Finlay's Casebook*
that was on television some years ago – except that her accent

is Irish, of course! I make a little joke of it – asking her the whereabouts of Doctor Cameron, or Doctor Snoddy – characters in the television series – or some other witticism along those lines. It's jolly good fun.

Just about everybody else had gone off into the stimulating al fresco ambience of the Zocalo – I had stayed in the hotel deliberately to catch Lady Cairncross. Isabel was still changing in our room and I had ignored her plea to wait for her.

I did not, of course, launch into the fascinating topic of the British aristocracy. I spoke of the ruins we had seen that morning – comparing them unfavourably with the overwhelming architecture of Angkor Wat and the punctilious masonry of Chaco, New Mexico. Maureen claimed to have visited a surprising number of places including Singapore, Antigua and the Hindu Kush – equally surprisingly, Lady Cairncross grunted that this was her first trip outside Europe. Her husband, though – she referred to him, thrillingly, as simply 'Cairncross' – has been absolutely everywhere – like me, she flatteringly said. 'And a fat lot of good it's done him,' she added. Her brown, wrinkled face could be that of a Russian peasant or a Paris concierge were it not for her fine, haughty, moody eyes in which reside centuries of fastidious breeding and ruthless politics. Enraptured by her civility I took up the theme of how experiences may mould an individual – *the child is father to the man* – in order to introduce the topic of my years at Cloisterhouse – I wanted her to know that I been to a decent school and was eager to know what school she had attended and how it compared with my Alma Mater. I told her about the super fun it was – the hampers from home and the candle-lit dares – Lucinda up on the wardrobe with her nightie round her waist! – but also a bit about the cruelty – the peppers and suppositories – the caltrops on the parquet – the dunkings in the loo.

Suddenly, without a word of explanation, Lady Cairncross rose to her considerable height – her fish salad untouched – and quit the dining-room, with her stooped and stumbling gait of one no longer sound of limb who proudly scorns the use of a stick. I deduced that something in my speech or manner had offended her. It is painful for aristocrats – obliged as they are to uphold the dignity of their heritage – to mix with classless democrats such as I who insist on treating all we meet as part of a great Brotherhood and Sisterhood.

'Have I offended her Ladyship?' I asked Maureen. She looked at me as if I had spoken in a foreign tongue. I reiterated: 'Do you think I have offended Lady Cairncross?' Maureen narrowed her eyes and looked very cunning. 'Annabel? She isn't a Lady.' I understood at once, and said with a tactful and complicit twinkle – 'Righto Maureen! Roger and out!' She shrugged and carried on eating her meal rather more hastily than before – either eager to escape interrogation or fearful that her presence might be required elsewhere.

Anxious to reassure Maureen – and through her Lady Cairncross – that they were dealing with a person of delicacy – I went on – 'I'll ask her forgiveness. She mustn't mind the way I am. My zest and spontaneity sometimes have an unfortunate effect on those unable to share it. It was the same at Cloisterhouse. I was a *limber elf*, a sunbeam, yet my chirrupy love of Being made me enemies. There were times when this resentment became . . . I can remember not wanting to go back to school after the vac. Hilary Kyriakos used to spit in my food. I know it sounds incredible at a pukkah place like Cloisterhouse. She was food monitor, too!'

Just then Isabel joined us and at the same time Maureen rose and excused herself. I could see that she had done justice neither to her meal nor to what I was saying – in her panic that she was acting contrary to the expectations of Lady Cairncross by remaining with me in the dining room.

I thought it would be pleasanter to go to the market with Lisa – sometimes, even for peregrine spirits like mine, it is more relaxing to have the tour leader deal with the natives – but there was no hide nor hair of Lisa to be seen! She's a sprightly, perky sort of lass after my own heart – a sweety-pie – but she does have this pesky habit of sloping off when she should be earning her shekels. Just about everybody on this trip seems content to let her get away with it – but I've had a lot of experience of tour leaders – amid the gorges of Calabria – the minarets of Trebizond – the guano-crusted rocks of the Galapagos – and know that they benefit from a bit of unabashed correction when they are failing to *play up, play up and play the game*. I strode to Lisa's room and boldly beat the door. 'Come out of there, Lisa!' I cried commandingly – though my voice was bubbling with mitigating mirth. 'Some of us need you!' I thought I heard movement within the room so I beat louder on the door and cried, 'What are you up to in there? I bet it's something naughty!' Isabel was mortified, some passing Americans stared and a couple of doors opened further down the corridor – all of which I thought hilarious – but Lisa didn't let out a peep.

Not that I was fazed by having to visit the market unguided. I have walked without escort in the bazaars of high Kashmir, through an enchantment of silks and peppers and piled, ravishingly coloured powdered dyes – I have winced at the embryos of Arequipa and the skinned snakes of Shanghai – I have played the uproarious game of haggling from the shanties of Bolivia to the souks of Marakesh. I strode blithely enough into the covered market of Oaxaca, with Isabel dragging along in her somewhat abject way.

Lisa had mentioned, in the course of her Oaxaca briefing, two specialities of the market – a sugary, fudgy chocolate which she herself did not recommend and a watery ice-cream she declared delicious. The chocolate we found first – on a little stall next to a shoe-shine stand – wrapped into white paper packets and clearly priced so that we were able to purchase it by pointing and paying. Both Isabel and I disagreed with Lisa – finding it scrumptious as we wandered round the market in search of the ice-cream.

I was resolved not to buy souvenirs – seasoned travellers know to buy such items at the last port of call – in this case Cancun in the Yucatan. Silly Isabel has already bought a ridiculous amount of clutter to supplement her excessive wardrobe – including a hammock and a voluminous Mexican hat – which for the rest of the trip will be a nuisance both to her and anyone in her vicinity. In Mexico City she bought a great rug – practically a carpet – which she left at the hotel and plans to collect by taxi during the two-hour gap when we change planes between Cancun and Heathrow. I bet her house is full of didgeridoos and Zulu shields and other dust-attracting junk – whereas I understand full well that memories – *in the deep heart's core* – are the best and most portable souvenirs – and with the aid of my Lifebooks my memories are more decorative and rewarding than all the ethnic paraphernalia and keepsake gimmicks that money can buy. *See the little tippler leaning against the Sun!* Poor inarticulate Isabel has to amass material objects as her means of expression.

I was less interested in feeding future memories than in thoroughly and ecstatically absorbing the life-enhancing experience of Oaxaca market. Isabel, though, could not keep away from the clothing stalls – especially those offering white cotton tops with square yolks – embroidered with brilliantly coloured flowers – in which Mexican women look so beguiling. She speaks no Spanish – or any language but the Queen's English, as she proudly calls it – and is incapable of conducting the simplest transaction without an interpreter. I for my part relish the challenge of Babel and have always had a gift for languages – dating from when I had a pash for dusky, dreamy Fabienne – the French assistante – when I was in Fifth Remove at Cloisterhouse. As well as an acquaintance with Spanish, French, Italian, German and Greek I have smatterings of more exotic tongues such as Urdu, Thai, Quetchua, Basque and Matabele – picked up in the course of my enthralling argosies. Added to which I always equip myself with a phrase book – for this trip the Berlitz *Latin-American Spanish for Travellers* – and am adept at a little sign-language of my own which enables me to breach communication-gaps from fronded Venezuela to the shopping malls of Glasgow.

Isabel impulsively lunged onto a stall and addressed the dumpy and submissive matron who was tending the merchandise and a grubby infant at the same time.

'How much are the mantillas?' She was following advice I gave her at the beginning of the trip. In most of the world these days, in hotels and other tourist locations – and especially in a country like Mexico which borders onto the United States – one can get by speaking English slowly and distinctly if one doesn't have the local lingo. But Isabel seemed under the impression that volume was more pertinent than clarity – she let out a bossy yell that made the woman wince but otherwise communicated nothing – particularly as she had used the wrong word – there were no mantillas for sale – silly Isabel!

'Kwantoah kwaystah?' I asked. For this dependable expression I could use the Latin-American pronunciation without resource to the phrase-book. I pointed up at one of the blouses that was displayed on a coat-hanger.

The woman stared at me with the same half-blank half-fearful look which she had given Isabel. Talking to foreigners in their own tongue can be a challenge. My French, for instance, is sound enough – I got a B at A level – but even in sophisticated Paris – under the Heavenward-aspiring twin towers of Notre Dame – I have known the frustration of having to repeat the same banal phrase until the light of comprehension dawns on the features of the person I am addressing – who then gives the phrase back to me – as if correcting my pronunciation – exactly as I have said it several times!

'Kwantoah kwaystah?' The woman rose – deposited the baby in a sort of nest of rags that she had beside her – reached down the blouse from the coat-hanger and handed it to me.

'How much are they?' Isabel shouted – then to me, 'Look – ask what they cost, will you?'

'Kwantoah kwaystah?' I held out the palm of my left hand and pretended to pick coins out of it. The woman stared intently at the palm of my hand as if she could see something growing there. Meanwhile Isabel was admiring the blouse, which was extremely low-cut, with a broidery of scarlet flowers – she would look appalling in it! Her choice of clothes and hairstyle seems deliberately calculated to accentuate the sag of her face and the shrivelling of her figure. It is pitiful that one so concerned about her appearance should deteriorate so helplessly – I thank my stars I am more or less as firm and fit of body as when Roly Poly used to call me his Bouncing Babe.

'Ask her where the fitting-room is,' Isabel commanded, looking around her. It was evident that there was not one, though there looked to be some sort of den or galley behind a curtain of sacking at the back of the stall. While I leafed through my phrase book she set to examining other blouses – picking them up and sneering at them and flinging them down in her insolent way. A small number of Mexicans – two elderly women and several schoolchildren – had come to a halt in the thoroughfare between the stalls and were watching the antics of the gringos as if we were on a stage.

'Donday aystah ayl proabahdoar?' I asked – but the last part of this was drowned by Isabel letting out a yell. She was pointing at a small pink dog which had appeared from behind the sacking screen and was sniffing around the baby's nest. The poor creature had some sort of mite infestation which had stripped away much of its fur, revealing sore flesh and suppurating scabs.

The woman called out something I couldn't fathom – the animal's name? – and the dog dipped its head, wagged its tail wearily and ambled back through the curtain.

Isabel stood transfixed for several seconds, shifting her gaze between the stall-keeper woman and the dog's point of egress. Then – as I knew she was going to – she swung round towards me.

'Rose! Tell her she must do something about that dog! She must take it for treatment!' She was so distressed and peremptory that it seemed kinder to obey. I cast around among my Castilian. '*El perro es malo*,' I said.

The woman had continued to look daunted by Isabel's stridency and my easy air of authority – but when I uttered these innocuous

words her face contorted into an expression of extreme malevolence. Maybe she misheard some spectacular insult. She clenched
her fists and began to shout – in a deafening, coarse, masculine
voice that made Isabel's previous noisiness seem as nothing. I
couldn't understand anything – if it was Spanish it was in an
indecipherable dialect – but both Isabel and I were intimidated
by the racket she was making and the wrath that made her look
so evil. Furthermore, the sacking curtain moved again and a man
lurched out – as if summoned to an entertainment – and lolled
and leered – a drunken fellow with a skin disease that puckered
up one side of his face – as though the dog had taken human
form behind the curtain, a werewolf in reverse! And the audience
in the thoroughfare had swelled – a beggar on crutches, a couple of
cold-eyed young hoodlums – and others were arriving every second
as the woman's rough bellows permeated the purlieus.

I was aware – as I have been among the hovels of Calcutta,
the shanties of Lima, the kraals of Africa – of the impoverished
and unprincipled scrutiny of the undeveloped world. Fortunately,
Rhodesia – my childhood and half my adult life spent there –
trained me in the importance of retaining poise in the presence
of native insolence. *If you can keep your head when those about
you* . . . I just laughed my merry laugh and said, 'Goodness! What
a fuss she is making! Come along, Isabel.'

I took the blouses out of Isabel's hands and dumped them on a
tabletop. The drunken man said something – showed his broken
teeth – pointed at the mound of blouses and rubbed two fingers
together in the mime suggesting payment which earlier I had failed
to remember. I took Isabel by the arm and we stepped into the
thoroughfare – where it was necessary for some of the little crowd
to back off to make space for us. The woman stopped shouting
to spit at us – I am glad to say it was a dry, figurative gesture
of contempt rather than a launch of real spittle. I couldn't resist
a jaunty little wave as we left – but it was a relief to get out into
the Zocalo – then off the suddenly sinister streets of Oaxaca and
back into the hotel.

It was not a new experience for either of us. Isabel has an awful manner with anybody she considers subservient – air-hostesses, shop-assistants, hotel staff – and there must be many occasions when it backfires on her. I on the other hand have been vouchsafed Enlightenment – treat all my fellow humans however abject as my brothers and sisters – but my natural candour and high spirits give rise to irrational antipathy once in a while.

Isabel was quite overcome – to the extent of becoming snivelly when we got back to the hotel and going to lie down. I am made of sterner stuff, *I thank whatever God may be for my indomitable soul.* I went into the bar and ordered a gin and tonic – una toaneekah koan kheenaybrah – then wrote up the incident in my diary, adding: *Even as I record this rather perturbing encounter – such is the therapeutic power of the literary art! – I feel better and better about it – until I am actually glad that it happened! It is with such blundering, hilarious little adventures – fraught with contretemps and doubtless dismaying at the time – that the joy of the rest of the trip – the serenity of fellowship amid the breathless delight of discovery – is given spice and savour – as Nature in Her wisdom will often emphasise, by means of an awkward little cloudlet, the blueness of a summer sky.*

Brian and Millie came into the bar and ordered coffee – at first they were reluctant to join me, then decided – as I closed my Lifebook and beamed at them – that it would seem rude not to do so. I was delighted because – even on this trip full of engrossing and attractive characters – they are two of my favourite people. Tonia told me that Brian and Millie are on their honeymoon. This is quite wrong – they have different surnames and have been together for six years – but one can understand why she made the mistake. Brian absolutely dotes on his 'Little Millie' as he calls her – and she is just as fond of him, in her quieter way. The Love-Birds, as I call them, fortify and justify my faith in humanity and its vagaries which has never left me though bruised by betrayal and vicissitude.

I asked if they had yet visited the museum and they answered simultaneously – Brian saying, 'Yes we have,' whereas Millie answered, 'No, we're off there this afternoon' – then they stared at each other for a moment or so till Brian said, 'The museum here in Oaxaca? No we haven't. I thought you meant the Museum of Anthropology in Mexico City.'

'Might I come with you?' I asked. 'Isabel isn't well and I'm nervous of going on the streets here alone.'

Brian answered – with quite good grace – 'No problem.' I didn't resent the fact that he hadn't wanted me along – any more than I resented their reluctance to sit with me when they came into the bar. I can remember the time when for me also two was company and I wanted myself and Roly Poly to be shut away from the rest of the world forever. *And wilderness were Paradise enow* . . . All the same I was not going to let their yen for privacy prevent me from seeing the Mixtec treasure from tomb 7 at Monte Alban – or have me run the hazard of the Oaxaca streets alone.

I had a dreamy afternoon! On the way to the museum I regaled Brian and Millie with a side-splitting account of the events in Oaxaca market and their effect on poor Isabel. The Mixtec treasure was spiffing – a hoard of beautifully worked silver – turquoise – coral – jade – amber – jet – rock crystal – pearls – jaguar and eagle bone – and above all gold. Gazing upon these wonders made it easy to sink deep into mystical reveries. *Our birth is but a sleep* . . . Furthermore I bought a darling little book on pre-Columbian cookery at the museum book-shop and entertained Brian and Millie over drinks and a snack by reading them extracts so hysterically amusing that I had to keep breaking off to weep with mirth and clean my spectacles.

When I got back to the hotel room Isabel had got over her funk – *wee, sleekit, cowering, timorous beastie* – and was livid with rage. She had been ringing Lisa's room – without success – to complain about what had happened – and now she wanted me to contact the police – or the local tourist board – or the Mayor of Oaxaca – about the market-woman's behaviour – and the condition of the dog. I tried to divert her with an account of the Mixtec treasure – till she lay on her bed with her back to me and sulked – I swear she was sucking her thumb – then I read some extracts from the cookery book to entertain her – but she complained that I was giving her a headache.

I crossed out my account of the incident in Oaxaca market, and wrote instead: *There were stalls bedecked with every example of the exotic garb of the native Mexican – ponchos and serapes, sombreros and panamas, mariachi jackets and leather boots, frilly skirts and tops – as well as more practical and inexpensive clothing such as jeans and nylon shirts. There were cafés and bars and ice-cream parlours – though they all looked so squalid – as did the customers – that we were daunted from sampling their wares! The same was true of the butchers' stalls where utterly unrecognisable cuts of meat – as if the poor creatures had been hacked up at random by madmen – were dangling from hooks and smelling too ripe for our European taste. This was even more the case with the fish-mongers stalls, which Isabel was forced to pass at a trot holding her nose and saying 'Pooh!'. I did the same – just for the fun of it – then collapsed against a stall counter giggling – but Isabel wasn't amused, poor sombre soul. And there were stalls for fruit, vegetables and general groceries, with the produce painstakingly arrayed into decorative cones – chillis, figs, dates, and – ugh! – roasted grasshoppers. All this panoply was bedizened by the thrilling, teeming populace of Mexico – the shaggy macho of the males, the glossy locks of the senoritas, the big eyes and white teeth of the cheeky bambinos. I opened my thirsty soul to the multifarious plenitude of the experience.*

Soon afterwards I was a disappointment to Isabel – when the group were assembled prior to dinner in the bar next to the hotel. When Lisa showed up – twenty minutes late, with a flushed, pink face – as if she had been over-exerting herself – or drinking – or crying – or all three – Isabel pitched straight into her – relating the 'awful, distressing' market occurrence – and demanding to know what Lisa proposed to do about it. Dissatisfied with the flippant nature of Lisa's response – four or five others were belabouring our tour leader with complaints about the hotel and questions about future arrangements – Isabel called on me to give witness. I'm afraid I began to regale the company – as far as my chuckles of irrepressible mirth would let me – with a sprightly, fiddle-de-dee account of our adventure that found no favour with Isabel – who rudely interrupted with further demands that Lisa should take action – particularly over the dog. At this Lisa let out a snort and said, 'I don't give a sod about some scabby dog.' This caused us all to go quiet – except Sunita, who laughed. Isabel went red and looked to be on the point of tears. Lisa hesitated for a moment – as if she was thinking of retracting or qualifying her remark – then gave a shrug – said briskly, 'Come along!' – and set off across the square, leaving us to drink up, pay and follow as best we could.

The restaurant to which she led us was really rather special – posher and pricier than most of the others on the trip – all dark, delicious Spanish wood and mystic candlelight and fascinating Moorish furnishings. It also boasted the sauciest and wittiest waiters even in Mexico – the one who took the main order had me in stitches – and a menu full of authentic Mexican specialities, from which I selected a chicken baked in banana leaf that was meltingly and utterly divine.

Our tables were alfresco on a balcony, so that as we ate I could gloat on the fun-fair seethe and hubbub of the Zocalo. The fountain, the triangles of verdure and the criss-crossing little alleyways were lit by orange globes on wrought-iron stands and there were also festoons of coloured bulbs on the palm trees, conifers and surrounding buildings. All four sides of the square were resplendent with stalls of multicoloured textiles and blankets spread to display shimmering gewgaws. There were booths – tents – kiosks on wheels – selling drinks, lollipops, candy-floss and walking-sticks made out of what looked just like English seaside rock. Vividly caparisoned people were everywhere – whole families, with fat old grannies wheezing and bambinos cavorting – tourists nosing and questing with their cameras and bum-bags and their spectacles secured on pieces of string – balloon-sellers wheedling and shoe-shine boys proclaiming and armed soldiers and policemen patrolling macho and serene. An international medley of music outpoured from cafés and stalls and car radios – and there was an urchin playing a jaunty accordion – and a blind old man cajoling rapture from a violin. And there was romance in the air – teenagers horsing about, young bucks loitering, couples talking gravely, señoritas strolling arm in arm. The whole square was thronged and vibrant, clamorous and rejoicing, an enchanted island of noise and colour in the velvet night.

The conviviality of our little group did not match the thrilling turmoil of the vista. Brian and Millie were not with us – nor Lady Cairncross and Maureen – nor Martin, who Dennis says has got a 'gastric affliction' – nor Tonia and Sunita, though they had been with us for apéritifs. Lisa was scowly and pouty – like on the last night in Mexico City but worse. I had a stab at jollying her out of her gloom – saying brightly, 'Cheer up Lisa, it might not happen! A smile wouldn't crack your face, hmm?' She didn't give me the civility of an answer – just stared at me then insolently away. Piqued by this petulance, I cried, 'Come, come! It won't do for the tour leader to be down in the dumps!' The sprightliness of my tone did not disguise the reprimand – Lisa's eyes narrowed but she contented herself with muttering, 'I'm tired, that's all,' before turning emphatically from me to pretend to talk to Stephanie and Katrin.

Namby-pamby Isabel was miserable all evening – drinking a bottle of wine to herself and not even complaining about the food! I am proud to say – *no coward soul is mine* – I can face affliction without the shameful crutch of alcohol – and I do not need to artificially boost my joviality with booze in order to be the life and soul of a party – any more than I need cosmetic help to enhance the glorious natural complexion which I was granted as a child and have kept for the rest of my life.

Simon insisted on talking politics even after I protested that politics are unsuitable for a social occasion. He got into a heated argument with Dorothy – who is some sort of commie like weirdo Augustine at Cloisterhouse – though he kept looking at dear old

Donald all the time – dreamy Donald, I call him – as if it was him he was really addressing. Leaning forward aggressively as far as his bulk permitted, he did not listen to Dorothy's twaddle but waited impatiently for a chance to interrupt with his pompous spiel. Pamela just sat there beaming at her lord and master as if she were his dusky slave! I shouted across to her, in a joky tone, 'Is he always like this?' – which got no response from her and an irascible blink from him. Some insecurity deeper than mere chauvinism makes him resent women of character. For all his glittering career as a property magnate I find it hard to see him other than as a great, cross, fattypuff, bearded baby – and my heart responds to him with scornful compassion.

He felt the need to be rude to me three times in the course of the evening. Once when I tried to change the subject by introducing the brilliant but controversial theories of Erich von Daniken he cut me short by snapping, 'Von Daniken is utter drivel and not worth discussing.' Another time, when I interpolated the snippet – culled first-hand from Joan Bullivant, an erstwhile secretary in Westminster – that Margaret Thatcher was considerate to those who worked for her – Simon snorted, 'We all know what it was like to work for that bitch.' The third time I was actually supporting him against Dorothy's woolly notions – whatever our personal compassion, we simply can't afford to give free medical treatment to everyone who demands it – when he turned on me with, 'You'd just let people die, would you?' – then went on to something else without giving me a chance to reply. The glance he flashed – the tilt of his chin – the confident tone – reminded me of Roland, and for a moment I quailed. Which is ridiculous, because Roland was lean and hard and dangerous, whereas Simon is a harmless heap of blubber and bluster like Billy Bunter.

Luckily, on the other side of me was sweety-pie Dennis, though more subdued than usual – missing his buddy Marty, I kidded him. He entertained me with an account of proposed transport modifications in Cardiganshire and North Wales – I riposted with comical accounts of my adventures – and misadventures! – on the

Trans-Siberian Express, the Barcelona Funicular and the mule trek on the 'Secrets of the Bosphorus' tour. As for Wales – too near to home for the yearning scope of my wanderlust? – I have never set foot there, but its lakes and valleys beckoned as I listened to Dennis, till I teased him by asking for his address – only half joking! He looked horrified but I think he was secretly pleased. He is a cultured and well-mannered young man, dashing and athletic in appearance – Isabel claims that he suffers from body odour, but I can't say I have noticed. The sort of young man – I'm such a flirt and tease! – that could make me wish I was twenty years younger – or even feel twenty years younger – I told him with a wink – and made him blush!

The wine did nothing for Isabel's spirits – by the time we got back to the hotel she was practically blubbing with ill-humour. I considered dawdling downstairs until she had snivelled herself to sleep – but we had to be up very early next morning for the long journey south to Chiapas – so nobody took up my suggestion of a nightcap in the hotel bar. I went up to the room and wrote in my Lifebook as best I could, while Isabel raged about Lisa – not just the offensive way Lisa had spoken to her earlier in the evening – though there was sufficient about that – but about our tour leader's general lack of response to our wishes and needs. I found myself acting the diplomat – which isn't my style at all! – saying Lisa is maybe under stress – hadn't meant to sound so abrupt – and in any case it wasn't worth bothering about when one could be steeping one's Being in Mexico.

Meanwhile I had written in my Lifebook: *On all the tours it has been my privilege to join – in all the exotic and enthralling places – the sculpted splendour of the Mountains of the Moon – the crisp air of Lapland where herds of reindeer glide like ghosts across the tundra – the mellow bells and bridges and buildings of Prague in autumn – the sultry silver sands of the Carib Sea – there have always been people like Isabel, deaf and blind to the miracles around them, demanding my time and care.*

Befuddled with drink and distracted by temper she had donned her tarty nightie and got into bed without washing the make-up out of her wrinkles. Now she was sitting up looking grotesque – like a sort of geriatric nymphet – round-shouldered, with her bottom lip pouted out in an infantile manner and her ill-advised henna haircut looking like a cheap wig plonked on slightly askew.

Tears besmeared her tainted face as she answered my last point by saying she hated all foreign countries. She had only come on the stinking tour because she was miserable in the big bungalow since the death of her husband – with her son lost somewhere in Canada and the East Finchley Bridge Club full of decrepit men and sarcastic Jewish bitches – and she was too scatterbrained for bridge, anyway . . .

I cried out, 'Isabel, you are in denial! Open yourself to the wonders of Being!'

This had the same effect as Lisa's grumpy outburst. Isabel sniffed up and swallowed her mucal grief then flumped down with her back to me and switched off her light. I could still see to write because of my own bedside lamp.

I have shut her up – not handled it well – I never claimed to be a social worker or therapist! Yet I have been tactful, by my standards! I nearly told her what a pitiful coward she is.

Today has been a tad disappointing – the morning frolics, the majesty of Monte Alban, the kaleidoscope of throbbing life in Oaxaca market, the magic trove of the museum, the fun with Brian and Millie, the delicious fare and ambience of the evening, offset – but not much – by the assault of the market woman, the antipathy of Simon, the snivelling of Isabel.

Those blots on the panoply of fun and wonder will not loom large in retrospect. Nothing will darken my dauntless spirit or mar the magical merriment for the last few miles of the Pilgrimage. 'Laugh and be merry, remember, better the world with a song.' If I can cope with my appalling schooldays – the disgusting nightmare of marriage to Roland – the menace of Rhodesia – exile, spinsterhood, lonely decay – doors shutting, options dwindling – and on top of it all the news Doctor

Goodrich gave me last month – I can surely take Simon and Isabel in my stride and get a contretemps with a Mexican stall-holder into perspective.

SUNITA RAVIKUMAR

The sun slanted in through the dusty windows of the bus. In spite of how early it was it seemed warm to me but Tonia said it was cold. She was in her padded jacket. 'Christ, it's cold!' she boomed. 'Freezes your ass!'

Rose said to Mario, 'Wakey wakey driver! Up with the lark this morning, hm?'

He grinned at her in the way people do when they don't understand what's said. Rose threw back her head and laughed loudly, showing her white teeth. Simon, who was with Pamela on the seats just behind us, drew in his breath and said 'Christ!'

Tonia said, 'I sure feel bad about last night, Nita.'

Isabel demanded, 'Can somebody tell me what we're waiting for?'

Rose responded, 'Clueless Kate of course. What else?'

Tonia asked me, 'Did you hear what I just said?'

At that point Lisa clambered onto the bus carrying a day-sack and a clip-board. She had washed her hair and slept off her bad mood. 'Everybody on board?'

Several voices chimed in with the news about Katrin. When the chorus had died down Simon spoke out sarcastically. 'Whatever happened to your threat to go without people who weren't on time?'

Dennis had been rearranging luggage on the long back seat. He takes great care to stack it securely with the larger and heavier cases at the bottom. Now he said, 'It is not legally viable to deliberately leave a paid-up member of the group for whom the tour company has accepted responsibility. Unless there were exceptional circumstances it would be a violation of contractual obligations.'

Simon snorted and said, 'In that case why make the threat in the first place?' Meanwhile Lisa had got off the bus and disappeared through the side door of the hotel.

'Stephanie, where's Katrin?' Isabel shouted accusingly. Stephanie didn't look up from her *Lonely Planet* guidebook. Brian and Millie were fiddling with bird-books and binoculars. Dorothy was studying a map. Donald was engrossed with his little magnetic chess-set.

Dennis asked, 'Time did you say you made it? I only make it quarter past.' Several people looked at their watches but nobody said anything, so he went on, 'I reckon we all ought to synchronise our chronometers. Time do you make it, Martyboy?'

'Five thirty,' said Martin. 'Talisman time.'

Tonia turned round with her smirky smile on her face. 'Marty's got a clock in his gut. Happy hour, huh, Marty?'

At first it seemed he was not going to answer, then he said, just loudly enough for us to hear, 'Weekdays and Saturdays only.'

Katrin came briskly up the street and got on the bus. She must have come out of the hotel by the main entrance on the Zocalo. 'Where is Lisa?' she enquired before anybody could say anything.

'Gone to look for you,' said Isabel rudely and Annabel asked icily, 'Do you know what time it is?'

'I have need of her,' said Katrin. 'My baggage has been pilfered.' She was about to get off the bus again when Simon shouted commandingly, 'It has not been stolen. It has been loaded into the back of the bus.'

'Provided it was deposited in the foyer by seven forty-five in accordance with briefing instructions,' Dennis added.

Stephanie then surprised everybody by saying without lifting her eyes from her guidebook, 'She doesn't mean her case. She's talking about her day-sack.'

'Containing my monies and personal effects including my contact lenses,' said Katrin in her chanting, foreign voice. It was hard to tell how shaken she was because she always looks aghast.

Lisa appeared round the corner. She had been all through the hotel and out at the main entrance. Climbing onto the bus she said pleasantly, 'Ah! There you are!'

'My baggage has been pilfered,' Katrin repeated.

'She's lost it again!' said Simon.

Rose shouted, 'She'd lose her head if it was loose!'

I said to Tonia, 'Isn't that Katrin's day-sack? The red one on top of the pile to the left.'

Katrin said firmly to Lisa, 'You shall come with me into the hotel. If necessary you shall apprise the police.' This was greeted with gasps and snorts. If it had been somebody else rather than Katrin we would have been more sympathetic.

'When do you last remember having it?' Lisa asked.

'I don't know!' said Katrin, as if it was a stupid question.

'She'd lose her head if it was loose!' Rose shouted again.

Tonia exclaimed loudly, 'Hey, lookee! On the rear seat, top of the heap!'

Katrin's face twitched and she peered suspiciously down the bus, like somebody trying to make out something at sea. Stephanie said, 'She doesn't see too good without her lenses.'

Lisa said, 'Often referred to as a Mixtec capital, Mitla was a Zapotec settlement from 1,000 AD to modern times. It is mostly famous for the magnificent geometrical designs in the Hall of Mosaics.'

Tonia whispered to me, 'Hey, there's Lee!'

I had to move my head to see through the wing-mirror of the bus. Sure enough, Lee was just behind us in a little green Volkswagen that seemed jammed full of him.

Tonia said into my ear, 'Guess we're not talking today, huh?' She was sitting next to me in the gangway seat for the first time on the trip. Usually she got on the bus first and bagged a window seat then I sat next to her. 'Shit, Nita! What am I reckoned to have done, anyway?'

I said, 'Shh!'

In front of us Maureen said, 'Ploat? What's that?'

Annabel said, 'I don't know but it's in the book.'

Lisa recited, 'Before lunch we stop in Tule to look at a two-thousand-year old cypress tree. This afternoon we descend to cross the narrow Isthmus of Tehuantepec, a rain-forest area between the Atlantic and Pacific oceans. Then we climb again into the state of Chiapas.'

The bus was winding through brown, cactus-covered mountains. Brian said, 'It's a kite is that. Just look at the tail. I reckon it's Elanus Leucurus.'

Millie said, 'Maybe Gampsonyx Swainsonii.'

Brian said, 'Millikins sweetie, you should read your Schub and Wedlock. Gamsonyx Swainsonii is only about nine inches long!'

Rose declaimed, 'I love these ancient Indian names! Chimborazo, Cotapaxi! Poetry is a source of unending delight to me!'

Lisa was saying, 'Chiapas is the poorest state in Mexico, with a large Indian population. After the EZLN rising in 1994 the state was dangerous, but at present there is a cease-fire between the Zapatistas and the army.'

Dennis called from the back, 'According to the current edition of the *Globetrotter Megaguide to Mesa-America* there have been no instances of the insurrectionary forces adopting an aggressive attitude to tourists.'

Lisa said, 'Marcos and his guerrillas have stopped the odd bus, but just to give a propaganda lecture and pass a hat round.'

'How exciting!' cried Rose. 'I should dearly love that to happen!'

Simon behind me said to Pamela, 'The stupid bitch!'

Millie was trying to watch the kite through her binoculars but the bus kept swerving round mountain bends. 'You can't tell its size,' she complained to Brian, 'because you can't judge how high it is.'

Tonia said to me in an intense whisper, 'I've put a lot of dough into this vacation, Nita, and I'm gonna have fun. I'm not gonna let your moods and hang-ups wreck it.'

As I turned to answer her I was shaken by how close her face was to mine. I could see at very close quarters the freckles that cover her cheeks and forehead. 'That's how I feel too,' I said. 'Shut up. People are listening.'

It was true enough that the bus was hushed just then, so that I could even hear the tinny sound of an orchestra from Katrin's earphones. Lisa, kneeling on the front seat to face us all, was leafing through her notes.

Tonia got up, reached her day-sack from the rack and left me. I saw through the driver's mirror that she went to Martin, who grudgingly shifted his stuff off the gangway seat to let her sit down. He likes two seats to himself. Tonia handled it pretty well, as if she had gone back there because she'd suddenly thought of some topic she wanted to chew over with Martin.

In front of me Annabel said, 'Goaf and Filo with the F on a treble. Thirty eight.'

Maureen said, 'I challenge both of them.'

Dennis called from the back, 'Howsabout a photo-stop soon, Lisa?'

Rose said, 'Ooh goody, yes!'

Mitla didn't look much from the carpark. All I could see were walls, about ten feet high, of grubby salmon-coloured stone.

'Church Group to the left. House of Mosaics on the right. Back in the bus at ten sharp, okay?'

We didn't have a guide on this occasion. Lisa had bought our tickets at the ticket-office, then given us a brief lecture about the mosaics.

'Aren't you accompanying us?' Simon asked her nastily.

'I'd love to but I've got a bit of paperwork to see to. Okay?'

I dawdled at the back on my own, wandering towards the House of Mosaics, then made up my mind and turned back to the bus. On the way back I passed Lee, who was on his way to the ruins with a ticket in his fist. Our eyes met and I thought for a moment that he was going to speak.

Lisa wasn't doing paperwork. She was sitting on the steps on the shady side of the bus and smoking a cigarette. Mario was inside the bus, settling onto the front seat to have a quick snooze. Lee's Volkswagen was at the other side of the carpark, about twenty yards away.

'I want to split with Tonia,' I said.

She offered me a cigarette though she knows I don't smoke. Then she said, 'I don't follow.'

'I don't want to share a room with her. I want you to put me with somebody else.'

'Had a tiff, have you?' I didn't answer. Mario was grinning and winking at me through the window. It put me off my stride, though he probably couldn't hear what we were saying and doesn't understand much English anyway. Lisa took a drag and let out a plume of smoke. 'My advice, Nita, is let it ride for now. This isn't the first time you two have had a tiff, is it? You'll have made it up by tomorrow.'

'I don't want to make it up!' I blurted. I'd thought that it would be fairly easy to talk to Lisa but it wasn't. Maybe the sighting of Lee had spoiled her early-morning mood.

She cocked her head on one side and gave me a sideways, searching look. 'What have you fallen out over?'

'I haven't a clue.' I could hear the irritation in my voice. 'Tonia's always reckoning to fall out. Then she makes up. It's how she operates.'

Lisa spread her arms and smiled brightly. 'Falling out, making up. That's life. Par for the course in most relationships.'

She was assuming that I'm stupid, probably because of my colour. I'd not noticed that sort of racist crap in Lisa but I'd never tried to hold a serious conversation with her before.

'Tonia and me don't have a relationship. We never met before this trip.'

Now she gave a tinkly little laugh. 'Come off it, Nita! Anybody can see you and Tonia have really hit it off together.'

'That's what everybody says including Tonia and I don't like it.

I don't like Rose calling us "the Terrible Twins" and I don't like Martin's cracks about us being dykes. Tonia and me haven't got anything in common. I don't like discos. I don't like going round town after midnight boozing and looking for pigs to pester me. I don't like liars and stupid power-games.'

It had all come out wrong, which is what happens with me. I go along with things I should complain about until when I do complain it comes out wrong because I'm too worked up over it.

The smile had gone from Lisa's face. When she spoke her voice had a sort of rhythm to it, as if she was reciting verse, which I've noticed before when she is rattled. 'Yes, okay Nita, all that's between you and Tonia and no business of mine. But changing rooms isn't as easy as all that. There's nowhere to put either of you unless you can find someone else who's willing to swap.'

A savage-looking dog – there were any number of them around the Mitla ruins and carpark – was circling around near us with its head low. Lisa flicked her fag viciously at the dog which gave a sneeze and cringed off. 'I don't want any hassle. I can't start shuffling people round without the full knowledge and permission of everybody concerned.'

I had to hurry round Mitla. The mosaics were okay. I was last on the bus, by which time Tonia was in my window seat expecting me to sit next to her. I went down the bus past her. All the window seats were claimed so I asked Stephanie if I could sit next to her.

'Righto.'

'It's a bit draughty up the front of the bus.'

Dennis leant over from behind and talked to us for a long time about the Samarkand tour he went on, where some of the terrain was similar to the part of Mexico we were travelling through. He quoted a lot of statistics about rainfall and temperatures. After he had shut up I said to Stephanie, 'There certainly are a lot of cactuses. Cacti, I mean.' I spoke fairly loudly because I had worked out that I was on her deaf side.

She spun round on me and said, 'Hey! You don't have to yell! I'm not deaf.'

'Another of Tonia's bloody fibs.'

Dennis behind us and Donald and Dorothy in front might be eavesdropping, but I wasn't bothered. In any case our conversation was being given a certain amount of privacy by the Mexican music that was now being piped through the bus radio.

Stephanie leaned towards me and lowered her voice. 'Y'had a barney with Tonia? Wouldn't want to swap rooms, would yer?'

'I would! I've already talked to Lisa. She says I've to find somebody who wants to swap.'

'I'd be chuffed to room with Tonia if it's all right with her. I've had my share of Katrin, I reckon. I should warn yer, she makes a lot of noise in her sleep, talking and . . . kind of . . . but y'aren't gonna swap rooms if I say more!'

Just then Dennis leant forward again and started telling us about some lectures he attended at the Extramural Department of the University of Wales in Aberystwyth.

We stopped at Tule to look at a cypress that was supposed to be 2,000 years old, an enormous tree full of hundreds of sparrows. We had a cup of coffee in a café there. Some people bought tortillas and other grub, because we weren't scheduled to have lunch until three o'clock. Behind the café was a recreation area with a hammock, for some reason, and a deer in a cage. Stephanie and I had come out to get away from Dennis and were looking at the deer when I broached my topic again. 'Listen Stephanie, I've got to admit I don't fancy sharing with Katrin.'

'Don't blame yer.' She was pushing a twist of several long blades of grass through the chicken-wire of the cage. The deer took them into its muzzle and munched them carefully. I liked the way Stephanie watched it do this. She pushed her own face forward and seemed to become a deer herself for a fraction of a second.

'But I don't want to share with Tonia either. So why shouldn't I share with you?'

She thought about it. Her eyes may be misaligned but there is a calm in them that shows she is strong. 'That's great with me, but how about Tonia and Katrin?'

'All we do is say we want to share a room. If there's a problem, Lisa's got a double room. She can share with either Tonia or Katrin and let the other have a room to herself.'

The bus took us down out of the mountains onto the Isthmus of Tehuantepec. It was hot, dusty and windy, as Lisa had said it would be. We passed a lot of windmills and Dennis explained how they were being used to power a generator. This part of Mexico was supposed to be full of jungle, and Brian and Millie were ready to start spotting lots of rain-forest birds, but there wasn't any jungle where the road went. There was just grass, scrub, cactus and flowers that Dorothy said were Californian poppies.

Lunch was at a roadside self-service. I had chick pea and vegetable soup. There was a cold box in the café and Martin bought half a dozen beers to take on the bus. He's permanently semi-sloshed.

On we went over the windy plain past Tehuantepec Town. Rose shouted, '"In that November off Tehuantepec . . ." It's a poem by an American, William Tennessee Williams. "Mile-mallows that a mellow sun cajoles . . ."'

Stephanie said to me, 'She reckons yer been circumcised!'

'Circumcised!'

'Customary with you people, she said.'

'That's Africa, not India.'

'Yeah. And she said how you had an arranged marriage, seven years old, to a creepy old bloke that died.'

'She's a pathological cowing liar. She's the one that spread the stories about Annabel being a duchess and Simon a millionaire.'

'Yeah, and how Katrin's ma an' pa met in Belsen. And how Lisa's got a psycho on her tail.'

'That last one's true, some of it.'

*　　*　　*

At five o'clock in the afternoon we were on a stretch of windy road from the coast to the mountains of Chiapas when the bus stopped at the back of a long line of traffic. Lorries, cars and petrol tankers were all at a standstill for as far as could be seen up the road and over the next ridge. Drivers and passengers were out of the vehicles, talking in the road and walking about. Nothing was coming down the road from the opposite direction, except for a couple of vehicles that had just turned round to head back the way we had come. Lisa stood up and exchanged a meaningful glance with Mario. 'Shit!' she said.

Mario switched on a CB radio. Lisa leant over to listen as well, then she and Mario spoke to each other in Spanish. He spoke into his microphone then they both listened to a voice on the radio. This went on for some time while the rest of us stayed quiet, some people craning up in their seats as if they would be able to make out what was happening like that.

Tonia speaks Spanish so well that I believe her when she says she's spent time in Barcelona. Now she called out, 'It's a road-block. Something political.' Lisa, who was still trying to listen, shut her up with a frantic gesture.

I looked at Stephanie, dismayed. 'Wow!' she said. 'A road-block! That's terrific!' I must have looked surprised because she went on to explain. 'The other girls on the ward – well – none of them go on flash trips like me. I reckon it's my one claim to fame. This kind of thing – a road-block – makes a great story, y'see?'

Lisa had turned to talk to us all. 'There's a road-block at a bridge about two kilometres on.'

Rose said, 'What a bally nuisance!'

Lisa said, 'This sort of thing is always happening in Chiapas. Sometimes it's over in an hour or two, but sometimes it lasts days.'

'Terrorists?' Isabel quavered.

Lisa said, 'I'm going to walk along to the bridge.'

Dorothy suggested, 'Take somebody with you. Tonia, you speak Spanish.'

'Excuse me if this remark seems to smack of chauvinism,' Dennis interposed, 'but I think you ought to have a man along.'

Annabel said, 'Take Simon!' and laughed. The rest of us were gobsmacked by this sudden shaft of malice.

Simon said testily, 'The obvious person to take is the driver.'

Lisa said, 'Mario stops here in case the traffic starts to move. Dennis, I want you to look after the bus. Don't let anybody on it who isn't in our party.'

There are some don't rate Lisa as a tour leader but this was brilliant. Dennis blushed and his tash seemed to bristle with bliss. 'Don't worry about it, skipper,' he said, giving her a thumbs-up sign. 'Nobody who is not an accredited member of the tour will be permitted to board this vehicle in your absence.'

As Lisa went up the road with Tonia Annabel asked, 'Isn't there another road we can take to avoid this nonsense?'

Dennis responded, 'Not according to my *Bartholomew Conic Projection Routemaster Atlas of Mexico*.'

Simon said, 'Then we must return to Tehuantepec Town and Baluth Tours must charter an aircraft.'

Maureen gasped, 'That's a good idea!'

'They are legally contracted to provide us with the advertised itinerary,' Simon said.

Brian said, 'No they aren't, are they Millie? They've lots of let-out clauses about unforeseen events and local conditions.'

Maureen groaned, 'Oh yes. That's true.'

Dennis declared, 'If anybody wants to stretch their legs that's okay. I'll stay here and ensure that no unauthorised strangers board the bus. Best if you don't wander too far from the bus in case we have to set off at short notice.'

Millie was peering into the sky through her binoculars. Martin was drinking a can of Tecate. Donald was staring at his little magnetic chess-set. Katrin had her headphones on and her eyes shut.

The traffic started moving. Everybody cheered and those who were on the road scrambled back into the bus. But we only went a hundred yards before we stopped again. We were just filling in spaces in the queue that had been left by those who had turned round and gone back towards Tehuantepec.

Stephanie was exactly the sort of friend I had hoped to run into. 'You look after sick babies?' I asked her.

'Sick kids up to seven years old.'

'I wish I did something useful like that. Instead of selling holidays to people who don't really need them.'

'Everybody needs a holiday. That's a nice job, fixing holidays for folk. I'm obliged to the girls in Cahoon who fixed mine.'

'Cahoon?'

'It's a district of Sydney. It's not spelt how we say it.'

'When I was little we lived in a place they called Karma. It's spelt Caldmore.'

'Cahoon's a tough district.'

'So was Karma. People called us jungle bunnies and peed through our letterbox.'

Lisa and Tonia were gone for an hour. When they got back Lisa said, 'The bridge ahead is blocked by a couple of trucks slewed across it. Nothing can move. The town across the bridge is jammed with traffic coming this way.'

Annabel asked, 'Isn't there another road?'

Dennis said, 'Not according to my *Bartholomew Conic Projection Routefinder Atlas of Mexico*.'

Lisa said, 'The locals are protesting about the state cutting off their electricity.'

'We met a couple of Yankee truckers who said they were fixing to spend the night in their trucks,' said Tonia. 'A Mexican guy said the block would most likely be lifted soon – but then as he went off he said he was heading back to Tehuantepec.'

Rose said, 'Surely you could explain to these people that we are tourists who have no part in their dispute? Ask them to be good sports and let us through.'

'I don't think that would be a very good idea,' said Lisa.

'What we should do,' Isabel announced, 'is what Tonia's Mexican fellow is doing. Go back to Tehuantepec and find a hotel.'

Simon added, 'And charter a plane to fly us to the next point in our itinerary first thing in the morning.'

Dennis said emphatically, 'What is most essential in this predicament is that we keep our heads and maintain morale. We must not let panic or impatience precipitate a course of action which is later a cause for regret.'

Lisa had given her tinkly little laugh at Simon's suggestion as if he intended it as a joke. Now she turned away to talk in Spanish to Mario.

Rose cried out, 'We can only hope these silly people soon tire of their demonstration.'

Annabel nodded. 'Or the army turns up and knocks the buggers for six.'

Dorothy said, 'If the poor sods have had their electricity cut off I hope they can stick it out till they get some sort of deal.'

Isabel whined, 'It's not our fault they haven't paid their rates.'

Dorothy said, 'It is. Marcos is right. The Indians shouldn't be forced to play the capitalist game.'

Simon snorted, 'For Christ's sake! It's capitalism that's given them their bloody electricity!'

'It's not just because of the electric that they're blocking the highway,' Dorothy said. 'It's because of centuries of injustice.'

Lisa announced, 'Mario has been busy on his CB. He's contacted a coach on the other side of the road-block with a view to swapping passengers. If the plan proceeds we'll carry our luggage over the road-block and take over the other coach.'

'Brilliant!' exulted Rose. 'I'd never have thought it of Mario! He's so dopey!'

'Do you mean to say that we are going to have to hump all our own luggage?' Simon protested.

Lisa went on, 'One problem is that the other coach is bigger than us and carrying a lot more passengers. However there is a small coach – an Italian tour – a couple of hundred yards behind us.'

Rose crowed, 'Are those the same ones we saw at Mitla? It's so jolly when you keep bumping into the same people!'

'The Italian tour leader and their driver are coming here. Then the five of us – the tour leaders and drivers and Tonia who can speak Italian – are off to find the other coach and work out arrangements. We'll have to get clearance from our tour companies, coach firms and what have you . . .'

The road ran between steep banks that were hard to climb because of the sandy soil and the cactus and thorn bushes. Just the same we all climbed them at one time or another during our wait, so we could go to the toilet out of sight of the road. All that could be seen from the bank-top were dunes of prickly plants for miles. No more of the road could be seen from up there than from down below. There was a ridge behind us and a ridge in front. Between the ridges were about sixty vehicles drawn up on our side of the road – buses, petrol tankers, lorries, articulated trucks and private cars. There was a lot of noise, as usual in Mexico. Music was coming from various vehicles and Mario's CB that he had left on was bleating away at the front of the coach. On top of that there were people chatting as they walked by. They passed in pairs or larger groups towards the road-block and the town beyond the ridge. Later they would come back towards their vehicles, some of them with carrier-bags.

Tonia said, 'I'm going up the road to chew the fat with the spaghetti-heads. Who's coming?' She had not been needed as an interpreter because the Italian tour leader spoke excellent English. She had listened to the CB and told Brian and Millie what was being said, but she tired of that almost as soon as they did. I don't think she could understand the local dialect as well as she pretended. Then she had chatted to Martin and drunk one of his cans of beer, to his horror. But now he had fallen asleep.

She was looking at me as she spoke but it was Maureen who answered. 'I wouldn't mind. For something to do.'

From near the top of the bank Rose called, 'Ahoy there down below!'

Annabel said severely to Maureen, 'Don't you dare, Maureen Corrigan! You're booked for another game of Scrabble!'

It was hard to tell if she was joking. In any case Tonia and Maureen had set off. Beyond them, about ten vehicles behind our bus, I could see Lee's little green Volkswagen. He was sitting in the front passenger seat and reading or writing. Earlier he had been stretching his long legs on the road and looking towards us, but he had shown no sign of approaching our bus or of going after Lisa and the others to the bridge.

Simon announced, 'Pamela and I are off to have a look at the town.'

Annabel said, 'Lisa and Tonia said it's a dire dump with absolutely nothing there.'

'It can't be worse than here,' retorted Simon.

Dennis had been explaining anti-erosion techniques to me and Stephanie until we left the bus saying we wanted fresh air. He now came to join us on the road and declared, 'It is not advisable in these circumstances for individuals to wander away from the group and lose contact. Furthermore, it is necessary that all members of the group should remain in the vicinity of the coach.'

Simon said, 'Rubbish. Where's the coach going to go without a driver?'

'Help!' Rose shouted from the top of the bank. 'Mayday! Mayday!' Then she couldn't speak for shrieking with mirth. 'I'm stuck! How do I get down?' she finally managed to splutter.

'Sideways like a crab is best,' Dennis instructed her. 'Move slowly and methodically, consolidating each foothold and endeavouring not to look down in order to avoid the possibility of vertigo.'

But Rose was already slithering down feet first on her bottom. 'Yow! Ouch! My bum!' she yelled. Then she brushed herself down and giggled. 'In the First Year at Cloisterhouse I was always getting into trouble for having dirty knickers.'

'Are we off then?' Simon demanded of Pamela.

Pamela answered quietly, 'I don't think so. It's a bit far to walk.'

'I wouldn't mind coming along,' said Isabel.

Simon stared up and down the road, then up at the sky. Then he scratched his beard and climbed back onto the bus.

'You only have to look at Simon and Pamela. She's hardly a word to say for herself.'

'Yeah, but look at Donald an' Dorothy!'

'I've had a lot of hassle from my mum. Always trying to fix me up with a nice Indian boy. The friend of some cousin, or the cousin of some friend . . . The whole Hindu culture, to me, is . . . I just don't feel Indian. All my friends are white.'

'You never been to India?'

'Once as a kid, but all I remember is the houses of relatives. My parents have been back since, but I refused to go.'

Katrin had rescued us from Dennis. She had loomed up to him on the road. 'I want you to tell me what is going on,' she had said in her careful voice. He doesn't like Katrin, but all the same hadn't been able to resist. He had spread his vast *Bartholomew Conic Projection* map on the roadway and was squatted over it pointing and explaining. Katrin was pacing around him in that zombie-like way she has. She didn't seem to be either looking or listening. Stephanie and I had sneaked back onto the bus.

Stephanie said, 'I had a boyfriend, Howard, for a couple of years, but it was never . . . just good mates, y'know. He got a job in Brisbane.'

I whispered, 'Hey! Look at that!' I pointed through the gap between the seats in front of us. Dorothy was reading a book about the Mexican Revolution. Donald had put his chess-set away and got out a notebook. I had seen him with this before and had assumed that he was keeping some sort of diary, like Rose. But now I could see there was nothing on the page but a few unreadable scribbles and a big weird doodle, quite a careful drawing, that he was working on. It seemed to be a drawing of a vulture that was sitting on the head of another vulture that was sitting on the head of a man in braces who was smoking a pipe.

Stephanie shrugged, then went on: 'But you're good-looking, Nita. Must have had lots of sweethearts.'

'Lots of pigs, but not a lot of sweethearts.'

'Don't y'want to marry, have kids?'

'I can't see me living with a bloke, they're so pathetic. I wouldn't mind a kid but my mum'd die of shame.'

Word about the traffic hold-up had got round the district by now. Locals were walking up and down the line of vehicles selling. One lad came by with a lidless plastic cold-box full of cans. Martin miraculously woke up and tugged open a window. 'Beer! *Cerveza!*' he shouted.

The lad grinned and shook his head. Two girls came heaving a big plastic pail of chicken stew. A third girl carried a carton of plastic mugs. I didn't fancy the stuff but Isabel and Dennis bought it and of course said it was delicious. Simon bought a pineapple from another trader, then stood with it in his hand looking baffled. The driver of the petrol tanker in front of us produced a knife and paper plate and skilfully dissected the fruit. Simon then brought the plate aboard the bus without even thanking him. Pamela took the plate back and offered fruit to the driver who refused with a gracious little mime.

Maureen and Tonia had come back from their visit to the Italians. 'They got the heebie jeebies back there,' Tonia said. 'They figure bandits are fixing to strike in the small hours. Rape and pillage and all that stuff.'

'This is insupportable!' cried Isabel. 'Somebody must find Lisa at once and tell her we insist on returning to Tehuantepec!'

Simon was about to say something, then he shut his mouth and turned away. I expect he agreed with Isabel but didn't want to support her because he hates her. Dennis said, 'In these sort of situations alarmist rumours are commonplace and invariably best ignored.'

Dorothy said to Donald, 'Look!' He took no notice. She was pointing down the road. An open truck was coming from the direction of the blockade. 'Perhaps the blockade has been lifted,' she added.

We watched the truck pass. It was full of Mexican workers who were sitting still and silent. If the blockade had been lifted and they were the first through they would surely have been looking cheerful, even shouting and waving to the rest of us. It was obviously just another truck that had left the line to turn back to Tehuantepec. This still happened every so often but now nobody was bothering to move up and fill the gaps.

'Tonia was lying,' I said to Stephanie.

'Dunno. Maureen's there to back her up.'

'Maureen didn't contradict her but didn't agree with her either. I wonder how much Italian Maureen can understand.'

'I reckon the Eyeties were messing around, trying to put a scare on Tonia an' Maureen.' She wasn't bothered. She was enjoying herself. 'This is really something!'

'It's a bit . . .'

'Scared?'

'I feel a long way from home.'

She looked out of the window along the road and smiled. 'If it comes to that, there's plenty to scare me in Cahoon.'

Brian had switched off the CB, which had been getting on everybody's nerves, but had given up trying to find the switch to put the lights on in the bus. Dennis had advised against this in case it flattened the battery. One or two people were using torches to read. Most people were out of the bus, lying on the road which was still warm. Katrin had cottoned on to this. She was lying straight on her back with her earphones on and at first we thought she was either having a stroke or had finally gone crazy. Then we understood how warm and comfortable the road was, and Rose shouted, 'Good old Katrin! Not so dumb after all!'

Now Brian was saying, 'That's Orion's belt. Those three bright stars in a line.'

Dennis said, 'Stellar parallax is used to measure the distance to the stars that are relatively close to the earth. Once the angle of shift of the star is determined this can be used with the known shift in position of the earth to work out the distance to the star.'

Isabel said, 'Tonia, tell that man to stop smoking at once! He's standing next to gallons of inflammable material!'

The petrol tanker driver's cigarette glowed brighter as he took a deep drag at it. 'It's okay,' Tonia lied. 'He told me his tanker is empty.'

Brian said, 'If you follow the line of the belt you should see the Pleiades. A fuzzy little bunch of seven stars. They'll get clearer later on.'

'Guess what everybody!' Rose yelled. 'Isabel and I have some gin and tonic stashed away! Drinks are on us the minute this road-block's lifted!'

Simon said, 'I detest gin.'

Martin asked Tonia, 'Is that right, about bandits coming to rape and pillage?' He sniggered. 'Some of these old bags won't be able to believe their luck.'

Lisa arrived with the Italian tour leader, a handsome bloke with prematurely white hair. Isabel said, 'Thank God! At last!' but otherwise Lisa wasn't met by any protests. Everybody was glad to see her. Rose shouted, 'Hurrah!'

'We must take all our stuff off the bus,' Lisa announced. 'Mario and the Italian driver will be along soon with the passengers off the other bus.'

Simon asked, 'Are you proposing that we hump all our own luggage for two kilometres?'

'Further than that,' Lisa retorted. 'The bus is through the town, about a kilometre past the bridge.'

Dennis said, 'If everyone will vacate the vehicle and the blokes then form a chain as instructed by me on previous occasions we'll soon have the luggage extricated.'

Brian stood up rather reluctantly but none of the other men budged. Lisa said, 'It would be best if we each got our own stuff off the bus and were responsible for it.'

Isabel wailed, 'There's no way I can carry all my things. It's a physical impossibility.' Some minutes later when we were all camped among our bags on the warm road she tried again. 'Unless somebody helps me I don't know what I shall do. I simply can't carry it myself.'

Pamela said, 'We're in an even worse fix. It's medically danger-ous for Simon to over-exert himself. He's under doctor's orders.'

Annabel said, 'Don't look at us. It will be all I can do to get my old bones there. Maureen will have to carry one of my cases.'

Maureen looked startled. Simon said, 'Baluth Tours are contrac-tually responsible for the transporting of our heavier baggage.'

Stephanie said, 'Hey! Listen!'

She had cupped her hand to her ear. Everyone looked at her curiously, especially those who had been told she was a bit deaf. We could hear people coming along the road shouting. Soon four or five Mexicans ran past in the dark, one of them wobbling along on a bicycle. They were laughing and shouting. 'The road-block has been lifted!' Tonia cried.

Lisa came out of the bus and confirmed it. 'The blockade is lifted. It just came through on the CB.'

Rose yelled, 'Yippee!'

We loaded all our luggage back onto the bus, then took our seats and waited for Mario to arrive and the queue to move. Lisa had put the lights on inside the bus. Rose and Isabel had opened their bottle of gin and a small bottle of tonic. They had also furnished themselves with a couple of plastic cups from somewhere. Either they had forgotten the promise to give everybody a drink or they had decided they only had enough for themselves. Everybody was in too good a humour to complain about this. We were relieved that the waiting was over and glad we didn't have to carry our luggage through miles of darkness and past the menace of the blockade.

'It's all been super fun!' Rose declaimed. 'A life-enhancing experience! This is what it's all about!'

Lisa, sprawling on the front seat drinking warm lemonade, called over her shoulder, 'Do you all know it's Isabel's birthday today?'

Isabel flushed pink. 'Christ! Is it?'

Rose sang a chorus of 'Happy Birthday To You' and quite a few people joined in. Then Rose tried 'Why Was She Born So Beautiful?' but got no support so tailed out at the end of the first line.

I had moved to the front next to Lisa. 'Hey Lisa, when we get to the hotel, put me and Stephanie in the same room.'

Lisa grinned at me. 'All that fuss and bother. Hours of fixing and phoning. I might as well have sat on my bum in the bus. Still, it's best.'

'Did you hear what I just asked you?' Our conversation in the carpark at Mitla seemed a long time ago. 'From now on Stephanie and me want to share a room.'

'Leave it with me, Nita. I'll talk to the others.'

'What others?'

She was looking beyond me, out of the open doorway of the bus. I turned and saw that a Mexican woman was holding a large white bundle and staring into the bus. Even as I looked at her another woman joined her. This one had a smaller, grey bundle under her arm. Looking out of the window I saw that our bus was surrounded by Mexican peasants who were all carrying baskets or bundles. Even before Mario climbed onto the bus I had worked out that these must be the passengers from the bus beyond the blockade.

Mario leant across me. For some reason he smelt of kerosene. He and Lisa talked in Spanish for some time. Lisa said, 'Shit!' She turned round and announced to everybody, 'The blockade is still on!'

*   *   *

We waited for the Italians. 'Safety in numbers,' Lisa said. 'And it's important that we all try to keep together.'

Dennis said, less bouncily than usual, 'Those at the front don't go too fast. Those at the back don't dawdle and get left behind.'

Meanwhile two Mexicans had arrived by magic with a two-wheeled trailer on which people balanced any baggage they weren't prepared to carry. I had only my case and day-sack and preferred to carry them.

The Italians made a lot of noise, trundling a couple of luggage trolleys and talking loudly to each other, so it was easy to hear them coming. When the first of them came level Lisa said, 'Right! Let's go!' Dennis said, '*Vamos!*' and we set off. Once we were on the move the advice of Lisa and Dennis was forgotten even by them. Everybody went as fast as they could until they were slowed by lack of puff and the weight they were carrying. The noise of all the feet and voices and the feeling of being in a large group were comforting. It was an almost cloudless night with moon and stars, and there were lights in some of the vehicles we passed. Sometimes people called out to us in what sounded a friendly fashion, and one or two trucks seemed to put their headlights on so that we could see the road better. But then one truck turned its lights off and pulled out onto the road in front of us. I was one of the first, trying to keep up with Lisa who knew where the bus was. The truck pulled right across to block us, so that we had to pick our way through a little gap he had left behind him. Maybe the driver was in sympathy with the demonstrators and didn't see why the gringos should beat the road-block. Or maybe he was just bloody-minded. Whatever it was, it seemed deliberately hostile and was frightening. After that even the Italians were quieter. The dark was speckled with the lights in the sky and lights along the way but none of these lights were enough to let you see much around you.

I looked at Stephanie, who was trotting along next to me. She was bent forward under a huge sausage of a kit-bag which she had perched on top of her day-sack but even so, in a sudden beam of light, I could see from her parted lips and shining eyes that none of this was scary or even a nuisance to her. It was a once-in-a-lifetime adventure, better than all the archaeological sites and museums. It was the bit she was going to brag about to the gang in the Paediatric Unit in Cahoon.

It was confusing when we came to the bridge. There was a lot of light. Trucks and cars had their headlights on, including a couple of police vehicles. I think that there was also a service station there which was lit up with electric lights. Somebody told me later that it was not in this town that the electricity had been cut off but in one or two surrounding villages. There was certainly a great crowd there, mostly men with shiny black Indian hair. They jeered at us as we hurried over the bridge. Some of the Italians shouted defiance and this scared me, but the demonstrators were put in a good humour by the sight of the gringos having to carry their own luggage. Nobody tried to stop us and soon we were passing through a town that was jammed with vehicles.

It was a boom town just for that night. The bars and cafés were packed and noisy. So were a number of ordinary houses that had turned themselves into bars or cafés at short notice. Musicians and beggars and food-stalls and trash-sellers had appeared out of nowhere to take advantage of the blockade – as many as in the Zocalo at Oaxaca.

The bus had somehow been turned round and was facing in the opposite direction to the rest of the traffic, ready for a quick getaway. The driver had as many as three assistants, probably all friends of his who he was giving a lift. They were all leaner than Mario, with blue-black tresses and hairless Indian lips. They helped us shove our baggage into the vast space under the bus, then Stephanie and I claimed the front seats behind the driver.

Lisa was already on the bus, kneeling on the front seat opposite us next to the Italian tour leader. They were getting on well, beaming and smirking at each other as they counted their parties aboard.

Brian and Millie arrived together as always. He helped her up onto the bus. Brian may be fussy and soppy but he is the sort I could tolerate if I ever have to have a man. Tonia came next and stared hard at me, ignoring Stephanie. Then she went and sat behind Brian and Millie, who had sat behind Stephanie and me. The Italians were taking the other side of the bus. Dennis got on and peered down the bus and nodded his head as if everything was working out according to his plan.

Maureen got on and said, 'That was one of the most unpleasant half-hours of my life!'

Stephanie said, 'Wow, you must have had it soft!'

Isabel hooted, 'Pooh! It stinks in here!'

'I did this to those jerks on the bridge,' Rose exulted. She screwed her finger into her temple. 'I did that and I said, "*Loco! Loco!*"'

'It was stupid,' said Dorothy, who was immediately behind Rose. 'Things could quickly have turned nasty. It's not a game to them.'

Donald, who was immediately behind Dorothy, said nothing. Martin got on, winked at Lisa, swayed, and went down the bus. Annabel wheezed up the steps and gave a haughty shout. 'Maureen Corrigan! What have you done with my suitcase?'

Pamela helped Simon up the steps. The hair that usually hides his pate was dangling over his ears. There were beads of sweat all over his face and whiskers but he managed to find breath enough to snap at her, 'Don't fuss, don't fuss!'

Last came Katrin. Her pale face loomed up out of the dark. It was a bit like a corpse coming out of a canal. She didn't acknowledge our greeting or Lisa's. She stared down the dim interior of the big bus as if it was a spooky cave. Her hand crept up and slightly adjusted the black woolly hat that she was wearing jammed down on her forehead. Then her face twitched, the hand crept down again and she went down the bus to find somewhere to sit.

There was hardly any lighting in the bus. The seats were hard and threadbare. Everything rattled and quivered as we bounced up the dark road into the hills. The engine was very loud and there were terrible grinding noises whenever the driver changed gear. Every now and then we were striped by the headlights of an oncoming truck on its unsuspecting way to the blockade. Apart from the rattling and the racket from the engine it was quiet once Isabel had made Lisa ask them to turn off the Mexican music. They hadn't switched it off altogether but had turned it right down so that it now sounded a long way away. Even the Italians were not doing a lot of talking. After the long day and the last hour of crisis everybody had flopped. People had their eyes shut and were either sleeping or trying to sleep.

'I'm an only child.'

'Wow, you lucky dog! I got two sisters and three brothers. I'm the youngest. I used to dream about being the only kid.'

'No, it's terrible. I was lonely. On top of which I was just about the only Paki in the school.'

'My brothers and sisters are married now except Clark. I got seven nephews and nieces.'

'If you're an only child your parents count on you too much. I've made my mum miserable by not marrying. And my dad wanted me to be a genius and go to University.'

'You've got to be prepared to disappoint people.'

The bus was stopped and boarded by two soldiers in camouflage gear. One of them, a little bloke who looked like an Apache out of a Western, was holding a rifle and scowling down the bus as if he was looking for somebody to shoot. The other was slim with a neat moustache. He was clearly in charge. First he went up and down the bus shining a torch under the seats, then he interrogated the driver, asking long, complicated questions. His manner was haughty and threatening but the driver and his buddies didn't seem intimidated. They looked as though it had all happened many times before.

'I'm not very sociable and never have a lot of friends. I've one good friend, Sheila, my flat-mate. She was going to come on this trip. We planned it together. But now she's getting wed in July.'

'Me, I still live with Ma and Pa.'

'My mum tries to make me feel guilty about that, too.'

'I don't have a lot of time for friends.'

I glanced across at Stephanie, not sure what she meant. Why had she never had her eye fixed? Perhaps it couldn't be fixed.

Brilliant golden light was being provided by carriage-lamps in the forecourt of a roadside hotel. The Italians were thronging off the coach into the hotel, which looked very posh, all white walls, black woodwork and red tiled floors. Dennis got off with them, 'to ensure that none of our luggage is erroneously disembarked'. Katrin was already off the coach, roaming about and taking deep breaths. Lisa was out there too, puffing at a cigarette while swapping contact addresses and telephone numbers with the Italian tour leader. I suddenly thought of Lee, who was now stuck on the other side of the road-block and would have lost our trail.

'I'm not Tonia's type. Even when I was a teenager I didn't like discos and parties. I go to Keep Fit twice a week with Sheila but I stop in most nights. I like reading. Nothing highbrow, just detective stories and romances. And I'm a telly addict. I'm missing *EastEnders* and *Brookside*.'

'Yer got good leisure interests. I don't get time for any of that.'

'You work long hours?'

'An' Ma and Pa are old, y'see. Ma was forty-five when she had me. And Clark's Spina Bifida. He can't do a lot for himself.'

'So you . . .'

'Once a year I come on a trip. They don't like it so they have to lump it.'

I woke to hear Lisa arguing with the driver. We were in a network of narrow streets and he didn't want to take his coach up an even narrower alley to our hotel.

Stephanie looked as wide-awake as ever. 'We've been past a landfall,' she said. 'Covered half the highway. We just about squeezed by.'

It was half past two by the time we got into the hotel. Lisa put me and Tonia in the same room! I didn't say anything immediately, but as soon as she had finished giving out the keys, when she wasn't the focus of everybody's attention, I went up to her.

Brian got to her just before me. 'Did I hear you right, Lisa?' His voice was several notches higher than usual. 'Did I hear you say the trip to the Zoo tomorrow is cancelled?'

She was pale and her eyes were bleary. Instead of answering him she looked at me, then put her hand over her mouth like people do when they know they've made a gaffe.

'Leave it for tonight, Nita, eh?'

BRIAN SINGLETON

1. SYNOPSIS

1. SYNOPSIS

2. ASSESSMENT KEY

3. ITINERARY

3.1. General

    3.1.1. Modifications
    3.1.2. Transport
    3.1.3. Food
    3.1.4. Lodging
    3.1.5. Ambience

3.2. Sumidero Canyon
3.3. San Cristobal de Las Casas

4. BIRD LIFE

4.1. General & Miscellaneous
4.2. Waterfowl

5. SOCIAL & PERSONAL

5.1. Note
5.2. General Comments
5.3. Individual Assessments.

5.3.1.	Notes
5.3.II.	Lisa
5.3.III	Dorothy
5.3.IV.	Donald
5.3.V.	Simon
5.3.VI.	Pamela
5.3.VII.	Annabel
5.3.VIII	Maureen
5.3.IX.	Isabel
5.3.X.	Rose
5.3.XI.	Katrin
5.3.XII.	Stephanie
5.3.XIII.	Sunita
5.3.XIV.	Tonia
5.3.XV.	Martin
5.3.XVI.	Dennis
5.3.XVII.	Millie
5.3.XVIII.	Brian

2. ASSESSMENT KEY

++ EXCELLENT
+ GOOD
+/= ABOVE AVERAGE
= AVERAGE
=/– BELOW AVERAGE
– POOR
– – UNACCEPTABLE

Also see Note 5.1. to Section 5.

3. ITINERARY

3.1. GENERAL

3.1.1. Modifications (– –)
(A) A serious modification to the itinerary was announced

by Lisa last night. We slept in this morning to compensate for late arrival. This entailed cancellation of a trip to Tuxtla Zoological Gardens, reputedly the best in Mexico if not in the whole of Latin America. They contain only creatures from Chiapas, wild and in captivity. The vast majority of the 641 bird species in the state can be seen there, including *quetzales*. (B) My Millie and I were therefore greatly disappointed, particularly since we had already, on Lisa's advice, forgone a visit to Chapultepec Zoo on Sunday. (C) I raised the matter with Lisa last night, and again this morning. She resisted my protest on both occasions, pointing out that the zoo trip was an 'unofficial extra' not mentioned in the Tour Dossier, and that nobody else was complaining. (D) She did, however, offer to obtain bus-tickets if we wish to return from San Cristobal tomorrow. The journey will take two hours each way, cost six dollars each and entail us missing an Indian village as well as other sights of San Cristobal. My Millie and I must make the trip but are not happy.

3.1.2. Transport (=/−)

3.1.2.1. The Toyota Minibus that carried us today was the most up-to-date vehicle that we have used, but most of us missed the roominess of the coach from Oaxaca. The baggage piled high on the Toyota roof-rack rendered us unstable in the mountain winds, and both the seats and the leg-room between them seem to have been calculated with trim little oriental physiques in mind.
3.1.2.2. The speedboats on the river trip were inconvenient for sightseeing and highly unsuitable for the serious observation of wild life. See one's further comments in 3.2.

3.1.3. Food (+)

3.1.3.1. Breakfast (=/−)
Breakfast at the Hotel Bonampak in Tuxla was just about

par for the course. (A) The scrambled egg was a little too dry for one's taste and the beans too soggy. (B) The coffee was less insipid than is usual in Mexico.

3.1.3.2. Lunch (+)

The fish lunch at the Sumidero Canyon was highly palatable as well as good value. (A) The main dish was a white sea-fish (which none could confidently identify), split down the middle and fried then served with chips and sweet corn. (B) Little Millie discovered *taxcalate*, a maize-based chocolate and cinnamon drink which she reckons is the best thing since Horlicks!

3.1.3.3. Dinner (++)

(A) In the evening the group ate at a restaurant called 'La Parrila' and brought back good reports of it. (B) My Millie and I decided upon a tête-à-tête aside from the main party. We found a little vegetarian café for back-packers – 'Los Payasos', run by a Dutchman – where the food was a welcome change, cheap and simple and wholesome. (See 5.3.XVII.G1 below.) The soya loaf was excellent and the lentil soup with hot little nuggets of brown bread floating on the surface was particularly delicious.

3.1.4. Lodgings. (=)

(A) The Hotel Moctezuma in San Cristobal is highly attractive, with a quaint and cottage-like/colonial ambience. There is an inner courtyard full of jungle plants whence our room is reached via a wooden staircase and balcony. (B) The room, though, is somewhat dank and gloomy. (C) Service and facilities are average.

3.1.5. Ambience. (+/=)

The day has afforded a number of charming glimpses of Mexico, (A) beginning with the little lad, about nine years old, who climbed aboard our bus and serenaded us with an ethnic ditty before we left the hotel in the morning. Other highlights were (B) lunch under the awning of a riverside café at the *embarcadero* of the Sumidero Canyon and (C) the scenic drive through the mountains to San Cristobal. For further remarks about the Sumidero Canyon and San Cristobal see 3.2. and 3.3. below.

3.2. SUMIDERO CANYON (+/=)

3.2.1. Fast passenger-launches took us on a two-hour trip, 35 kilometres, through the canyon, a spectacular geographical feature. The walls are about 1,000 metres high. Looking up from water level at the sheer rock faces (that have plants or even trees growing out of them, clinging from little crevices) is a memorable if vertiginous experience. The point at which the tribe of Indians are supposed to have flung themselves to their doom is particularly impressive. The riverbanks along the bottom of the canyon are lined with tropical foliage and inhabited by caymans as well as considerable bird life. (See 4.2.)

3.2.2. Negative aspects were (A) the school-trip-like constraint of sitting in the launches and (B) (see 3.1.2.2. above) the unsuitable speed of the vehicles. This was exacerbated by the (C) antics of the drivers: skimming us under low bridges, bobbing in each other's wakes and other foolishness presumably intended to amuse us. It made serious bird-spotting (see 4.2.) very difficult; and (D) the points at which the boats were brought to rest were never those my Millie and I would have chosen. (E) Furthermore, the water of the River Grivalja was polluted by hundreds of plastic bottles. (One understands it is not recommended for swimming.)

3.3 SAN CRISTOBAL DE LAS CASAS (+)

3.3.1. This is the colonial capital of the region and was the centre of the Zapatista rising in 1994. Lisa says that a lot of people compare it with Cuzco, the old Inca Capital in the Andes. My Millie and I have never been to Peru, but are charmed by San Cristobal to the extent of being crosser than ever about the cancellation of the Zoo trip which means that one is going to miss time here.

3.3.2. It is a place full of piquant contrasts: bustling markets and tranquil corners. Among the impressions that will persist in one's memory are the clear mountain atmosphere, the odours of wood-smoke and paraffin, and the sight of Indians stealthily traversing the Zocalo in their vivid tribal costumes. From dawn till long after midnight music ranging from Strauss to Bob Marley is discreetly whispered out by the Zocalo loudspeakers. The atmosphere is relaxed and bohemian because there are a lot of young back-packers here from all over the world, whereas in Mexico City and Oaxaca most of the tourists seemed to be wealthy Americans.

3.3.3. It should be said, though, that there are considerable indications of poverty within the picturesque ambience of San Cristobal. The streets, cafés and pool-halls are infested by beggars and layabouts.

4. BIRD LIFE

4.1. GENERAL AND MISCELLANEOUS (+/=)

4.1.1. General
Today provided two serious spotting sessions: the riverside habitat in Sumidero Canyon (see 4.2.) and the drive through the mountains of Chiapas. The riverside was the more exciting since it provided us with species not previously available on this trip. Between Tuxla and San Cristobal most sightings were of birds encountered in the uplands between Oaxaca and Tehuantepec.

4.1.2. Birds of Prey.

A) At last we made a positive and unanimous sighting of the black-shouldered kite *Elanus leucurus*. (B) We saw several examples of a greyish-rufous hawk, a hulking bird perched on telegraph poles along the route, which could only be *Buteo magnirostris*. (C) In addition we surprised a couple of yellow-headed caracaras *Miluago chimachima* that were busy on roadside carrion.

4.1.3. *Phaethornis superciliosus* (?)

At a mountain photo-stop little Millie sighted a humming-bird quite unlike any previously seen: a greenish-brown bird with rufous breast, longish tail and slightly curved beak. The only bird approaching this description in either Dunstable or Zabal-Galgathor is the long-tailed hermit humming-bird *Phaethornis superciliosus* but these are categorised in Zabal-Galgathor as lowland forest dwellers.

4.1.4. North American migrants (?)

A brushy successional area in a valley bottom yielded no less than three intriguing sightings that plunged us into our field guides. Our tentative conclusion was that all three specimens were most likely North American migrants: (A) a grey catbird *Dumetella carolinensis*, (B) a northern yellow throat *Geothlypis trychas* and (C) a yellow breasted chat *Icteria virens*.

4.1.5. Miscellaneous.

There is a splendid green macaw *Ara ambigua* in the courtyard of the Hotel Moctezuma.

4.2. WATERFOWL (+)

4.2.1 General Comment.

Our sightings in the Sumidero Canyon were a creditable haul, given the difficulties and distractions. (See 3.1.2.2. and 3.2.2. above.)

4.2.2. *Ardenidae*
(A) The egrets seen were without exception common egrets *Egretta alba*. (B) We sighted two great blue herons *Ardea herodias* though Millie claims one of them was a little blue heron *Egretta caerulea*.

4.2.3. *Coraciiformes*
The two kingfishers we saw (perhaps the same bird sighted twice) were iridescent green above with rufous breasts. We identified them from a photograph in Dunstable as *Chloroceryle inda*, only to discover in Zabal-Galgathor that this species is not found so far north as Mexico. What we saw was almost certainly *Chloroceryle americana* – the rufous tinge being either an optical illusion or a freak mutation.

4.2.4. *Jabirou mycteria*
At the spot where the Indians leapt to their doom my Millie and I were distracted by a large bird making lazy circles. Impulsive little Millie declared it to be a heron. I pointed out that (a) while the bird was undoubtedly of the order *Ciconiiformes* (b) it was flying with its neck outstretched – a characteristic not of the *Ardenidae* but of the family *Ciconiidae*. One is confident that it was a Jabirou *Jabirou mycteria*, which is among the largest storks, topping 4 feet in height when standing. I looked through the binoculars for the characteristic black neck, at the base of which there should be a red patch, but was not able to satisfactorily verify these details.

4.2.5. *Ixobrychus exilis* (?)
When the boats were stopped to photograph the caymans little Millie got ten out of ten for a squatting bittern. It was sitting very still and its brown, black, yellow and white plumage was affording almost perfect camouflage in the reed-clump it had selected. This sighting, though,

led to further altercation and perplexity. We thought it was the little bittern *Ixobrychus minutus* which my Millie has brilliantly spotted a couple of times in Europe – but neither Dunstable nor Zabal-Galgathor include this species. Instead they list the least bittern *Ixobrychus exilis*, which from both the photograph in Dunstable and the description in Zabal-Galgathor seems to be identical in appearance, but which differs from its European cousin in that it is diurnal. It should have been fishing, not squatting, when little Millie spotted it!

4.2.6. *Piciformes*

Also at the cayman stop we observed a slender bird with long tail and sharp bill sitting motionless on the exposed branch of a submerged tree. Its colouring was dull, brackish brown with a white lower breast and belly. One is pretty confident that it was a Jacamar, family *Gabulidae*, order *Piciformes*, but which of the 16 known species is impossible to say before one gets home and consults one's Schub & Wedlock.

5. SOCIAL & PERSONAL

5.1. NOTE

Unlike the symbols in the objective assessment key (see Section 2 and passim) the marks out of ten given as fractions in 5.3 are intended to be set against each individual's personal scale of mood and morale, with 5/10 the norm. They are not to be compared each with another.

5.2. GENERAL MORALE (– –)

5.2.1 Communal bonding development on group holidays
In one's experience (which admittedly only extends to two previous trips), (A) one begins by being irritated and repelled by the foibles of most of those with whom one

is to share the expensive experience. (B) As the holiday progresses, ((B1) because one is sharing unusual and sometimes disconcerting experiences, and (B2) because one's education and career have accustomed one to adapt to the idiosyncrasies of others), what at first seemed unacceptable is made tolerable by familiarity. (C) One gets along better and better with people whom one didn't like until by the end of the holiday one is exchanging addresses and sincerely warm goodbyes.

5.2.2. Current group morale
(A) One might have supposed that (A1) the initial constraints and antipathies of the present group would be dispersing by this stage, and (A2) the ordeal of yesterday's road-block would have accelerated the development of a sense of community. (B) Yet this group seems proof against any such process. Personalities and the relationships between them deteriorate slightly but remorselessly each day. (B1) The grumblers grumble more. (B2) The bores get louder. (B3) The drunks get drunker. (B4) Those who don't have much to say for themselves are saying less and less.

5.2.3. Reasons for current group morale
Whatever one thinks of (A) Lisa as a tour leader, or (B) the tour so far, the main reason for this steady worsening of morale is to be found in (C) the unfortunate constitution of the group. (C1) There are too many on the trip whose conduct is intolerable, and (C2) not enough normal human beings to set behavioural standards. All the extroverts are predatory stereotypes who in another group would either modify their ways or become pariahs, whereas those who should be the normalising majority are nearly all introverted loners: either (C21) meekly self-effacing like Pamela, Stephanie, Sunita and Maureen, or (C22) pathologically imploded like Donald and Katrin, or (C23)

absorbed in their own concerns and relationships like Millie and me.

5.3 INDIVIDUAL ASSESSMENTS

5.3.I. Notes

5.3.I. 1 See the comment on the scores out of 10 in 5.1.

5.3.I. 2 Some of the individual assessments that follow are not based on extensive observation.

5.3.II. Lisa. (–) (3/10)

Today did nothing to qualify one's low opinion of her as a tour leader:

(A) Several people have expressed their satisfaction at her performance yesterday, missing the fact that it was the shrewd initiative of the driver Mario that got us out of our difficulties.

(B) Fresh from this spurious triumph, one would have expected Lisa to be on top form; especially as the road-block has rid her of the young American whose (supposedly unwelcome) pursuit of her has (supposedly) been depressing her spirits and interfering with her duties.

(C) Yet she has been morose and inert all day, not even bothering to summon that brittle brightness of manner with which she sometimes cloaks her idle egotism.

(D) See also, 5.3.XIV.C and 5.3.XV.B&E (below).

5.3.III. Dorothy (=/–) (5/10)

(A) Dorothy was roused again at lunch when somebody made a slighting comment about the Zapatistas. She launched into an archaic Trotskyite diatribe that made others either gaze at their plates or exchange derisory glances. One wonders whether her constant, embarrassing need to bear witness is contributory to her husband's retreat into himself.

(B) One actually sympathises with many of her views, from

a rational standpoint as distinct from her emotional and dogmatic approach.

(C) But politics is an unappealing topic and one hesitates to support her utterances in case it incites or prolongs discussion.

5.3.IV. Donald (=) (5/10)

(A) I did not hear him say anything all day.

(B) Simon made a rather baffling attempt to talk to him in the minibus through the mountains. Donald was as usual ignoring the scenery in favour of his travelling chess-set when Simon leant across the gangway to him and informed him that the Armada Playhouse in Plymouth is shortly to stage a play about a mad chess grand-master. Donald raised an eyebrow.

(C) See also my comment in 5.3.XI.C.

5.3.V. Simon (– –) (7/10)

(A) His 'unacceptable' rating seems harsh, because today he made efforts to restrain or conceal his misanthropy. Examples were: (A1) the incident referred to below in 5.3.VI. B; (A2) the conversation mentioned above in 5.3.IV.B; (A3) at the place where the Indians did their suicide leap he actually cracked a joke about mariachi music; (A4) at lunch he held a brief but civil conversation with Rose, which admittedly consisted of each trying to prove they knew more about Egypt than the other did.

(B) Which is why one still gives him (– –). When he is not whingeing he is annoyingly boastful.

5.3.VI. Pamela (+/=) (4/10)

(A) Everybody likes Pamela because she is: (A1) dignified, (A2) polite, (A3) quiet, (A4) serene, (A5) black and (A6) unlike her husband.

(B) One observed a tiny flaw in her image this morning on the minibus outside the hotel. Simon had tutted and grunted throughout the performance of the Indian lad who had boarded the bus to serenade us (see 3.1.5.A above), but at the end of the song he fished a handful of coins from his pocket. Pamela put out her hand over Simon's fist and quelled his impulse.

5.3.VII. Annabel (–) (5/10)

(A) The latest news on the tour grapevine is that Annabel is not Lady Cairncross, nor is Maureen some sort of feudal retainer.

(B) One doubts this, because today we witnessed an incident in which the pair of them behaved uncannily true to stereotype. As the high-powered launches sped us along the river Annabel requested, 'Maureen, would you mind changing places? It's too draughty this side for my liking.' Maureen glanced across at her but did not respond. Annabel went on to say, 'The draught is actually hurting my shoulder.' This time Maureen did not look round but gazed out over the water sullenly. Annabel shouted, 'MAUREEN, WOULD YOU MIND CHANGING PLACES?' so loudly that everybody on the boat went silent. Maureen blinked, breathed out down her nose in a disgusted manner, then to the astonishment of us all changed places with Annabel.

5.3.VIII. Maureen (=) (5/10)

(A) See above, 5.3.VII.

(B) Maureen seems to be almost a complete cipher.

(C) One is intrigued by her.

(D) Today little Millie told me something that Tonia told her – that Maureen, beneath her air of subservient reserve, is haunted by a torrid and disreputable past.

5.3.IX. Isabel (–) (5/10)

(A) Isabel pouted and complained her way through yet another expensive day in Mexico.

(B) There is a pairings syndrome within the group which

one cannot be bothered to examine in great detail. Suffice it to say that just as (B1) Pamela is admired in contrast to Simon (5.3.VI.A6 above) and (B2) Dorothy is pitied because of Donald, so (B3) Isabel, a fairly crashing person, is not thought quite so crashing next to Rose.

(C) One suspects, too, that one's attitude to Isabel is influenced by a sense of gratitude that she rooms with Rose and keeps her partly occupied so that she has less time for the rest of us.

5.3.X. Rose (– –) (5/10)

(A) As their speedboat overtook ours she broke safety regulations by rising in her seat and waving both arms in the air. 'Oho! Tally ho!' she whooped, then collapsed back pealing with mirth.

(B) At the Indian leap her boat was close enough for us to hear her interrupting their driver's commentary to correct his halting English, until she reduced him to silence by saying, 'I'm sorry old chap, but you really must speak more clearly.'

(C) See 5.3.V.A4 for her crashing lunch-time conversation with Simon.

(D) As the minibus wound into San Cristobal she yelled, 'I have been here before! I have and yet I haven't! Oh, I so pity those of you who cannot attain to my mystic meaning!'

5.3.XI. Katrin (=/–) (5/10)

(A) Today she was last onto the minibus on all occasions. Outright hostility to her is increasing until it is bordering on persecution. Though she was not far behind, and did not hold up the bus, her entry was invariably greeted with sighs of wasted patience, and a shout of 'Come on, Slowcoach!' from Rose.

(B) My Millie is convinced that Katrin is clinically insane; in a state of traumatic amnesia or chronic shock. The evidence she gives for this is: (B1) speech impairment,

(B2) basic facial expression, (B3) involuntary movements and muscular twitches.

(C) One is inclined to demur from little Millie's diagnosis, especially if one compares Katrin with Donald, whose appearance is unexceptional but whose behaviour is pathologically reclusive. Katrin's weird appearance and manner tend to disguise the fact that her behaviour is that of a normal tourist: (C1) she looks at what there is to see and listens to the commentaries of the guides; (C2) she buys souvenirs, usually items of clothing, so long as they are black; (C3) she joins the group for evening meals and (C4) she tries the local drinks and dishes.

(D) One concludes that Katrin's real problem, discounting the disorganised tardiness that has made her unpopular but is not evidence of insanity, is that she does not speak or understand English fluently.

5.3.XII. Stephanie (=) 7/10

(A) She continued to sit with Sunita today, and when we got to the Hotel Moctezuma in San Cristobal Lisa gave one room key to Stephanie and Sunita, another to Tonia and Katrin.

(B) One observes a blossoming in Stephanie now that she has obtained an acceptable companion and been rescued from Katrin. (B1) Her Antipodean whine as she chatted with Sunita was a constant background noise on the bus today. (B2) She has been beaming at everything and everybody, clearly happy.

5.3.XIII. Sunita (=/−) (6/10)

(A) This physically attractive and vain young woman was looking smug all day, presumably because she knew she was going to get her own way and have Stephanie for a room-mate instead of Tonia.

(B) One has the impression, both from her general deportment and from what her erstwhile friend Tonia has let slip, that Sunita is used to a hectic social and sexual life. Her presence on this trip is a mystery: she clearly finds both Mexico and her companions dull. This is why she is trying to amuse herself with girlish intrigues, making and breaking alliances and so forth.

(C) One cannot think that she will prefer Stephanie's company to Tonia's for long. Certainly she won't find Stephanie as easy to drag round discos at night in search of male attention.

5.3.XIV. Tonia (+) (4/10)

(A) Today, despite being a bit subdued, Tonia's contribution to the group was as valuable as ever: (A1) efficiently and discreetly tipping the drivers etc., (A2) making coherent and interesting contributions to group response, and (A3) putting her excellent Spanish at the disposal of others in shops and eating-places.

(B) She would, one surmises, make a much better tour leader than Lisa.

(C) The room-switch at the Hotel Moctezuma clearly came as a total surprise to Tonia: her eyes widened and her jaw dropped. It is incredible that Lisa, even in today's apathetic mood, could take such a step without consulting all those concerned.

(D) See also 5.3.XV.B below.

5.3.XV. Martin (–) (2/10)

(A) Martin's morale is plummeting. (A1) He has come to realise that he is intellectually and culturally too 'lower deck' for this trip. He wishes he was back in Manchester drinking warm beer and chatting to barmaids. (A2) His earlier attempts to foist himself onto Tonia and Sunita as part jester and part sugar-daddy have now failed. He relates to nobody, and nobody relates to him, apart from Tonia's generosity as related below in (B) of this section.

(B) Tonia is patient and generous towards Martin beyond

his merits, fulfilling in this as in other matters what should surely be Lisa's function. She (B1) sits next to him on the bus, (B2) laughs at his sodden sallies and (B3) continues to treat him, in face of all the evidence, as if he is an amusing and likeable 'character'. (B4) If she sometimes pokes fun at him, even to the extent of temporarily offending him, one can see that this is not merely a 'distancing' mechanism applied for her own convenience, but also a genuine and kindly attempt to get the hapless fellow to see himself through the eyes of others.

(C) Martin is now drinking constantly. (C1) Whenever we stop at a café or store he buys beer from a cold-box to drink on the bus. (C2) Whenever we reach a destination he disappears first into the hotel bar then into the bars of the town. (C3) In addition he has a little hip-flask filled with (I think) tequila, and presumably one or more bottles from which he supplies this flask.

(D) He is obviously a practised drinker who remains polite and mostly amiable. His symptoms are of dogged long-term drinking: (D1) stertorous breathing, (D2) slow reactions, (D3) blurred speech, (D4) dithering hands.

(E) Martin is an accident waiting to happen. One wonders how Lisa is able to ignore him or be breezily dismissive if he is mentioned.

5.3.XVI. Dennis (– –) (5/10)
He has attached himself to Tonia and Sunita at present, which is a relief to Millie and me.

5.3.XVII. Millie (++) (4/10)
My little love has not been in top form today because what I fondly call her Millie-mood has been on her. One is usually careful not to speak of it so to her in case one hurts her feelings by seeming to accuse her. One is by no means an expert on feminine psychology, but one is not alone in having observed that most women seem subject

to such involuntary and contrary 'vapours', sometimes as a direct result of physiological functions. My Millie is by nature quiet and self-controlled, so her Millie-mood may only be noticed by somebody very close to her. On the other hand, one suspects she is more strongly affected than most women; because Millie is a very feminine woman and now in her thirties and childless: a decision which we have taken voluntarily but which doubtless has psychological repercussions in her case, offending as it does against female instincts and procedures.

(A) (A1) Before we left the hotel room this morning she was brushing her fluffy fair hair while I was making sure that we had packed everything, when I noticed that she was wearing the waxed jacket that I bought for her at the Outward Bound in Billericay. 'I think that you should wear something lighter, Petal Pie,' I said. 'It will be very hot later in the day.' To my surprise she puckered her forehead and pouted. 'Then as soon as it gets hot I shall take the blessed thing off, shan't I? Stop fussing, Brian!' Despite her lightness of tone and smile, I cast my mind back over recent events to see if one might in any way have irritated her by too much officious concern. (A2) And it was provoking, as the morning progressed, to watch the stubborn person keep on her waxed jacket long after it had become a discomfort to her, rather than admit that one's advice had any validity. Even after the stifling minibus had forced her to remove it, Little Miss Perversity donned it again when we came to the speedboats, supposing that it might be chilly on the water (in the tropics, at almost noon!).

(B) One observed, too, that she was more than usually contentious when it came to ornithological sightings and identification. (B1) This was particularly obvious in the case of *Ardea herodias* (see 4.2.2.above) and *Chloroceryle americana* (see 4.2.3. above), when her refusal to accede to one's verdict even caused her to bring the accuracy of the Field Guides into question. (B2) This reluctance to accept one's authority is beginning to cast a slight but regrettable shadow upon our ornithological pursuits. When I first introduced Millie to the delights of bird-spotting we quickly became an efficient team: combining her quick eyes and flair with the binoculars with my knowledge and judgement. If she now becomes discontent with what she subconsciously considers a subordinate role we shall risk spoiling our observation, and even missing important sighting, while we engage in futile dispute over identification. (B3) Aware that her contrariness was merely a Millie-mood, one was careful not to overreact to her annoying little mutinies. In fact I began to respectfully submit to some of her opinions, and in the case of our last waterfowl sighting (see 4.2.6. above) I deliberately withheld my conviction that it was a Jacamar, not even demurring from Millie's risible suggestion that it might be 'a species of cormorant'. (There is nothing remotely of the *Pelicaniformes* in the Jacamar.)

(C) Because of my care my darling's mood was temporarily lightened. (C1) By lunchtime she was her placid and com-panionable self, amusing me by pulling her comic goblin face of evil delight as she slurped at her *taxcalate* (see 3.1.3.2. above). (C2) Our ornithological teamwork was mostly smooth and amicable on the drive to San Cristobal. (C3) At two photo-stops, though, she annoyingly produced her camera and went to snap the scenery, leaving one to man the ornithological binoculars alone.

(D) It was 16.40 by the time we were settled into the Hotel Moctezuma: we were due for a briefing about the attrac-tions of San Cristobal in the hotel bar at 19.00. My Millie said, 'There's not a lot of point us going to the briefing is there, since tomorrow we won't . . .' Anybody else might have let this remark pass as an innocent statement of fact. But I know my little Millie well, and the tell-tale lift of her voice, and the way she trailed her remark into the air in mid-sentence. I cast a keen glance across at where she was perched up cutely in the cushioned window-nook of our room overlooking the fronded courtyard of the hotel (see 3.1.4.A above). I saw the delicate little vein that shows on her temple even if she is only very slightly in the dumps. I asked her, 'Is something the matter with Petal Pudding?' She shook her head and said, 'Nothing at all,' but one saw that her lovely blue eyes were small and bird-like through her spectacles, the eyes of a Millie-mood. I said, 'I don't agree, Munchkin. If we set off for Tuxtla good and early in the morning we should be able to spend a couple of hours at the zoo, grab lunch somewhere and be back here for the bulk of the afternoon. All the more reason, then, to go to the briefing, so we can be selective and decisive about what we see in San Cristobal tomorrow.' Little Millie shook her head again so that her fluffy fair hair bobbed against her ears. She said, 'You know what it will be like once we get to the zoo. We won't want to be rushed.' 'I'm sure we can restrict ourselves to two hours,' I said, 'or three at the most. That will be more than we would have had if the original trip had not been cancelled. Which reminds me that Lisa needs to be told to arrange our tickets for tomorrow. I'll tell her we want a very early start.' With which I turned and walked to the door. But ever sensitive to my Millie's responses and emotions I sneaked a look at her. One could see only passive acceptance, no indication of agreement and certainly no enthusiasm in her round-shouldered, cross-legged stillness as she pretended to gaze out of the window. So I went back and said, 'Unless, of course, little Millie would prefer not to go to the zoo.' Then she turned to look at me. 'That's rubbish!' she said. 'You're set on going. It's one of the high spots of the whole trip for you.' One was a little hurt that one's generous offer had been dismissed as rubbish. Also one was exasperated by my darling's feminine lack of logic and justice, which had now transformed the zoo visit into something solely for my pleasure and at my initiative, whereas one knew full well that up to now my Millie had been anticipating it with as much zest as I had. 'If Millie does not wish to go to the zoo,' I said sincerely, 'then we shall not go, my blossom. We shall go round the Indian markets and the other tourist attractions of San Cristobal with the others.' She did not answer immediately, which is usually a sign that she thinks what she is about to say might be distasteful to one. She gazed out of the window again, while I was left hovering in the middle of the room, uncertain whether to press her for a response or to assume that her silence was a form of acceptance of the original plan and to set off in search of Lisa. Then she said quietly, almost as if she was talking to herself, 'We've seen a lot of zoos, haven't we? One zoo is like another.' One was able to control one's annoyance, replacing it with concern as one thought what a severe bout of the dumps this must be to make my Millie so contrary. My answer was gentle and reasonable. 'Indeed, Poppet, zoos do tend to resemble each other. But then, so do zocalos and markets and museums and Mexican towns. And it should be said in fairness that the Tuxtla Zoo is unique in that it is dedicated to the birds and animals of this state, offering us a precious opportunity to see many extremely rare species in what is virtually their natural habitat.' My Millie has a fine intelligence even when her Millie-mood is upon her. Instead of entrenching herself in the arbitrary position she had adopted, or resorting to an emotional display as many women would do, she now succumbed to my superior reason. 'Exactly,' she said, as though she had not just been expressing a view diametrically opposed to mine. 'Go and find Lisa.' In case this surrender of hers, too sudden to be complete, might leave a residue of resentment to cloud my darling's delight tomorrow, one could not quite leave the matter so. I said, 'Only if Millie is quite sure she wants to go to the zoo. I know if she goes at all reluctantly she won't enjoy it and I won't either.' 'For goodness sake go!' my darling now cried out impatiently, 'or we shall waste what little time we have in San Cristobal today by mithering and maundering about tomorrow.' 'I'll go to find Lisa then,' I said. Now fairly certain that the conversation had been concluded to our mutual benefit, I edged towards the door. 'Be quick!' said little Millie. 'Maybe we can get to an Indian village this afternoon.' 'I rather think not, Petalkin,' I said, 'because we really do need to have a sort-out of our clothes and find a laundry.'

(E) The Millie-mood continued when we got back from the laundry. (E1) Even a tour of the intriguing Zocalo (see 3.3.2. above) did not restore her to her chirpy Millie-self and smooth the little vein on her temple. (E2) I took her into a café and pressed her to have another *taxcalate* but she said that it was not so delicious as the first (see 3.1.3.2.B and 5.3.XVII.C1 above) and would not pull her goblin faces while she drank it. (E3) To buck her up I suggested that we didn't go to dinner with the group but sneaked off together, just the two of us, and treated ourselves to somewhere special and private. 'We'll find some secret Millie-munchery,' I said, 'like we do at home, and like we did in Quito and Bombay.' She adjusted her spectacles slightly on her nose, another tell-tale code that lets only her lover know that all is not quite well. Then she said, 'That would be nice,' but in a drab little voice that seemed to mean the opposite. I said, 'After all, we've been to a lot of group dinners this trip. They've seen more of little Millie than they deserve. And we were cooped up with them all day yesterday in the coach and at the road-block.' She took a sip of her *taxcalate* and dabbed her lips with the back of her hand: all a ruse in order to give herself time to think

BRIAN SINGLETON

what to say. 'But we shall be on our own at Tuxtla,' she said. One couldn't believe one's ears. 'Does that mean little Millie prefers to dine with the group again tonight?' She hesitated. The vein was so prominent on her forehead that one could imagine one could see it throbbing and it filled one with tenderness. She said, 'We shall be on our own most of tomorrow, shan't we?' Perturbed by some of the implications of this remark, I couldn't help saying, 'On the Marvels of Central India trip we almost always ate alone in the evenings. We only ate with the group twice on the whole holiday.' Now she was looking away from me again, staring across the Zocalo, nursing her Millie-mood and excluding me from her Millie-mind. I went on, 'Yet on this trip, for some reason, we have tended to go with the group. And silly Millie was saying only yesterday how she didn't like these people as much as the ones in India, yet today she can't abide to be separated from them for a single evening!' Millie let out a little sigh that was near enough to a gasp of impatience to risk wounding one's feelings. 'If you want us to dine alone tonight we shall, Brian,' she said. My jaw dropped again. I perceived that she had worked her feminine trick on me, illogical, unjust and infuriating. The tête-à-tête in some secret Millie-munchery which one had proposed entirely as a treat for her, to divert her from her dumps, was now transformed into something one had thought up for one's own entertainment and was imposing on her.

(F) Back at the hotel things improved. She said she thought she would lie down and rest for a while and not attend the briefing in the bar. I said, 'Fair enough my prettypot. It won't need both of us at the briefing. Little Millie got the tummywobbles?' 'No but I've had a slight headache for most of today.' This delighted one because one knew that she was apologising, in her own stubborn feminine little way, for any pain and worry her Millie-mood had given one. It meant

209

that she had come to recognise the mood in herself, even if she could not bring herself to admit it directly to one. There was now every likelihood that with one's discreet assistance the mood would disperse and we would be like two nestling love-birds for the rest of the evening.

(G) Sure enough, in Los Payasos (see 3.1.3.3. above) the Millie-mood was gone at last and things were as they almost always are between my poppet and me. (G1) The café was intimate yet jolly, with candles in bottles on the tables and brightly coloured murals of clowns on every wall – clever Millie explained to me that *payaso* is Spanish for clown – and the food, as I stated in 3.1.3.3. above, was delicious. (G2) Furthermore, we were both doing something that gives us delight, which is being nice to someone whom we dearly love. (G21) I was congratulating myself that my care had helped rescue my petal-pot from the dumps that had troubled her day. One was also glad not to have to share her, for once, with the likes of Tonia and Dorothy, who fill her head with girly gossip and political junk. (G22) Millie was pulling her comical faces and laughing and pretending to spill her wine. The silly sweet biddy was a bit guilty about the distress her Millie-mood might have caused one, and was now deter-mined to pamper and indulge one as she felt one deserved. (G3) We talked about (G31) other members of the tour group (see 5.3.VIII.D and 5.3.XI.B,C&D above), (G32) about events at the road-block yesterday, (G33) about our past trips to Central India and the Galapagos Islands and (G34) about future holiday plans. Millie surprised me by announcing that she would next like to go to Peru (the little goose has been influenced by Dorothy's Inca propaganda), whereas previously she has always agreed with one that the absolute priority must be Puerto Rico, the ornithologist's heaven. But I said nothing, partly because one had no wish to fracture the harmony of the evening by objecting, but mostly because I had a secret (see 5.3.XVIII below) which made argument unnecessary. (G4) While we talked we played our game. Neither of us was allowed to mention home, work, religion, politics, science or technology. As usual, this became a bit silly. For example, when I mentioned the Galapagos trip, Millie clapped her hands and cried (a bit like Rose) 'Galapagos! That's Darwin! That's science! One to me!' (G5) By this time she had drunk at least half of a bottle of red wine, whereas normally she only has one glass and I drink the rest. Rejoicing to see her in a happier mood, one by no means begrudged her this little act of gluttony; nor was one disaffected by her schoolgirlish tipsiness, which can be grotesque in someone like Rose.

(H) Tipsy she certainly was. Her cheeks had that tell-tale flush, and she leant on my arm with a woozy giggle as we walked the short distance between Los Payasos and our hotel. Her voice was even a little indistinct: I called her Millie Mumblekins. From the way she was pressing her fingers into one's arm, it was clear to one that a little nooky-wooky was to be on the agenda. Normally we make it a rule to be strict with ourselves and not have nooky-wooky while on trips like this. After a long and emotionally difficult day one rather regretted not having insisted on a greater share of the red wine. But I remembered my secret (see 5.3.XVIII below) and all went well.

5.3.XVIII. Brian (=) (5/10)

(A) One is planning to sunder oneself from one's little Millie: a project for which one can find several sources. (A1) The political doctrine that every society must contain within itself the seeds of its own destruction is derived from a commonplace in biology, that death is an essential part of the life process. (A2) I do not hold with poets: I agree with whoever said, *'they trouble their waters so that they seem deep'*. Nor have I ever caught Millie reading poetry, but for some reason I opened one of her books last Summer when I was hanging around the flat waiting for decorators. I read a brief, morbid poem in which the poet claimed he wished his only love was dead and he was coming away from her grave in the rain. When I flicked to another page a phrase leapt out at me from a longer poem, *'Death is the mother of beauty'*. The coincidence of these sentiments stuck in my mind. In particular, *'Death is the mother of beauty'* is of interest, not as a philosophical utterance (the terms of reference not being sufficiently clarified) but as an exemplar of a psychological process. (A3) Yet such propositions as in A1 and A2 do not provide a motive so much as an intellectual justification for an impulse which has been present since one was a child. The notion of a perverse and pure alternative would impinge on one's most cherished delights and thrive in one's mind until it became inseparable from the delight. (A31) One would know that sooner or later one was going to smash to fragments the intricate balsa-wood model that one had been assembling for weeks and adoring. (A32) Then one would continue the assembly even more painstakingly, with the devotion of an Aztec priest nurturing a victim for sacrifice. (See 5 3 XVIII.C below.)

(B) I intend to tell her some time during this trip. I want to choose the moment so as to help us both as much as possible; so that I can be loving and she can be brave. (B1) Thursday was a fairly typical day in this respect. (B11) On Wednesday night (it was actually half past two on Thursday morning before we finally got into bed) we were tired after the long day of travel and the five hours at the road-block. It occurred to me to tell her then: get it over with while our senses were blunted, and in the hope that physical weariness would prevent a night of pleas, accusations and demands for explanations. But I decided against it. I decided that one would need all one's wits about one whenever one broached the topic; and I was daunted by the fact that we were alone and compelled to remain shut together for several hours. It seemed then that the morning might be the best time to deliver the terrible message, when one would be able to set out at once into the new day, taking refuge from the grief of personal collision in the sights to see and the surrounding crowd of fellow-tourists. (B12) But in the morning, as I watched her (in her wax jacket) brush her hair in front of the hotel mirror (see 5.3.XVII.A1 above), the morning seemed much less suitable than the evening for such a revelation. If one told her then, at the beginning of the day, her whole day would be made disconsolate and her delight in it murdered. This seemed crueller than telling her at night and giving her the chance to cry herself to sleep then wake refreshed and resolute. (B13) On one or two occasions in the course of the day I found Millie provoking. (B131) During some or all of these interludes, [(B1311) her stubbornness over the bird identifications (see 5.3.XVII.B1 above); (B1312) her failure to share the stint with the binoculars during photo-stops (see 5.3.XVII.C3 above); (B1313) her vapours in the hotel room (see 5.3.XVII.D above); (B1314) her contrariness in the café on the Zocalo, (see 5.3.XVII.E above)] it flashed through my mind that one might take the chance, while the relationship was relatively cool, to divulge one's callous secret. (B132) But there were a number of factors preventing me from acting on the impulse. (B1321) The drastic thunderbolt I was to let drop was out of all proportion to the tiny degree of annoyance that Millie was causing and the tepid nature of the dispute. To create a suitable context of animosity one would have to contrive some vicious quarrel such as I and my Millie have never had and which would hardly seem credible to either of us. (B1322) Furthermore, it was impossible for one to reveal one's secret to Millie when fortified by temporary annoyance because the mere thought of the secret was enough to remove any irritation one felt with her, replacing it with chivalrous adoration (see 5.3.XVIII.C below). (B14) Yet when our relationship is harmonious it is too tempting to prolong the delightful suspense. (B141) If the secret played its part in the intimate tryst at the new Millie-munchery (see 5.3.XVII.G above), it was not as a looming conversational option but as a psychological ingredient that heightened my response to the occasion (see 5.3.XVIII.C below). (B142) The observation made above in sub-section B141 of this paragraph is also true of the events referred to in 5.3.XVII.H above. (B2) Furthermore, a constant problem confronting me on all the occasions mentioned in 5.3.XVIII B1 above is that one cannot be sure how Millie will react to one's secret when one finally manages to get it off one's chest. I have often undergone the painful but perversely fascinating experience of rehearsing the scene in my mind, and the conduct of my co-star has been bewilderingly various in these dramas. (B21) The protectiveness I feel towards my little Millie makes me fear that the news will be too terrible for her to sustain. She might (B211) drop dead of a broken heart, (B212) suffer brain damage as a result of traumatic shock or (B213) take her own life in revenge or despair. (B22) On the other hand, there are plenty of documented cases of even such equable angels as Millie, when deprived of the lover with whom they were besotted, having resource to less passive grief, destroying or maiming their lover rather than themselves. (B23) More likely, and endurable, than B21 or B22 above, is an emotionally turbulent but not physically dangerous response: a scene, or several scenes. (B24) Yet Millie is normally disinclined to make a public display of her feelings. It is quite likely that she will act as she has done before, to one's knowledge, when something has upset her: a death in the family or an incident at work. In this case she may become terribly silent. (B25) On the other hand it should be remembered that my fluffy little poppet has a fine intelligence. She has a better degree than I have and is highly regarded by the senior partners in her practice. Her feminine scorn for logic does not preclude relentless argument when she is motivated. She might submit me to searching interrogation, which will stump me, because the processes recounted in 5.3.XVIII.A above are not conducive to explanation in Millie's terms. She could never appreciate how aptly the notion of quitting and losing her answers the needs of our relationship. (B26) Other scenarios are only vaguely envisaged because they conflict strongly with one's idea of Millie. But sometimes things that Millie does or says make one wonder if one has constructed an illusory version of her in one's mind, designed to appeal to one's own self-pride. Maybe the real Millie will greet my spilled secret with relief. (B3) As a result of these perplexities the process described in 5.3.XVIII.B1 above has been going on since the beginning of the holiday and looks like continuing indefinitely. (B31) I will keep insisting to myself that since one is to tell her sooner or later on the trip (one has solemnly promised oneself this), then later will be less cruel for my poor darling, and for me too, because little Millie will be happy for longer. (B32) From my point of view, and also from hers as I see it, it would be best if we could always be happy while together and only know guilt and grief and loneliness when we are apart. So one suspects that as the plane is circling Heathrow I will still be wanting to avoid or postpone the moment of unhappiness together, and will persuade myself that it will be best to give the news to Millie when we are both back at work in Basildon and have our careers to absorb us and dilute the sorrow. (B33) Just as

I told myself before the holiday that the best time to tell her was during the Mexico trip when she would be relaxed and distracted. I also judged that being in a group of people when I told her would be better for both of us than if I told her at home where we are either eyeball to eyeball in our flat or more or less solitary in our respective places of work. (B34) One perceives that all my compassionate strategy is cowardice. Eventually I may deem it best for both of us if I leave her without warning, employing the dismal ruse of a letter: *Dear little Millie, I love you so much and have left you for ever. Don't expect to understand, any more than I do.* This will entail considerable preparation, to vanish from her world without her prior knowledge. So I will keep putting off this departure, just as I now keep postponing the simpler matter of telling her of my decision. I may decide that after all one needs to tell her first in order to commit oneself to action . . .

(C) My decision to leave Millie has enriched our relationship. (C1) Prior to the adoption of my notion, sexual relations between myself and Millie were (C11) not always satisfactory. [This was (C111) partly the result of her emotional reticence, which stemmed in turn from (C1111) her sheltered childhood and (C1112) her religious convictions and made her sexual arousal difficult; and (C112) partly because one was sometimes afflicted with (C1121) premature ejaculation or (C1122) impotence due to the disparity between little Millie and the succubi of one's fantasies.] (C12) We were good chums with a lot in common, well-motivated to continue our relationship and honour its commitments despite these hiccups. (C13) But since I decided that I am going to quit it is as if I am the ogre in some rollicking old yarn and Millie's docile body is the prisoner over whom I gloat. The result is highly satisfactory for both of us. (C2) Nor is the enrichment of our relationship confined to the sexual act. It is usual for a bereft friend, relative or lover to discover qualities in the departed which went either unnoticed or unappreciated. There is a Woody Allen film in which the final sequence is a montage of shots from earlier in the action, all wistfully and affectionately featuring the woman now lost to the foolish hero. Watching somebody one is shortly to lose can enhance their attractions and flatter their weaknesses even more poignantly. I used to take my little Millie for granted but now dote on her with guilty obsession. (C21) I have always accepted that Millie is not a beautiful or prestigious girlfriend, just as I see myself as not conventionally attractive to women but a short, plump nonentity who beautiful women ignore. Glamour was for me a sheepish fantasy, a form of mild self-abuse. Millie was merely available and compatible. But now every item of her appearance is tenderly registered and enhanced with the glamour of loss. (C211) Her pale complexion never seems to respond to the sun, though wine can put a hectic flush on her cheekbones (see 5.3.XVII.H above). (C212) Her small blue eyes are made to seem even smaller and more piercing by the special spectacles she has to wear. (C213) She has narrow hips and (C214) bony toes and fingers. (C215) Her legs are thin, with prominent knee-caps (C216) When she is undressed she looks undernourished, with her flesh stretched by her rib-cage and shoulder-blades. (C217) She is almost breastless, with pale, perfectly symmetrical nipples. (C218) There is a little vein on her temple that becomes emphasised by stress (see 5.3.XVII.D above). All these features are lovely to me now, and (C22) her psychological features equally dear. (C221) Her habits and mannerisms: (C2211) her ungainly stance, with spine curved and face thrust out, when she is watching or hearing something that absorbs her; (C2212) her way of betraying the tensions beneath her surface serenity by rolling little pellets of bread in restaurants of shredding drip-mats in pubs; (C2213) her habit of adjusting her spectacles on her nose with her forefinger (see 5.3.XVII.E3 above); (C2214) and her habit of addressing herself in the second person, often chidingly, when she thinks she is alone: *'What do you think of that, then, Millie?'* or, *'Millie Robinson, you fool!'*. (C222) Her tastes and predilections: (C2221) her (C22211) love of cats and (C22212) fear of dogs; (C2222) her (C22221) taste for tea and (C22222) dislike of coffee; (C2223) her (C22231) liking for popular music that was already old-fashioned when she was a child (the Beatles, Simon and Garfunkel) and (C22232) her dismissal of anything produced since as either (C222321) talentless imitations or (C222322) tasteless experiments; (C2224) her religious beliefs which her intellect cannot justify. (C23) Most dear and poignant of all is her behaviour towards myself: (C231) making the baby-talk and the comic goblin faces that I say amuse me (see 5.3.XVII.C1, 5.3.XVII.E2 and 5.3.XVII.G22 above); (C232) squeezing my forearm shyly from a sudden impulse of attraction (C233) leaning over me with my bed-time cocoa, nearly spilling it as she softly kisses my forehead. (C24) Even her clothes are subject to the magic of this premeditated elegy. One can become aware of a sentimental constriction in one's throat, a little globe of grief that one finds it necessary to swallow, when one sees items of clothing she has discarded, in the untidy way that used to irritate one, on floor and chair and bed. Sporty unfeminine garments, with popular brand-names, that might have belonged to anybody; but her tenure of them has given them significance, as if they were now murder clues that one must identify. (C241) A purple and orange shell suit which she has always suspected is a bit too garish. (C242) Reebok trainers, children's size, with the heels worn over. (C243) Sloggi knickers, faintly daring. (C244) A Heineken T-shirt won in a pub raffle. (C245) That foolish Barbour waxed jacket which she so perversely adores (see 5.3.XVII.A above).

SIMON FIELDING

'Yesterday I made a mammoth effort. Not a cavil crossed my lips, I was abjectly charming to everyone. I even spoiled my lunch by chatting with that obnoxious hag.'

Pam continued to pack the cases placidly, humming. Sometimes it is like being married to a psychiatric nurse. We are vastly incompatible, in that she has a policy of banishing difficulties, however urgent, to a remote turret of consciousness while she potters at something more congenial – whereas my only way with a problem, even a minor irritation, is to abandon everything and lunge at it, lambaste it with rhetoric and bluster, worry it to death. This incompatibility, unlike that of Jack Spratt and his wife, causes one or other of us distress most of the time.

'I did my damnedest, and you were one hundred per cent wrong, as usual when you prescribe for me. If it were possible for something as unremittingly crapulous as this tour to have a low point, yesterday would be it. All that stopped me cutting my throat was the prospect of our evening meal together away from that dismal circus.'

Shutting her eyes and parting her lips, Pam winced, less at my tirade than at an appalling squawk from the chained bird in the yard under our window. I could feel my jowls wobble with the violence of my vociferation as I went on: 'Yet today I'm supposed to endure the same purgatory sustained by the prospect of the shoddy hell of a group meal at the end of it.'

I was being monstrously unjust to Pam, since I myself had proposed, the previous night after a bottle of Pomerol, that our next evening meal should be with the group. Conscious of the helpless bad humour embedded in me by detestation of this Baluth squalor and the riff raff that infest it, I had ascribed to Pam a distress at my conduct for which there was no evidence. Having then resolved to reform my behaviour to spare her this imaginary distress, I was now resenting her innocent part in my self-imposed penance.

Pam murmured, as she too often does, 'Remember your blood-pressure.' She has persuaded me to give up cigars and keeps trying to put me on a diet, which discredits my first wife's assertion that Pam only married me for my wealth (or Ruth's wealth, as Ruth sees it).

'I'll make a deal,' I said, raising a hand in a plea for abeyance as though she had just subjected me to a torrent of eloquence. 'I'll be moronically nice to everybody all morning. Then we shun them for the rest of the day.'

She nodded her acceptance of this scheme with offensive prompt-titude, betraying indifference to my torments and scepticism about my resolutions. Then she mentioned breakfast and I immediately reneged on the deal.

'For Christ's sake let's get out of the hotel! You can't expect me to start being sociable half-awake on an empty stomach!'

We breakfasted in a drab hippie café, the walls lurid with incompetent pictures of clowns and the owner continually grinning at us as if he was a failed clown himself or an expatriate Brit. The worthy, crumbly toast and the sour, organic butter left me as hungry as when I began; on the other hand it was no hardship to be denied, for once, that carbonised fat that Americans call bacon and that brown gunge, like the stool of a diarrhoeal duck, which Mexicans call beans. Disdaining a fill-up of impotent coffee we dashed back to the hotel late for the rendezvous, then languished through a half-hour of Dennis's erudition and Rose's enthusiasm while waiting for the others to deign to appear.

There are those on trips like this who exercise starved egos by deliberately keeping others waiting. Katrin is the worst; Tonia is not much better, yet seems to escape criticism. Martin becomes less and less bothered about timetables as slurred speech and the stink of alcohol settle permanently on him. This morning he was next to the last to arrive, his grey mop tousled, his blue chin stubbled, the whites of his eyes khaki, his eyelids rimed with gore. He had stanched a shaving-cut with a bloody shred of newspaper and a twist of crisp mucus dangled from a nostril.

He grinned slyly and offered Pam a cigarette. This stalwart racist is fascinated by my wife and pesters her with his attention when he is not ogling Tonia, who encourages him perversely, or Lisa, who brushes him off as briskly as she brushes off the rest of us. His claim on Pam is that she smokes occasionally. When she refused his offer he nonetheless chose to favour her with conversation: leered, waved a packet of Mexican cigarettes under her nose and asked if she had tried the brand. Though I had no intention of interfering, I barked out, 'No she has not!' whereat Pam mortified me by producing from her bag an identical packet to his and holding it up, snap.

Lisa was last to arrive, not bothering with apology or excuse; nor did anyone dare a comment as, except for Brian and Millie who had gone to a zoo, we set off in a humiliating crocodile. At least Dennis has given up trying to marshal us as if he was a sheep-dog.

Globus hystericus was, mercifully, dormant. The spots were in front of my eyes – the delicate, distinct one shaped like a ballerina, and the fuzzy, unfocused spider – but the flashes in the east-south-east of my field of vision were not evident. The Zocalo was spruce in morning sunshine, with its pink-tiled floor and grey buildings.

Banks having opened, a number of people discovered the need to cash travellers' cheques – then were not prepared to cash them quickly at the nearest point but insisted on shopping around for the most favourable rate of exchange, dragging the rest of us from bank to bank. Once again we were proceeding at the speed of the most disorganised and incompetent. I cannot count the expensive hours lost waiting for somebody to conduct private business such as buying food, film, toothpaste, trash, obtaining money, or even going to the toilet – things any reasonable person expects to do in their own time without inconveniencing others. We are even subjected to the insulting experience of waiting for smokers (Lisa, Martin, Tonia and, alas, sometimes Pam) to finish their cigarettes.

When at last we were moving from the Zocalo towards where the *colectivos* were scheduled to start for San Juan Chamula, Lisa, with the aid of the lungs of her odious Welsh sergeant, called us to a halt. Katrin had forgotten to hand in her hotel room key and wanted us to wait while she returned to the hotel.

'What does it matter if she holds on to the damned key?'

Dennis supported me, which made me suspect I was talking piffle. 'We shall only be absent for a few hours and they presumably have duplicate keys to which they can have resource in such temporary exigencies.'

Even coming from Dennis this made too much sense to appeal to Katrin, who would go no further until the key had been returned. For some unfathomable reason Lisa concurred. 'They can be funny about keys in Mexican hotels.'

'Eh? What is that supposed to mean?' I could feel *globus hystericus* forming like a fur-ball in the pit of my throat. Pam put her hand on my arm: I turned and spoke quietly, as if to her alone. 'I know too well what it means. It means we're going to hang around while Katrin creeps to the hotel and back and probably gets lost.'

Katrin was holding the key up in front of her white face as though it was a crucifix and we were all vampires. Lisa reached out and plucked the item from Katrin's hand, then issued decisions in a rattled staccato. Lisa herself would return. The rest of us were to move on up the street to a small square where there was a bar. There we were to wait for Lisa.

Pam looked at me beseechingly. If anybody else noticed that the arrangements were blatantly stupid, Lisa's tone discouraged protest. Only after she had left us did Tonia say mildly, 'I don't see why we couldn't have waited here. It's a quiet street, we're not causing an obstruction.'

As we trudged uphill Isabel took it upon herself to castigate Katrin, saying Katrin should have taken the key herself and the rest of the group not waited for her. If unable to catch up she should have missed the Indian village trip. Rose intervened on behalf of sweetness and light: 'Don't be too hard on poor Katrin, Isabel. Experience teaches us to be gentle with the inadequacies of others.'

Katrin drooped her head lower and walked more slowly, so that the other two had to fall back to continue their prosecution. We toiled up past a couple of intersections without finding the square with the bar. The third intersection was with a wide dirt road; on the corner a church was set back with a paved area in front of it.

'This is the place!' Dennis announced confidently, as he struggled his special, heavy duty, commando-issue, utterly fatuous day-sack off his shoulders and perched his buttocks on a low wall. 'Deploy yourselves comfortably and so that you cause no obstruction to traffic.'

Martin asked, 'Where's the bar?'

Dennis pointed to a building, decorated with an ancient Coca Cola sign, that looked like a grocery that had been closed for years.

Tonia put her arms akimbo, as she does when she has something emphatic to say. 'That's no bar, and she never said nothing about a church. It's further up the hill.'

Dorothy said, 'What's it matter? Lisa will find us here when she comes up.'

There is intrigue and chicanery among the younger women. On Friday Tonia, previously Sunita's room-mate, was put with Katrin, which led to spirited negotiations between Tonia and Lisa, which have concluded in Tonia sharing with Lisa while Katrin is on her own and, alas, responsible for her own door-key. Rejection by Sunita and the insult of being lumped in with Katrin has put iron into Tonia's soul. Now she marshalled her freckles into a scowl at Dorothy's insubordination. 'Lisa may not pass this way. She

225

may know a short cut. It sticks out a mile this is not the place. I'm going on up.'

Dennis chanted, 'This is the place all right, and the first rule of any party negotiating foreign terrain is that the group should stick together.'

Tonia took a few remorseless steps then looked round commandingly. It was like a dispute between Arctic explorers or conquistadors in the Matto Grosso. Martin crossed the line to join her, as did Dorothy and Donald. Tonia was crestfallen that everybody else stayed put but there was no chance of her backing down and accepting Dennis's authority. 'I'm going on up,' she repeated, like a character in a bad adventure movie, and the four set off.

Rose sided with Dennis, whom she sometimes ogles grotesquely. Isabel stayed with Rose. Sunita voted against Tonia because there is a rift between them. Stephanie stayed with Sunita. Katrin stayed for indecipherable and possibly arbitrary reasons. While I marginally preferred Tonia's arguments, and certainly prefer her trite and vulgar personality to that of Dennis, I had done enough uphill walking on that warm morning. Pam stayed with me. At the last minute, just before the defecting quartet went out of sight round the corner of the church, Annabel went looming after them. 'Come along, Maureen Corrigan,' she called. Maureen, bearing a weighty shoulder-bag which I imagine to be full of syringes and crepe bandages, followed without discussion. There was an interval, after which anybody who set off would have seemed hopelessly indecisive. We had therefore divided 8–6: I could not help noticing that our majority contained most of the nincompoops.

Fifteen minutes of hiatus ensued, wherein Isabel and Rose continued to berate and counsel Katrin, like an angel and a fiend at strife for her soul, till they saw that she had donned her cassette earphones. Dennis moralised triumphantly apropos the folly of Tonia's faction and congratulated us and himself that there had not been more desertions. Sunita and Stephanie went into the church but soon emerged with wry faces. Rose went to investigate. My wife talked with Isabel about infant allergies.

Lisa came with narrow eyes and pursed lips: either she was resenting the unnecessary trouble she had voluntarily taken, or some off-stage event had distressed her. In any case she is a moody baggage.

'Why are you waiting here?'

Despicably, Dennis said nothing. Lisa adopted a stance of utter incredulity, round-eyed and slack-jawed, as Isabel related the details of the schism.

'Come along!'

Stephanie fetched Rose out of the church and we followed Lisa round the corner of the building and up the hill, a mere fifty yards to an intersection with a main road. Here the wide pavement and set-back houses gave a fleeting impression of a square, but there was nothing remotely like a bar.

Lisa scowled towards all points of the compass before demanding accusingly, 'Where are they?'

Isabel riposted with a question of her own. 'Is this where we were supposed to wait?'

'Of course it is. Where are the others?'

'Where is the bar?'

'What bar?'

'You said there was a bar.'

'Shit, this is no time for boozing! We're late for the *colectivos*. Where are the others?'

I said to Pam, 'This is wonderful. Surreal.'

She stared at me obtusely, then smiled. 'You're doing very well,' she said, as if to a child.

We turned left and followed the road down until it was a busy thoroughfare between shops and stalls. Compared to the Zocalo and tourist quarter this was a slum region where tradespeople and customers alike looked squalid and delinquent.

Lisa led us into an alley where several battered vans were surrounded by evil-featured Indians and mestizos, young and old, male and female. She vanished into a kiosk while the rest of us loomed self-consciously among the leering dwarves.

'Now we've lost one of the fucking *colectivos*!' she shouted as she re-emerged. The vulgarity caused Rose to give a melodramatic gasp and put a hand to her mouth. 'Because we're so fucking late. So we've all got to jam onto the other. It's just as well some silly sods have got lost.'

There were ten of us, including two old men, plus a sack of grain they were taking up the mountain, whereas the van had been cobbled up with uncomfortable seating for eight passengers. Lisa decreed that Pam should sit on my lap – a hasty, ignorant decision and blatantly impracticable. My legs are so fat that I must spread them when I sit: Pam would have been constrained to ride side-saddle on one thigh, to the ungainly discomfort of us both. I therefore broke silence at last, reminding Lisa forcibly that the Indian village trip was featured in the Baluth brochure, therefore proper transport to and from the village, provided and paid for by the company, was contractually obligatory.

Lisa bared her teeth like a cornered rat that was planning to tear out my jugular but before she could retort Rose exclaimed that what it was all about was mucking in with the gang, even if it meant sacrificing comfort and modesty, and furthermore it was all jolly good fun and she was game to sit on anybody's knee. She pounced her considerable bulk forthwith on the appalled Dennis, who I must admit bore the imposition with better grace than I could have mustered. There was still not enough room on the vehicle so Lisa, upbraiding both my girth and my unreasonableness with a series of meaningful glances, took Sunita onto her lap.

The fifteen-minute journey to San Juan Chamula was intolerable, a microcosm of the entire trip. Rose was in a state of embarrassing arousal, even for her: whooping and giggling, whenever the van swerved or went over a *tope* or pot-hole, in a manner that was unsubtly obscene, and proclaiming in her vibrant voice what instructive bliss was in the whole mindless shambles. There was a stench in the stifling confines of the vehicle that may have been a legacy from earlier passengers but which I suspect was Dennis's sebaceous glands expressing their horror and embarrassment at Rose's incubal antics. I was cramped between Pam and Isabel: the latter kept cringing from the pressure of my helplessly spread leg and making reproving noises in case I was assaulting her. At the same time she quizzed me about my success as a property magnate, perplexing me with a disbelieving sniff when I told her that I had nothing to do with property but ran a theatre company in Plymouth. Tinnitus was tormenting my left ear and south-south-east of my retina there were mad lights dancing. It all made a suitable prologue to the depressing experience of the Indian village.

Nowadays romantic and sentimental notions attach themselves to any indigenous population. Cultured opinion, not content with grossly inflating the achievements of primitive civilisations such as the Inca and the Aztec in preference to their conquerors, must look for achievements and virtues where there are none whatsoever. Australian aborigines, the most dejected and retarded human beings on the planet, are envied for 'intuitive wisdom' and 'pictorial intelligence'. Primitive and sadistic killers like the nineteenth-century Apache and Cheyenne are ascribed such purely imaginary qualities as 'dignity' and 'rapport with nature'. So the tribal Indians in Mexico, still sunk in the torpor of drudgery and credulity that trapped them under the bloodthirsty pre-Colombian priests, are permitted to pose as disinherited victims, in some way more worthy and less privileged than the rest of Mexico's poor.

Baluth literature, as one would expect of a profit-making tourist organisation, devoutly reflects these fashionable pro-Indian attitudes. Lisa either naïvely or cynically subscribes to them, praising the doctrinaire posturings of Marcos and inviting us to rejoice in how the tribal villages have 'won' a degree of self-government. There was evidence of this autonomy outside the church, in the persons of two swarthy hoodlums in uniform white ponchos and panamas, brandishing rifles and wearing pistols in holsters. Lisa told us that they were there to ensure that visitors 'respected the village'. On no account should we use cameras inside the church, and it was disrespectful to photograph anywhere in the village without asking permission – and offering to pay. There had been cases, she said approvingly, of tourists being 'roughed up' who had failed to show sufficient respect.

The church was practically full, the floor covered with candles, flowers, branches of pine and blankets for the worshippers to kneel on, so that we had to pick our way around, conscious that inside as outside native Gestapo in their rudimentary uniforms were standing with folded arms and daring us to be disrespectful. The light, provided by thousands of little candles, seemed to pulse to the mumbling rhythm of rat-poor Indians who were wasting the hours of daylight by worshipping an amalgam of ancient demons and Catholic saints. In a fog of incense, tawdry images were surrounded by mirrors and decked with shabby vestments. For all the obsessive credulity on display the whole scene was a commercial performance, with plenty of opportunities for visitors to buy candles of all sizes and lots of offering boxes and donation plates conspicuous. The aborigines have eagerly assimilated the unattractive features of the conquistadors: economic greed and a morbid religion that mixes effortlessly with their own drastic superstitions.

Cupidity unalloyed by religion awaited us when we emerged gasping and blinking into the bright air. Once the church had been visited there was precious little else to San Juan Chamula apart from the stalls that thronged the plaza and surrounding streets. The ambience was of a shoddy and grudging theme-park rather than a viable community. Maybe there were people actually working fields somewhere out in the hills – but the impression I got was that the bulk of the population were around the plaza, either on show as worshippers in church or milking visitors on the stalls. Sunday is supposed to be market day in San Juan Chamula, and this was merely Saturday ... I suspect that every day is market day during the tourist season.

The contents of the stalls were uninteresting. The textiles were slightly cheaper but much less impressive than at the weavers' co-operative in San Cristobal which we visited yesterday afternoon. (Nevertheless Pam to my horror bought a *rebozo* to further swell our unwieldy luggage.) Otherwise, apart from a few food stalls for the natives, everything was the usual keepsake trash: leather-work and lace-work, silver jewellery, embroidered skirts and tops. Lisa bought a macabre, black-masked Zapatista doll.

Whining children, some of them selling worthless bracelets of twisted wool, most of them merely thrusting their cupped and filthy hands under one's face, made an ordeal out of a drink at an al fresco café. A couple of girls wanted to insert little plaits into Pam's devastatingly expensive coiffure, obviously in the hopes of a tip, and were insolently difficult to dissuade.

Lisa flopped into a chair at our table – spoke in Spanish to the children, who either went away at once or backed off and fell silent – and took one of Pam's cigarettes: unlike Pam, she made no effort to keep her smoke out of my face.

'You haven't ordered a meal have you?'

I said, 'You're joking.'

Lisa didn't smile at all. 'Because the bus goes on to Zinacanta in fifteen minutes' time.'

I said, 'I rather think I've seen enough Indians for one day.'

Pam dismayed me by saying, 'I wouldn't mind going to look at the textiles.'

'You go then. My eyes are bad and I have stomach cramps. I want to get back to the hotel and lie down.' I asked Lisa, 'Is there a bus back to San Cristobal?'

'No there isn't. You'll have to take a taxi, over there. It'll cost you about half a buck.'

I heaved myself to my feet. 'I prefer you to do the negotiating. I have hardly a word of Spanish, as you know.'

Lisa grimaced and did not budge. 'All you have to say is "San Cristobal". You don't have to be much of a linguist to manage that.'

Ascribing her rude reluctance to residual resentment of our dispute on the *colectivo*, I assumed that if I insisted she could not refuse. Annoyance sent my voice into its upper register. 'All the same I am requesting your help,' I piped. 'Are you the tour leader or not?'

She returned my gaze coolly and I perceived abruptly that she hated me, hated her job and was not going to back down. Lights were exploding in the corner of my eye and the globus furball was rising towards my tonsils.

Pam said to Lisa, 'What do you think? Will there be a good choice of textiles at the next village?'

Lisa continued to meet my gaze for a couple of seconds, then said, 'I doubt it. The quality stuff is in the shops and co-operatives. The best of the rest is on the plaza in San Cristobal. What they sell off in the villages are mostly rejects and sub-standards.'

'Thanks for the tip,' Pam put out her cigarette and rose and ranged herself next to me. 'I'll go back with Simon.' She gave Lisa a winning smile.

Lisa rose too. Whereas she detests me enough to risk her job rather than oblige me, she likes Pam enough to help her even at the cost of letting me seem to have triumphed. We had to share the taxi she found us with two middle-aged mestizo males who stank of methylated spirits and clumsily consumed tortillas out of straw baskets.

At a small restaurant just north of the Zocalo free rolls and butter were provided in abundance. French onion soup came with real Parmesan, parsley and other herbs, in capacious bowls. Roquefort salad proved a delight: a plate of very lightly boiled potato, beetroot and carrot with fresh tomato and Roquefort cheese on top. My main course was a filet steak wrapped in bacon and stuffed with yet more cheese and green vegetables. I topped it off with a large slice of superbly sticky lemon meringue pie and two Coca-colas – so far this trip I have managed to accede to Pam's wish that I don't drink alcohol before dinner. The irritations that countered this restorative feast were the compulsory ten per cent service charge, the gross overpricing of Pam's Perrier water and the stultitude of the waiter whose unjustified boast that he could speak English lured us into unenlightening conversation about items on the menu: 'Adobo Cristobalo? Like how make in Cristobalo. Eet same adobo Guatamalo.'

Over coffee Pam announced that she wouldn't mind going back to the co-operative we visited on Friday afternoon – or to another textile emporium recommended in the guidebook. Seeing the horror that immediately contorted my features she added, 'You needn't come. You could have that lie down you've been talking about.'

Since Pam is enjoying herself, whereas I am enduring the tepid tortures of cut-price Hell, it is ironic to think that she came on this trip at my bidding to please me, just as she went to Egypt and Angkor Wat. She has no interest in the humanist sciences and suffers from prompt vertigo on pyramids. Apart from the superficial parade of people and places her chief pleasure is in gathering ethnic materials with which to decorate our home and her person.

'I don't want to lie down!' I sounded petulant. 'I want to look at Na Bolom – the place I showed you in the guidebook – as we agreed last night.'

'You said you'd had enough of Indians.'

'Enough direct contact, but they still intrigue me as anthropological phenomena.'

'Fine, you go there and I'll go shopping.'

Her facial expression indicated that she knew what I would say next. I was briefly tempted to leave my case unstated in order to prove her wrong.

'Shopping? We're already overloaded with impulse-purchase paraphernalia and clothes you'll never wear! And you'll buy at least three rugs and two hammocks when we get to Yucatan.'

'Remember your blood pressure.' Then she dropped her bomb, which had been prepared and aimed by the foregoing conversation.

'I'll do a deal. I'll come with you to the Blollum place this afternoon if we eat with everybody else this evening.'

'You're joking!' The roof of my mouth started to tingle and my nose itched.

'It might be entertaining.'

'Entertaining?' Beyond the tinkling irritation in my ear I could hear the pulse of a drum that corresponded to the throb of my temple.

'You said yourself you want to be less negative. You want to change your mindset and find things entertaining. That's what you said last night.' Her serene, sweet tones were finely calculated to plunge me into half-crazed paroxysms of wrath. Then she would comfortably win the long-term argument, however crass her case, simply by not losing her temper.

'We've made one deal today, and I kept to my part of it all morning.'

'No you didn't. You sneered and snarled as usual and made no effort to enjoy anything.'

'There was something to enjoy?' My eyes were flashing and dithering, my vision further obstructed by the spider, the ballerina and an inverted seagull that I had never seen before. I lunged to my feet, nearly dragging the tablecloth and coffee-cups with me, and shouted, 'Sorry! I seem to have failed to appreciate that the only problem with this otherwise delightful holiday is my curmudgeonly self. I suggest that I fly home immediately, leaving you with your new-found circle of chums and relieving you of any further need to insult me, double-cross me or set me social assignments and endurance tests that I'm certain to fail!'

I then left the restaurant with such speed and dignity as my bulk permitted. In addition to all aforementioned symptoms of stress, which were still in full swing, there was a throttling hand on my gullet and my stomach, swollen alike with lunch and rage, seemed to have risen to try to invade my lungs. An ulcer glowed somewhere in my small intestine and the fangs of a goblin were fixed in my thigh.

I needed a holiday, which this is not. This is like putting on a shabby farce ('Mexican Mess-Around') with the most refractory and talentless cast in the world.

Pam is a foolish, inconsistent bitch and an appalling cheat. On Monday she regales me with shredded celery and lettuce telling me that my obesity is a health crisis that must be urgently tackled; on Tuesday she feeds me lasagne, pommes frites and crème brûlée informing me that my diet is my own problem and I must not impose it on others. She stops me smoking, limits my drinking, nags me to exercise, manipulates my moods and modifies my behaviour until I hardly recognise myself, then disclaims all responsibility and accuses me of blaming her for my self-induced condition. Though I have rescued her from a disastrous marriage, ensconced her in affluence and been incredibly patient with and generous towards her children, her comportment towards me often reflects an infuriating, gingerly tolerance, as if she were a social worker who has been abducted by an ogre.

Reaching the Hotel Moctezuma I flounced into the bar, determined to soothe myself with a gin and tonic and even contemplating declaring insurrection with a cigar. But Martin was installed on a bar-stool, blotto enough to hail me with an affectionate grin, and my curiosity as to what had become of the splinter group that morning was not enough to tempt me into the thicket of his blurred platitudes, so I turned on my heel without bothering to pretend that I had not seen him.

Up in our room I lay on the bed clutching my beard after consuming a generous dose of Valium, addiction to which Pamela is happy to permit since it doesn't have the social stigma of alcohol and is not as much fun. From time to time the chained bird screamed in the fronded courtyard beyond the blinds. As I waited for the stress-symbols to abate self-justified wrath was replaced by the ooze and cringe of guilt. Scenes such as the one I had just enacted were what finally persuaded Ruth to divorce me.

When footsteps clopped on the wooden stairs and along the

balcony I opened the door before Pam had time to knock. 'I hoped I'd grown out of that sort of tantrum.' I said.

'At least this time I had my own credit-card and was able to pay the bill.' She drew the curtains back, opened the window, took off her shoes and sat on her bed. A wave of relief quelled all my twitches, dimmed the pangs and bells. Perhaps it was just the Valium taking effect.

'I've had enough of Indians. We'll both go shopping.'

'No, I've bought too much stuff as it is. We'll go to that Blobbum place.'

'Only on condition that we eat with the rest of the group tonight.'

She laughed uncertainly, wondering if I was being sarcastic. The bird screamed below us, an even more appalling racket now that the window was open. I said, 'Why do you put up with me? I'm awful.'

'No you're not.' She smiled at me. 'Not compared to Colin, anyway.' Colin was her first husband, bless him.

The Casa Na Bolom (House of the Jaguar) used to be the home of a couple of European Jews, Frans and Trudy Blom – there is a sprightly effort at a pun in the name of the house. He was an archaeologist working on Mayan sites until his death in 1963: she lasted until 1993, an anthropologist mostly studying the Lacandon Indians of Eastern Chiapas. The Casa is now run by a trust that attempts to succour this hapless, fragile tribe, whose rain-forest is being devastated by slash-and-burn settlers and timber merchants.

The Lacandons have been much featured on TV travelogues and brochure photographs; striking-looking Indians who seem at first glance like escapees from an old B-feature science fiction movie. Men and women wear long white gowns that contrast dramatically with their long black hair. The poetical appeal of their appearance, allied to the fashionable, ecological cause they represent, makes them irresistible to scruffy left-wing do-gooders;

all the volunteers I saw at Na Bolom fell decidedly into that category.

The three-dollar guided tour in English was scheduled to last an hour and a half. After a brisk tour of the handsome house we were led into the less impressive garden by a Home Counties youth in an Australian bush-hat complete with those foolish dangling corks. He lectured us there for half an hour on the plight of the Lacandons, claiming plausibly that Na Bolom was endeavouring merely to soften the impact of civilisation on the Indians and make sure that they had friends as well as enemies. It has not occurred to him that protective patronage can be as destructive as antagonism or exploitation, nor is he aware of the banal and dubious motives that underlie his own work at Na Bolom. The forty-five minutes that were left us after his lecture were enough to twice exhaust the display rooms of photographs and scientific relics, as well as the usual tacky video in painful colours with voice-overs from 'Listen with Mother'. There is a library of 14,000 books at Na Bolom, including one of the world's biggest Mayan collections, but that is a separate rip-off, open only in the mornings and on Mondays when the tour does not take place.

Ten of our group were there for the 4.30 tour: the absentees were Annabel and Maureen, Brian and Millie, of course Lisa, understandably Martin and incredibly Dennis. I greeted everybody so warmly that I perplexed and embarrassed some: at one point snide Pamela chuckled and said to me, 'Don't overdo it, Simon!'

While we were waiting for the tour to begin, consuming expensive chocolate cake and coffee, Dorothy and Tonia complained about 'being deserted' by Lisa in the morning. It seems the six defectors had coincidentally found a square with a bar a few blocks north of where Lisa intended. They had waited there a good while, until Martin was inextricably locked in conversation with a Dutch drunkard and Annabel, losing patience, took a taxi (and Maureen) back to the hotel. Tonia, utilising her efficient Spanish, had then led Dorothy and Donald to San Juan Chamula.

I listened to this intently, emitting small cries of sympathy and wonder. I then delighted in Rose, who was in captivating form during the guide's lecture, interrupting so impulsively with questions about his home town, Dagenham, and how its facilities compared with those of Wimbledon, that he was hard pressed to maintain his spiel. I told myself that if I can run a theatre company for twenty-five years I can endure a fortnight with a bunch of tourists for whom I am not responsible. I even managed to be civilly unresponsive to Isabel, who had seen somebody lying in a gutter outside Na Bolom and wondered if I might report it to the police. I did not point out to anyone, not even Pamela, that the Casa Na Bolom stinks of self-righteous left-wing dogma and like all such doctrinaire dens is unapologetic about not giving value for money – visitors being supposed to feel privileged to be allowed to contribute their guilty wealth to the cause.

But I could not resist teasing Dorothy. 'I suppose you think this is terrific.'

'It's a drop in the ocean. It isn't the answer.'

'What is the answer then? Marcos? Lenin?'

'Why not?' she snapped, and swung away from me like a saint abjuring a demon.

Donald gave me a lopsided grin but there was nothing behind his eyes. I envy his insulated stupor: a resource which I assume he developed while teaching in some comprehensive-school hell – or while seeking a modus vivendi with his assertive and opinionated spouse.

Two hours later in the Madre Tierra restaurant I went to sit next to Dorothy, planning to incite her by asking what she thought of San Juan Chamula. The only other time Pam and I dined with the others I had spent most of the evening arguing politics with Dorothy – but this time I was to be granted no such palliative, since Dorothy has clearly become wary of exposing her callow opinions to my hostile fire. When she saw I was beside her she blatantly changed her mind about the seat, taking herself and Donald off to the other end of the table. Tonia and Sunita took the places next to us.

Having indulged in a couple of Margaritas in the Moctezuma bar where we assembled, I ordered a bottle of Pichon-Lalande '92 to continue the therapy and a glass of Californian rosé for Pamela who is neither a toper nor a connoisseur. I was also able to bolster my euphoria with food that was surprisingly edible for a Baluth eatery though hardly Cordon Bleu. I began with a chicken and chick-pea soup that also contained avocado, cheese, onions and peppers, accompanied, as I believe is traditional, with hot tortillas rather than bread. A couple of *empanadas* stuffed with minced beef, tomatoes and sultanas then tided me over until the main course of pork and rice with chilli peppers, pine-nuts, tomatoes, sultanas and sausage-meat. I concluded with a heavy pudding of bread and milk soaked with honey and sherry.

The restaurant was a complex of little rooms with a ranch theme: chunky wooden furniture, saddles for bar-stools and so forth. All our group except Martin and Katrin was assembled round one long table in a narrow, blind room that might have started existence as a corridor. As soon as the food had been ordered Lisa left so discreetly and abruptly that her departure was not generally noted or commented upon for a while.

Beer- and wine-bottles thronged the table, and most people had already drunk at least one apéritif at the hotel: Annabel and Dorothy were flushed, Stephanie and Sunita giggly. In the course of the evening the alcohol had its normal adverse effect on manners but not the beneficial effect upon tempers that is sometimes claimed for it.

Clockwise from one extremity of the table: Stephanie, Sunita, Me, Pamela, Annabel, Maureen, Dennis, Rose, Isabel, Dorothy, Donald, Tonia, Millie, Brian.
    Tonia has taken responsibility both for general procedure

and the instigation of good cheer. She distributes a benevolent smirk around the table.

TONIA (*her deep voice jovial*) Y'all ordered? There's a crowd of us tonight! (*Shouts to Dennis*) Where's Marty?

SUNITA (*to Stephanie*) She should know! She's his buddy!

Stephanie's good eye twinkles. Throughout this scene Sunita and Stephanie behave like two children at a show: meeting each other's gaze and simpering, sharing hilarious whispered secrets, nudging each other and pointing to various comic features of the entertainment . . .

DENNIS (*his officious jargon, as ever, made more irritating by his sing-song Welsh voice*) His inebriation was such that all my endeavours to maintain his contact with the group en route from the Hotel Moctezuma—

TONIA (*cutting him short and turning away*) He sloped off into a bar.

ROSE (*shouts out as if suddenly vouchsafed a vision*) Marty's a card! A real character! The salt of the earth!

ANNABEL A disgusting drunk.

This forthright comment sends a wave of shock through the gathering. Several people look at Annabel and register the fact that she is in a savage temper. Her jowls are relentless. Her eyes are baleful slits.

MAUREEN (*supporting Annabel*) At least we're being spared his drunken . . .

ISABEL (*to Rose but loudly enough for everyone to hear. The group contains several skilled exponents of stage whispers and ringing asides*) It's disgraceful. It's time Lisa did something about him.

ANNABEL Lisa does not consider herself responsible for the welfare of members of the group.

ROSE (*bellows cheerily*) Ooh, I'm sure you don't mean that, your ladyship. Lisa's doing a spiffing job. Three cheers for Lisa! Where is she?

BRIAN (*sardonically*) She has a headache.

STEPHANIE (*to Sunita*) Or some paperwork to do.

Sunita and Stephanie bend their heads together and wheeze with mirth.

ANNABEL (*grimly braggadocio*) I expect she guessed I've something to say to her. So she's scarpered.

TONIA Her boyfriend's showed up. The one we lost on the road block.

Rose claps her hands and emits a gratified squeal.

DENNIS The importunate swain would seem to be as indefatigable as he is ardent.

ROSE (*hoots like an owl*) True, too true! How clever of him to find us so quickly in the whole of Mexico!

MAUREEN Yes, isn't it?

STEPHANIE (*to Sunita*) That's stupid. Anybody would know we were coming to San Cristobal.

A pause indicates the passage of time. Waiters remove the soup plates and serve the second course.

ANNABEL Does nobody else think it disgusting?

DOROTHY What's disgusting about it? They're consenting adults.

ISABEL She is not being paid to be a 'consenting adult'.

MAUREEN That's right! Her neglect of us is what is disgusting.

ME (*to Annabel*) I expect you're furious about this morning.

ANNABEL (*correctly suspecting my attitude*) Are you suggesting that I should not be furious?

DENNIS It should be borne in mind—

MAUREEN We missed our entitlement.

ANNABEL Shut up, Maureen.

Maureen flinches and is quelled, her lips pursed and her nose quivering. Stephanie and Sunita look at each other and seem about to explode with bottled hilarity.

ANNABEL The trip to the Indian village is unconditionally promised in the dossier.

DENNIS (*after clearing his throat*) It should be borne in mind—

ME There was nothing to stop you going by yourselves this afternoon.

ANNABEL (*outraged*) Why should we have to—

BRIAN That's what we had to do, isn't it, little Millie? All the way back to Tuxtla, at a cost of twelve dollars, though the zoo also featured in the dossier.

DENNIS (*plonkingly*) It should be borne in mind that the priority regulation for any group negotiating unfamiliar terrain is that they should maintain—

ME (*impulsively*) Exactly! It wasn't Lisa's fault that you went off and got lost!

Pamela lays a hand on my arm.

TONIA I like that! We were the only guys who followed Lisa's orders!

ANNABEL (*with a scorching scowl for me*) The tour leader did not take the trouble to give proper directions.

ROSE (*oblivious to the mounting tension*) The rest of us didn't get lost, though. Not even Katrin! Not then, anyway. Where is she now?

ISABEL She could be anywhere! It's Lisa's responsibility.

ROSE It's a sad thing to have to say, but it's jollier without Katrin, isn't it? The poor dear is a bit of a wet blanket.

Another pause indicates a further passage of time. Waiters clear away the starter plates and bring the main course.

BRIAN Everything is left so carelessly vague. It's the same with Bonampak and Yaxchilan on Monday.

ISABEL Bonamp . . . ?

DENNIS (*as if he has been lurking in wait for the cue*) As explained by Lisa in the course of yesterday's briefing, Bonampak and Yaxchilan are Mayan sites in the jungle, most conveniently accessible by light aircraft from Palenque.

ROSE (*thrilled and aghast*) Ooh, a light aircraft!

DENNIS (*brandishing four fingers and a thumb to help with the mathematics*) If five among us elect to take the trip then the hire of plane and pilot will cost us approximately one hundred and twenty United States dollars per person. If more than five but less than ten wish to make the trip then we must draw lots.

ISABEL I absolutely refuse to draw lots! The trip is stated as an option in the Baluth tour dossier and the company is obliged—

ME I agree with that.

PAMELA (*quietly*) Simon!

DENNIS I think you will find that the precise wording in the dossier is always to the effect that such a trip 'may be possible', the company thus safeguarding themselves against any contractual obligation.

TONIA As far as Lisa's concerned, if anybody backs out of drawing lots the whole deal falls through.

BRIAN (*slyly subversive*) Typical, eh, Millie?

DOROTHY That's not right! Why should those of us who are prepared to co-operate and draw lots be penalised? If Simon won't draw lots then he shouldn't be considered for the trip.

She trains on me, through her heavy spectacles, a glower of personal distaste and political animosity.

ISABEL In any case the trip is far too expensive.

ROSE (*shouts*) You can say that again!

TONIA If Lisa drops out, there's nothing to stop five of us getting together and hiring a plane.

ME We come on group tours like this expressly to be spared such hassle.

MAUREEN (*tentatively, with a nervous glance at Annabel, who is now paying peevish attention to her plate*) In any case, the trip is far too expensive.

ROSE (*shouts*) You can say that again!

DOROTHY (*to me, sarcastically*) This is Baluth, not Magic Carpet. If you want everything laid on to your taste you'll have to dig deeper into your wallet.

PAMELA (*laughs and nudges me*) She's right, you know.

In a third pause, waiters clear away the main course plates and bring the puddings. When conversation resumes, the strident emphasis of most of the speakers reveals a leap in the level of inebriation.

TONIA Lisa's quitting Baluth after this trip.

ROSE Oh what a shame!

SUNITA (*to Stephanie*) Don't believe a word of it.

BRIAN (*to Millie*) That won't be a great loss to tourism, Petalkin.

TONIA (*smirking around her, holding her hand level with her bottom lip*) She figures she's had it up to here. And this bunch is the last straw, she says.

DOROTHY Let's face it, we're a pretty difficult group.

ANNABEL Speak for yourself.

ISABEL How dare she blame us! Her lack of enthusiasm's been obvious from the start.

DENNIS (*after clearing his throat*) In the interests of justice I feel I ought to say something to qualify, if not—

ANNABEL (*her patrician snarl taking effortless precedence over Dennis's whine*) She has been disgustingly neglectful and her manner towards us throughout has been that of someone who considers she is doing us a favour.

ROSE (*cries out*) No, no, you can't say that, Lady Cairngorm! Oops! I mean, Lady Cairncross!

ANNABEL (*like a tipsy actress going over the top playing Lady Bracknell*) Are you being deliberately offensive?

ROSE (*blushing furiously*) Not at all. Just a slip of the silly old tongue. I do beg your ladyship's pardon!

STEPHANIE (*to Sunita*) Hey, this bit's really terrific!

DENNIS I feel it incumbent upon me to interpose a couple of remarks on the subject of—

ANNABEL All this 'your Ladyship', 'Lady Cairncross'. Is it some kind of joke? Or is it supposed to be sarcastic?

ROSE I'm terribly, terribly, terribly sorry! I realise that you don't want everybody to . . . I'm such a blabbermouth . . . so spontaneous and impulsive . . .

SUNITA (*calls down the table to Rose*) Annabel isn't a lady. (*Giggles, but carries on determinedly*) Not an aristocrat, I mean. It's just a story somebody's . . . (*tails off into a splutter of mirth*).

ANNABEL Why would anybody spread a story like that? And what is so amusing about it?

DENNIS If I might be permitted to intervene—

ANNABEL (*in thudding, slow contralto*) Be quiet, you tedious oaf! *Stephanie and Sunita almost break into applause. Dennis's slack jaw drops another half inch. His small eyes glisten behind his metal-rimmed Infralux Varitints.*

ROSE (*timidly*) It was Tonia told me.

TONIA You're kidding!

ISABEL Yes it was. I was there. (*to Annabel*) She also said that Maureen is your paid companion.

ME (*to Annabel*) You are supposed to be travelling incognito.

TONIA It was a joke.

MAUREEN And what is so amusing about it?

ISABEL (*to Maureen*) Tonia said that it was you that told her.

Annabel, Maureen and Tonia speak simultaneously:

ANNABEL Maureen!

MAUREEN I didn't!

TONIA Not me!

Isabel and Rose speak simultaneously:

ISABEL (*to Tonia*) Yes you did!

ROSE (*to Annabel*) Yes she did!

TONIA I was just passing on something that Marty said. (*Tearful*) I never figured anybody would believe it.

ANNABEL Apparently all these blithering idiots did.

Annabel turns to indicate the assembled company. As she does so her gaze meets mine and becomes more particularly truculent.

ME If any of us believed it, it was because your conduct and Maureen's made it seem all too credible.

Annabel's eyes widen and her mouth becomes an O of outrage, so that she resembles a deep-sea carnivore in a blue-rinsed wig.

TONIA (*sullen*) I didn't make up nothing about anybody. Some-body is spreading lies about me.

ME (*ignoring the distant tinnitus in my ear-drum and the hand of Pamela*) All this bitchiness—

PAMELA (*sternly*) Shut up, Simon!

DOROTHY Bitchiness! Listen to the sneer of the chauvinist pig!

ME (*there is a tormenting tingle in my antrum and the goblin has its teeth in my thigh again*) What has chauvinism to do with it, silly woman?

SUNITA (*to Stephanie, but not quietly enough*) He can't deny the pig bit, can he?

Stephanie makes a pig noise then puffs out her cheeks to amusingly portray the imbecility of a pig.

ME (*my jowls quivering and my voice fluting with petulance*) Cannot anyone silence those sniggering schoolgirls?

Stephanie and Sunita laugh outright as if I have cracked a joke.

DOROTHY (*to me*) It's because Lisa is a woman that you've criti-cised every aspect of the tour.

ISABEL No, he'd have moaned whoever was in charge.

ROSE (*in a normal speaking voice, subdued by her débâcle*) Once a moaner, always a moaner. Mister Grumpy!

ANNABEL (*retaliating at last*) How you treat your own wife is your own affair but you mustn't expect to talk to us how you like.

MAUREEN (*popping her head round the bulky headland of Annabel*) Hear hear!

ME How I treat my . . . ?

Globus hystericus maximus prevents further utterance. I clutch my beard, look down into the bread and honey pudding and wonder if I am about to vomit but am too proud to advertise my discomfiture by leaving the table.

BRIAN (*in his bleating Essex voice*) That's not entirely fair. While nobody could accuse me of chauvinism, I agree with most of Simon's criticisms of the tour, don't we, little Millie?

DOROTHY It's unbelievable! He's even worse than Simon. He treats Millie like—

MILLIE (*with sober composure*) Is it your business, Dorothy?

PAMELA (*sweetly to Millie, but for everybody to hear*) We haven't had the dubious pleasure of meeting Lord Cairncross – but we wouldn't want Brian and Simon to behave like Donald, would we?

A pause, the silence of shock and mortal offence:

TONIA I know who's spreading these lousy . . . It's that brown-skinned bitch over there.

STEPHANIE (*with a squeal of amusement*) Wow! She's priceless!

TONIA Marty's right about coloureds. I was dumb enough to make friends with her at the start of the trip. Then when I wouldn't wear her oriental scheming she swung against me and has been slandering me ever since.

Sunita suddenly emerges from her role of disrespectful spectator and speaks directly to everyone with alcohol-enhanced aplomb.

SUNITA (*her Midlands accent unapologetic*) I shouldn't pay a lot of attention to what Tonia says if I was you. According to her Donald has had a lobotomy.

STEPHANIE (*joining in promptly like part of a recitation*) Sunita's been circumcised.

SUNITA (*bubbling with laughter*) Stephanie's deaf.

STEPHANIE (*exactly imitating Tonia's Detroit baritone*) Katrin's parents met in Belsen.

SUNITA (*enjoying herself, her eyes and teeth flashing*) Brian and Millie are having fertility treatment.

STEPHANIE (*exactly imitating Tonia's confidential tone*) Simon's made a hundred million bucks doing shady deals.

SUNITA (*mercilessly hilarious*) Pamela was his secretary who seduced him for his money.

STEPHANIE (*even managing to look like Tonia*) Maureen has an illegitimate kid that she gave to an orphanage.

Tonia springs up with a snarl like an exorcised fiend, her square freckled features beslobbered with confusion.

TONIA It's all lies! There are laws against slander y'know!

Exit Tonia in disarray.

ISABEL Who's going to pay her bill?

ANNABEL (*after a sigh of perverse satisfaction*) I have never in all my days experienced such ill-natured, disagreeable . . .

ME (*pluckily, through the cacophonous chorus of my symptoms*) That's rich, coming from you.

BRIAN (*judicially, to Millie*) This is Lisa's fault, Plopkin. It's part of her job to see that these social occasions run smoothly.

KATRIN BAUM

I have read about a writer whose name I cannot remember who used to hire rooms in London over a century ago. He would fill the room with books and manuscripts and a medley of possessions. He allowed nobody to tidy the place or otherwise interfere. Then he would lock the room and go away for ever to locate somewhere else to hire.

It seemed in my dream as if I had come to some such room of my own.

The door fell open. Had I forgotten to lock it when I left? Had the lock been picked or forced by intruders like the tomb-robber varlets of Egypt? I was burgled twice in Camden Town. That was when I was living alone on Arlington Road where the drunkards used to sing in the early hours of the morning. Before I met Rodney. I remember how the burglar's terror and malevolence still lingered to violate the flat though he was gone from the premises before I returned.

The room in the dream was looted long ago and there was nothing to show me that it had once been mine. I searched in vain for any recollection in the musty stink and the yellow paper. I examined the mouldy floorboards and the vacuous grate. I picked up an omnibus ticket and uncrumpled it and read that it was for thirty pence but the date on the ticket was smudged and illegible.

Suddenly I saw that the room was disgustingly bestrewn with used condoms and sodden garments and slobbered filtertips and apple cores. There was a brown paper parcel untidily wrapped and wound with hairy twine that I did not dare to open for it had the consistency and sticky texture of meat. In a corner was a cracked and scalped doll but it was not Heidi that my grandmother burned for ever when I had typhoid fever.

I recognised nothing through the curtainless window. There were council houses and privet hedges. Gardens full of wrecked prams and rusty bicycles. A jet trail in the sky. Astride the wall next to my window was a small boy rather like my brother Otto except he had a shaven head defaced by some disease of the scalp. He was staring down and jabbing with a stick into bushes on the remote side of the wall. I could hear an animal scrambling and whimpering in throes of pain and it was clear to me that the boy had something trapped down there and was tormenting it.

I rapped on the dusty pane but he did not look up. I banged with the flat of my hand and shouted at him to stop though I feared him. Otto used to inflate frogs and swing cats by their tails. I could not move the rusted catch that held the window shut. I picked at it in panic and bruised my fingers.

The bird screamed just outside and I woke.

The room was like a lot of other rooms at the terrible hour of almost dawn. I remembered a childhood room where stains of damp put goblins on the wallpaper. The pitch dark of my college cell with its blind window. The Camden Town bedroom striped by the moon through Venetian blinds. I could see that this was none of those rooms nor the desolate room of my dream but I could not at first conjecture where I was. Then I knew that I was in the Hotel Moctezuma in San Cristobal in Mexico.

It was a room that had come to meet me across centuries and oceans. Galleons had made landfall and conquistadors had hacked their way through Aztec flesh along the causeways of Tenoctitlan. My grandmother had smuggled my mother into Switzerland in her womb. I had tobogganed down a sloping pasture aghast and out of control with the others cheering. I had laughed in Camden Library and wept outside Euston Station. The entire history of everything had to have been just as it was so that I could wake up there in that ashen gloam and face another day of trial.

The furnishings loomed like wrecks from a swamp. The wardrobe was immense and dark like the wardrobe that leads into a snowbound forest in the children's book that my mother loved and I hated. I was in a ground floor room whose window was darkened by the foliage of trees in the courtyard. It was later than it seemed.

Perhaps I was keeping everybody waiting again. The coach throbbing like a transparent host under a microscope and the parasites within pulsing to their own rhythm as they merged into a single entity ready to greet me with rage and scorn. My mother said that I would never be grown up until I could take responsibility for my own deficiencies.

Raising myself onto my elbow I stared through the twilight at the unused bed next to mine. The bird screamed again. They used to have me share a room with Stephanie but it has been arranged that she now shares with Sunita who used to share with Tonia. Tonia has refused to share with me in order that I shall be alone. If loneliness is all there is to endure I shall cope with it.

But I prefer not to be alone in a hotel room for there is no privacy in the solitude. The spoor of a thousand casual paying customers lingers to disgust me. It is worse than the burglar's aura in the violated security of my Camden room. If I am not vigilant my fancy can summon ghosts of previous occupants until the room is packed. The beds are mounded like tumbrils with inert or writhing cadavers. Countless thighs and buttocks crush for their turn on the lavatory seat. Violent and obscene collision is only prevented by the laws of sequence and the stupidity of time.

So far it is only in hotel rooms that this afflicts me. I dread it spreading to buses and beaches and everywhere in the universe of my consciousness. Rodney said that time and space are illusions. Everything is happening in the same place at the same time.

Scores of toothbrushes were crammed into the glass on the washbasin. I focused on my own face in the mirror ignoring all the strangers who were craning to get into the picture like fools at a television broadcast. But even my own solitary face became thousands of faces if I looked too closely. All the faces were there which I had worn in all my moments back through childhood to oblivion. They all had yellow hair and brown eyes and pinched nostrils. They all had fat lips that met in a grim line. All the faces of age and death were lurking below the surface ready to emerge. There was the past dwindling away and the future zooming towards me. There were all my other past and future faces of lost possibility.

I closed my eyes and my mother pushed her big face close to mine. I could see the mole on her lip and the trace of a moustache. She said *if you look too long into the mirror you will see the fiend.*

It was true but not how she meant it.

I stepped from my sepia room into the coloured world. In the yard of dark green rubbery leaves the bird screamed. I saw that he was watching me from the perch where he was chained. He was a big lime-green bird with a yellow head and a black tongue. He lifted and flexed a long grey claw that was like the hand of a corpse. He looked at me with his cold and mindless eye and screamed. I did not flatter myself that he had any message for me but I quailed under his scrutiny.

Since I came to Mexico I have undergone this hostile examination. I have endured the cavern eyes of beggars and the stone eyes of the carved god at Teotihuacan and the golden eyes of the office blocks in Mexico City. Mexico has detested me from the first. That is so that I shall be at the mercy of the others.

Before I got here I thought that the others would not matter. I thought that if I did not like them I need have little to do with the group but could explore alone speaking to Mexicans in their own tongue. Then the trip might be as therapeutic as Doctor Stevenson foretold. But Mexico detests me with its greed and squalor. Its glib music. Its strutting and sentimental passions. It is like the loud and morbid operas which my grandmother loved except that the suffering is abrupt and real. In Mexico City a three-legged dog ran doomed in heavy traffic. I saw it and let out a cry and the others sniggered and pronounced me insane because they did not know what I had seen. I did not tell them. I was listening to the squeal of brakes that was like the scream of a bird and the cry of the dog that was like my cry.

My mother said that nothing happens by accident.

Within the swollen pain of modern Mexico is the blood and pus of history. Ancient Mexico looms through like a face inside another in a mirror. In the Olmec room in Mexico Museum there are statuettes of flayed beings with agonised square mouths and deformed heads. There is a grotesque creature that seems to be half human infant and half jaguar. There is a baby stuffed inside the skin of another baby. And what began in Olmec horror has endured through three thousand years of Mexican artifice. The steps of the pyramids are steep so that the corpses of the victims will bounce all the way down to the earth. When you look more closely at the friezes you see that the ribbons of the dancers are the entrails of the disembowelled.

In the black and yellow dining-room of the Hotel Moctezuma there was a waiter whose face was discoloured by a mulberry birth-mark like a Zapatista mask.

Yesterday the group had sat in fours or even sixes for breakfast. Today those present were placed strategically around the room in pairs and threes. Dorothy and Donald. Dennis and Rose and Isabel. Brian and Millie and Tonia. Sunita and Stephanie. This novel distribution was so that I might be accorded my first test of the day. I needed to think very promptly and accurately if I was not to wear the dunce's cap once more.

Last night I had dared to dine alone for the first time on the trip and would not yet be forgiven. It would seem a further defiance of tour etiquette and an even weirder departure from my own routine if I now chose to sit alone. I hovered between the tables until I had managed to eliminate other choices. Rose and Isabel have always been openly hostile towards me and Dennis's initial friendliness was only a ruse to render me absurd. Nor must I sit with Sunita and Stephanie for the former has a devilish light in her dark eyes and the latter has repudiated me. Brian and Millie were a safer choice but Tonia was deployed with them and she had insulted me by refusing to take Stephanie's place in my room. I thus selected Donald and Dorothy and fell into the trap. I had taken such anxious account of every other aspect of the conundrum but failed to observe that they had just finished breakfast. They rose to leave as I approached their table and left me sitting alone in ignominy.

Normally I prefer to shield myself from scrutiny by simply pointing at the menu but flustered by my failure of the first test of the day I ordered aloud in Spanish *un hueva pasado por agua*. I listened for the sniggers and exclamations of surprise but heard nothing. Isabel and Dennis and Rose were uncommonly quiet. Rose for once did not call out to me derisively asking me why I had neglected dinner last night or telling me not to keep everybody waiting this morning. She did not flash her white teeth at me as if she was planning to bite into my flesh. Tonia was talking in a fast and pressing whisper to Brian and Millie. Sunita and Stephanie were silent and seemed to be trying to eavesdrop on Tonia.

For nine days I have watched the throes and fluctuations. Sometimes they are the contortions of an embryo. Sometimes they are the swirl of merging fluids in a retort. Sometimes I think of the shuffled permutation of letters and numbers in search of an enabling code. Sometimes I am reminded of the joining and sundering of cells in the formation of a biological entity.

My mother said that we live on Satan's planet.

I do not believe that the fiend can exist independent of humans. Nor can any one human being personify or evoke the fiend. The fiend has to be constructed by the confluence and interaction of human predators and victims. The fiend is a concentrate of deadly trespasses and suffering and stupidity in greater quantities than any single individual can provide.

Last night I could not endure a group gathering. I could not endure to watch as the fiend waxed and flexed its spleen. I stayed in my hotel room consuming bananas because if carefully peeled they are devoid of contamination. I listened to the lucid Third Orchestral Suite until the room became unbearably crowded with previous occupants whose antics drove me out into the dining room. Only a couple of aged Americans skulked on a corner table there as I toyed my way through several courses of a meal that I did not relish because I had just eaten the bananas.

I got my luggage onto the mound in the hotel foyer at 9 a.m. in time for it to be loaded into the coach with the rest. I watched that it was not removed from the pile as has happened in order to cause me distress and shame. I would have been one of the first to board the bus but then I cringed back against the wall of the hotel.

I was afraid of falling up into the sky. I was aware of myself suspended over a blue abyss and attached to the pavement only by the tentative contact of the soles of my sandals and the theory of gravity.

Sometimes when there was nothing to watch on television Rodney would amuse himself by perplexing me with preposterous theories. Once he said that the number of incidents of things falling downwards towards the centre of the earth rather than upwards into the sky makes an insignificant fraction when placed over the denominator of infinity. However many times a coin comes down heads has no bearing on the chances involved in the next toss of the coin. At any moment the coincidence of gravity might terminate and we would fall up into the sky.

Another time he maintained that there is no such thing as gravity but that anyone who spun a bowl of liquid or a wet wheel can understand the principle of centrifugal force. If we were on the outside of the world as most people believe then centrifugal force would send us whirling off into the universe. It is clear that we are held against an inner surface. The sun and moon and stars are motes floating in the void that divides North from South Pole and England from Australia. Our world is a pocket of atmosphere containing the universe and surrounded by revolving rock. All photographs from space are propaganda fakes. Sunrise and sunset and the seeming apparition of ships over horizons are optical illusions which afflicted nobody until the geometry of Copernicus challenged the idea that the earth is flat.

This was flippant rubbish culled from the science fiction which Rodney enjoyed but I was unable to refute his sophistry because I was distressed by the smug and playful malice which came into his face as he spoke. It was the same as that of Otto when he would nudge me to deliberately spoil a whole page of painstaking writing or would throw my bicycle into a winter pond.

There was a voice imploring me. An Indian child was brandishing a little doll that he wanted to sell me. Looking down into his grubby face and narrow eyes made it possible for me to ignore the sky. I stared hard at the doll and detested it. It was made of a mixture of fabrics and wire bound round with twine. The skirts it wore and the child strapped onto its back made it clear that a woman was being depicted. She was holding a length of wood in such a way that it might be either a rifle or a musical instrument. Her head was horrible. It looked like a stuffed black rubbish sack tied with green rope. A slit on the sack showed a segment of white material on which two green eyes and the bridge of a nose had been stitched with cotton. The papoose that peered over her shoulder was wearing the same mask of an anonymous killer or a demon in a pageant.

On the bus I was shielded from the threat of the sky but a variant of the test I failed at breakfast was imposed on me. There were no window seats available. I knew that whoever I sat beside would more or less suppress a grimace and I would hear sniggers of relief and sympathy from the others. I chose Tonia who gave a blatant wince before turning sullenly from me.

I imagined that Otto was sitting on the back seat next to Dennis. He had that brutal haircut he used to have when he was fourteen and I was nine. Whenever I looked round he was peering up the bus at me. He used to watch me very closely for evidence of tears.

At each swerve of the road brilliant pictures were drawn on the windows of the bus by the blue air and sunlit vistas. Within the bus was the evolving fiend. The seven deadly sins my mother warned of were around me. Martin was occupying the two seats across the gangway and depicting lust and gluttony. His face was crinkly grey and his clothes tousled as if he had spent the night with a whore in a ditch. Wrath and envy were exuded by Tonia who every so often dispatched a scowl like a missile towards where Sunita and Stephanie were chatting unaware. Each of the thousand freckles on her face was a little island of self-pity. In the seat in front of me that fortress of sloth and pride Donald was playing with himself on his little magnetic chess-set. Avarice was the only deadly sin I could not immediately diagnose in the features of a neighbour. This is ironical because our entire group is an emblem of avarice according to Dorothy. As a communist she blames avarice for everything and would solve the fix the world is in by replacing avarice with wrath.

Terror has been my contribution. The fiend thrives on my terror and is now almost strong enough to destroy me again.

The evil breeds and festers as we gloat our way through a world of ancient crime and alien demons. That world is like a picture show on the windows of our coach as if the coach was a capsule isolating us from the perilous air. It is not only necessary for our protection but propitious for the incubation of the evil we bring which must be brought to maturity before it marries with the native devils to create Hell.

Some new stage has been reached in the construction of the fiend. This morning Dennis did not concern himself with the luggage or offer advice about the itinerary. Rose was not emitting her whoops of delight and fatuous comments. The only people showing any animation were Sunita and Stephanie who talked to each other and ignored the rest of us. Even when Lisa produced her American lover who has been dogging our steps and had him sit next to her there was little reaction. Those who are most outspoken were discreet. The more kindly disposed gave him no greeting though he grinned at us sheepishly and mumbled *Hi*. Nobody seemed interested in Lisa's antics.

They had other work for their minds.

We stopped on the rim of a vista but hardly anybody got out of the coach to take photographs or smoke. Martin got out of the coach and was sick beside the road. I stayed on the coach. I do not take photographs because I think that cameras are liars.

And I was still afraid of the sky.

I never feared the sky until I stood on the Pyramid of the Sun at Teotihuacan and remembered Rodney. Now I cringe from Palenque. I have seen pictures of pyramids towering from the jungle like steep stairways down into the sky. Even if I shun the steps I am afraid of my brain sooner or later losing its footing and falling into the dark void of Mexico. Could I endure Mexico if it was not for the others? I am too afraid of Mexico to stray far from the others. Yet the others are worse.

It is as if my raft was a carnivorous beast.

Our coach was stopped by a police car and two policemen boarded us. They looked exactly like the two soldiers who boarded us on the night of the road block. One of them stared at us through superstitious Indian eyes while the other questioned Lisa and the driver. He inspected some documents then bluntly asked for money. The driver gave him a bank-note but the policeman made a sign with his fingers that that was insufficient. The driver handed over another bank-note as if we were smuggling some crime or shame.

We passed a man beating a donkey. The donkey was too heavily loaded to budge. The man was drunk even at that time in the morning. He was staggering round the beast as he beat it with a heavy stick. The donkey bellowed. Nobody noticed.

It was for my eyes only.

We passed a coach travelling in the opposite direction and I thought I saw Rodney. Our eyes met. At Teotihuacan he descended the Pyramid of the Sun towards me but when he came close I saw that it was somebody wearing Rodney's anorak to tease me.

Rodney said that the human race is a cancer eating earth. *See from an aeroplane the night lights of a conurbation scabbing the planet. Humanity is a disproportionate growth destroying a larger organism. The faulty atom infects the cell and so on until the fatal sickness rules the galaxies.*

This morning I was determined to swim at Agua Azul as the guidebook recommended. I love to swim. But I was not prepared to submit to the ordeal of changing under the sardonic regard of the others. So I put on my one-piece swimsuit under my long dress and had a pressing need to urinate for most of the journey between San Cristobal and Agua Azul. The toilets in the garages and roadside cafés of Chiapas are unhygienic and in my swimming costume I would have to strip nearly naked to urinate. My mind saw my predicament and like a cunning bully tormented the weakness.

I have never had proper control of my mind.

When I was a child in bed at night my mind would combine filthy words and images with everything my mother had conjoined me to hold sacred. I was helpless to prevent my mind from entertaining these blasphemies which I was convinced would damn me to Hell.

I cried out in panic for my mother or my grandmother but when one of them came I did not tell the truth. I said that I was afraid of the dark. My mother would scold me for childishness and lack of consideration. She would tell me to have faith in my guardian angels. *One to watch and one to pray and two to carry my soul away.* I drew no comfort from the concept of this awesome quartet. Grandmother would leave on the light or leave the bedroom door open so that my room was half lit from the landing. As soon as she was gone the demon in my mind would assail me again with filthy blasphemies. The extra light made it even less likely that I would escape into sleep.

These episodes caused my brother Otto to devote a lot of time and energy to what he presumed were terrifying tricks. If I was reading at night he would silently creep his hand round the door to the light switch and plunge me into darkness. Once when we were left alone in the house together he went to the trouble of extracting all the light bulbs before he stalked me growling and wailing. Even in stark daylight he would endeavour to provoke my terror by coming behind me and obstructing my eyes with his rough hands while making spooky noises into my ears. My unfeigned tears and screams were satisfactory to him because I was afraid of him and distressed by his malevolence. I did not let him know that I was not bothered by darkness. It suited me to let him torture me with that rather than hit on something more germane. He believes to this day that I am afraid of the dark.

I never told anyone about my blasphemies and my certainty of damnation. This was not only from shame but from the need to keep my weaknesses from my family in case Otto should discover them. My mother and grandmother were indiscreet and trusted Otto. They preferred to think well of him because they could not control him. I never dared to complain of him to them because I knew they would do nothing. Whereas I believed all his threats because I knew the sort of creature that he was.

Lisa had told us to provide ourselves with a picnic to eat at the waterfall. I had forgotten to do this but it did not matter as girls were parading the riverbank with baskets of fruit on their heads. From these I bought bananas which I left on the bus for the time being so that they would not be stolen. I was not able to lunch immediately because the flush and swirl of water down the falls was torturing my urgent need to urinate.

There was a restaurant against which we had been warned by Lisa at the briefing and a stall selling tortillas and drinks. I had nothing to do with these. I read about Mexico before I came and have been careful about my diet. I wipe my cutlery with medicated tissues. I wipe the lips of cans and bottles before I drink out of them. Even in expensive restaurants I prefer not to use the glasses provided. They have often been washed in infested water. Others mock me. They eat fruit without peeling it and sordid specimens of meat that have been standing for ages. They eat slices of fly-ridden mango and plates of raw fish salad. Yet none of them has had a serious gastronomic complaint whereas I have not felt fully well since I came to Mexico.

There were two or three coaches at Agua Azul and the riverbank was being utilised by a small crowd of Americans and Mexicans. There was not so much a waterfall as a series of dazzling turquoise cascades tumbling over white limestone. Downstream of the falls the river spread to pools with blue tranquil water in the shallows.

It was now that I was glad that I had had the resolve to put on my swimming costume beneath my dress before leaving San Cristobal. There was no suitable cover here for people who wished to put on swimming gear unless they were to change in the coach under the leering eyes of the driver.

In full view of everyone I simply removed my dress and sandals and walked into the water.

Even in their present subdued mood I caused a small excitement among those of our group who were on the nearby bank starting their picnics and watching the falls. Rose let out a brief cheer and a couple of people clapped their hands. It was not easy for me to see who applauded because I had left my contact lenses on the bus and was dazzled by the sun. When I looked towards the bank all that I could see was a seethe of pigments. It was as if a gaudy monster was sprawling and stirring at the water's edge.

I knew that the applause was sarcastic and that I had no well-wishers. They were scorning the cringing way I have of moving my limbs as I walk into water. They were noting my niggardly breasts and my pale and scrawny thighs. They were hoping that I would stub my toe or cringe and squeal at the cold of the water. Best of all if I slipped and fell in a shame of spray and terror.

I could hear that Dennis was emitting some advice or warning but I did not distinguish the words. Then it occurred to me that it was not advisable to swim at this spot. The only other swimmers were two little Mexican girls in their knickers. The suitable swimming facilities were at Misol-Ha which was where the rest of our group intended to swim. I had made a faux pas that would bring me humiliation.

There was nothing that I could do about it now. To return and retreat from the water would have been abject even if the urgent pressure on my bladder had not made it unthinkable. I turned my face from the near shore and gazed intrepidly across the pool. I was diligent not to look up at the sky or to show any hesitation in my steady progress into the water. The water was chill on my shins and then on my thighs. The bank shelved smoothly but my feet were slipping in shallow mud. When the water was tickling my waist I launched myself forward without pausing to become accustomed to the cold.

Suddenly my ordeal terminated in bliss. I was employing my slow breast-stroke which is a more fluent gesture than any my limbs perform on terra firma. With their sleek heads popped up like periscopes the Mexican children were doggy-paddling around me. It was as if they were a couple of ducklings and I was the mother duck. The sun was refulgent on the shout and splash of the falls. The sky was no problem. Luxuriantly and without haste I let my bladder empty into the brilliant blue water.

It was the happiest I have been in Mexico.

A Mexican male in a pair of garish shorts advanced into the pool. He had shaggy black hair and moustache. He had a fat brown body like a seal. He swam with snorting macho fury clubbing with his thick arms and flailing his legs to make a great disturbance in the water. There are people like this to spoil every stretch of placid water in the world. The small girls shrieked with protest as they bobbed in his wake. He flopped over in a turmoil of testosterone. He headed back towards us like a hunting shark. This time I was half submerged as he churned past. The lethal Mexican water which I have vowed never to drink stung my sinuses. I panicked. For a choking moment my feet touched into thick mud that was as if a pair of hairy hands had seized me by the ankles.

Then I was back on the surface gasping and coughing as I headed for the shore. Otto used to dive beneath me and drag me down or pounce on me and hold me under choking with a brutal hand on my nape.

I put my dress back over my wet swimsuit and went to the coach to collect my lenses and bananas. I intended to talk to Lisa about my objection to being in a hotel room alone. If she could alter arrangements at the request of others I did not see why she should not do so for me. Yet I knew that such an interview would be futile. I was glad that Lisa was not on the coach but had gone for a walk along the riverbank with her lover. Nobody in the group would consent to share with me. Lisa herself would find some grounds for refusal. Then she would tell the others and they would take delight in my confession of distress.

Occupying Lisa's seat in the coach was the Zapatista doll she bought yesterday in the Indian village. It was a stuffed fabric doll all in black wearing a balaclava and with a wooden rifle sewn into its hands. It was not so horrible as the doll which the child had tried to make me buy in San Cristobal but all the same I did not like it. It reminded me of the golliwog hand-puppet which Otto used to suddenly brandish in my face.

At the end of our stop at Agua Azul I was last onto the coach but a window seat was still free. Tonia had moved in order to sit with Martin across the gangway. She smiled at me and made an applauding gesture with her hands. *Well done Katrin!* I was bewildered. She had refused to share a room with me and was now avoiding sitting next to me on the coach. She preferred to sit with Martin whose speech was slurred and who stunk of beer and vomit. Ignoring her I put on the earphones and shut my eyes as though I was listening to music.

Then I worried in case I should not have ignored her.

Rodney said our smallest action or lack of action can have an impulse that makes globes of consequence ricochet for ever and galaxies collide. There is no way of tracing the results of folly or wisdom through the blizzard of consequential possibility. Ignorant helplessness can mitigate the guilt but not the distress. Good intentions are at best pointless and at worst a cowardly evasion. The murderer may be the benefactor of mankind. The destroyer of mankind may be the benefactor of the galaxy. In the long term every benefit is dubious and every judgement irrelevant.

With Lee's help Lisa had fixed up a microphone at the front of the bus. *You may as well all know that this is my fiancé Lee. You will be seeing something of him for the rest of this trip but I assure you that his presence will not interfere with your holiday.* Lee bobbed up and gave a little bow. He looked happy and disarming.

Nobody said anything.

I decided that Lisa had produced Lee at dinner last night. There had been a terrible argument between Lisa and the malcontents. She was now formally and defiantly repeating her announcement in the sober light of day. That would explain not merely the insolent voice in which she made the announcement but also the remarkable and embarrassing lack of response.

It amazed me that in my absence the group had discussed any-thing but the progress of my persecution and how best to continue it. My egotism makes it hard for me to accept my irrelevance which is more terrifying than any cosmic plot against me.

At Misol-Ha Annabel made Lisa order all the men including the driver out of the coach so that it could be used as a changing room for those women who wanted to swim. In the event only Annabel and Rose and Tonia elected to swim and none of them swam for long. I was glad that I had swum at Agua Azul. The waterfall at Misol-Ha was a tall cascade into a sunless pool. You had to descend by steep and treacherous steps to the pool. Then you could climb a similar stairway to a cave underneath the waterfall. I did not like that cave. It stank of Mexico. The dank interior and the water dropping past the entrance made me feel as if I was in the mouth of a gargoyle or a vomiting beast.

I imagined my grandmother sitting on the steps down to the pond. She was dressed like a Central European refugee. Her milky blue eyes were straining to see me. Even when she was eighty she was too vain to wear glasses. Then her eyes focused on me and she gave me a look of terrible reproof. I loved her when I was a child but then I was hardly aware of her existence until she died ten years ago. The old become invisible to the rest of us. It is a fate less dignified than death.

I watched the others swim. Rose swam a bit of breast-stroke and a bit of back-stroke and made a lot of fuss getting in and out of the water. With her grey plait wound inside a swimming cap and her squeals of terror and delight and her thick bright frolicking limbs she was more than ever like the dead schoolgirl she impersonates. Tonia swam like the man at Agua Azul. The pool was not wide or empty enough to accommodate her plunging butterfly and battering crawl. Annabel was dour. It was as if she was determined to partake of every experience included in the price of the trip despite her age and regardless of how unpleasant the experience was. It took her a long time to descend to the pool. She then encumbered Maureen with a number of towelling robes as she revealed her grey and wrinkled limbs and stooping shoulders. Unflinchingly entering that chill tarn that was the colour of spinach she swam a labouring breast-stroke with hardly any help from her legs. Two grim traverses of the pool then she heaved herself ashore with honour satisfied.

There was a café where I drank a dark unpleasant Mexican beer which I had not seen before. I do not know why the waiter brought it to me unless it was to play a trick on me. Others who ordered beer were given ordinary bottles of Corona.

Dorothy tried once more to question me about my work in genetic research. I was aware that she had no interest in the matter and therefore turned to Sunita and asked her what happened at dinner last night.

She shrugged and averted her face. I had been foolish to choose Sunita as a source of information. I saw that she did not wish to tell me or even to be seen talking to me.

It was terrific! Stephanie spoke with quiet relish. A furtive glance around the café and a flickering gesture with her fingers indicated that she could tell me no more in that public place.

The swim had enabled Rose to recover some of the bounce that had been absent all day so far. She declaimed about how super and bracing it had been and called the rest of us cowardy custards. Annabel was not in the café but Tonia who was leaning at the bar with Martin refused Rose's shouted demand for support for her opinion. Tonia called back that the water had been too freezing cold for fun and that she wished she had swum at Agua Azul. She perplexed me again by adding *Katrin was the only one with any sense.*

Martin reached out to flick ash into an ashtray that was too far along the bar for his purpose. His stool tilted and slipped from under him. He bounced off the bar counter and sprawled on the floor. Sunita laughed. Rose said facetiously *Whoops!* Then she immediately said *Oh! Sorry!* Otherwise we all watched without comment. For a moment he lay in a heap of long limbs and bony joints like a crippled grasshopper. Then he got to his feet without pain or annoyance. He righted his stool and climbed back onto it. He drank calmly from his beer-glass which his fall had left untouched on the bar. His shirt and trousers were soiled from the filthy floor. The cigarette he had dropped was burning a hole in the linoleum.

He is getting worse. Like me. Like the others.

Rodney said that none of us is the same person as yesterday since every single cell in the human body is renewed every seven years. This was a puerile simplification of a concept familiar to me from my work in genetics before I was ill. But what is said is often less important than why it is said. He said, *The legal system of the civilised world is ridiculous. It is folly to kill or imprison people for crimes committed by somebody else who no longer exists. And even those vanished criminals were not responsible for their actions. Every deed is compelled by either character or circumstances or sheer chance or a blend of the three. Free will and responsibility are hypocritical excuses for punishing the guiltless in pursuit of social order and control.*

My mother said that we live on Satan's planet.

We were offered a free Tequila Sunrise when we arrived at the Hotel Los Papagayos near Palenque. But I did not wish to be at the disposal of the others in the little bar under the umbrella of thatch near the hotel reception.

I was still wearing my swimsuit under my dress and there was a pool at the hotel but I was sure that the water would be infected. The water in the pool on the river had been enough of such danger for one day. I did not wish to be alone in my hotel room either. I put on my earphones and listened to Cello Suite number 2 in D minor while I walked out of the hotel.

I intended to explore the town centre of Palenque but discovered that the hotel was very much on the outskirts of town. On either side of the road were hotels and restaurants on lots that had been cleared from the rain-forest. Dirt roads gave access to these lots and connected them. There were bulldozers and timber-piles but nobody was around. It was Sunday. The air was dark and heavy with the threat of rain.

I was telling myself how pleasant it was to be alone when I saw that a huge and ghostly head was confronting me across the narrow traffic-way. It loomed abrupt and lurid as a nightmare in the lowering jungle light so that I almost let out a cry. Then I understood that it was a modern sculpture cast in concrete and painted white that depicted some ancient Mexican king or deity. But panic would not quit me and I was unnerved by the blind baleful eyes of the thing.

I turned away down a dank and fronded track that was littered with rubbish. Black bin-liners stuffed with kitchen refuse had been torn apart by animals. There were several brown sacks tied firmly with rope and a sodden parcel that looked very like the one in the room of my dream. A rusty cable. A shoe. A plastic lid with biro runes erased by rain.

Suddenly I switched off the cassette player because I thought I heard a harsh voice utter the syllables of my name. Creatures of the jungle were proclaiming an oncoming storm like a concert of demons. Several screamed with the voice of the chained bird in the dark hotel. Others that might have been monkeys let out guttural grunts of lust and lunatic wails. Another grated unappeased like a mechanical implement in a fortress cell.

I came to a halt. I could not turn the next blind corner between the dark green rubbery bushes.

Rodney said anything can happen at any given moment. If matter is infinite everything must be happening somewhere. If matter is finite everything must eventually happen. I must walk here millions of times. I must turn this corner and encounter everything. A tomb. A herd of buffalo. The sea. My dearest wish. My deepest dread.

My mother said that you need to understand about Original Sin. Then you will understand that some things are more likely to happen than others.

The omens were unpropitious.

It would most likely be something Mexican and mundane like the doll with the stuffed black rubbish-sack head. Perhaps it would be lying at the roadside propped in an old car tyre. Its lumpy limbs would seem to twitch in the dark green light and the green eyes in the mask would be fixed upon me as I went insane.

I remembered my thoughts as I woke this morning in San Cristobal. How all history had conspired to bring me to that room. And I reviewed the events of the day that had led intransigently from then to this moment in the jungle gloom. The distasteful dream and the screaming bird. The haunted room and the masked doll and the terrifying sky. The beaten donkey bellowing agony. The clumsy swimmer plunging towards me through the infected waters. Rejections and humiliations at the hands of the others. The animosity of the evolving fiend that had driven me from the others and the hotel towards this lonely encounter in the dusk with whatever was needed to destroy me.

Throughout my life and throughout the day I could not remember a single informed and voluntary act of mine. Rodney said that the illusion of free will vanishes as soon as one can step back to judge. But now at least I seemed to have a choice. I could go back or go on. Before me were the thirsty ancient gods and squalid modern menace of Mexico. Back in the hotel was the fiend which we have brought with us from Europe in our minds like the separate parts of a construction kit.

My mother said *Satan is everywhere. You must put your trust in God.* I removed my arm from her urgent clasp. Her two statements seemed to me to be contradictory and unhelpful. Rodney said that in the long run it did not matter what I did. Otto capered around in lederhosen with a chanting chorus of fellow-gremlins. *Katty's scared! Katty's scared!*

Better the devil you know my grandmother said. I turned back towards the hotel and switched on the Walkman. Concerto for piano and orchestra. The witty complexities of sophisticated Europe drowned out the screams and gibbers of Terra Incognita. I can anticipate every quirk and flourish of the piece because I have loved it for as long as I can remember. I can countenance the Baluth fiend because it is not the first time that I have watched it emanate and known its malice. It is implicit in my history and part of my ancestry.

Earlier I had listened to Isabel complaining because tonight was to be the first night when there was not a group dinner. It was unwelcome news to me too because it made of dinner the same ordeal that I had to suffer every breakfast and lunchtime. If I was first into the restaurant I would have to sit alone and wait for others to sit at my table. Some would insult me by sitting elsewhere. Others would submit me to a subtler and more long-term humiliation by taking their place next to me with a blatant show of pity and social constraint. But if someone else was already in place when I arrived the situation would be just as bad. If I ignored them and sat on my own I would be thought weird. If I sat next to them I would see their flinch and sneer.

What decided me to be first in the restaurant was that I could not abide my bedroom. It had been naïve of me to suppose that I would escape the jungle demons by returning to confront the fiend in the hotel. The room's ghosts were as nothing to the terror I had imported from the path between the dark green bushes of Palenque.

The drab room was everywhere and for ever.

I was fearing that there would be a knock on the door. Whatever was about to happen had followed me back to the hotel and was poised outside for the only moment which is eternity. Then I was afraid because the door was silent. Whatever was about to happen had come with me into the room. It was concealed in the narrow wardrobe or under the bed.

But I went into the restaurant armed with resolve and strategy. I chose a small table to proclaim that I chose to sit alone. I sat with my back to the door so that anybody who came in would not catch my eye and feel obliged to join me.

There were menus in both Spanish and English but the waitress spoke no English and did not understand the English menu. Put on my guard by the filthy cloth that wrapped the bread I ordered chilli con carne. It is a well-cooked dish and contains disinfecting spices.

It happened that my table was situated under a television set and my seat was directly opposite the screen. This was excellent because it seemed that I was engrossed in the television and not on the lookout for company.

Admittedly the television programme was not much to my taste. It was a game of football between Argentina and Uruguay. Yet I was able to find it therapeutic. I was able to transfer my lurking phobia to the screen. Everything could happen there too. I watched for the game to be disrupted by spaceships or buffalo. By an angel. Or a monster. I watched without apprehension. However devastating the apparitions they would be rendered remote and conventional in the little world beyond the screen.

Nothing unexpected happened. What Rodney called *the laws we assume from sheer coincidence* continued to function. The trajectories of the ball when it was kicked were comfortably within the usual range. The behaviour of all the humans was unexceptional. It occurred to me that whenever I was afflicted by philosophic terror I might try this trick.

Normally I find it difficult to watch television because I am tormented by what is happening just off-picture. In the same way great works of art are interrupted by the notional noise of bath-water gurgling away or the clink of coins as the model is paid. A visit to the Uffizi was tainted for me when I imagined Botticelli's Venus flopping onto the parquet in a mess of brine and entrails because only the front half of her exists.

Mind if I join you?

Tonia sat down opposite me with her back to the football match.

Mesera! Puedo ver la carta?

Her Spanish is good though her pronunciation is strongly Americanised. The waitress brought back the menu which had been on the table when I arrived.

Shall I put in your order for you Katrin? What would you like?

I told her that I had already ordered. She ordered meatball soup and a steak with avocado and beans.

Quisiero la lista de vinos. Have you ordered any wine?

She had already drunk at least one Tequila Sunrise as well as sundry beers earlier in the day. But you cannot tell how much Tonia has imbibed. It does not show in her speech and movements nor in her already ruddy complexion.

Shall we split a bottle? I'm pretty dry.

I agreed and told the waitress that I also would have meatball soup. Tonia gaped.

You're Spanish! I figured you were foreign – I mean not English – but I didn't know you were Spanish!

I said that I was not Spanish and can speak four languages. She made me list them. I could see that she was dashed by the fluency with which I had addressed the waitress. She has thrust herself forward from the first as a dab at the language. I have heard her tell people that her Spanish is better than that of Lisa. Which is untrue.

I told her that her Spanish was better than mine.

I don't think so!

Then she fell silent. As usual I could think of nothing to say. I asked her what had become of Martin and she scowled.

He's moseyed off into town but there was no way I was going along. He isn't my business.

I told her I thought she was very nice to him.

When he's only half canned he's a sweet old guy but he's been well over the top all of today and yesterday. He comes on corny, telling me I'm the type he always wanted for a daughter. Next minute he's saying if he was twenty years younger he'd marry me.

Rose and Isabel had claimed a table in the restaurant. Donald and Dorothy were on another. Everybody else must have gone off into the town of Palenque or to adjoining hotels.

I feel sorry for the old sap but I haven't come on vacation to be stressed with stuff like that. It's got to be embarrassing. I know the sort of crap that bitch Sunita's spreading about him and me.

I said nothing. Since she sat down I had already spoken more than I had for the rest of the day.

I feel sorry for the old sap but I'm not here to nurse a drunk. Did you know he's been done twice for sloppy drunk and once for indecency?

She filled two glasses with strong red wine. The soup had arrived.

No, that last bit's not true. At least . . . I got it from something

Marty let out when he was drunk but I'm pretty sure he was kidding.

Our group has more than its share of pariahs. Some of them are true pariahs who would be outcasts anywhere. They are not necessarily alone. Rose and Isabel are always together though they get no comfort from each other. Simon has Pamela. Others have only become pariahs because of particular and temporary conditions. When Martin is sober he is not thought detestable. Lisa is only unpopular because of her job. Donald is not an outcast at all but a wilful recluse who can claim full social status any time he chooses.

Dennis and I are true pariahs. He stinks of rejection. At the beginning of the trip I thought that we might be destined for each other's company. It is more or less how Rodney and I first got together. It is why I joined in Dennis's tequila challenge in Garibaldi Square and made myself ridiculous for ever. But Dennis like many true pariahs would be appalled to be confronted with his status. He would never willingly be seen consorting with another outcast. He would rather be quite alone if that permits him to preserve his illusions.

You're wised-up, Katrin. Not like me. I stick my chin out and ask for it. I take up folk and try to be nice to them and they shit in my face.

The chilli con carne was disappointing. It was minced beef instead of braising steak. The chillis had been seeded before use to weaken them for tourist palates.

I imagined Otto sitting at the table. He looked from Tonia to me and back again. His hair was cropped as short as when he had nits as a child. Under the stubble his scalp was mottled by a skin complaint or the results of abrasions. He winked his left eye at me and protruded his tongue in a prurient manner from the right hand side of his mouth. At the same time he indicated Tonia with a derisory jerk of his head. He clenched his fist and used it to make suggestive thrusting gestures.

She asked me how I became so proficient at Spanish. We

discovered that we had both spent the same twelve months of our youth in Barcelona without meeting. I had been working at the University. She said she had been giving English conversation courses to businessmen. She spoke the names of a number of clubs and bars that were unknown to me. I was surprised that she knew nothing of the art galleries and the Gaudí buildings.

You're brainy and well-qualified. It's lousy that bitches like Sunita and Stephanie laugh at you behind your back and even to your face. Because you speak with a foreign accent they figure you're a halfwit. It's sheer racism and coming from stinking Sunita that's rich!

I was sure that when she next ran out of chatter she would start to question me about my history. Then I would tell her about Rodney. I would tell her about the garden in the hospital. Later she would try to betray me by revealing my secrets to the others. But she would not be able to bring herself to tell the truth. She would tell them that I was traumatised by rape. She would tell them that I had killed my father with rat-poison when I was five years old.

Tell you what Katrin! I've a proposition to put you. Can I room with you tonight? Lisa is pressuring me to room with her but she won't be there if last night and the night before are any guide. She'll be with Lee for sure tonight because now he's got a pad in this hotel. I'm not scared on my own or any stuff like that but I can feel the chill of the fix that Sunita and Lisa have put me in and wouldn't say no to a bit of friendly company.

Tonia's face was thrust towards me. I noticed the vestigial moustache like my mother's and the out-thrust masculine jaw. There are so many freckles on her face that they seem to interfere with the expression of feeling but all the same I could see that she was as sincerely unhappy as I am. I could see what was going on.

Nothing happens by chance.

I stared at this treacherous emissary of the fiend. The fiend knows that I am aware and fears my awareness. Otherwise why has there been such hostility towards me? Why were they now trying to recruit me?

I said that I preferred to have a room to myself.

Otto pointed up at the television screen where there had either been dramatic developments or a change of programme. A buffalo was trundling through a sea of windswept grass.

DONALD HEMINGWAY

In Katrin's bedroom, a sparse room with spruce two-star fabrics and woodwork, sufficient sepia light was oozing between the curtains for Katrin to be seen, if there had been anybody to see her, humped in bed asleep. A bird screamed like the bird in the courtyard in San Cristobal but loud enough to be actually in the room or even inside Katrin's head. She sat bolt upright, clad in institutional pyjamas, gazing round aghast and listening intently to the silence, her eyes two brown buttons, the eyes of a small rodent or a teddy-bear, her podgy lips pursed upon the flat slit of her mouth like two halves of a muffin. She could hear a woodwind instrument far away playing something in the pentatonic scale.

Down the corridor Lisa was awake, lying on her back, unwilling to stir in case Lee was dozing. His crew-cut head was on her shoulder as his body lay against hers under the counterpane, his arm heavy across her belly. The room was all orange cotton and yellow pine. The light was orange too, through the filter of the curtains. By comparison Lisa looked pale and cool – her arms and shoulders, her tumble of coiffure, even her lips – a water-nymph or a fugitive from the dungeons of Dis. The leg not trapped by Lee emerged from under the orange counterpane, the knee raised so that the leg formed the two adjacent sides of an isosceles triangle: thigh, knee, calf, like the leg of Sharon that Martin remembered on day four. From Lee's vast radio-cassette-player that was perched on the bedside table the voice and guitar of Charley Patton could faintly be heard:

Some of these days you're gonna miss me Honey.
Some of these days I'm goin' away.

Some of these days you're gonna miss me Honey.
I know you're gonna miss me, sweet dreams, I'll be goin'
   away.

Lee nuzzled the flesh of Lisa's neck with his nose and lips then gave an appreciative groan, shattered and elated. 'Time to rise and shine, huh, Honey?'

'Sod that. Dennis will be showing them the video. We can steal another half hour at least.'

Sure enough in the lounge of the Hotel Los Papagayos Dennis had switched on the video. He had been glad to oblige although Lisa's suggestion, made the previous night, had not met with general enthusiasm and in fact only Donald, Dorothy and Brian were watching, with Sunita and Stephanie talking and laughing behind the potted plants.

The screen filled with hundreds of little figures from the Mixtec Codices in the Peabody Museum, coloured in shades of green and brown. They had manic vitality though their faces were impassive masks and their movements cumbered with shields and weaponry, body-armour and headdresses, symbolic creatures and emblems of personal history. They milled around the screen as the woodwind music became clearer and more sprightly. After a while it was evident that they had merged their colours and identities to form the chunky letters, RUTA MAYA: PALENQUE. The woodwind continued to play as the credits rolled, until Dennis turned down the sound.

Donald was nibbling his white whiskers, pushing the hairs into his mouth with a forefinger then cropping them with his front teeth. It was a habit he had when he was plunged into reverie.

The video began somewhat bewilderingly with Aztec Tenoctitlan: the sacred centre as reconstructed by Marquina. A multitude was assembled between the temple of Quetzalcoatl and the Templo Major. Sacrificial victims thronged the left-hand flight of steps of the great pyramid. On the platform priests busily stretched the victims backwards over stone slabs, then the chests were cut open and the hearts wrenched out and brandished before being dropped into receptacles. The bodies were tumbled messily down the right-hand flight of steps, the crowd swaying to greet the bouncing, flailing descent of each cadaver. Attendants at the bottom of the steps bore off each body as it flopped to earth. The steps and platform, the priests and attendants, were slimed with gore. Dennis said in his sing-song voice, 'Every dawn Huitzilopochtli is reborn, according to Aztec doctrine, climbing the sky on the back of a serpent of fire, and every night the Cihuateteo, the fearsome ghosts of women who have died in childbirth, carry the sun-god down to the Underworld. Unless he is constantly fed the hearts and blood of brave captives he will not have the strength to emerge to bless mankind with his vivifying rays. This was the reason for the constant human sacrifices in the Aztec capital. At the dedication of the great pyramid of Tenoctitlan in 1487 more than twenty thousand people were sacrificed.'

Dorothy let out a significant cough that brought Donald out of his ruminations and made him meet her stare. He thought he knew what was the matter. In her opinion his trick of eating his facial hair not only looked foolish as an activity but left the beard with a ravaged and uneven appearance. She also feared that it might be injurious to his health: she knew of a neurotic woman who died from eating her own tresses, the result being a throttling fur-ball such as less fatally afflicts cats. Yet neither of these considerations was the real basis for her aversion to her husband's habit. She saw his idiotic browsing on his beard as one further symptom of obsessive, self-absorbed behaviour; evidence of his disregard for both the opinion of the world and the wishes of his concubine. The stubbornness of the habit, though he was prepared to placidly desist (as now) whenever she protested, was another example of his remorseless truancy from the place and moment of her need.

But he was wrong. She hissed at him, 'It must be in Spanish. Dennis is going to recite his bloody guidebook all the way through. I might go away.'

Tonia's room was pale blue because the curtains were blue. Sitting up in bed, wearing a maroon nightie like that which Martin pictured Fiona wearing on day four, she looked across at the empty bed next to hers, then at her watch, then thought: *This can't be happening to me! Back home in Detroit I'm confident and popular. A responsible job with a pharmaceutical multinational. A full social life. Envied by strangers and valued by buddies.* She switched on the television, an early morning soap in Spanish, but gave it no attention. *Everybody likes me. Sal and Kelly. Rick and Sonia. Jerry kids me a bit about how I fantasise. Says he can see my nose growing, like Pinocchio's. I tell him it's the job, I got to be inventive to push the product.* She climbed out of bed, stretched, scratched, looked through the curtains, padded across the room to the bathroom. *Saturday night is Football Club with Jerry and his squad. Monday is bowling. Tuesday aerobics. Thursday is girls' night out, boozing and clubbing with Lo and Jeanette and Pinkie and Babs and Sonia. Friday I'm down the Boogie Bar with the whole gang.*

A game was in progress on a ball court in Ancient Mexico. The masonry was covered with white plaster and decorated with brilliant ochre and vermilion, the terraces thronged with spectators clad in textiles that were mostly creamy white or shades of brown. The players – half a dozen on a side – were loaded with protective gear: wide, heavy belts of wood and leather, hip-pads, knee-pads, gloves and headgear that resembled the jousting-helmet of medieval Europe. All this paraphernalia made the players look very like the little figures on the Mixtec codices. The ball was made of solid rubber and was about the size of a modern football. Despite their encumbrances the players displayed skill and agility as they propelled the volatile and lethal missile, playing it with their hips and flanks and haunches. The crowd that swayed and waved to accompany the events of the game seemed to be undergoing a religious experience rather than watching an athletic contest.

Dennis declaimed, 'The ball-game was no simple athletic contest but a form of religious observance, the court itself being a diagram of the cosmos, with the ball representing the sun, and the post-game ceremonies including the sacrifice of one of the teams. Authorities are not unanimous as to whether it was the winners or the losers who met with this fate.'

In the dining-room Millie and Pamela were sitting over the breakfast debris, Pamela smoking.

'Brian has a low sperm count but doctors say that all the same it's bad luck not one spermatozoon has got through. And they say there is no reason why artificial insemination shouldn't have worked.'

'I know very well that some of the others can't understand how I come to be married to Simon. They see him as too fat for a woman to desire, and his bluff and bluster repels them too. I'd like to let them know that at one time everybody used to envy me my husband.'

'We pretend now that we've decided not to have children, and Brian pretends to be content with this, for my sake, but I know that it constantly bothers him and he feels . . . to blame. It is easier for me to bear because the fault is not in me.'

'Colin was lean and handsome and most charming. He was a fond father, cuddling his children in public, unless they puked or shat when he would dump them on me. He was a good lover and an attentive husband, seeing to it that my needs were not neglected because of his other affairs. Then fat, grumpy Simon arrived, looking more like an ogre than a hero, and saved me and my children from that smirking liar.'

'Mexico is fine though the bird life is not a patch on . . . It would have been better if Brian and I had had the courage to come on our own. The others . . .'

'But Simon would hate me to defend him in front of this riff-raff.'

Suddenly the ball court was ruined and empty, as it is to be seen today. The scene changed to the Rivera frescoes in the Palacio Nacional. Then the frescoes seemed to come to life. Cannon fired, dignitaries posed, priests prayed, Indians implored, conquistador thugs went about their work. Details were picked out of the mêlée and savoured: a jungle Indian in a coat of drab nailed to a tree, his last shout of agony frozen onto his features; a gringo with hairy shoulders and a leather skull-cap fornicating with what seemed to be a corpse; another conquistador in a quilted coat and a morion laughing and drinking and spilling liquor; a dog which somebody had disembowelled for fun galloping round crazily with its tripes trailing.

On the steps outside the hotel Sunita and Stephanie were oblivious to their surroundings.

'Who's this, then?' Stephanie moulded her face into an ecstatic grin. 'Ooh! Super!' It was a remarkable impersonation.

Sunita laughed and clapped her hands, also imitating Rose. 'Rose, of course! Who's this?' She puffed out her cheeks and looked cross, intoning in a posh whine, 'How much longer are we expected to wait?'

'Isabel?'

'Of course it isn't, dumbo! It's Simon!'

'No! This is Simon.' Stephanie puffed out her cheeks and looked cross and moved her lips. The cast of her eye seemed to be momentarily rectified as the voice of Simon said, 'How much longer are we expected to wait?'

Sunita laughed and clapped her hands. 'Do Rose again!'

In the chamber she was sharing with Isabel, Rose cried, 'Come along, Slow-coach! Don't spend all day trying to improve on Nature!' Her voice, however, lacked some of its usual bounce.

Isabel had taken her chair into the bathroom in order to apply her make-up with the aid of the bathroom mirror and was concentrating on this task, seeming to address her remarks to her own reflection:

'Mexico is filthy and the tour group awful. Hardly anybody is speaking to anybody else. Now Lisa's boyfriend has blatantly joined the trip, which is surely against the regulations and means she will neglect us even more disgracefully.'

Rose, her pen poised over her open Lifebook, only half listening to Isabel, asked, 'Do you intend to complain to Baluth?'

Before replying Isabel mumbled her lips together to evenly distribute the lipstick – a gesture employed by twenty-two-year-old Dorothy in a reminiscence on day three.

'We should all phone the company headquarters in London today. If nothing is done, we should all take legal action.'

'You want your money back?'

Isabel chucked herself ruefully under the chin then lifted her head so that the extra chin temporarily vanished. She wished she was at home in East Finchley drinking sherry and watching *EastEnders* with her toes in the sheepskin rug.

'I was so looking forward to this holiday!' she blurted.

For once Rose could summon nothing up-beat and positive either to say to Isabel or write in the Lifebook. Sometimes the impermissible found its way through the rents left by the world's candour in the optimistic haze which cloaked her consciousness. She now remembered emerging from Doctor Goodrich's surgery onto the busy mall in Wimbledon, wearing sunglasses that more or less concealed from the world the horror of the news she had received, biting hard on the knuckles of her right hand as she walked straight across the road causing cars to break and horns to sound. Then she remembered the butchery stalls in Oaxaca market, the strange hunks of meat that looked as if they had been hacked by a madman and piled on counters or strung from hooks.

A cylinder of pottery, coloured in faded black and rust against an ochre background, turned slowly before the camera while Dennis recited: 'The two ball-players depicted are a human hero and a cthonic deity. The weird birds are the magic owls sent by the rulers of Xibalta to summon the humans to a ball-game in the Underworld. The glyphic text at the rim has yet to be decoded.'

Into Donald's head came a voice such as one hears on radio or TV arts programmes: a voice made vibrant by the percep-tive intelligence of its possessor. '*The Others*, a misanthropic meditation in ten fits, is Donald Hemingway's first published work, though we understand that he is no longer a young man and has a number of previous efforts languishing in his bureau. Rejection has not apparently qualified an assurance which redeems with sheer virtuosity what might otherwise be self-indulgent pretensions.'

While Donald's surroundings were a matter of almost complete indifference to him the claims on his attention made by the ineluctable processes of travelling were a nuisance. He therefore disliked travelling almost as much as he detested any sort of social interaction. His passively indulgent, benignly neglectful posture towards his wife had made it impossible for him to avoid the ghastly pitfall of this Baluth trip which combined relentless travel with suffocating social pressure. Moreover, Mexico was too vivid and his fellow travellers too obnoxiously assertive to be easily ignored. His usual refuges – chess-set, brace of unfinishable epics, morose recollections of domestic and professional failure – had proved inadequate to deal with the onslaught and for several days at the beginning of the trip he had been in real distress. Then he had hit on the wheeze of writing a book about the trip. Brilliant! It meant that those very details which had been importunately intrusive on his daydreams now became a generous source of diversionary fodder for his imagination.

Palenque had appeared at last on the screen: the sixty-nine steep steps to the five gaping doorways of the Temple of the Inscriptions. 'Palenque is located in the western lowlands of the Mayan region, approximately one hundred and forty kilometres from the town of Villahermosa, and is notable for the grace of the architecture and the quality of the stonework which emerges from a jungle setting. According to my *Globetrotter's Megaguide to Meso-America* all the important buildings at Palenque were originally painted vermilion – and don't forget either that everything here was achieved without the advantages of pack-animals, metal tools or the wheel. A characteristic of Palenque architecture is the latticed roof comb and stucco sculpture on mansard roof façades.'

'Shit!' said Dorothy. 'He must have been up all night rehearsing this!'

Eventually Dennis judged that there was no time for more video and reluctantly switched off, leaving a TV programme on the screen. Old, brown, jerky film of the Mexican revolution was accompanied by the almost inaudible strains of the Internationale. There were horsemen galloping, shell explosions, frantic machine-gunners, corpses swathed in bandoliers. General Huerta stepped out of a massive limousine, saluted the troops that were drawn to attention then swaggered into a bar. A train chugged along with Pancho Villa's army leaning out of the windows and crammed onto the roofs of the carriages. A couple of revolutionaries grinned piratically for the benefit of the camera and fired their pistols into the air. More soberly, the peasant army of Morelos, all in white with battered sombreros, advanced on foot through fields of maize towards the capital. Villa and Zapata were enthroned in the Presidential Palace, Zapata, surrounded by politicians and journalists, looking depressed and furtive. Then came the photograph of Zapata surrounded by his slayers, the blurred face zooming into close-up.

As they climbed onto the coach Lee was fingering Lisa's nape. He was finding it difficult to keep his hands off her even for a moment. If this embarrassed Lisa she showed no sign of it. She had jammed her flippant hairdo into Lee's baseball cap with a pony-tail of ringlets protruding from the back. Relaxed, having decided that this was her last Baluth trip, she had no difficulty in ignoring Simon's ostentatious consultation of his watch or Isabel's, 'Ah! At long last!' Grinning down the coach like a campaigning politician she cheerily yelled, 'Hi there! Is everybody on board?'

Her tone was so defiantly contrary to both the lowering weather and the sullen temper of the others that while there was no prospect of her touching hearts or disarming anybody she might have imposed a degree of gob-smacked civility by her impudence. But as it happened everybody was not yet on board, which gave her most strident customers the opportunity for an outburst of spleen.

'No such luck.'

'Katrin, wouldn't you know?'

'Clueless Katrin, I call her.'

'Ugh! She gives me the creeps.'

'She does it on purpose. Why should she get away with it?'

'We should leave without that zombie bitch!'

This last remark, uncharacteristically bellowed by Martin who was carried along by the pack emotion, coincided with the appearance of Katrin's pale visage between Lee and Lisa in the doorway of the coach.

The vehicle was soon rolling through the jungle murk past the roadside sculpture spotted last night by Katrin – an Indian head with impassive blank eyes – on the outskirts of Palenque. Donald closed his eyes and saw the coach being tracked from the cockpit of a helicopter. The lens angle widened until the Palenque ruins, surrounded and half obscured by the greenery of the rain-forest, could be seen. At first there were tendrils of mist curling among the outcrops of exotic architecture then it began to rain hard, drops and rivulets on the window interfering with the view. Charley Patton's incongruous voice strove against the din of the helicopter:

You will never know what your friend will do
Till he's gone away.
You will miss him 'fore he returnin'.
You will miss him for goin' away.
You will miss him aw little Honey.
I know you gonna miss me, sweet dreams, I'll be goin' away.

The song was actually being played on the coach cassette-player, having been introduced there by Lee and Lisa whose respectively cropped and curly heads were leaning together just in front of Donald and Dorothy.

As the holiday had progressed Donald had come more and more
to appreciate the convenience for his purposes of a screenplay
rather than a novel. The latter demanded a detailed observation
of motives and mannerisms that was not compatible with Donald's
temperament, whereas a screenplay allowed him full liberty to
trifle with entertainingly juxtaposed images and events without
having to give much attention to human psychology.

Dorothy had her guidebook on her knees, as was often the
case, open at a photograph of a brown terracotta statue, its
mouth a black rectangle of agony. 'Xipon Totec, the flayed god,
the god of vegetation and harvest. His human impersonators
wore the flayed skin of a sacrificial victim.' As Donald looked
down at the picture then at his wife next to him she turned her
face and met his gaze. Her initial expression was one of fleeting
hope: then the disillusioned folds settled and the brackets became
pronounced round her parched lips as she understood that his
regard was mechanical and purposeless. It was like when, at
home, he caught her looking through her photograph albums.

In Donald's mind the statue of the flayed god blended and
changed into a photograph of a yelling girl-child next to an
upturned toboggan in a field of snow. Then came photographs
of Alison ringleted and in a white dress for somebody's birthday,
in shorts on a camp-site bouncing a beach-ball a thousand times
to set a record, in a yellow sweater and jodhpurs astride a
piebald pony, tipsy at Christmas with a tilted paper crown –
always with a fake grin of starlet glamour that concealed both
her intellect and her poisonous turbulence. There was Jonathan
smirking in his secondary school uniform before he decided that
it was part of the plot to humiliate him, then in the rugger kit he
dreaded his parents watching him play in because by then he was
morbidly ashamed of them. There was Jonathan with his face a
moonscape of acne, home from University, remarkable for the
prim way his lips disrelished the food he was consenting to
eat and the slovenliness with which he flung his conversational
pearls into his parents' sty. He had the sort of bleached hairdo his

father despised and wire-framed spectacles such as were associated with homosexuals. And there were photos of Donald himself, posed against vineyards and wedding-banquets and seascapes and ancient stones, always wearing the same expression of tolerance towards the importunate photographer. There were no group or family pictures and no pictures of Dorothy.

In the Palenque reception area rain was slanting down splashing onto the coach park and the dirt road between the dejected-looking stalls of the Indians. Several of the Baluth group sat at tables in the snack bar which was sheltered by a corrugated metal roof perched on four posts of timber. Rain was drumming on the roof. Martin, sitting alone, very carefully and methodically emptied a bottle of beer into a glass and lit a cigarette. Sunita and Stephanie and Rose had bought waterproofs made out of black bin-liners from a stall and Rose, her morning malaise of spirit banished, was dancing like an infant in the rain, her bulky frame engulfed in the bin-liner. Lee and Lisa and Tonia were buying arrows from some Lacandon Indians as described by Simon on day eight. Simon, Pamela, Isabel, Katrin and Dennis were queuing at a tortilla stand.

Dorothy said, 'Shit, I wish they'd hurry up! They had all yesterday afternoon to get something to eat for today. Here we are again wasting our sodding time waiting for the others. We've only got a few hours in Palenque.'

Maureen and Annabel were side by side at a wooden table in the snack bar, opposite Brian and Millie. Bearing witness, setting the record straight, they spoke out in turn as if scripted and rehearsed, to the accompaniment of birds and howler monkeys:

'This is the first time my sister-in-law and I have been on a trip like this.'

'Another of my bad ideas.'

'People are always telling me I should stand up to Annabel.'

'Maureen is a ninny. She has no mind of her own.'

'We have seen a lot of each other since our children grew up and Lewis died.'

'And Cairncross went so peculiar. The swine should be in a booby hatch.'

'I sold my flat in Dublin and the pair of us set up house together in Kilabee.'

'Beare Peninsula. Another of my brainwaves.'

'There are lovely walks through heathery hills.'

'There were until my knee packed up on me.'

'And there's a nice pebble beach and a rocky coast where seals bask.'

'Until the bloody campers scare them off. In summer it's unbelievable. Van-loads of unwashed louts from the length and breadth of Europe playing guitars all night long.'

'It's a bit rowdy in summer but it's quiet in winter.'

'Apart from the wind and the rain.'

'Yes, though the climate is quite mild in the south west . . .'

'The climate is abominable. Maureen is a ninny.'

'The weather is a bit of a problem. So we decided—'

'I decided I needed a break from bloody Kilabee.'

Donald was meanwhile toying with the notion of turning his project into a murder mystery. 'Two apparently unconnected members of the tour are dead by the end of day two, in what at first do not seem suspicious circumstances. The trip continues while the bodies remain in Mexico City, but there are one or two close misses as it gradually transpires, through the investigations of Sunita, a detective-story devotee, that almost everybody on the trip has prior cognisance of at least one of the others and has a rival or witness to eliminate or a score to settle. The multiple conundrum involves an eccentric will, a family vendetta, a drugs cartel and a government minister. All the deadly sins feature in the motives real or professed of the candidates for culprit-hood. There are runes to decode, diagrams to examine and time-zones to take into account. At last there is a mass showdown in Lord Pakal's tomb. Alibis are refuted, confessions disregarded and devastating secrets brought to light. Several members of the group peel off their disguises to reveal that they are actually international criminals, police officers, murder victims who were shamming or simply other members of the group. There are scampering feet on the steps of the tomb, a pistol-shot, wild laughter.'

Eventually the group set out from the reception area behind their new guide, Ramon, a lean and cadaverous fellow in blood red waterproofs. Lee became temporarily separated from Lisa (who was left trying to settle a dispute at the tortilla stand) and promptly started confiding in Stephanie, for some reason.

'I've been waiting for Lisa all my life and now my life is full of sunshine at last. Hers too, I guess. She'll give up her lousy job and find fulfilment as a wife and mother. I'll give up study and take paid employment if that's what she wants, though there's not a lot of need for that since I'm heir to the Eezispool patents that are worth millions of bucks.'

Stephanie said nothing because just then Ramon gathered the group around a site map of Palenque and gave a remorseless twenty minute résumé of guidebook information which made Dorothy grind her teeth and hiss with impatience, particularly since a number of people then asked questions which proved they had not been listening and permitted Ramon to repeat a large portion of his glib lore.

When they at last set off again – Lisa, who was having a beer at the tortilla stand, still being absent from the group – Lee carried on talking to Stephanie as if there had been no interruption. The heightened emotion which now threatened to disrupt his speech indicated that rather than listening to Ramon he had been engaged in a maudlin gloat over his own state of bliss.

'She can decide whether we have a quickie wedding in Mexico or a slap-up do in the States, or we can cross to England for the ceremony if that suits her. For me the devastating night of loneliness is over.' He let out a sob, put his hand to his mouth, bravely recovered composure. 'We'll have lots of kids and raise them so they never suffer what I've suffered.' He laughed, then snivelled, then laughed again, his face glistening with mawkish happiness.

Stephanie walked for a while in silence, hunched in her bin-liner, digesting Lee's utterance, before responding: 'People are okay, you know – life is okay – so long as you don't tense up.'

The Temple of Inscriptions conformed faithfully to the video and Dennis's commentary, except that it was still raining as the group set to climbing, negotiating the slippery steps with care; Dennis, who had adjusted his Microfeather Monsoonproof so that it enfolded his Screemarcher Routepack, leading the way. Dorothy recited, in flat, neutral tones:

> 'We are not in the world for ever.
> Gold shall fade and jade shatter.
> Let us have our songs.
> Let us have our flowers.
> We are not in the world for ever.'

Donald recollected the poem, entitled, 'Aztec Poem', written with yellow chalk on a school blackboard. At first the classroom was empty. The bookshelves were packed with space-saving piles so that no titles were visible. Soft-boards on the mustard-coloured walls exhibited sheets of stimulating material or exemplary writing. Through the tumbled wreck of a venetian blind the window disclosed a bungalow, a tower block and some humped bourgeois homes in the distant hills. Then the desks were populated: red, brown, bottlegreen, beetroot-coloured uniforms; donkey jackets, parkas, Harringtons, ski-jackets; hooped skirts, miniskirts, mesh stockings, lurid leg-warmers; crops, tresses, ringlets, spikes, pigtails. A yob with a face like the skull of a psychopath showed his teeth. 'Fucking old tosser. Get stuffed.' A prim-faced bitch made her mouth even smaller, complaining, 'You should have better discipline, sir, then we'd learn more.' An eleven-year-old lad gave a confidential leer. 'Pooh, sir, you stink of booze!' Alison said, 'Dad's drunk again!' and swooped her contemptuous eyelids and curled her lip.

As one moved onto the platform of the Temple of Inscriptions the steps by which one had ascended became invisible, the platform seeming to end abruptly over an abyss of grey space and green foliage. Anybody subject to vertigo was going to find it difficult to go close enough to the edge of the platform for the steps to come back into sight – and as soon as some had finished the climb they began to wish they had stayed at ground level. Katrin, who had climbed in wilful blindness, now stood holding her breath, suppressing any expression of an agoraphobic panic that was shortly to be dispelled in a hell of claustrophobia. Martin was pale green, the colour of swallowed vomit: when Pamela asked him, 'How much do you reckon a rescue helicopter will cost?' he failed to smile. Annabel came doggedly stumping up last, shouting for Maureen in her posh voice that contrasted strangely with her canvas hat and wizened mariner's face. Then she turned back to look out from the platform and gave an audible gulp.

Most of the group were unaffected: taking off their waterproofs, getting their breath back after the climb and serenely admiring or photographing the view. Simon, in a blue shirt and khaki shorts, looked like a bearded greedy boy from a cautionary tale. Pamela, in a black satin trouser suit and sunglasses, looked like a jazz diva. Rose spread her arms like a priest, exulting over the vista. 'This is what it's all about! It makes me feel ecstatically privileged and humble to witness such life-enhancing wonders!' Isabel scowled up at her from where she was sitting in a doorway with a shoe in her hand. 'I think I've sprained my ankle.'

Some were already at the stairhead looking down into the interior of the pyramid where a string of bare bulbs along a flex stapled to the stone lit the descent to the tomb of Pakal. The roof was composed of tall trapezoid arches; the steps were steep and narrow and there were no handrails to assist the descent. Ramon said, 'This steep staircase is open only from ten a.m. until twelve noon and from fourteen hundred to sixteen hundred hours. It descends inside the pyramid to the tomb of Lord Pakal which is at ground level and remained undiscovered until 1957 when the archaeologist Alberto Ruz, while excavating the staircase, found a sealed stone passageway in which were seated several skeletons. These victims of religious sacrifice were intended to serve Pakal in death and were buried with pottery, jewellery and tools for his journey to the next world.'

Donald sat on a low stone plinth in the Temple of Inscriptions after deciding not to make the descent to the tomb. His little travelling chess set was open on his knee but for once he paid no attention to it, instead watching the others as they queued at the stairhead to pick their way carefully down the steps and out of sight. Having conceived what struck him as an effective way to end his book/screenplay he was now blinking his eyelids in imitation of a camera lens, taking a still photograph of each of the group as they began the descent: Ramon, Dennis, Brian, Millie, Stephanie, Sunita, Dorothy, Tonia, Martin, Lee, Lisa, Katrin, Rose, Isabel, Maureen, Annabel, Pamela, Simon.

When they had all sunk out of sight Donald shut his eyes and pictured the tomb in the depths as seen that morning on the video. Deep inside the pyramid, at the bottom of the steps to the tomb, was a small rectangle of space, about nine feet by five feet, eight feet high, lit by one dim electric bulb, the last in the string on the stairway. A low wall and a sheet of glass divided this space from the sarcophagus of Lord Pakal. Above the sarcophagus a large stone slab had been slanted so that the design on it could be seen. Bats were flittering in the darkness beyond the sarcophagus. Looking back up the steps one could not see the top because of the angle of the roof. There was nobody either on the steps or in the tomb. One could imagine the scrambling noise of the bats and hear the voice of Dennis: 'The sarcophagus lid remains here but Lord Pakal's jewel-decked skeleton and jade mosaic death-mask were taken to the Museo del Antropologia in Mexico City where we have seen the re-creation of the tomb, although the death-mask was stolen from the Museo del Antropologia in 1985. The designs on the carved stone slab include the image of Pakal encircled by serpents, mythical monsters, the sun god and glyphs recounting

Pakal's reign. Carved on the wall yonder are the nine lords of the underworld.'

A young Mexican couple climbed the outer steps of the Temple of Inscriptions in the rain, their Indian blood evidenced by their black hair and the epicanthic folds above the eyes. He was stocky, she slender. Their jeans and T-shirts were sodden. The most remarkable thing about them was their footwear, which was totally unsuitable for climbing those daunting and precipitous steps: he had cowboy boots with Cuban heels, she was in high-heeled slippers. Yet they clattered up the slippery steps in a practised and unhesitating zig-zag, chattering and laughing as they came, apparently heedless of the death or dreadful injury that would result from a missed footing. They passed Donald, stepped nimbly into the aperture at the head of the stairway to the tomb and disappeared.

Perfect, thought Donald. He filmed the Baluth group descending the steps towards Pakal's tomb. This was at first presented as a swift succession of monochrome photographs similar to that of the dead Zapata. There were views from above of their backs and shoulders as they descended, then they were seen from below as they groped down towards the lens. The camera reverted to colour and motion as they all descended cautiously, sideways, putting both feet on each step. Fat Simon, old Annabel, drunken Martin, clumsy Katrin and timid Isabel were particularly tentative.

A fire-engine with a blue light flaring and a siren wailing dashed past the huge impassive white head of the sculpture on the outskirts of Palenque. There was an ambulance there that had crashed into a truck: the door of the ambulance had buckled open and a distraught male nurse was peering out and shouting, brandishing a drip-bag with severed leads. The truck-driver was slumped at his wheel looking prey to chagrin. A small boy, presumably the truck-driver's son, was disloyally leaving the scene of the crime as fast as his chubby little legs would function.

Captain Gomez was behind a cursory desk in a fly-ridden police station. He was something of a caricature; fat, with a scruffy uniform and a droopy moustache. Jaunty mariachi music was in the background and while the captain was trying to be solemn, in view of the tragic circumstances, his irrepressible cheerfulness kept breaking to the surface. He spoke English well but carefully, with an American accent. 'The stairs are steep, see, and no handrail. A slip of the foot . . . It was gonna happen someday.' He grinned disgracefully, displaying several gold teeth. 'There are a lotta casualties. There were a lotta people on the steps, see. They were knocked down like tenpins into the tomb and there is no space. Many were rubbed out or wounded on the steep stairs and others in the panic below. There was no space and only those on top were able to move. Some were squashed and some were suffocated.' He grinned again. 'There should have been an attendant to ensure safety but his wife was giving birth to their first . . . You know how it is. The names of the dead and injured will be released . . .' He gave a furtive glance sideways as if seeking a prompt.

At the back of the Temple of Inscriptions, which was built on a hillside, there was an alternative route to the platform, less splendid and daunting than the steps. Bodies that had been brought out of the tomb were being carried down by soldiers or lowered with ropes to ground level where there were army trucks, fire-engines, several private ambulances flashing and bleeping through the mercilessly falling rain that was churning the ground into mud.

In a large bare room with whitewashed walls and a red-tiled floor a row of corpses was arrayed on mortuary trolleys, naked except that they were wrapped in transparent plastic like super-market chickens. As the camera panned down the row some of the corpses could be recognised: the enormous mound of Simon, Pamela's darker colouring, Rose's long grey plait . . .

'Hey, Don, wake up!'

Dorothy had re-emerged from the stairs and come across the

platform to accost him. He could see the excitement of Pakal and Palenque already diminishing in her pale eyes; being ousted by the disappointed, almost mortified expression that seemed to invade them whenever her husband was their target. Behind her, out of the tomb, escaping from the craw of doom, came the others: Brian helping his Millikins up the last step, Tonia helping Martin, Lee's fingers kneading Lisa's nape. Katrin surfaced slowly and creepily like an upfloating corpse (an image that occurred to Sunita on day six), that stark look on her face as if she had just swallowed hemlock. Behind her, still invisible on the steps, Rose was exclaiming, for about the seventh time, 'Ooh, spooky!'

Donald grimaced at this confirmation of his long-standing conviction as to the inferiority of life to art. Where art would concoct a conclusion, life went brainlessly on. The tour would continue. 'The Others II: The Rest of the Trip likewise consists of ten episodes, begun by Lisa and concluded by Donald. Lisa lollops through the flight to Yucatan and an insomniac night in a hot hotel. Maureen mewls through the gutters of Merida and on the vertiginous plinths of Uxmal. The insalubrious deities of Chichen Itza are allotted to the jaundiced jargon of Isabel. Manic Millie meanders us through the baffling carvings and fat iguanas of Tulum. We travel with paranoid Pam to a paradisal plage where we bask and bluster with agonised Annabel, wind-surf with loomingly lunatic Lee, snorkel half-drowning with traumatic Tonia, before Stephanie takes us snivelling to Cancun airport whence we tunnel through space to land, most of us, phew, at Heathrow. Homecoming cameos, apt and snide, are deployed by deceptively dozy Donald in a fascinating finale.'

The tour went on. Carrot and potato soup at the café in the Palenque reception area was pronounced delicious by all those who were sufficiently on speaking terms with their neighbours to make pronouncements. Most people then took the bus back through persisting drizzle to the hotel.

Dorothy and Donald of course returned to the site, where she quizzed and cherished the weird buildings in the damp and lurid gloom, re-scaled the steps of the Temple of Inscriptions, descended again to the tomb of the club foot lord. Donald ambled around after her with the air of somebody reluctantly supervising the antics of a child or exercising a dog. From time to time she photographed him in front of an edifice or alongside a carving to give an idea of the size of the item. Eventually they were driven off by the worsening rain and shared a combo back to the hotel zone with a couple of equally soggy Germans who spoke English nearly as well as Dorothy and French better.

Everybody was back in the Hotel Los Papagayos by half past four that afternoon. The excursion to Bonampak and Yaxchilan by light aircraft had of course been cancelled because of the weather.

Rose and Isabel had been horse riding – another optional extra – through half-cleared jungle in the rain. Rose, who was now singing hymns in a hot bath, was of course ecstatic about an experience that had been both physically bracing and spiritually profound. Isabel, who was composing a postcard message for somebody to shout at her vacantly nodding younger son, had just as predictably been appalled by the costly brevity of the jaunt and the gaunt rib-cages of the ponies.

On a plastic poolside chair under a sunshade that was acting as an umbrella Katrin was watching Annabel and Maureen wallow in the grey-green murk of the swimming-pool. While Katrin was herself in her swimming costume, which for some reason she had worn all morning under her frock, she had no intention of entering that insalubrious water. For the time being she was going to stay where she was – just out of reach of solitude without having to endure anybody's company.

Martin was in bed, awake, sweating, unsuccessfully essaying his bachelor trick of sleeping off the lunchtime booze before embarking on the evening's drinking. Having forgone this afternoon nap since Fiona stopped him drinking at lunchtime, he had lost the knack of it. Now he was trying to evoke a sprightly succubus but was mostly aware of a burgeoning need to urinate.

Millie was in bed too, with Brian watching over her forty winks. *Milliwinks.* He told himself how indulgently he tended her, how tenderly he indulged her, remembering himself in a large department store, 'Jingle Bells' and tinsel festoons, buying a giant green Snoopy dog which the shop assistant had trouble wrapping. His eyes filled with compassion as he foresaw Millie when he had left her at last, wrapped in her cute quilted dressing-gown, poring over a monster jigsaw of the Temple of Inscriptions with Snoopy on the bedside table seeming to supervise her efforts.

Dennis was watching the rest of the Palenque video in the lounge. He was not providing his scrupulously prepared commentary because nobody had taken up his invitation to watch with him. Instead he had turned up the sound and told himself that he was passing his time productively by improving his Spanish. Tonia glanced in and half considered joining him, since he was one of the few people who were not now her enemies either because of the lies she had told about them or because of the truth they had told about her.

Simon was dictating to a Baluth answerphone in England. 'I strongly recommend that in Merida you replace the foolish hussy with a competent tour leader, but in any case my wife and I wish to cancel the Yucatan extension and claim full reimbursement since both your tour arrangements and your clientele are utterly insufferable. I rang twice this morning during your normal office hours but—' A series of bleeps indicated that the tape had come to an end. He listened to the bleeps, then to silence, swallowing his globus and shutting his eyes so that he looked like a reptile digesting its lunch. The specks of wrath continued to flicker in dayglo colours on the inside of his eyelids.

Lee, Lisa, Stephanie, Sunita and Pamela were drinking at the thatched al fresco bar near the hotel reception.

Lee lolled his head on Lisa's shoulder and almost took her ear between his teeth as he purred, 'Howsabout that . . . y'know . . . siesta, Honey, huh?'

'You go ahead, Sweetypie. I'll have another beer with the girls.'

Lee narrowed his eyes as if he had not properly caught the gist of her blithe response then moved his head off her shoulder and sat motionless.

Stephanie declared, 'This tour's a wow! The best yet! And Mexico's great! There's plenty of tough luck and misery here but that's no problem. In my job I've learned not to get involved. Kids die in the Unit and there's a lot of pain. I used to get too involved, questioning the purpose of it all and that sort of thing. Father Damien told me I was taking too much personal responsibility and committing the sin of pride. He said I'd got to let it go, have faith in God. But it's not just religion, because everybody in the Unit acts the way I do whether they're Catholics or not. I guess you'd think us pretty callous if you could witness how we crack jokes and mess around. It's how we survive.'

Sunita said, 'Stephanie, don't be sincere, it's boring.'

Lee loomed abruptly onto his feet, his lips in a petulant crescent that resembled the mouth of an Olmec were-jaguar and his big hands shaking slightly as they dangled at the end of his powerful forearms. His voice shook too, with disproportionate outrage.

'Lisa, Honey, in view of the gravity of our commitment I'm very disappointed that you are not . . . amenable to my . . . sympathetic to my . . .'

He flung out of the thatched bar area and lunged off past the pool towards the bedrooms. Seen from the back the peevish set of his shoulders and the injured droop of his crew-cut cranium detracted from the impressiveness of his other physical attributes.

Bugger! thought Lisa as she turned her head to watch him go. This New World prince was threatening to prove an even wartier toad than Dean. *When will somebody I shag turn out to be a human being?*

*   *   *

In the Hemingways' room that night after dinner a news programme showed candid vignettes of modern Mexico. People
scavenged and squabbled on a rubbish tip. A legless beggar
propelled himself on a little trolley. A mad woman clutched her
rags and leered. A lost and filthy child bellowed inconsolably.
The scabby pink dog sloped by that so upset Isabel in Oaxaca
on day five.

Dorothy and Donald were propped on pillows against the head
of the big double bed but only Dorothy was watching. Donald
was nibbling his beard with his eyes shut, intent on the film in
his head. His camera found Martin, whose long and bony frame
was perched precariously on a high bar stool such as he fell from
on day nine.

As Martin was about to drink his glass slipped through his
fingers and splashed to the floor. The barman, squat with long
Indian hair, came resolutely round the bar to expel the drunk.
Outside, the world was seen through the drunken eyes of Martin:
a mad accordion played as the camera registered a dizzy dance
of moony globes and Zocalo balloons and the zooming signs of
neon bars.

Then it was quiet enough for Donald to hear his own stumbling
feet. The amber street-lamps were blurred that curved away uphill
past privet hedges and wrought-iron gates, a bungalow under
construction with a stack of bricks and a cement mixer . . . The
quiet was emphasised by a dog barking across the house-tops and
the stars. When he came to the junction the pub he disliked was
entirely unlit, as were all the shops on the little precinct apart from
the fish and chip shop, where there were just a couple of customers.
Crumbs of batter were all that was left in the display compartment
and there was no fat bubbling in the range. The woman behind
the counter had her back to him, conducting some transaction
with the till. He was leaning to see if any chips remained when
a clear voice called, 'Mr Hemingway!' A customer who had just
been served, a fair-haired lass, was smiling at him with lipsticked
lips and offering him a chip. Dorothy Clifford was wearing a

tawny sweater, a tight white skirt, bright red high-heeled shoes. Her boyfriend, a dark young fellow with mannered sideburns, was holding the door open for her exit but she seemed to have entirely forgotten his existence. Her pale eyes were brilliant with the delight of meeting Donald then an expression of tender tact invaded her features as she realised how sad and drunk he was.

Donald was roused from his reverie by American voices. Dorothy had switched to an English-speaking channel with an interview with Marcos, who was wearing his woollen mask and smoking his pipe, looking a bit like the doll that frightened Katrin on day nine. The interviewer spoke in English – there was then a pause during which one could faintly hear the Spanish translation – then as Marcos answered in Spanish his soft and reasonable voice was drowned under the simultaneous English translation by someone with a haughty, irascible delivery who sounded like Simon speaking with an American accent.

'You do not think that the Government's offer is a fair one?'

'The Government has made many offers and many promises. All the offers have been fair. All the promises have been broken.'

'Is it revolution you want? Are you Marxists?'

'Many of us are not Marxists but I personally accept most of Marx's propositions.'

'Looking round the world, hasn't Marxism failed?'

'If Marxism fails it is no reason for us to give up the struggle. We are Indians fighting centuries of abuse by Europeans.'

Dorothy was rapt. 'Doesn't he make us seem crass? With our money and arrogance and idle curiosity, our love of safe romantic old stones, piddling selfish . . . Doesn't he make us seem futile and irrelevant?'

Donald did not reply because he was now remembering the beginning of the morning video, with the frantic figures from the Mixtec codices which he thought he might incorporate into his own screenplay. But the cartoon profiles turned towards the camera and the faces and voices became those of Yorkshire schoolchildren on a cloudy Friday afternoon:

'Sir, can we watch a video?'

'Can I go to the bogs? I'm bursting.'

'Sir, he's farted! Pooh! Pooh!'

'Sir, can you borrow me a pen?'

'I can see Paula's knickers!'

'Tell him, sir, the dirty sod!'

'This lesson is boring.'

'Can we have the window open? It's boiling in here.'

'Wayne's squeezing his boil, sir.'

'Can I go to the bogs? I'm bursting.'

'Tell him! He's flegged on my desk!'

'Why can't we watch a video? It's not fair.'

'Sir, Darren says he's going to rape me.'

'Shut the window, sir. It's freezing in here.'

'Tracy's eating, sir.'

'I aren't. See.'

'She's hid it under her tongue.'

'Sir, can you borrow me a pen?'

Dorothy shouted, louder than any of the children, 'Don! I'm talking to you!'

He gaped at her, shocked. She seemed really upset rather than just irritated and depressed by his inattention as usual.

'Sorry?' he murmured.

To his horror she said, 'I'm lonely, Don.'

He was scared that she was going to burst into tears but instead she shouted violently, 'I feel like the last person in the fucking universe!'

A bit thick that, he thought, when he let her drag him everywhere, Gascony, Mexico, disturbing his schedules and interfering with his creative processes.

The camera zoomed in crudely onto her distressed face and her wild white hair that had dropped out in patches like a half blown dandelion clock. Donald could see the empty sacs of her breasts in the green and white thermal pyjamas identical to his own. He spoke gently, thinking of the vivid girl in the chip shop who had pitied him and given herself to his plight.

'You're never alone, Dottie. I love you and need you.'

Patting her arm, he added, 'I was thinking.'

White Mice
NICHOLAS BLINCOE

'Models are like white mice – they are cute, they all look identical, and they all sleep with each other.'

Jamie and Louise Greenhalgh look more like twins than brother and sister. He has just turned twenty and should be in college. She is twenty-three, a born diva and a desperately failing model. Jamie loves her whatever face she chooses to wear, whether she is charming or seductive or suicidal. But he also knows that she is the empress of deceit.

As Louise drags Jamie from Paris to Milan and back as part of the entourage of an ageing couturier, her career mysteriously re-ignites. Jamie is suddenly the brother of Europe's most talked-about model. But then he learns what they are talking about . . .

Praise for Nicholas Blincoe and his previous novel, The Dope Priest:

'One of England's most gifted writers . . . entertaining and challenging his readers with an intelligence that is both embracing and unforced' Alex Garland

'Manic, funny, hugely imaginative . . . Blincoe is a terrific talent' *The Times*

'It has become customary to compare every young novelist who writes thrillers set in exotic climes to Graham Greene, but Blincoe is perhaps most deserving of that tag . . . [His] brave decision to set his thriller in one of the most charged political climates takes his sharp storytelling to new heights' *Literary Review*

'One of the sharpest young writers around, and far more intelligent than the caperish plots of his novels might suggest' *Guardian*

'Combines intelligence, pace and simple prose to produce an intriguing yarn' James Hopkin, *The Times*' Books of the Year

'Deceptively light-hearted with an artfully hidden persuasive agenda' *Express*

SCEPTRE

Home
FRANK RONAN

Growing up on a commune in the sixties, Coorg learns to love peace and brown rice, abide by the lessons of the I Ching, accept his mother's indifference and respect the feelings of cabbages. He also bears the burden of destiny – from birth he has been acclaimed as the new messiah. Then Merlin bursts on to the scene in the form of Marc Bolan.

Temporarily downgraded to messiah-in-waiting at the age of six, Coorg finds worse is to come. His grandparents track him down and abduct him to Ireland where he is renamed Joseph. In a seaside village he learns to love sweets and abide by the rules of the Church. Unloved by all except a brace of kindly aunts, he spends his affection on an abused pony. Vaguely conscious of a duty to put the world to rights, he still has to deal with the pitfalls of adolescence.

In this vibrant and immensely engaging novel, Frank Ronan depicts the delusions of faith with infectious humour, and tells the poignant story of a boy who grows up trying to fit in but somehow always being the odd one out, caught in the collision between the old ways and the permissive modern age.

Praise for Frank Ronan and his previous novel, Lovely:

'Frank Ronan has a clarity of style and sharpness of vision that make him an anatomist of feeling' *The Times*

'Overwhelming – a rich, provocative, hopeful and hopeless vision of "everlasting love"' *Irish Times*

'Engaging, funny and moving . . . *Lovely* consolidates Ronan's reputation as a witty, honest observer of the vagaries of the human heart' *Scotsman*

'A powerful picture of unregeneracy' *Times Literary Supplement*

'Ronan captures the class struggle between his protagonists with tremendous elegance, and the rapid disintegration of their romance is as enthralling as a good thriller . . . a fascinating and insightful read' *Punch*

SCEPTRE

number9dream
DAVID MITCHELL
Shortlisted for the Booker Prize

The days of summer are numbered. As Eiji Miyake's twentieth birthday nears, he arrives in Tokyo with a mission – to find the father he has never met.

number9dream follows Eiji on a search that leads through the seething city's underworld, its lost property offices and video arcades; through his own imaginings, dreams and memories; via his alcoholic mother's letters, the manuscript of an attic fabulist, and the journal of a wartime human torpedo pilot; to encounters with a syndicate of organ harvesters, John Lennon, and the god of thunder; and finally back to the rainy southern island of Yakushima, where everything that matters to Eiji began and ended.

David Mitchell's second novel belongs in a Far Eastern, multi-textual, urban-pastoral, road-movie-of-the-mind, cyber-metaphys-ical, detective/family chronicle, coming-of-age-love-story genre of one. It is a mesmerising successor to his highly acclaimed and prize-winning debut, *Ghostwritten*.

'Unique: clever, unusual, gripping and beautifully written'
Literary Review

'The novel's imaginative power re-energises everything it touches' *The Face*

'Resounds to the same marvellous chatter of voices that marked out *Ghostwritten*' *Observer*

'Wildly inventive' *Sunday Times*

'Captures aspects of modern Japan with a compelling authenticity and beauty' *Daily Telegraph*

'Dangerously addictive' *Big Issue*

'Mitchell is an amazing stylist' *Esquire*

'The wonderfully energetic prose is constantly entertaining, filled with daring imaginative stunts and the crackling rhythms of the digital age' *Evening Standard*

SCEPTRE

He Kills Coppers
JAKE ARNOTT

August 1966 – the long hot summer of World Cup euphoria is abruptly shattered when three policemen are gunned down in a West London street. A bewilderingly senseless crime that shocks a nation seemingly at ease with itself and brings an end to the victory celebrations. Yet it also marks a beginning for three men, whose fates are irrevocably bound up with the event and its consequences, which come to a head thirty years on:

Frank Taylor – an ambitious detective struggling with the conflicts between career and conscience as he is drawn into intrigues of corruption.

Tony Meehan – a gutter press journalist with a nose for a nasty story, using scandal and exposé as a cover for his own dark secrets.

Billy Porter – a disaffected petty thief, haunted by a violent past, pushed over the edge to commit the ultimate crime.

From the heady sixties to the Thatcherite eighties, *He Kills Coppers* spans three decades of profound social change as it looks at morality and corruption on both sides of the law and at the very heart of the state.

'A wonderful mix of period detail and atmosphere, this is a fine, evocative novel' *Independent*

'Propels Arnott further into a league of his own' *Independent on Sunday*

'Easily as good as, if not better than, the superb *Long Firm* . . . The novel is a stylish tour-de-force' *Big Issue*

'Arnott's tough and streetwise novel packs a powerful punch' *Mail on Sunday*

'Many thought that Jake Arnott's debut, *The Long Firm*, was good but not quite as good as the hype tried to convince us it was. Frankly, Hemingway, Hammett and Greene together would have been hard pressed to come up with anything that good. His eagerly awaited follow-up, *He Kills Coppers*, has arrived – and it's better' *Time Out*

$\int$

SCEPTRE

A selection of other books from
Sceptre

White Mice	Nicholas Blincoe	0 340 75046 4	£10.99 ☐
Home	Frank Ronan	0 340 82056 X	£14.99 ☐
number9dream	David Mitchell	0 340 74797 8	£6.99 ☐
He Kills Coppers	Jake Arnott	0 340 74880 X	£6.99 ☐
Carter Beats the Devil	Glen David Gold	0 340 79499 2	£6.99 ☐

All Hodder & Stoughton books are available at your local bookshop or newsagent, or can be ordered direct from the publisher. Just tick the titles you want and fill in the form below. Prices and availability subject to change without notice.

Hodder & Stoughton Books, Cash Sales Department, Bookpoint, 39 Milton Park, Abingdon, OXON, OX14 4TD, UK. E-mail address: orders@bookpoint.co.uk. If you have a credit card you may order by telephone – (01235) 400414.

Please enclose a cheque or postal order made payable to Bookpoint Ltd to the value of the cover price and allow the following for postage and packing:
UK & BFPO: £1.00 for the first book, 50p for the second book and 30p for each additional book ordered up to a maximum charge of £3.00.
OVERSEAS & EIRE: £2.00 for the first book, £1.00 for the second book and 50p for each additional book.

Name . . . .

Address . . . .

. . . .

. . . .

If you would prefer to pay by credit card, please complete:
Please debit my Visa / Access / Diner's Club / American Express (delete as applicable) card no:

Signature . . . .

Expiry Date . . . .

If you would NOT like to receive further information on our products please tick the box. ☐